THE PREFECT DREYFUS EMERGENCIES

(within the Revelation Space universe)
Aurora Rising (previously published as The Prefect)
Elysium Fire
Machine Vendetta

SHORT STORY COLLECTIONS

Diamond Dogs, Turquoise Days
Galactic North
Zima Blue
Beyond the Aquila Rift
The Revelation Space Collection: Volume 1
The Revelation Space Collection: Volume 2

Praise for Alastair Reynolds:

'The span here is mind-boggling, cosmos-spanning concepts, a breath-taking journey' *Good Book Guide* on *Chasm City*

'[A] wonderfully entertaining puzzle wrapped inside an adventure story' *The Guardian* on *Eversion*

'A fabulous and satisfying novel' *SF Crowsnest* on *Revenger*

'An excellent adventure that's sure to keep readers on their toes' *Publishers Weekly* on *Revenger*

'A fun, character focused bottle mystery that shifts settings like a chameleon walking across a rainbow carpet' *The Quill to Live* on *Eversion*

'Entertaining and thought-provoking' *Locus* on *Revelation Space*

'Pirates in space, full of peril and high-jinks . . . This is a novel that's elegantly plotted, full of surprises and, as first time round, rip-roaring fun' *SFX* on *Revenger*

'Reynolds is one of the modern masters of science fiction' *Starburst*

'This is a story to break hearts and make you turn pages. It's great stuff; pick it up, you'll want to know what happens next' *SF&F Reviews* on *Century Rain*

'Reynolds is a master singer of the Space Opera' *The Times*

Also by Alastair Reynolds

NOVELS

Century Rain
Pushing Ice
House of Suns
Terminal World
The Medusa Chronicles (with Stephen Baxter)
Eversion
Halcyon Years

REVELATION SPACE

Revelation Space
Redemption Ark
Absolution Gap
Chasm City
Inhibitor Phase

POSEIDON'S CHILDREN

Blue Remembered Earth
On the Steel Breeze
Poseidon's Wake

REVENGER

Revenger
Shadow Captain
Bone Silence

THE REVELATION SPACE COLLECTION: VOLUME 2

This paperback first published in Great Britain in 2026 by Gollancz
First published in Great Britain in 2025 by Gollancz
an imprint of The Orion Publishing Group Ltd
Carmelite House, 50 Victoria Embankment
London EC4Y 0DZ

An Hachette UK Company

The authorised representative in the EEA is Hachette Ireland, 8 Castlecourt Centre, Castleknock Road, Castleknock, Dublin 15, D15 XTP3, Republic of Ireland (email: info@hbgi.ie)

1 3 5 7 9 10 8 6 4 2

A CIP catalogue record for this book is available from the British Library.

ISBN (Mass Market Paperback) 978 1 399 61198 5
ISBN (eBook) 978 1 399 61199 2
ISBN (Audio) 978 1 399 61200 5

Typeset by Born Group
Printed in Great Britain by Clays Ltd, Elcograph S.p.A

www.gollancz.co.uk

THE REVELATION SPACE COLLECTION: VOLUME 2

Alastair Reynolds

Contents

TURQUOISE DAYS

'Set sail in those Turquoise Days'

Echo and the Bunnymen

ONE

Naqi Okpik waited until her sister was safely asleep before she stepped onto the railed balcony that circled the gondola.

It was the most perfectly warm and still summer night in months. Even the breeze caused by the airship's motion was warmer than usual, as soft against her cheek as the breath of an attentive lover. Above, yet hidden by the black curve of the vacuum-bag, the two moons were nearly at their fullest. Microscopic creatures sparkled a hundred metres under the airship, great schools of them daubing galaxies against the profound black of the sea. Spirals, flukes and arms of luminescence wheeled and coiled as if in thrall to secret music.

Naqi looked to the rear, where the airship's ceramic-jacketed sensor pod carved a twinkling furrow. Pinks and rubies and furious greens sparkled in the wake. Occasionally they darted from point to point with the nervous motion of kingfishers. As ever, she was alert to anything unusual in movements of the messenger sprites, anything that might merit a note in the latest circular, or even a full-blown article in one of the major journals of Juggler studies. But there was nothing odd happening tonight, no yet-to-be catalogued forms or behaviour patterns, nothing that might indicate more significant Pattern Juggler activity.

She walked around the airship's balcony until she had reached the stern, where the submersible sensor pod was tethered by a long fibre-optic dragline. Naqi pulled a long hinged stick from her pocket, flicked it open in the manner of a courtesan's fan and then waved it close to the winch assembly. The default watercoloured lilies and sea serpents melted away, replaced by tables of numbers, sinuous graphs and trembling histograms. A glance established that there was nothing surprising here either, but the data would still form a useful calibration set for other experiments.

As she closed the fan – delicately, for it was worth almost as much as the airship itself – Naqi reminded herself that it was a day since she had gathered the last batch of incoming messages. Rot had taken out the connection between the antenna and the gondola during the last expedition, and since then collecting the messages had become a chore, to be taken in turns or traded for less tedious tasks.

Naqi gripped a handrail and swung out behind the airship. Here the vacuum-bag overhung the gondola by only a metre, and a grilled ladder allowed her to climb around the overhang and scramble onto the flat top of the bag. She moved gingerly, bare feet against rusting rungs, doing her best not to disturb Mina. The airship rocked and creaked a little as she found her balance on the top and then was again silent and still. The churning of its motors was so quiet that Naqi had long ago filtered the sound from her experience.

All was calm, beautifully so.

In the moonlight the antenna was a single dark flower rising from the broad back of the bladder. Naqi started moving along the railed catwalk that led to it, steadying herself as she went but feeling much less vertigo than would have been the case in daylight.

Then she froze, certain that she was being watched.

Just within Naqi's peripheral vision appeared a messenger sprite. It had flown to the height of the airship and was now shadowing it from a distance of ten or twelve metres. Naqi gasped, delighted and unnerved at the same time. Apart from dead specimens this was the first time Naqi had ever seen a sprite this close. The organism had the approximate size and morphology of a terrestrial hummingbird, yet it glowed like a lantern. Naqi recognised it immediately as a long-range packet carrier. Its belly would be stuffed with data coded into tightly packed wads of RNA, locked within microscopic protein capsomeres. The packet carrier's head was a smooth teardrop, patterned with luminous pastel markings, but lacking any other detail save for two black eyes positioned above the midline. Inside the head was a cluster of neurones, which encoded the positions of the brightest circumpolar stars. Other than that, sprites had only the most rudimentary kind of intelligence. They existed to shift information between nodal points in the ocean when the usual chemical signalling pathways were deemed too slow or imprecise. The sprite would die when it reached its destination, consumed by microscopic organisms that would unravel and process the information stored in the capsomeres.

And yet Naqi had the acute impression that it was watching her: not just the airship, but *her*, with a kind of watchful curiosity that made the hairs on the back of her neck bristle. And then – just at the point when the feeling of scrutiny had become unsettling – the sprite whipped sharply away from the airship. Naqi watched it descend back towards the ocean and then coast above the surface, bobbing now and then like a skipping stone. She remained still for several more minutes, convinced that something of significance had happened, though aware too of how subjective the experience had been; how unimpressive it would seem if she tried to explain it to Mina tomorrow. Anyway, Mina was the one with the special bond with the ocean, wasn't she? Mina was the one who scratched her arms at night; Mina was the one who had too high a conformal index to be allowed into the swimmer corps. It was always Mina.

It was never Naqi.

The antenna's metre-wide dish was anchored to a squat plinth inset with weatherproofed controls and read-outs. It was century-old *Pelican* technology, like the airship and the fan. Many of the controls and displays were dead, but the unit was still able to lock onto the functioning satellites. Naqi flicked open the fan and copied the latest feeds into the fan's remaining memory. Then she knelt down next to the plinth, propped the fan on her knees and sifted through the messages and news summaries of the last day. A handful of reports had arrived from friends in Prachuap-Pangnirtung and Umingmaktok snowflake cities, another from an old boyfriend in the swimmer corps station on Narathiwat atoll. He had sent her a list of jokes that were already in wide circulation. She scrolled down the list, grimacing more than grinning, before finally managing a half-hearted chuckle at one that had previously escaped her. Then there were a dozen digests from various special interest groups related to the Jugglers, along with a request from a journal editor that she critique a paper. Naqi skimmed the paper's abstract and thought that she was probably capable of reviewing it.

She checked through the remaining messages. There was a note from Dr Sivaraksa saying that her formal application to work on the Moat project had been received and was now under consideration. There had been no official interview, but Naqi had met Sivaraksa a few weeks earlier when both of them happened to be in Umingmaktok. Sivaraksa had been in an encouraging mood during the meeting, though Naqi couldn't say whether that was because she'd given a good impression or because Sivaraksa had just had his tapeworm swapped for a nice new one. But Sivaraksa's message said she could expect to hear the result in a day or two. Naqi wondered idly how she would break the news to Mina if she was offered the job. Mina was critical of the whole idea of the Moat and would probably take a dim view of her sister having anything to do with it.

Scrolling down further, she read another message from a scientist in Qaanaaq requesting access to some calibration data she had obtained earlier in the summer. Then there were four or five automatic weather advisories, drafts of two papers she was contributing to, and an invitation to attend the amicable divorce of Kugluktuk and Gjoa, scheduled to take place in three weeks' time. Following that there was a summary of the latest worldwide news – an unusually bulky file – and then there was nothing. No further messages had arrived for eight hours.

There was nothing particularly unusual about that – the ailing network was always going down – but for the second time that night the back of Naqi's neck tingled. Something *must* have happened, she thought.

She opened the news summary and started reading. Five minutes later she was waking Mina.

'I don't think I want to believe it,' Mina Okpik said.

Naqi scanned the heavens, dredging childhood knowledge of the stars. With some minor adjustment to allow for parallax, the old constellations were still more or less valid when seen from Turquoise.

'That's it, I think.'

'What?' Mina said, still sleepy.

Naqi waved her hand at a vague area of the sky, pinned between Scorpius and Hercules. 'Ophiuchus. If our eyes were sensitive enough, we'd be able to see it now: a little prick of blue light.'

'I've had enough of little pricks for one lifetime,' Mina said, tucking her arms around her knees. Her hair was the same pure black as Naqi's, but trimmed into a severe, spiked crop which made her look younger or older depending on the light. She wore black shorts and a shirt that left her arms bare. Luminous tattoos in emerald and indigo spiralled around the piebald marks of random fungal invasion that covered her arms, thighs, neck and cheeks. The fullness of the moons caused the fungal patterns to glow a little themselves, shimmering with the same emerald and indigo hues. Naqi had no tattoos and scarcely any fungal patterns of her own; she couldn't help but feel slightly envious of her sister's adornments.

Mina continued, 'But seriously, you don't think it might be a mistake?'

'I don't think so, no. See what it says there? They detected it weeks ago, but they kept quiet until now so that they could make more measurements.'

'I'm surprised there wasn't a rumour.'

Naqi nodded. 'They kept the lid on it pretty well. Which doesn't mean there isn't going to be a lot of trouble.'

'Mm. And they think this blackout is going to help?'

'My guess is official traffic's still getting through. They just don't want the rest of us clogging up the network with endless speculation.'

'Can't blame us for that, can we? I mean, everyone's going to be guessing, aren't they?'

'Maybe they'll announce themselves before very long,' Naqi said doubtfully.

While they had been speaking the airship had passed into a zone of the sea largely devoid of bioluminescent surface life. Such zones were almost as common as the nodal regions where the network was thickest, like the gaping voids between clusters of galaxies. The wake of the sensor pod was almost impossible to pick out, and the darkness around them was absolute, relieved only by the occasional mindless errand of a solitary messenger sprite.

Mina said: 'And if they don't?'

'Then I guess we're all in a lot more trouble than we'd like.'

For the first time in a century a ship was approaching Turquoise, commencing its deceleration from interstellar cruise speed. The flare of the lighthugger's exhaust was pointed straight at the Turquoise system. Measurement of the Doppler shift of the flame showed that the vessel was still two years out, but that was hardly any time at all on Turquoise. The ship had yet to announce itself, but even if it turned out to have nothing but benign intentions – a short trade stopover, perhaps – the effect on Turquoise society would be incalculable. Everyone knew of the troubles that had followed the arrival of *Pelican in Impiety*. When the Ultras moved into orbit there had been much unrest below. Spies had undermined lucrative trade deals. Cities had jockeyed for prestige, competing for technological tidbits. There had been hasty marriages and equally hasty separations. A century later, old enmities smouldered just beneath the surface of cordial intercity politics.

It wouldn't be any better this time.

'Look,' Mina said, 'it doesn't have to be all that bad. They might not even want to talk to us. Didn't a ship pass through the system about seventy years ago without so much as a by-your-leave?'

Naqi agreed; it was mentioned in a sidebar to one of the main articles. 'They had engine trouble, or something. But the experts say there's no sign of anything like that this time.'

'So they've come to trade. What have we got to offer them that we didn't have last time?'

'Not much, I suppose.'

Mina nodded knowingly. 'A few works of art that probably won't travel very well. Ten-hour-long nose-flute symphonies, anyone?' She pulled a face. 'That's supposedly my culture, and even I can't stand it. What else? A handful of discoveries about the Jugglers, which have more than likely been replicated elsewhere a dozen times. Technology, medicine? Forget it.'

'They must think we have something worth coming here for,' Naqi said. 'Whatever it is, we'll just have to wait and see, won't we? It's only two years.'

'I expect you think that's quite a long time,' Mina said.

'Actually—'

Mina froze.

'Look!'

Something whipped past in the night, far below, then a handful of them, then a dozen, and then a whole bright squadron. Messenger sprites, Naqi realised – but she had never seen so many of them moving at once, and on what was so evidently the same errand. Against the darkness of the ocean the lights were mesmerising: curling and weaving, swapping positions and occasionally veering far from the main pack before arcing back towards the swarm. Once again one of the sprites climbed to the altitude of the airship, loitering for a few moments on fanning wings before whipping off to rejoin the others. The swarm receded, becoming a tight ball of fireflies, and then only a pale globular smudge. Naqi watched until she was certain that the last sprite had vanished into the night.

'Wow,' Mina said quietly.

'Have you ever seen anything like that?'

'Never.'

'Bit funny that it should happen tonight, wouldn't you say?'

'Don't be silly,' Mina said. 'The Jugglers can't possibly know about the ship.'

'We don't know that for sure. Most people heard about this ship hours ago. That's more than enough time for someone to have swum.'

Mina conceded her younger sister's point. 'Still, information flow isn't usually that clear-cut. The Jugglers store patterns, but they seldom show any sign of comprehending actual content. We're dealing with a mindless biological archiving system, a museum without a curator.'

'That's one view.'

Mina shrugged. 'I'd love to be proved otherwise.'

'Well, do you think we should try following them? I know we can't track sprites over any distance, but we might be able to keep up for a few hours before we drain the batteries.'

'We wouldn't learn much.'

'We won't know until we've tried,' Naqi said, gritting her teeth. 'Come on – it's got to be worth a go, hasn't it? I reckon that swarm moved a bit slower than a single sprite. We'd at least have enough for a report, wouldn't we?'

Mina shook her head. 'All we'd have is a single observation with a little bit of speculation thrown in. You know we can't publish that sort of thing. And anyway, assuming that sprite swarm did have something to do with the ship, there are going to be hundreds of similar sightings tonight.'

'I just thought it might take our minds off the news.'

'Perhaps it would. But it would also make us unforgivably late for our target.' Mina dropped the tone of her voice, making an obvious effort to sound reasonable. 'Look, I understand your curiosity. I feel it as well. But the chances are it was either a statistical fluke or part of a global event everyone else will have had a much better chance to study. Either way we can't contribute anything useful, so we might as well just forget about it.' She rubbed at the marks on her forearm, tracing the paisley-patterned barbs and whorls of glowing colouration. 'And I'm tired, and we have several busy days ahead of us. I think we just need to put this one down to experience, all right?'

'Fine,' Naqi said.

'I'm sorry, but I just know we'd be wasting our time.'

'I said fine.' Naqi stood up and steadied herself on the railing that traversed the length of the airship's back.

'Where are you going?'

'To sleep. Like you said, we've got a busy day coming up. We'd be fools to waste time chasing a fluke, wouldn't we?'

An hour after dawn they crossed out of the dead zone. The sea below began to thicken with floating life, becoming soupy and torpid. A kilometre or so further in and the soup showed ominous signs of structure: a blue-green stew of ropy strands and wide, kelplike plates. They suggested the floating, half-digested entrails of embattled sea monsters.

Within another kilometre the floating life had become a dense vegetative raft, stinking of brine and rotting cabbage. Within another kilometre of that the raft had thickened to the point where the underlying sea was only intermittently visible. The air above the raft was humid, hot and pungent with microscopic irritants. The raft itself was possessed of a curiously beguiling motion, bobbing and writhing and gyring according to the ebb and flow of weirdly localised current systems. It was as if many invisible spoons were stirring a great bowl of spinach. Even the shadow of the airship, pushed far ahead of it by the low sun, had some influence on the movement of the material. The Pattern Juggler biomass scurried and squirmed to evade the track of the shadow, and the peculiar purposefulness of the motion reminded Naqi of an octopus she had seen in the terrestrial habitats aquarium on Umingmaktok, squeezing its way through impossibly small gaps in the glass prison of its tank.

Presently they arrived at the precise centre of the circular raft. It spread away from them in all directions, hemmed by a distant ribbon of sparkling sea. It felt as if the airship had come to rest above an island, as fixed and ancient as any geological feature. The island even had a sort of geography: humps and ridges and depressions sculpted into the cloying texture of layered biomass. But there were few islands on Turquoise, especially at this latitude, and the Juggler node was only a few days old. Satellites had detected its growth a week earlier, and Mina and Naqi had been sent to investigate. They were under strict instructions simply to hover above the island and deploy a handful of tethered sensors. If the node showed any signs of being unusual, a more experienced team would be sent out from Umingmaktok by high-speed dirigible. Most nodes dispersed within twenty to thirty days, so there was always a need for some urgency. They might even send trained swimmers, eager to dive into the sea and open their minds to alien communion. Ready – as they called it – to *ken* the ocean.

But first things first: chances were this node would turn out to be interesting rather than exceptional.

'Morning,' Mina said when Naqi approached her. Mina was swabbing the sensor pod she had reeled in earlier, collecting the green mucus that had adhered to its ceramic teardrop. All human artefacts eventually succumbed to biological attack from the ocean, although ceramics were the most resilient.

'You're cheerful,' Naqi said, trying to make the statement sound matter-of-fact rather than judgemental.

'Aren't you? It's not everyone gets a chance to study a node up this close. Make the most of it, sis. The news we got last night doesn't change what we have to do today.'

Naqi scraped the back of her hand across her nose. Now that the airship was above the node she was breathing vast numbers of aerial organisms into her lungs with each breath. The smell was redolent of ammonia and decomposing vegetation. It required an intense effort of will not to keep rubbing her eyes rawer than they already were. 'Do you see anything unusual?'

'Bit early to say.'

'So that's a "no", then.'

'You can't learn much without probes, Naqi.' Mina dipped a swab into a collection bag, squeezing tight the plastic seal. Then she dropped the bag into a bucket between her feet. 'Oh, wait. I saw another of those swarms, after you'd gone to sleep.'

'I thought you were the one complaining about being tired.'

Mina dug out a fresh swab and rubbed vigorously at a deep olive smear on the side of the sensor. 'I picked up my messages, that's all. Tried again this morning, but the blackout still hasn't been lifted. I picked up a few short-wave radio signals from the closest cities, but they were just transmitting a recorded message from the Snowflake Council: stay tuned and don't panic.'

'So let's hope we don't find anything significant here,' Naqi said, 'because we won't be able to report it if we do.'

'They're bound to lift the blackout soon. In the meantime I think we have enough measurements to keep us busy. Did you find that spiral sweep program in the airship's avionics box?'

'I haven't looked for it,' Naqi said, certain that Mina had never mentioned such a thing before. 'But I'm sure I can program something from scratch in a few minutes.'

'Well, let's not waste any more time than necessary. Here.' Smiling, she offered Naqi the swab, its tip laden with green slime. 'You take over this and I'll go and dig out the program.'

Naqi took the swab after a moment's delay.

'Of course. Prioritise tasks according to ability, right?'

'That's not what I meant,' Mina said soothingly. 'Look, let's not argue, shall we? We were best friends until last night. I just thought it would be quicker . . .' She trailed off and shrugged. 'You know what I mean. I know you blame me for not letting us follow the sprites, but we had no choice but to come here. Understand that, will you? Under any other circumstances—'

'I understand,' Naqi said, realising as she did how sullen and childlike she sounded; how much she was playing the petulant younger sister. The worst of it was that she knew Mina was right. At dawn it all looked much clearer.

'Do you? Really?'

Naqi nodded, feeling the perverse euphoria that came with an admission of defeat. 'Yes. Really. We'd have been wrong to chase them.'

Mina sighed. 'I was tempted, you know. I just didn't want you to see how tempted I was, or else you'd have found a way to convince me.'

'I'm that persuasive?'

'Don't underestimate yourself, sis. I know I never would.' Mina paused and took back the swab. 'I'll finish this. Can you handle the sweep program?

Naqi smiled. She felt better now. The tension between them would still take a little while to dissipate, but at least things were easier now. Mina was right about something else: they were best friends, not just sisters.

'I'll handle it,' Naqi said.

*

Naqi stepped through the hermetic curtain into the air-conditioned cool of the gondola. She closed the door, rubbed her eyes and then sat down at the navigator's station. The airship had flown itself automatically from Umingmaktok, adjusting its course to take cunning advantage of jet streams and weather fronts. Now it was in hovering mode: once or twice a minute the electrically driven motors purred, stabilising the craft against gusts of wind generated by the microclimate above the Juggler node. Naqi called up the current avionics program, a menu of options appearing on a flat screen. The options quivered; Naqi thumped the screen with the back of her hand until the display behaved itself. Then she scrolled down through the other flight sequences, but there was no pre-program spiral loaded into the current avionics suite. Naqi rummaged around in the background files, but there was nothing to help her there either. She was about to start hacking something together – at a push it would take her half an hour to assemble a routine – when she remembered that she had once backed up some earlier avionics files onto the fan. She had no idea if they were still there, or even if there was anything useful amongst the cache, but it was probably worth taking the time to find out. The fan lay closed on a bench; Mina must have left it there after she had verified that the blackout was still in force.

Naqi grabbed the fan and spread it open across her lap. To her surprise, it was still active: instead of the usual watercolour patterns the display showed the messages she had been scrolling through earlier.

She looked closer and frowned. These were not her messages at all. She was looking at the messages Mina had copied onto the fan during the night. Naqi felt an immediate prickle of guilt: she should snap the fan shut, or at the very least close her sister's mail and move into her own area of the fan. But she did neither of those things. Telling herself that it was only what anyone else would have done, she accessed the final message in the list and examined its incoming time-stamp. To within a few minutes, it had arrived at the same time as the final message Naqi had received.

Mina had been telling the truth when she said that the blackout was continuing.

Naqi glanced up. Through the window of the gondola she could see the back of her sister's head, bobbing up and down as she checked winches along the side.

Naqi looked at the body of the message. It was nothing remarkable, just an automated circular from one of the Juggler special-interest groups. Something about neurotransmitter chemistry.

She exited the circular, getting back to the list of incoming messages. She told herself that she had done nothing shameful so far. If she closed Mina's mail now, she would have nothing to feel really guilty about.

But a name she recognised jumped out at her from the list of messages: Dr Jotah Sivaraksa, manager of the Moat project. The man she had met in Umingmaktok, glowing with renewed vitality after his yearly worm change. What could Mina possibly want with Sivaraksa?

She opened the message, read it.

It was exactly what she had feared, and yet not dared to believe.

Sivaraksa was responding to Mina's request to work on the Moat. The tone of the message was conversational, in stark contrast to the businesslike response Naqi had received. Sivaraksa informed her sister that her request had been appraised favourably, and that while there were still one or two other candidates to be considered, Mina had so far emerged as the most convincing applicant. Even if this turned out not to be the case, Sivaraksa continued – and that was not very likely – Mina's name would be at the top of the list when further vacancies became available. In short, she was more or less guaranteed a chance to work on the Moat within the year.

Naqi read the message again, just in case there was some highly subtle detail that threw the entire thing into a different, more benign light.

Then she snapped shut the fan with a sense of profound fury. She placed it back where it was, exactly as it had been.

Mina pushed her head through the hermetic curtain.

'How's it coming along?'

'Fine,' Naqi said. Her voice sounded drained of emotion even to herself. She felt stunned and mute. Mina would call her a hypocrite were she to object to her sister having applied for exactly the same job she had . . . but there was more to it than that. Naqi had never been as openly critical of the Moat project as her sister. By contrast, Mina had never missed a chance to denounce both the project and the personalities behind it.

Now that was real hypocrisy.

'Got that routine cobbled together?'

'Coming along,' Naqi said.

'Something the matter?'

'No,' Naqi forced a smile, 'no. Just working through the details. Have it ready in a few minutes.'

'Good. Can't wait to start the sweep. We're going to get some beautiful data, sis. And I think this is going to be a significant node. Maybe the largest this season. Aren't you glad it came our way?'

'Thrilled,' Naqi said, before returning to her work.

*

Thirty specialised probes hung on telemetric cables from the underside of the gondola, dangling like the venom-tipped stingers of some grotesque aerial jellyfish. The probes sniffed the air metres above the Juggler biomass, or skimmed the fuzzy green surface of the formation. Weighted plumb lines penetrated to the sea beneath the raft, sipping the organism-infested depths dozens of metres under the node. Radar mapped larger structures embedded within the node – dense kernels of compacted biomass, or huge cavities and tubes of inscrutable function – while sonar graphed the topology of the many sinewy organic cables which plunged into darkness, umbilicals anchoring the node to the seabed. Smaller nodes drew most of their energy from sunlight and the breakdown of sugars and fats in the sea's other floating microorganisms but the larger formations, which had a vastly higher information-processing burden, needed to tap belching aquatic fissures, active rifts in the ocean bed kilometres under the waves. Cold water was pumped down each umbilical by peristaltic compression waves, heated by being circulated in the superheated thermal environment of the underwater volcanoes, and then pumped back to the surface.

In all this sensing activity, remarkably little physical harm was done to the extended organism itself. The biomass sensed the approach of the probes and rearranged itself so that they passed through with little obstruction, even those scything lines that reached into the water. Energy was obviously being consumed to avoid the organism sustaining damage, and by implication the measurements must therefore have had some effect on the node's information-processing efficiency. The effect was likely to be small, however, and since the node was already subject to constant changes in its architecture – some probably intentional, and some probably forced on it by other factors in its environment – there appeared to be little point in worrying about the harm caused by the human investigators. Ultimately, so much was still guesswork. Although the swimmer teams had learned a great deal about the Pattern Jugglers' encoded information, almost everything else about them – how and why they stored the neural patterns, and to what extent the patterns were subject to subsequent post-processing – remained unknown. And those were merely the immediate questions. Beyond that were the real mysteries, which everyone wanted to solve, but right now they were simply beyond the scope of possible academic study. What they would learn today could not be expected to shed any light on those profundities. A single data point – even a single clutch of measurements – could not usually prove or disprove anything, but it might later turn out to play a vital role in a chain of argument, even if it was only in the biasing of some statistical distribution closer to one hypothesis than another. Science, as Naqi had long since realised, was as much a swarming, social process as it was something driven by ecstatic moments of personal discovery.

It was something she was proud to be part of.

The spiral sweep continued uneventfully, the airship chugging around in a gently widening circle. Morning shifted to early afternoon, and then the sun began to climb down towards the horizon, bleeding pale orange into the sky through soft-edged cracks in the cloud cover. For hours Naqi and Mina studied the incoming results, the ever-sharper scans of the node appearing on screens throughout the gondola. They discussed the results cordially enough, but Naqi could not stop thinking about Mina's betrayal. She took a spiteful pleasure in testing the extent to which her sister would lie, deliberately forcing the conversation around to Dr Sivaraksa and the project he steered.

'I hope I don't end up like one of those deadwood bureaucrats,' Naqi said, when they were discussing the way their careers might evolve. 'You know, like Sivaraksa.' She observed Mina pointedly, yet giving nothing away. 'I read some of his old papers; he used to be pretty good once. But now look at him.'

'It's easy to say that,' Mina said, 'but I bet he doesn't like being away from the front line any more than we would. But someone has to manage these big projects. Wouldn't you rather it was someone who'd at least *been* a scientist?'

'You sound like you're defending him. Next you'll be telling me you think the Moat is a good idea.'

'I'm not defending Sivaraksa,' Mina said. 'I'm just saying—' She eyed her sister with a sudden glimmer of suspicion. Had she guessed that Naqi knew? 'Never mind. Sivaraksa can fight his own battles. We've got work to do.'

'Anyone would think you were changing the subject,' Naqi said. But Mina was already on her way out of the gondola to check the equipment again.

At dusk the airship arrived at the perimetre of the node, completed one orbit, then began to track inwards again. As it passed over the parts of the node previously mapped, time-dependent changes were highlighted on the displays: arcs and bands of red superimposed against the lime and turquoise false-colour of the mapped structures. Most of the alterations were minor: a chamber opening here or closing there, or a small alteration in the network topology to ease a bottleneck between the lumpy subnodes dotted around the floating island. Other changes were more mysterious in function, but conformed to other studies. They were studied at enhanced resolution, the data prioritised and logged.

It looked as if the node was large, but in no way unusual.

Then night came, as swiftly as it always did at those latitudes. Mina and Naqi took turns, one sleeping for two or three-hour stretches while the other kept an eye on the read-outs. During a lull Naqi climbed up onto the top of the airship and tried the antenna again, and for a moment was gladdened when she saw that a new message had arrived. But the message itself turned out to be a statement from the Snowflake Council stating that the blackout on civilian messages would continue for at least another two days, until the current 'crisis' was over. There were allusions to civil disturbances in two cities, with curfews being imposed, and imperatives to ignore all unofficial news sources concerning the nature of the approaching ship.

Naqi wasn't surprised that there was trouble, though the extent of it took her aback. Her instincts were to believe the government line. The problem, from the government's point of view at least, was that nothing was yet known for certain about the nature of the ship, and so by being truthful they ended up sounding like they were keeping something back. They would have been far better off making up a plausible lie, which could be gently moulded towards accuracy as time passed.

Mina rose after midnight to begin her shift. Naqi went to sleep and dreamed fitfully, seeing in her mind's eye red smears and bars hovering against amorphous green. She had been staring at the read-outs too intently, for too many hours.

Mina woke her excitedly before dawn.

'Now I'm the one with the news,' she said.

'What?'

'Come and see for yourself.'

Naqi rose from her hammock, neither rested nor enthusiastic. In the dim light of the cabin Mina's fungal patterns shone with peculiar intensity: abstract detached shapes that only implied her presence.

Naqi followed the shapes onto the balcony.

'What,' she said again, not even bothering to make it sound like a question.

'There's been a development,' Mina said.

Naqi rubbed the sleep from her eyes. 'With the node?'

'Look. Down below. Right under us.'

Naqi pressed her stomach hard against the railing and leaned over as far as she dared. She had felt no real vertigo until they had lowered the sensor lines, and then suddenly there had been a physical connection between the airship and the ground. Was it her imagination, or had the airship lowered itself to about half its previous altitude, reeling in the lines at the same time?

The midnight light was all spectral shades of milky grey. The creased and crumpled landscape of the node reached away into mid-grey gloom, merging with the slate of the overlying cloud deck. Naqi saw nothing remarkable, other than the surprising closeness of the surface.

'I mean *really* look down,' Mina said.

Naqi pushed herself against the railing more than she had dared before, until she was standing on the very tips of her toes. Only then did she see it: directly below them was a peculiar circle of darkness, almost as if the airship was casting a distinct shadow beneath itself. It was a circular zone of exposed seawater, like a lagoon enclosed by the greater mass of the node. Steep banks of Juggler biomass, its heart a deep charcoal grey, rimmed the lagoon. Naqi studied it quietly. Her sister would judge her on any remark she made.

'How did you see it?' she asked eventually.

'See it?'

'It can't be more than twenty metres wide. A dot like that would have hardly shown up on the topographic map.'

'Naqi, you don't understand. I didn't steer us over the hole. It appeared below us, as we were moving. Listen to the motors. We're *still* moving. The hole's shadowing us. It follows us precisely.'

'Must be reacting to the sensors,' Naqi said.

'I've hauled them in. We're not trailing anything within thirty metres of the surface. The node's reacting to us, Naqi – to the presence of the airship. The Jugglers know we're here, and they're sending us a signal.'

'Maybe they are. But it isn't our job to interpret that signal. We're just here to make measurements, not to interact with the Jugglers.'

'So whose job is it?' Mina asked.

'Do I have to spell it out? Specialists from Umingmaktok.'

'They won't get here in time. You know how long nodes last. By the time the blackout's lifted, by the time the swimmer corps hotshots get here, we'll be sitting over a green smudge and not much more. This is a significant find, Naqi. It's the largest node this season and it's making a deliberate and clear attempt to invite swimmers.'

Naqi stepped back from the railing. 'Don't even think about it.'

'I've been thinking about it all night. This isn't just a large node, Naqi. Something's happening – that's why there's been so much sprite activity. If we don't swim here, we might miss something unique.'

'And if we do swim, we'll be violating every rule in the book. We're not trained, Mina. Even if we learned something – even if the Jugglers deigned to communicate with us – we'd be ostracised from the entire scientific community.'

'That would depend on what we learned, wouldn't it?'

'Don't do this, Mina. It isn't worth it.'

'We won't know if it's worth it or not until we try, will we?' Mina extended a hand. 'Look. You're right in one sense. Chances are pretty good nothing will happen. Normally you have to offer them a gift – a puzzle, or something rich in information. We haven't got anything like that. What'll probably happen is we'll hit the water and there won't be any kind of biochemical interaction. In which case, it doesn't matter. We don't have to tell anyone. And if we do learn something, but it isn't significant – well, we don't have to tell anyone about that either. Only if we learn something major. Something so big that they'll have to forget about a minor violation of protocol.'

'A minor violation—?' Naqi began, almost laughing at Mina's audacity.

'The point is, sis, we have a win-win situation here. And it's been handed to us on a plate.'

'You could also argue that we've been handed a major chance to fuck up spectacularly.'

'You read it whichever way you like. I know what I see.'

'It's too dangerous, Mina. People have died . . .' Naqi looked at Mina's fungal patterns, enhanced and emphasised by her tattoos. 'You flagged high for conformality. Doesn't that worry you slightly?'

'Conformality's just a fairy tale they use to scare children into behaving,' said Mina. '"Eat all your greens or the sea will swallow you up forever." I take it about as seriously as I take the Thule kraken, or the drowning of Arviat.'

'The Thule kraken is a joke, and Arviat never existed in the first place. But the last time I checked, conformality was an accepted phenomenon.'

'It's an accepted research topic. There's a distinction.'

'Don't split hairs—' Naqi began.

Mina gave every indication of not having heard Naqi speak. Her voice was distant, as if she were speaking to herself. It had a lilting, singsong quality. 'Too late to even think about it now. But it isn't long until dawn. I think it'll still be there at dawn.'

She pushed past Naqi.

'Where are you going now?'

'To catch some sleep. I need to be fresh for this. So do you.'

They hit the lagoon with two gentle, anticlimactic splashes. Naqi was underwater for a moment before she bobbed to the surface, holding her breath. At first she had to make a conscious effort to start breathing again: the air immediately above the water was so saturated with microscopic organisms that choking was a real possibility. Mina, surfacing next to her, drew in gulps with wild enthusiasm, as if willing the tiny creatures to invade her lungs. She shrieked delight at the sudden cold. When they had both gained equilibrium, treading with their shoulders above water, Naqi was finally able to take stock. She saw everything through a stinging haze of tears. The gondola hovered above them, poised beneath the larger mass of the vacuum-bladder. The life raft that it had deployed was sparkling new, rated for one hundred hours against moderate biological attack. But that was for mid-ocean, where the density of Juggler organisms would be much less than in the middle of a major node. Here, the hull might only endure a few tens of hours before it was consumed.

Once again, Naqi wondered if she should withdraw. There was still time. No real damage had yet been done. She could be back in the boat and back aboard the airship in a minute or so. Mina might not follow her, but she did not have to be complicit in her sister's actions. But Naqi knew she would not be able to turn back. She could not show weakness now that she had come this far.

'Nothing's happening . . .' she said.

'We've only been in the water a minute,' Mina said.

The two of them wore black wetsuits. The suits themselves could become buoyant if necessary – the right sequence of tactile commands and dozens of tiny bladders would inflate around the chest and shoulder area – but it was easy enough to tread water. In any case, if the Jugglers initiated contact, the suits would probably be eaten away in minutes. The swimmers who had made repeated contact often swam naked or near-naked, but neither Naqi nor Mina were yet prepared for that level of abject surrender to the ocean's assault. After another minute the water no longer felt as cold. Through gaps in the cloud cover the sun was harsh on Naqi's cheek. It etched furiously bright lines in the bottle-green surface of the lagoon, lines that coiled and shifted into fleeting calligraphic shapes as if conveying secret messages. The calm water lapped gently against their upper bodies. The walls of the lagoon were metre-high masses of fuzzy vegetation, like the steep banks of a river. Now and then Naqi felt something brush gently against her feet, like a passing frond or strand of seaweed. The first few times she flinched at the contact, but after a while it became strangely soothing. Occasionally something stroked one hand or the other, then moved playfully away. When she lifted her hands from the sea, mats of gossamer green draped from her fingers like the tattered remains of expensive gloves. The green material slithered free and slipped back into the sea. It tickled between her fingers.

'Nothing's happened yet,' Naqi said, more quietly this time.

'You're wrong. The shoreline's moved closer.'

Naqi looked at it. 'It's a trick of perspective.'

'I assure you it isn't.'

Naqi looked back at the raft. They had drifted five or six metres from it. It might as well have been a mile, for all the sense of security that the raft now offered. Mina was right: the lagoon was closing in on them, gently, slowly. If the lagoon had been twenty metres wide when they had entered, it must now be a third smaller. There was still time to escape before the hazy green walls squeezed in on them, but only if they moved now, back to the raft, back into the safety of the gondola.

'Mina . . . I want to go. We're not ready for this.'

'We don't need to be ready. It's going to happen.'

'We're not trained!'

'Call it learning on the job, in that case.' Mina was still trying to sound outrageously calm, but it wasn't working. Naqi heard it in her voice: she was either terribly frightened or terribly excited.

'You're more scared than I am,' she said.

'I am scared,' said Mina, 'scared we'll screw this up. Scared we'll blow this opportunity. Understand? I'm *that* kind of scared.'

Either Naqi was treading water less calmly, or the water itself had become visibly more agitated in the last few moments. The green walls were perhaps ten metres apart, and were no longer quite the sheer vertical structures they had appeared before. They had taken on form and design, growing and complexifying by the second. It was akin to watching a distant city emerge from fog, the revealing of bewildering, plunging layers of mesmeric detail, more than the eye or the mind could process.

'It doesn't look as if they're expecting a gift this time,' Mina said.

Veined tubes and pipes coiled and writhed around each other in constant, sinuous motion, making Naqi think of some hugely magnified circuitry formed from plant parts. It was restless, living circuitry that never quite settled into one configuration. Now and then chequerboard designs appeared, or intricately interlocking runes. Sharply geometric patterns flickered from point to point, echoed, amplified and subtly iterated at each move. Distinct three-dimensional shapes assumed brief solidity, carved from greenery as if by the deft hand of a topiarist. Naqi glimpsed unsettling anatomies: the warped memories of alien bodies that had once entered the ocean, a million, or a billion years ago. Here was a three-jointed limb, there the shieldlike curve of an exoskeletal plaque. The head of something that was almost equine melted into a goggling mass of faceted eyes. Fleetingly, a human form danced from the chaos. But only once. Alien swimmers vastly outnumbered human swimmers.

Here were the Pattern Jugglers, Naqi knew. The first explorers had mistaken these remembered forms for indications of actual sentience, thinking that the oceanic mass was a kind of community of intelligences. It was an easy mistake to have made, but it was some way from the truth. These animate shapes were enticements, like the gaudy covers of books. The minds themselves were captured only as frozen traces. The only living intelligence within the ocean lay in its own curatorial system.

To believe anything else was heresy.

The dance of bodies became too rapid to follow. Pastel-coloured lights glowed from deep within the green structure, flickering and stuttering. Naqi thought of lanterns burning in the depths of a forest. Now the edge of the lagoon had become irregular, extending peninsulas towards the centre of the dwindling circle of water, while narrow bays and inlets fissured back into the larger mass of the node. The peninsulas sprouted grasping tendrils, thigh-thick at the trunk but narrowing to the dimensions of plant fronds, and then narrowing further, bifurcating into lacy, fernlike hazes of awesome complexity. They diffracted light like the wings of dragonflies. They were closing over the lagoon, forming a shimmering canopy. Now and then a sprite – or something smaller but equally bright

– arced from one bank of the lagoon to another. Brighter things moved through the water like questing fish. Microscopic organisms were detaching from the larger fronds and tendrils, swarming in purposeful clouds. They batted against her skin, against her eyelids. Every breath that she took made her cough. The taste of the Pattern Jugglers was sour and medicinal. They were in her, invading her body.

She panicked. It was as if a tiny switch had flipped in her mind. Suddenly all other concerns melted away. She had to get out of the lagoon immediately, no matter what Mina would think of her.

Thrashing more than swimming, Naqi tried to push herself towards the raft, but as soon as the panic reaction had kicked in, she had felt something else slide over her. It was not so much paralysis as an immense sense of inertia. Moving, even breathing, became problematic. The boat was impossibly distant. She was no longer capable of treading water. She felt heavy, and when she looked down she saw that a green haze had enveloped the parts of her body that she could see above water. The organisms were adhering to the fabric of her wetsuit.

'Mina—' she called, 'Mina!'

But Mina only looked at her. Naqi sensed that her sister was experiencing the same sort of paralysis. Mina's movements had become languid; instead of panic, what Naqi saw on her face was profound resignation and acceptance. It was dangerously close to serenity.

Mina wasn't frightened at all.

The patterns on her neck were flaring vividly. Her eyes were closed. Already the organisms had begun to attack the fabric of her suit, stripping it away from her flesh. Naqi could feel the same thing happening to her own suit. There was no pain, for the organisms stopped short of attacking her skin. With a mighty effort she hoisted her forearm from the water, studying the juxtaposition of pale flesh and dissolving black fabric. Her fingers were as stiff as iron.

But – and Naqi clung to this fact – the ocean recognised the sanctity of organisms, or at least, thinking organisms. Strange things might happen to people who swam with the Jugglers, things that might be difficult to distinguish from death or near-death. But people always emerged afterwards, changed perhaps, but essentially whole. No matter what happened now, they would survive. The Jugglers always returned those who swam with them, and even when they did effect changes, they were seldom permanent.

Except, of course, for those who didn't return.

No, Naqi told herself. What they were doing was foolish, and might perhaps destroy their careers, but they would survive. Mina had flagged high on the conformality index when she had applied to join the swimmer corps, but that didn't mean she was necessarily at risk. Conformality merely implied a rare connection with the ocean. It verged on the glamorous.

Now Mina was going under. She had stopped moving entirely. Her eyes were blankly ecstatic.

Naqi wanted to resist that same impulse to submit, but all the strength had flowed away from her. She felt herself begin the same descent. The water closed over her mouth, then her eyes, and in a moment she was under. She felt herself a toppled statue sliding towards the seabed. Her fear reached a crescendo, and then passed it. She was not drowning. The froth of green organisms had forced itself down her throat, down her nasal passage. She felt no fright. There was nothing except a profound feeling that this was what she had been born to do.

Naqi knew what was happening, what was *going* to happen. She had studied enough reports on swimmer missions. The tiny organisms were infiltrating her entire body, creeping into her lungs and bloodstream. They were keeping her alive, while at the same time flooding her with chemical bliss. Droves of the same tiny creatures were seeking routes to her brain, inching along the optic nerve, the aural nerve, or crossing the blood-brain barrier itself. They were laying tiny threads behind them, fibres that extended back into the larger mass of organisms suspended in the water around her. In turn, these organisms would establish data-carrying channels back into the primary mass of the node . . . And the node itself was connected to other nodes, both chemically and via the packet-carrying sprites. The green threads bound Naqi to the entire ocean. It might take hours for a signal to reach her mind from halfway around Turquoise, but it didn't matter. She was beginning to think in Juggler time, her own thought processes seeming pointlessly quick, like the motion of bees.

She sensed herself becoming vaster.

She was no longer just a pale, hard-edged thing labelled *Naqi,* suspended in the lagoon like a dying starfish. Her sense of self was rushing out towards the horizon in all directions, encompassing first the node and then the empty oceanic waters around it. She couldn't say precisely how this information was reaching her. It wasn't through visual imagery, but more an intensely detailed spatial awareness. It was as if spatial awareness had suddenly become her most vital sense.

She supposed this was what swimmers meant when they spoke of *kenning.*

She *kenned* the presence of other nodes over the horizon, their chemical signals flooding her mind, each unique, each bewilderingly rich in information. It was like hearing the roar of a hundred crowds. And at the same time she *kenned* the ocean depths, the cold fathoms of water beneath the node, the life-giving warmth of the crustal vents. Closer, too, she *kenned* Mina. They were two neighbouring galaxies in a sea of strangeness. Mina's own thoughts were bleeding into the sea, into Naqi's mind, and in them Naqi felt the reflected echo of her own thoughts, picked up by Mina . . .

It was glorious.

For a moment their minds orbited each other, *kenning* each other on a level of intimacy neither had dreamed possible.

Mina . . . Can you feel me?

I'm here, Naqi. Isn't this wonderful?

The fear was gone, utterly. In its place was a marvellous feeling of immanence. They had made the right decision, Naqi knew. She had been right to follow Mina. Mina was deliciously happy, basking in the same hopeful sense of security and promise.

And then they began to sense other minds.

Nothing had changed, but it was suddenly clear that the roaring signals from the other nodes were composed of countless individual voices, countless individual streams of chemical information. Each stream was the recording of a mind that had entered the ocean at some point. The oldest minds – those that had entered in the deep past – were the faintest, but they were also the most numerous. They had begun to sound alike, the shapes of their stored personalities blurring into each other, no matter how different – how alien – they had been to start with. The minds that had been captured more recently were sharper and more variegated, like oddly shaped pebbles on a beach. Naqi *kenned* brutal alienness, baroque architectures of mind shaped by outlandish chains of evolutionary contingency. The only thing any of them had in common was that they had all reached a certain threshold of tool-using intelligence, and had all – for whatever reason – been driven into interstellar space, where they had encountered the Pattern Jugglers. But that was like saying the minds of sharks and leopards were alike because they had both evolved to hunt. The differences between the minds were so cosmically vast that Naqi felt her own mental processes struggling to accommodate them.

Even that was becoming easier. Subtly – slowly enough that from moment to moment she was not aware of it – the organisms in her skull were retuning her neural connections, allowing more and more of her own consciousness to seep out into the extended processing loom of the sea.

Now she sensed the most recent arrivals.

They were all human minds, each a glittering gem of distinctness. Naqi *kenned* a great gulf in time between the earliest human mind and the last recognisably alien one. She had no idea if it was a million years or a billion, but it felt immense. At the same time she grasped that the ocean had been desperate for an injection of variety, but while these human minds were welcome, they were not exotic enough, just barely sufficient to break the tedium.

The minds were snapshots, frozen in the conception of a single thought. It was like an orchestra of instruments, all sustaining a single, unique note. Perhaps there was a grindingly slow evolution in those minds – she felt the merest subliminal hint of change – but if that were the case, it would take centuries to complete a thought . . . thousands of years to complete the simplest internalised statement. The newest minds might not even have recognised that they had been swallowed by the sea.

And now Naqi could perceive a single mind flaring louder than the others.

It was recent, and human, and there was something about it that struck her as discordant. The mind was damaged, as if it had been captured imperfectly. It was disfigured, giving off squalls of hurt. It had suffered dreadfully. It was reaching out to her, craving love and affection; it searched for something to cling to in the abyssal loneliness it now knew.

Images ghosted through her mind. Something was burning. Flames licked through the interstitial gaps in a great black structure. She couldn't tell if it was a building or a vast, pyramidal bonfire.

She heard screams, and then something hysterical, which she at first took for more screaming, until she realised that it was something far, far worse. It was laughter, and as the flames roared higher, consuming the mass, smothering the screams, the laughter only intensified.

She thought it might be the laughter of a child.

Perhaps it was her imagination, but this mind appeared more fluid than the others. Its thoughts were still slow – far slower than Naqi's – but the mind appeared to have usurped more than its share of processing resources. It was stealing computational cycles from neighbouring minds, freezing them into absolute stasis while it completed a single sluggish thought.

The mind worried Naqi. Pain and fury was boiling off it.

Mina *kenned* it too. Naqi tasted Mina's thoughts and knew that her sister was equally disturbed by the mind's presence. Then she felt the mind's attention shift, drawn to the two inquisitive minds that had just entered the sea. It became aware of both of them, quietly watchful. A moment or two passed, and then the mind slipped away, back to wherever it had come from.

What was that . . .?

She felt her sister's reply. *I don't know. A human mind. A conformal, I think. Someone who was swallowed by the sea. But it's gone now.*

No, it hasn't. It's still there. Just hiding.

Millions of minds have entered the sea, Naqi. Thousands of conformals, perhaps, if you think of all the aliens that came before us. There are bound to be one or two bad apples.

That wasn't just a bad apple. It was like touching ice. And it sensed us. It reacted to us. Didn't it?

She sensed Mina's hesitation.

We can't be sure. Our own perceptions of events aren't necessarily reliable. I can't even be certain we're having this conversation. I might be talking to myself . . .

Mina . . . Don't talk like that. I don't feel safe.

Me neither. But I'm not going to let one frightening thing unnecessarily affect me.

Something happened then. It was a loosening, a feeling that the ocean's grip on Naqi had just relented to a significant degree. Mina, and the roaring background of other minds, fell away to something much more distant. It was as if Naqi had just stepped out of a babbling party into a quiet adjacent room, and was even now moving further and further away from the door.

Her body tingled. She no longer felt the same deadening paralysis. Pearl-grey light flickered above. Without being sure whether she was doing it herself, she rose towards the surface. She was aware that she was moving away from Mina, but for now all that mattered was to escape the sea. She wanted to be as far from that discordant mind as possible.

Her head rammed through a crust of green into air. At the same moment the Juggler organisms fled her body in a convulsive rush. She thrashed stiff limbs and took in deep, panicked breaths. The transition was horrible, but it was over in a few seconds. She looked around, expecting to see the sheer walls of the lagoon, but all she saw in one direction was open water. Naqi felt panic rising again. Then she kicked herself around and saw a wavy line of bottle-green that had to be the perimetre of the node, perhaps half a kilometre away from her present position. The airship was a distant silvery teardrop that appeared to be perched on the surface of the node itself.

In her fear she did not immediately think of Mina. All she wanted to do was reach the safety of the airship, to be aloft. Then she saw the raft, bobbing only one or two hundred metres away. Somehow it had been transplanted to the open waters as well. It looked distant but reachable. She started swimming, fear giving her strength and sense of purpose. In truth, she was well within the true boundary of the node: the water was still thick with suspended microorganisms, so that it was more like swimming through cold green soup. It made each stroke harder, but she did not have to expend much effort to stay afloat.

Did she trust the Pattern Jugglers not to harm her? Perhaps. After all, she had not encountered *their* minds at all – if they even *had* minds. They were merely the archiving system. Blaming them for that one poisoned mind was like blaming a library for one hateful book.

But still, it had unnerved her profoundly. She wondered why none of the other swimmers had ever communicated their encounters with such a mind. After all, she remembered it well enough now, and she was nearly out of the ocean. She might forget shortly – there were bound to be subsequent neurological effects – but under other circumstances there would have been nothing to prevent her relating her experiences to a witness or inviolable recording system.

She kept swimming, and began to wonder why Mina hadn't emerged from the waters as well. Mina had been just as terrified. But Mina had also been more curious, and more willing to ignore her fears. Naqi had grasped the opportunity to leave the ocean once the Jugglers released their grip on her. But what if Mina had elected to remain?

What if Mina was still down there, still in communion with the Jugglers?

Naqi reached the raft and hauled herself aboard, being careful not to capsize it. She saw that the raft was still largely intact. It had been moved, but not damaged, and although the ceramic sheathing was showing signs of attack, peppered here and there with scabbed green accretions, it was certainly good for another few hours. The rot-hardened control systems were alive, and still in telemetric connection with the distant airship.

Naqi had crawled from the sea naked. Now she felt cold and vulnerable. She pulled an aluminised quilt from the raft's supply box and wrapped it around herself. It did not stop her from shivering, did not make her feel any less nauseous, but at least it afforded some measure of symbolic barrier against the sea.

She looked around again, but there was still no sign of Mina.

Naqi folded aside the weatherproof control cover and tapped commands into the matrix of waterproofed keys. She waited for the response from the airship. The moment stretched. But there it was: a minute shift in the dull gleam on the silver back of the vacuum-bladder. The airship was turning, pivoting like a great slow weather vane. It was moving, responding to the raft's homing command.

But where was Mina?

Now something moved in the water next to her, coiling in weak, enervated spasms. Naqi looked at it with horrified recognition. She reached over, still shivering, and with appalled gentleness fished the writhing thing from the sea. It lay in her fingers like a baby sea serpent. It was white and segmented, half a metre long. She knew exactly what it was.

It was Mina's worm. It meant Mina had died.

TWO

Two years later Naqi watched a spark fall from the heavens.

Along with many hundreds of spectators, she was standing on the railed edge of one of Umingmaktok's elegant cantilevered arms. It was afternoon. Every visible surface of the city had been scoured of rot and given a fresh coat of crimson or emerald paint. Amber bunting had been hung along the metal stay-lines that supported the tapering arms protruding from the city's towering commercial core. Most of the berthing slots around the perimetre were occupied by passenger or cargo craft, while many smaller vessels were holding station in the immediate airspace around Umingmaktok. The effect, which Naqi had seen on her approach to the city a day earlier, had been to turn the snowflake into a glittering, delicately ornamented vision. By night they had fireworks displays. By day, as now, conjurers and confidence tricksters wound their way through the crowds. Nose-flute musicians and drum dancers performed impromptu atop improvised podia. Kick-boxers were being cheered on as they moved from one informal ring to another, pursued by whistle-blowing proctors. Hastily erected booths were marked with red and yellow pennants, selling refreshments, souvenirs or tattoo-work, while pretty costumed girls who wore backpacks equipped with tall flagstaffs sold drinks or ices. The children had balloons and rattles marked with the emblems of both Umingmaktok and the Snowflake Council, and many of them had had their faces painted to resemble stylised space travellers. Puppet theatres had been set up here and there, running through exactly the same small repertoire of stories that Naqi remembered from her childhood. The children were enthralled nonetheless; mouths agape at each miniature epic, whether it was a roughly accurate account of the world's settlement – with the colony ship being stripped to the bone for every gram of metal it held – or something altogether more fantastic, like the drowning of Arviat. It didn't matter to the children that one was based in fact and the other was pure mythology. To them the idea that every city they called home had been cannibalised from the belly of a four-kilometre-long ship was no more or less plausible than the idea that the living sea might occasionally snatch cities beneath the waves when they displeased it. At that age everything was both magical and mundane, and she supposed that the children were no more nor less excited by the prospect of the coming visitors than they were by the promised fireworks display, or the possibility of further treats if they were well behaved. Other than the children, there were animals: caged monkeys and birds, and the occasional expensive pet being shown off for the day. One or two servitors stalked through the crowd, and occasionally a golden float-cam would bob through the air, loitering over a scene of interest like a single detached eyeball. Turquoise had not seen this level of celebration since the last acrimonious divorce, and the networks were milking it remorselessly, over-analysing even the tiniest scrap of information.

This was, in truth, exactly the kind of thing Naqi would normally have gone to the other side of the planet to avoid. But something had drawn her this time, and made her wangle the trip out from the Moat at an otherwise critical time in the project. She could only suppose that it was a need to close a particular chapter in her life, one that had begun the night before Mina's death. The detection of the Ultra ship – they now knew that it was named *Voice of Evening* – had been the event that triggered the blackout, and the blackout had been Mina's justification for the two of them attempting to swim with the Jugglers. Indirectly, therefore, the Ultras were 'responsible' for whatever had happened to Mina. That was unfair, of course, but Naqi nonetheless felt the need to be here now, if only to witness the visitors' emergence with her own eyes and see if they really were the monsters of her imagination. She had come to Umingmaktok with a stoic determination that she would not be swept up by the hysteria of the celebrations. Yet now that she had made the trip, now that she was amidst the crowd, drunk on the chemical buzz of human excitement, with a nice fresh worm hooked onto her gut wall, she found herself in the perverse position of actually enjoying the atmosphere.

And now everyone had noticed the falling spark.

The crowd turned their heads into the sky, ignoring the musicians, conjurors and confidence tricksters. The backpacked girls stopped and looked aloft along with the others, shielding their eyes against the midday glare. The spark was the shuttle of *Voice of Evening*, now parked in orbit around Turquoise.

Everyone had seen Captain Moreau's ship by now, either with their own eyes as a moving star, or via the images captured by the orbiting cameras or ground-based telescopes. The ship was dark and sleek, outrageously elegant. Now and then its Conjoiner drives flickered on just enough to trim its orbit, those flashes like brief teasing windows into daylight for the hemisphere below.

A ship like that could do awful things to a world, and everyone knew it.

But if Captain Moreau and his crew meant ill for Turquoise, they'd had ample opportunity to do harm already. They had been silent at two years out, but at one year out the *Voice of Evening* had transmitted the usual approach signals, requesting permission to stop over for three or four months. It was a formality – no one argued with Ultras – but it was also a gladdening sign that they intended to play by the usual rules.

Over the next year there had been a steady stream of communications between the ship and the Snowflake Council. The official word was that the messages had been designed to establish a framework for negotiation and person-to-person trade. The Ultras would need to update their linguistics software to avoid being confused by the subtleties of the Turquoise dialects, which, although based on Canasian, contained confusing elements of Inuit and Thai, relics of the peculiar social mix of the original settlement coalition.

The falling shuttle had slowed to merely supersonic speed now, shedding its plume of ionised air. Dropping speed with each loop, it executed a lazily contracting spiral above Umingmaktok. Naqi had rented cheap binoculars from one of the vendors. The lenses were scuffed, shimmering with the pink of fungal bloom. She visually locked onto the shuttle, its roughly delta shape wobbling in and out of sharpness. Only when it was two or three thousand metres above Umingmaktok could she see it clearly. It was very elegant, a pure brilliant white like something carved from cloud. Beneath the mantalike hull complex machines – fans and control surfaces – moved too rapidly to be seen as anything other than blurs of subliminal motion. She watched as the ship reduced speed until it hovered at the same altitude as the snowflake city. Above the roar of the crowd – an ecstatic, flag-waving mass – all Naqi heard was a shrill hum, almost too far into ultrasound to detect.

The ship approached slowly. It had been given instructions for docking with the arm adjacent to the one where Naqi and the other spectators gathered. Now that it was close it was apparent that the shuttle was larger than any of the dirigible craft normally moored to the city's arms; by Naqi's estimate it was at least half as wide as the city's central core. But it slid into its designated mooring point with exquisite delicacy. Bright red symbols flashed onto the otherwise blank white hull, signifying airlocks, cargo ports and umbilical sockets. Gangways were swung out from the arm to align with the doors and ports. Dockers, supervised by proctors and city officials, scrambled along the precarious connecting ways and attempted to fix magnetic berthing stays onto the shuttle's hull. The magnetics slid off the hull. They tried adhesive grips next, and these were no more successful. After that, the dockers shrugged their shoulders and made exasperated gestures in the direction of the shuttle.

The roar of the crowd had died down a little by now.

Naqi felt the anticipation as well. She watched as an entourage of VIPs moved to the berthing position, led by a smooth, faintly cherubic individual that Naqi recognised as Tak Thonburi, the mayor of Umingmaktok and presiding chair of the Snowflake Council. Tak Thonburi was happily overweight and had a permanent cowlick of black hair, like an inverted question mark tattooed upon his forehead. His cheeks and brow were mottled with pale green. Next to him was the altogether leaner frame of Jotah Sivaraksa. It was no surprise that Dr Sivaraksa should be here today, for the Moat project was one of the most significant activities of the entire Snowflake Council. His iron-grey eyes flashed this way and that as if constantly triangulating the positions of enemies and allies alike. The group was accompanied by armed, ceremonially-dressed proctors and a triad of martial servitors. Their articulation points and sensor apertures were lathered in protective sterile grease, to guard against rot.

Though they tried to hide it, Naqi could tell that the VIPs were nervous. They moved a touch too confidently, making their trepidation all the more evident.

The red door symbol at the end of the gangway pulsed brighter and a section of the hull puckered open. Naqi squinted, but even through the binoculars it was difficult to make out anything other than red-lit gloom. Tak Thonburi and his officials stiffened. A sketchy figure emerged from the shuttle, lingered on the threshold and then stepped with immense slowness into full sunlight.

The crowd's reaction – and to some extent Naqi's own – was double-edged. There was a moment of relief that the messages from orbit had not been outright lies. Then there was an equally brief tang of shock at the actual appearance of Captain Moreau. The man was at least a third taller than anyone Naqi had ever seen in her life, yet commensurately thinner, his seemingly brittle frame contained within a jade-coloured mechanical exoskeleton of ornate design. The skeleton lent his movements something of the lethargic quality of a stick insect.

Tak Thonburi was the first to speak. His amplified voice boomed out across the six arms of Umingmaktok, echoing off the curved surfaces of the multiple vacuum-bladders that held the city aloft. Float-cams jostled for the best camera angle, swarming around him like pollen-crazed bees.

'Captain Moreau . . . Let me introduce myself. I am Tak Thonburi, mayor of Umingmaktok Snowflake City and incumbent chairman of the Snowflake Council of All Turquoise. It is my pleasure to welcome you, your crew and passengers to Umingmaktok, and to Turquoise itself. You have my word that we will do all in our power to make your visit as pleasant as possible.'

The Ultra moved closer to the official. The door to the shuttle remained open behind him. Naqi's binocs picked out red hologram serpents on the jade limbs of the skeleton.

The Ultra's own voice boomed at least as loud, but emanated from the shuttle rather than Umingmaktok's public address system. 'People of greenish-blue . . .' The captain hesitated, then tapped one of the stalks projecting from his helmet. 'People of Turquoise . . . Chairman Thonburi . . . Thank you for your welcome, and for your kind permission to assume orbit. We have accepted it with gratitude. You have my word . . . as captain of the lighthugger *Voice of Evening* . . . that we will abide by the strict terms of your generous offer of hospitality.' His mouth continued to move even during the pauses, Naqi noticed: the translation system was lagging. 'You have my additional guarantee that no harm will be done to your world, and Turquoise law will be presumed to apply to the occupants . . . of all bodies and vessels in your atmosphere. All traffic between my ship and your world will be subject to the authorisation of the Snowflake Council, and any member of the council will – under the . . . auspices of the council – be permitted to visit *Voice of Evening* at any time, subject to the availability of a . . . suitable conveyance.'

The captain paused and looked at Tak Thonburi expectantly. The mayor wiped a nervous hand across his brow, smoothing his kiss-curl into obedience. 'Thank you . . . Captain.' Tak Thonburi's eyes flashed to the other members of the reception party. 'Your terms are of course more than acceptable. You have my word that we will do all in our power to assist you and your crew, and that we will do our utmost to ensure that the forthcoming negotiations of trade proceed in an equable manner . . . and in such a way that both parties will be satisfied upon their conclusion.'

The captain did not respond immediately, allowing an uncomfortable pause to draw itself out. Naqi wondered if it was really the fault of the software, or whether Moreau was just playing on Tak Thonburi's evident nervousness.

'Of course,' the Ultra said, finally. 'Of course. My sentiments entirely . . . Chairman Thonburi. Perhaps now wouldn't be a bad time to introduce my guests?'

On his cue three new figures emerged from *Voice of Evening*'s shuttle. Unlike the Ultra, they could almost have passed for ordinary citizens of Turquoise. There were two men and one woman, all of approximately normal height and build, each with long hair, tied back in elaborate clasps. Their clothes were brightly coloured, fashioned from many separate fabrics of yellow, orange, red and russet, and various permutations of the same warm sunset shades. The clothes billowed around them, rippling in the light afternoon breeze. All three members of the party wore silver jewellery, far more than was customary on Turquoise. They wore it on their fingers, in their hair, hanging from their ears.

The woman was the first to speak, her voice booming out from the shuttle's PA system.

'Thank you, Captain Moreau. Thank you also, Chairman Thonburi. We are delighted to be here. I am Amesha Crane, and I speak for the Vahishta Foundation. Vahishta's a modest scientific organisation with its origins in the cometary prefectures of the Haven Demarchy. Lately we have been expanding our realm of interest to encompass other solar systems, such as this one.' Crane gestured at the two men who had accompanied her from the shuttle. 'My associates are Simon Matsubara and Rafael Weir. There are another seventeen of us aboard the shuttle. Captain Moreau carried us here as paying passengers aboard *Voice of Evening*, and as such Vahishta gladly accepts all the terms already agreed upon.'

Tak Thonburi looked even less sure of himself. 'Of course. We welcome your . . . interest. A scientific organisation, did you say?'

'One with a special interest in the study of the Jugglers,' Amesha Crane answered. She was the most strikingly attractive member of the trio, with fine cheekbones and a wide, sensual mouth that looked to be always on the point of smiling or laughing. Naqi felt that the woman was sharing something with her, something private and amusing. Doubtless everyone in the crowd felt the same vague sense of complicity.

Crane continued, 'We have no Pattern Jugglers in our own system, but that hasn't stopped us from focusing our research on them, collating the data available from the worlds where Juggler studies are ongoing. We've been doing this for decades, sifting inference and theory, guesswork and intuition. Haven't we, Simon?'

The man nodded. He had sallow skin and a fixed, quizzical expression.

'No two Juggler worlds are precisely alike,' Simon Matsubara said, his voice as clear and confident as the woman's. 'And no two Juggler worlds have been studied by precisely the same mix of human sociopolitical factions. That means that we have a great many variables to take into consideration. Despite that, we believe we have identified similarities that may have been overlooked by the individual research teams. They may even be very important similarities, with repercussions for wider humanity. But in the absence of our own Jugglers, it is difficult to test our theories. That's where Turquoise comes in.'

The other man – Naqi recalled his name was Rafael Weir – began to speak. 'Turquoise has been largely isolated from the rest of human space for the better part of two centuries.'

'We're aware of this,' said Jotah Sivaraksa. It was the first time any member of the entourage other than Tak Thonburi had spoken. To Naqi he sounded irritated, though he was doing his best to hide it.

'You don't share your findings with the other Juggler worlds,' said Amesha Crane. 'Nor – to the best of our knowledge – do you intercept their cultural transmissions. The consequence is that your research on the Jugglers has been untainted by any outside considerations – the latest fashionable theory, the latest groundbreaking technique. You prefer to work in scholarly isolation.'

'We're an isolationist world in other respects,' Tak Thonburi said. 'Believe it or not, it actually rather suits us.'

'Quite,' Crane said, with a hint of sharpness. 'But the point remains. Your Jugglers are an uncontaminated resource. When a swimmer enters the ocean, their own memories and personality may be absorbed into the Juggler sea. The prejudices and preconceptions that swimmer carries inevitably enter the ocean in some shape or form – diluted, confused, but nonetheless present in some form. And when the next swimmer enters the sea, and opens their mind to communion, what they perceive – what they *ken*, in your own terminology – is irrevocably tainted by the preconceptions introduced by the previous swimmer. They may experience something that confirms their deepest suspicion about the nature of the Jugglers – but they can't be sure that they aren't simply picking up the mental echoes of the last swimmer, or the swimmer before that.'

Jotah Sivaraksa nodded. 'What you say is undoubtedly true. But we've had just as many cycles of fashionable theory as anyone else. Even within Umingmaktok there are a dozen different research teams, each with their own views.'

'We accept that,' Crane said, with an audible sigh. 'But the degree of contamination is slight compared to other worlds. Vahishta lacks the resources for a trip to a previously unvisited Juggler world, so the next best thing is to visit one that has suffered the smallest degree of human cultural pollution. Turquoise fits the bill.'

Tak Thonburi held the moment before responding, playing to the crowd again. Naqi rather admired the way he did it.

'Good. I'm very . . . pleased . . . to hear it. And might I ask just what it is about our ocean that we can offer you?'

'Nothing except the ocean itself,' said Amesha Crane. 'We simply wish to join you in its study. If you will allow it, members of the Vahishta Foundation will collaborate with native Turquoise scientists and study teams. They will shadow them and offer interpretation or advice when requested. Nothing more than that.'

'That's all?'

Crane smiled. 'That's all. It's not as if we're asking for the world, is it?'

Naqi remained in Umingmaktok for three days after the arrival, visiting friends and taking care of business for the Moat. The newcomers had departed, taking their shuttle to one of the other snowflake cities – Prachuap or the recently married Qaanaaq-Pangnirtung, perhaps – where a smaller but no less worthy group of city dignitaries would welcome Captain Moreau and his passengers.

In Umingmaktok the booths and bunting were packed away and normal business resumed. Litter abounded. Worm dealers did brisk business, as they always did during times of mild gloom. There were far fewer transport craft moored to the arms, and no sign at all of the intense media presence of a few days before. Tourists had gone back to their home cities and the children were safely back in school. Between meetings Naqi sat in the midday shade of half-empty restaurants and bars, observing the same puzzled disappointment in every face she encountered. Deep down she felt it herself. For two years they had been free to imprint every possible fantasy on the approaching ship. Even if the newcomers had arrived with less than benign intent, there would still have been something interesting to talk about: the possibility, however remote, that one's own life might be about to become drastically more exciting.

But now none of that was going to happen. Undoubtedly Naqi would be involved with the visitors at some point, allowing them to visit the Moat or one of the outlying research zones she managed, but there would be nothing life-changing.

She thought back to that night with Mina, when they had heard the news. Everything had changed then. Mina had died, and Naqi had found herself taking her sister's role in the Moat. She had risen to the challenge and promotions had followed with gratifying swiftness, until she was in effective charge of the Moat's entire scientific programme. But that sense of closure she had yearned for was still absent. The men she had slept with – men who were almost always swimmers – had never provided it, and by turns they had each lost patience with her, realising that they were less important to her as people than what they represented, as connections to the sea. It had been months since her last romance, and once Naqi had recognised the way her own subconscious was drawing her back to the sea, she had drawn away from contact with swimmers. She had been drifting since then, daring to hope that the newcomers would allow her some measure of tranquillity.

But the newcomers had not supplied it.

She supposed she would have to find it elsewhere.

On the fourth day Naqi returned to the Moat on a high-speed dirigible. She arrived near sunset, dropping down from high altitude to see the structure winking back at her, a foreshortened ellipse of grey-white ceramic lying against the sea like some vast discarded bracelet. From horizon to horizon there were several Juggler nodes visible, webbed together by the faintest of filaments – to Naqi they looked like motes of ink spreading into blotting paper – but there were also smaller dabs of green within the Moat itself.

The structure was twenty kilometres wide and now it was nearly finished. Only a narrow channel remained where the two ends of the bracelet did not quite meet: a hundred-metre-wide sheer-sided aperture flanked on either side by tall, ramshackle towers of accommodation modules, equipment sheds and construction cranes. To the north, strings of heavy cargo dirigibles ferried processed ore and ceramic cladding from Narathiwat atoll, lowering it down to the construction teams on the Moat.

They had been working here for nearly twenty years. The hundred metres of the Moat that projected above the water was only one-tenth of the full structure – a kilometre-high ring resting on the seabed. In a matter of months the gap – little more than a notch in the top of the Moat – would be sealed, closed off by immense hermetically tight sea-doors. The process would be necessarily slow and delicate, for what was being attempted here was not simply the closing-off of part of the sea. The Moat was an attempt to isolate a part of the living ocean, sealing off a community of Pattern Juggler organisms within its impervious ceramic walls.

The high-speed dirigible swung low over the aperture. The thick green waters streaming through the cut had the phlegmatic consistency of congealing blood. Thick, ropy tendrils permitted information transfer between the external sea and the cluster of small nodes within the Moat. Swimmers were constantly present, either inside or outside the Moat, *kenning* the state of the sea and establishing that the usual Juggler processes continued unabated.

The dirigible docked with one of the two flanking towers.

Naqi stepped out, back into the hectic corridors and office spaces of the project building. It felt distinctly odd to be back on absolutely firm ground. Although one was seldom aware of it, Umingmaktok was never quite still: no snowflake city or airship ever was. But she would get used to it; in a few hours she would be immersed in her work, having to think of a dozen different things at once, finessing solution pathways, balancing budgets against quality, dealing with personality clashes and minor turf wars, and perhaps – if she was very lucky – managing an hour or two of pure research. Aside from the science, none of it was particularly challenging, but it kept her mind off other things. And after a few days of that, the arrival of the visitors would begin to feel like a bizarre, irrelevant interlude in an otherwise monotonous dream. She supposed that two years ago she would have been grateful for that. Life could indeed continue much as she had always imagined it would.

But when she arrived at her office there was a message from Dr Sivaraksa. He needed to speak to her urgently.

Dr Jotah Sivaraksa's office on the Moat was a good deal less spacious than his quarters in Umingmaktok, but the view was superb. His accommodation was perched halfway up one of the towers that flanked the cut through the Moat, buttressed out from the main mass of prefabricated modules like a partially opened desk drawer. Dr Sivaraksa was writing notes when she arrived. For a few moments Naqi lingered at the sloping window, watching the construction activity hundreds of metres below. Railed machines and helmeted workers toiled on the flat upper surface of the Moat, moving raw materials and equipment to the assembly sites. Above, the sky was a perfect cobalt-blue, marred now and then by the passing green-stained hull of a cargo dirigible. The sea beyond the Moat had the dimpled texture of expensive leather.

Dr Sivaraksa cleared his throat and, when Naqi turned, he gestured at the vacant seat on the opposite side of his desk.

'Life treating you well?'

'Can't complain, sir.'

'And work?'

'No particular problems that I'm aware of.'

'Good. Good.' Sivaraksa made a quick, cursive annotation in the notebook he had opened on his desk, then slid it beneath the smoky-grey cube of a paperweight. 'How long has it been now?'

'Since what, sir?'

'Since your sister . . . Since Mina . . .' He seemed unable to complete the sentence, substituting a spiralling gesture made with his index finger. His finely boned hands were marbled with veins of olive green.

Naqi eased into her seat. 'Two years, sir.'

'And you're . . . over it?'

'I wouldn't exactly say I'm over it, no. But life goes on, like they say. Actually I was hoping . . .' Naqi had been about to tell him how she had imagined the arrival of the visitors would close that chapter. But she doubted she would be able to convey her feelings in a way Dr Sivaraksa would understand. 'Well, I was hoping I'd have put it all behind me by now.'

'I knew another conformal, you know. Fellow from Gjoa. Made it into the élite swimmer corps before anyone had the foggiest idea . . .'

'It's never been proven that Mina was conformal, sir.'

'No, but the signs were there, weren't they? To one degree or another we're all subject to symbiotic invasion by the ocean's microorganisms. But conformals show an unusual degree of susceptibility. On one hand it's as if their own bodies actively invite the invasion, shutting down the usual inflammatory or foreign cell rejection mechanisms. On the other, the ocean seems to tailor its messengers for maximum effectiveness, as if the Jugglers have selected a specific target they wish to absorb. Mina had very strong fungal patterns, did she not?'

'I've seen worse,' Naqi said, which was not entirely a lie.

'But not, I suspect, in anyone who ever attempted to commune. I understand you had ambitions to join the swimmer corps yourself?'

'Before all that happened.'

'I understand. And now?'

Naqi had never told anyone that she had joined Mina in the swimming incident. The truth was that even if she had not been present at the time of Mina's death, her encounter with the rogue mind would have put her off entering the ocean for life.

'It isn't for me. That's all.'

Jotah Sivaraksa nodded gravely. 'A wise choice. Aptitude or not, you'd have almost certainly been filtered out of the swimmer corps. A direct genetic connection to a conformal – even an unproven conformal – would be too much of a risk.'

'That's what I assumed, sir.'

'Does it trouble you, Naqi?'

She was wearying of this. She had work to do: deadlines to meet that Sivaraksa himself had imposed.

'Does what trouble me?'

He nodded at the sea. Now that the play of light had shifted minutely, it looked less like dimpled leather than a sheet of beaten bronze. 'The thought that Mina might still be out there . . . in some sense.'

'It might trouble me if I were a swimmer, sir. Other than that . . . No. I can't say that it does. My sister died. That's all that mattered.'

'Swimmers have occasionally reported encountering minds – essences – of the lost, Naqi. The impressions are often acute. The conformed leave their mark on the ocean at a deeper, more permanent level than the impressions left behind by mere swimmers. One senses that there must be a purpose to this.'

'That wouldn't be for me to speculate, sir.'

'No.' He glanced down at the compad and then tapped his forefinger against his upper lip. 'No. Of course not. Well, to the matter at hand—'

She interrupted him. 'You swam once, sir?'

'Yes. Yes, I did.' The moment stretched. She was about to say something – anything – when Sivaraksa continued, 'I had to stop for medical reasons. Otherwise I suppose I'd have been in the swimmer corps for a good deal longer, at least until my hands started turning green.'

'What was it like?'

'Astonishing. Beyond anything I'd expected.'

'Did they change you?'

At that he smiled. 'I never thought that they did, until now. After my last swim I went through all the usual neurological and psychological tests. They found no anomalies; no indications that the Jugglers had imprinted any hints of alien personality or rewired my mind to think in an alien way.'

Sivaraksa reached across the desk and held up the smoky cube that Naqi had taken for a paperweight. 'This came down from *Voice of Evening*. Examine it.'

Naqi peered into the milky-grey depths of the cube. Now that she saw it closely she realised that there were things embedded within the translucent matrix. There were chains of unfamiliar symbols, intersecting at right angles. They resembled the complex white scaffolding of a building.

'What is it?'

'Mathematics. Actually, a mathematical argument – a proof, if you like. Conventional mathematical notation – no matter how arcane – has evolved so that it can be written down on a two-dimensional surface, like paper or a read-out. This is a three-dimensional syntax, liberated from that constraint. Its enormously richer, enormously more elegant.' The cube tumbled in Sivaraksa's hand. He was smiling. 'No one could make head or tail of it. Yet when I looked at it for the first time I nearly dropped it in shock. It made perfect sense to me. Not only did I understand the theorem, but I also understood the point of it. It's a joke, Naqi. A pun. This mathematics is rich enough to embody humour. And understanding *that* is the gift they left me. It was sitting in my mind for twenty-eight years, like an egg waiting to hatch.'

Abruptly, Sivaraksa placed the cube back on the table.

'Something's come up,' he said.

From somewhere came the distant, prolonged thunder of a dirigible discharging its cargo of processed ore. It must have been one of the last consignments.

'Something, sir?'

'They've asked to see the Moat.'

'They?'

'Crane and her Vahishta mob. They've requested an oversight of all major scientific centres on Turquoise, and naturally enough we're on the list. They'll be visiting us, spending a couple of days seeing what we've achieved.'

'I'm not too surprised that they've asked to visit, sir.'

'No, but I was hoping we'd have a few months' grace. We don't. They'll be here in a week.'

'That's not necessarily a problem for us, is it?'

'It mustn't become one,' Sivaraksa said. 'I'm putting you in charge of the visit, Naqi. You'll be the interface between Crane's group and the Moat. That's quite a responsibility, you understand. A mistake – the tiniest gaffe – could undermine our standing with the Snowflake Council.' He nodded at the compad. 'Our budgetary position is precarious. Frankly, I'm in Tak Thonburi's lap. We can't afford any embarrassments.'

'No, sir.'

She certainly did understand. The job was a poisoned chalice, or, at the very least, a chalice with the strong potential to become poisoned. If she succeeded – if the visit went smoothly, with no hitches – Sivaraksa could still take much of the credit for it. If it went wrong, on the other hand, the fault would be categorically hers.

'One more thing.' Sivaraksa reached under his desk and produced a brochure that he slid across to her. The brochure was marked with a prominent silver snowflake motif. It was sealed with red foil. 'Open it; you have clearance.'

'What is it, sir?'

'A security report on our new friends. One of them has been behaving a bit oddly. You'll need to keep an eye on him.'

For inscrutable reasons of their own, the liaison committee had decided she would be introduced to Amesha Crane and her associates a day before the official visit, when the party was still in Sukhothai-Sanikiluaq. The journey there took the better part of two days, even allowing for the legs she took by high-speed dirigible or the ageing, unreliable trans-atoll railway line between Narathiwat and Cape Dorset. She arrived at Sukhothai-Sanikiluaq in a velvety purple twilight, catching the tail end of a fireworks display. The two snowflake cities had only been married three weeks, so the arrival of the off-worlders was an excellent pretext for prolonging the celebrations. Naqi watched the fireworks from a civic landing stage perched halfway up Sukhothai's core, starbursts and cataracts of scarlet, indigo and intense emerald green brightening the sky above the vacuum-bladders. The colours reminded her of the organisms that she and Mina had seen in the wake of their airship. The recollection left her suddenly sad and drained, convinced that she had made a terrible mistake by accepting this assignment.

'Naqi?'

It was Tak Thonburi, coming out to meet her on the balcony. They had already exchanged messages during the journey. He was dressed in full civic finery and appeared more than a little drunk.

'Chairman Thonburi.'

'Good of you to come here, Naqi.' She watched his eyes map her contours with scientific rigour, lingering here and there around regions of particular interest. 'Enjoying the show?'

'You certainly seem to be, sir.'

'Yes, yes. Always had a thing about fireworks.' He pressed a drink into her hand and together they watched the display come to its mildly disappointing conclusion. There was a lull then, but Naqi noticed that the spectators on the other balconies were reluctant to leave, as if waiting for something. Presently a stunning display of three-dimensional images appeared, generated by powerful projection apparatus in the *Voice of Evening*'s shuttle. Above Sukhothai-Sanikiluaq, Chinese dragons as large as mountains fought epic battles. Sea monsters convulsed and writhed in the night. Celestial citadels burned. Hosts of purple-winged fiery angels fell from the heavens in tightly knit squadrons, clutching arcane instruments of music or punishment.

A marbled giant rose from the sea, as if woken from some aeons-long slumber.

It was very, very impressive.

'Bastards,' Thonburi muttered.

'Sir?'

'Bastards,' he said, louder this time. 'We know they're better than us. But do they have to keep reminding us?'

He ushered her into the reception chamber where the Vahishta visitors were being entertained. The return indoors had a magical sharpening effect on his senses. Naqi suspected that the ability to turn drunkenness on and off like a switch must be one of the most hallowed of diplomatic skills.

He leaned towards her, confidentially. 'Did Jotah mention any—'

'Security considerations, Chairman? Yes, I think I got the message.'

'It's probably nothing, only—'

'I understand. Better safe than sorry.'

He winked, touching a finger against the side of his nose. 'Precisely.'

The interior was bright after the balcony. Twenty Vahishta delegates were standing in a huddle near the middle of the room. The captain was absent – little had been seen of Moreau since the shuttle's arrival in Umingmaktok – but the delegates were talking to a clutch of local bigwigs, none of whom Naqi recognised. Thonburi steered her into the fray, oblivious to the conversations that were taking place.

'Ladies and gentleman . . . I would like to introduce Naqi Okpik. Naqi oversees the scientific programme on the Moat. She'll be your host for the visit to our project.'

'Ah, Naqi.' Amesha Crane leaned over and shook her hand. 'A pleasure. I just read your papers on information propagation methods in class-three nodes. Erudite.'

'They were collaborative works,' Naqi said. 'I really can't take too much credit.'

'Ah, but you can. All of you can. You achieved those findings with the minimum of resources, and you made very creative use of some extremely simplistic numerical methods.'

'We muddle through,' Naqi said.

Crane nodded enthusiastically. 'It must give you a great sense of satisfaction.'

Tak Thonburi said, 'It's a philosophy, that's all. We conduct our science in isolation, and we enjoy only limited communication with other colonies. As a social model it has its disadvantages, but it means we aren't forever jealous of what they're achieving on some other world that happens to be a few decades ahead of us because of an accident of history or location. We think that the benefits outweigh the costs.'

'Well, it seems to work,' Crane said. 'You have a remarkably stable society here, Chairman. Verging on the utopian, some might say.'

Tak Thonburi caressed his cowlick. 'We can't complain.'

'Nor can we,' said the man Naqi recognised as quizzical-faced Simon Matsubara. 'If you hadn't enforced this isolation, your own Juggler research would have been as hopelessly compromised as everywhere else.'

'But the isolation isn't absolute, is it?'

The voice was quiet, but commanding.

Naqi followed the voice to the speaker. It was Rafael Weir,

the man who had been identified as a possible security risk. Of the three who had emerged from Moreau's shuttle, he was the least remarkable looking, possessing the kind of amorphous face that would allow him to blend in with almost any crowd. Had her attention not been drawn to him, he would have been the last one she noticed. He was not unattractive, but there was nothing particularly striking or charismatic about his looks. According to the security dossier, he had made a number of efforts to break away from the main party of the delegation while they had been visiting research stations. They could have been accidents – one or two other party members had become separated at other times – but it was beginning to look a little too deliberate.

'No,' Tak Thonburi answered. 'We're not absolute isolationists, or we'd never have given permission for *Voice of Evening* to assume orbit around Turquoise. But we don't solicit passing traffic either. Our welcome is as warm as anyone's, we hope, but we don't encourage visitors.'

'Are we the first to visit since your settlement?' Weir asked.

'The first starship?' Tak Thonburi shook his head. 'No. But it's been a number of years since the last one.'

'Which was?'

'The *Pelican in Impiety*, a century ago.'

'An amusing coincidence, then,' Weir said.

Tak Thonburi narrowed his eyes. 'Coincidence?'

'The *Pelican*'s next port of call was Haven, if I'm not mistaken. It was en route from Zion, but it made a trade stopover around Turquoise.' He smiled. 'And we have come from Haven, so history already binds our two worlds, albeit tenuously.'

Thonburi's eyes narrowed. He was trying to read Weir and evidently failing. 'We don't talk about the *Pelican* too much. There were technical benefits – vacuum-bladder production methods, information technologies . . . but there was also a fair bit of unpleasantness. The wounds haven't entirely healed.'

'Let's hope this visit will be remembered more fondly,' Weir said.

Amesha Crane nodded, fingering one of the items of silver jewellery in her hair. 'Agreed. All the indications are favourable, at the very least. We've arrived at a most auspicious time.' She turned to Naqi. 'I find the Moat project fascinating, and I'm sure I speak for the entire Vahishta delegation. I may as well tell you that no one else has attempted anything remotely like it. Tell me, scientist to scientist, do you honestly think it will work?'

'We won't know until we try,' Naqi said. Any other answer would have been politically hazardous: too much optimism and the politicians would have started asking just why the expensive project was needed in the first place. Too much pessimism and they would ask exactly the same question.

'Fascinating, all the same.' Crane's expression was knowing, as if she understood Naqi's predicament perfectly. 'I understand that you're very close to running the first experiment?'

'Given that it's taken us twenty years to get this far, yes, we're close. But we're still looking at three to four months, maybe longer. It's not something we want to rush.'

'That's a great pity,' Crane said, turning now to Thonburi. 'In three to four months we might be on our way. Still, it would have been something to see, wouldn't it?'

Thonburi leaned towards Naqi. The alcohol on his breath was a fog of cheap vinegar. 'I suppose there wouldn't be any chance of accelerating the schedule, would there?'

'Out of the question, I'm afraid,' Naqi said.

'That's just too bad,' said Amesha Crane. Still toying with her jewellery, she turned to the others. 'But we mustn't let a little detail like that spoil our visit, must we?'

*

They returned to the Moat using the *Voice of Evening*'s shuttle. There was another civic reception to be endured upon arrival, but it was a much smaller affair than the one in Sukhothai-Sanikiluaq. Dr Jotah Sivaraksa was there, of course, and once Naqi had dealt with the business of introducing the party to him she was able to relax for the first time in many hours, melting into the corner of the room and watching the interaction between visitors and locals with a welcome sense of detachment. Naqi was tired and had difficulty keeping her eyes open. She saw everything through a sleepy blur, the delegates surrounding Sivaraksa like pillars of fire, the fabric of their costumes rippling with the slightest movement, reds and russets and chrome yellows dancing like sparks or sheets of flame. Naqi left as soon as she felt it was polite to do so, and when she reached her bed she fell immediately into troubled sleep, dreaming of squadrons of purple-winged angels falling from the skies and of the great giant rising from the depths, clawing the seaweed and kelp of ages from his eyes.

In the morning she awoke without really feeling refreshed. Anaemic light pierced the slats on her window. She was not due to meet the delegates again for another three or four hours, so there was time to turn over and try and catch some proper sleep. But she knew from experience that it would be futile.

She got up. To her surprise, there was a new message on her console from Jotah Sivaraksa. What, she wondered, did he have to say to her that he could not have said at the reception, or later this morning?

She opened the message and read.

'Sivaraksa,' she said to herself. 'Are you insane? It can't be done.'

The message informed her that there had been a change of plan. The first closure of the sea-doors would be attempted in two days, while the delegates were still on the Moat.

It was pure madness. They were months away from that. Yes, the doors could be closed – the basic machinery for doing that was in place – and yes, the doors would be hermetically tight for at least one hundred hours after closure. But nothing else was ready. The sensitive monitoring equipment, the failsafe subsystems, the back-ups . . . None of that would be in place and operational for many weeks. Then there was supposed to be at least six weeks of testing, slowly building up to the event itself . . .

To do it in two days made no sense at all, except to a politician. At best all they would learn was whether or not the Jugglers had remained inside the Moat when the door was closed. They would learn nothing about how the data flow was terminated, or how the internal connections between the nodes adapted to the loss of contact with the wider ocean.

Naqi swore and hit the console. She wanted to blame Sivaraksa, but she knew that was unfair. Sivaraksa had to keep the politicians happy, or the whole project would be endangered. He was just doing what he had to do, and he almost certainly liked it even less than she did.

Naqi pulled on shorts and a T-shirt and found some coffee in one of the adjoining mess rooms. The Moat was deserted, quiet except for the womblike throb of generators and air-circulation systems. A week ago it would have been as noisy now as at any other time of day, for the construction had continued around the clock. But the heavy work was finished; the last ore dirigible had arrived while Naqi was away. All that remained was the relatively light work of completing the Moat's support subsystems. Despite what Sivaraksa had said in his message there was really very little additional work needed to close the doors. Even two days of frantic activity would make no difference to the usefulness of the stunt.

When she'd calmed down, she returned to her room and called Sivaraksa. It was still far too early, but seeing that the bastard had already ruined her day she saw no reason not to reciprocate.

'Naqi.' His silver hair was a sleep-matted mess on the screen. 'I take it you got my message?'

'You didn't think I'd take it lying down, did you?'

'I don't like it any more than you do. But I see the political necessity.'

'Do you? This isn't like switching a light on and off, Jotah.' His eyes widened at the familiarity, but she pressed on regardless. 'If we screw up the first time, there might never be a second chance. The Jugglers have to play along. Without them all you've got here is a very expensive mid-ocean refuelling point. Does that make political sense to you?'

He pushed green fingers through the mess of his hair. 'Have some breakfast, get some fresh air, then come to my office. We'll talk about it then.'

'I've had breakfast, thanks very much.'

'Then get the fresh air. You'll feel better for it.' Sivaraksa rubbed his eyes. 'You're not very happy about this, are you?'

'It's bloody madness. And the worst thing is that you know it.'

'And my hands are tied. Ten years from now, Naqi, you'll be sitting in my place having to make similar decisions. And ten to one there'll be some idealistic young scientist telling you what a hopeless piece of deadwood you are.' He managed a weary smile. 'Mark my words, because I want you to remember this conversation when it happens.'

'There's nothing I can do to stop this, is there?'

'I'll be in my office in—' Sivaraksa looked aside at a clock, 'thirty minutes. We can talk about it properly then.'

'There's nothing to talk about.'

But even as she said that she knew she sounded petulant and inflexible. Sivaraksa was right: it was impossible to manage a project as complex and expensive as the Moat without a degree of compromise.

Naqi decided that Sivaraksa's advice – at least the part about getting some fresh air – was worth heeding. She descended a helical staircase until she reached the upper surface of the Moat's ring-shaped wall. The concrete was cold beneath her bare feet and a pleasantly cool breeze caressed her legs and arms. The sky had brightened on one horizon. Machines and supplies were arranged neatly on the upper surface ready for use, although further construction would be halted until the delegates completed their visit. Stepping nimbly over the tracks, conduits and cables that criss-crossed each other on the upper surface, Naqi walked to the side. A high railing, painted in high-visibility rot-resistant sealer, fenced the inner part of the Moat. She touched it to make sure it was dry, then leaned over. The distant side of the Moat was a colourless thread, twenty kilometres away, like a very low wall of sea mist.

What could be done in two days? Nothing. Or at least nothing compared to what had always been planned. But if the new schedule was a fait accompli – and that was the message she was getting from Sivaraksa – then it was her responsibility to find a way to squeeze some scientific return from the event. She looked down at the cut, and at the many spindly gantries and catwalks that spanned the aperture or hung some way towards the centre of the Moat. Perhaps if she arranged for some standard-issue probes to be prepared today, the type dropped from dirigibles . . .

Naqi's eyes darted around, surveying fixtures and telemetry conduits.

It would be hard work to get them in place in time, and even harder to get them patched into some kind of real-time acquisition system . . . But it *was* doable, just barely. The data quality would be laughable compared to the super-sensitive instruments that were going to be installed over the next few months . . . But crude was a lot better than nothing at all.

She laughed, aloud. An hour ago she would have stuck pins into herself rather than collaborate in this kind of fiasco.

Naqi walked along the railing until she reached a pair of pillar-mounted binoculars. They were smeared with rot-protection. She wiped the lens and eyepieces clean with the rag that was tied to the pedestal, then swung the binoculars in a slow arc, panning across the dark circle of water trapped within the Moat. Only vague patches of what Naqi would have called open water were visible. The rest was either a verdant porridge of Juggler organisms, or fully grown masses of organised floating matter, linked together by trunks and veins of the same green biomass. The latest estimate was that there were three small nodes within the ring. The smell was atrocious, but that was an excellent sign as well: it correlated strongly with the density of organisms in the nodes. She had experienced that smell many times, but it never failed to slam her back to that morning when Mina had died.

As much as the Pattern Jugglers 'knew' anything, they were surely aware of what was planned here. They had drunk the minds of the swimmers who had already entered the sea near or within the Moat, and not one of those swimmers was ignorant of the project's ultimate purpose. It was possible that that knowledge simply couldn't be parsed into a form the aliens would understand, but Naqi considered that unlikely:

the closure of the Moat would be about as stark a concept as one could imagine. If nothing else, geometry was the one thing the Jugglers did understand. And yet the aliens chose to remain within the closing Moat, hinting that they would tolerate the final closure that would seal them off from the rest of the ocean.

Perhaps they were not impressed. Perhaps they knew that the event would not rob them of every channel of communication, but only the chemical medium of the ocean. Sprites and other airborne organisms would still be able to cross the barrier. It was impossible to tell. The only way to know was to complete the experiment – to close the massive sea-doors – and see what happened.

She leaned back, taking her eyes from the binoculars.

Now Naqi saw something unexpected. It was a glint of hard white light, scudding across the water within the Moat.

Naqi squinted, but still she could not make out the object. She swung the binoculars hard around, got her eyes behind them and then zigzagged until something flashed through the field of view. She backed up and locked onto it.

It was a boat, and there was someone in it.

She keyed in the image zoom/stabilise function and the craft swelled to clarity across a clear kilometre of sea. The craft was a ceramic-hulled vessel of the type that the swimmer teams used, five or six metres long from bow to stern. The person sat behind a curved spray shield, their hands on the handlebars of the control pillar. An inboard thruster propelled the boat without ever touching water.

The figure was difficult to make out, but the billowing orange clothes left no room for doubt. It was one of the Vahishta delegates. And Naqi fully expected it to be Rafael Weir.

He was headed towards the closest node.

For an agonising few moments she did not know what to do. He was going to attempt to swim, she thought, just like she and Mina had done. And he would be no better prepared for the experience. She had to stop him, somehow. He would reach the node in only a few minutes.

Naqi sprinted back to the tower, breathless when she arrived. She reached a communications post and tried to find the right channel for the boat. But either she was doing it wrong or Weir had sabotaged the radio. What next? Technically, there was a security presence on the Moat, especially given the official visit. But what did the security goons know about chasing boats? All their training was aimed at dealing with internal crises, and none of them were competent to go anywhere near an active node.

She called them anyway, alerting them to what had happened. Then she called Sivaraksa, telling him the same news. 'I think it's Weir,' she said. 'I'm going to try and stop him.'

'Naqi . . .' he said warningly.

'This is my responsibility, Jotah. Let me handle it.'

Naqi ran back outside again. The closest elevator down to sea level was out of service; the next one was a kilometre further around the ring. She didn't have that much time. Instead she jogged along the line of railings until she reached a break that admitted entry to a staircase that descended the steep inner wall of the Moat. The steps and handrails had been helpfully greased with anti-rot, which made her descent that much more treacherous. There were five hundred steps down to sea level but she took them two or three at a time, sliding down the handrails until she reached the grilled platforms where the stairways reversed direction. All the while she watched the tiny white speck of the boat, seemingly immobile now that it was so far away, but undoubtedly narrowing the distance to the node with each minute. As she worked her way down she had plenty of time to think about what was going through the delegate's head. She was sure now that it was Weir. It did not really surprise her that he wanted to swim: it was what everyone who studied the Jugglers yearned for. But why make this unofficial attempt now when a little gentle persuasion would have made it possible anyway? Given Tak Thonburi's eagerness to please the delegates, it would not have been beyond the bounds of possibility for a swimming expedition to be organised . . . The corps would have protested, but just like Naqi they would have been given a forceful lesson in the refined art of political compromise.

But evidently Weir hadn't been prepared to wait. It all made sense, at any rate: the times when he had dodged away from the party before must have all been abortive attempts to reach the Jugglers. But only now had he been able to seize his opportunity.

Naqi reached the water level, where jetties floated on ceramic-sheathed pontoons. Most of the boats were suspended out of the water on cradles, to save their hulls from unnecessary degradation. Fortunately, there was an emergency rescue boat already afloat. Its formerly white hull had the flaking, pea-green scab patterning of advanced rot, but it still had a dozen or so hours of seaworthiness in it. Naqi jumped aboard, released the boat from its moorings and fired up the thruster. In a moment she was racing away from the jetty, away from the vast, stained edifice of the Moat itself. She steered a course through the least viscous stretches of water, avoiding conspicuous rafts of green matter.

She peered ahead through the boat's spray-drenched shield. It had been easy to keep track of Weir's boat when she had been a hundred metres higher, but now she kept losing him behind swells or miniature islands of Juggler matter. After a minute or so she gave up trying to follow the boat, and instead diverted her concentration to finding the quickest route to the node.

She flipped on the radio. 'Jotah? This is Naqi. I'm in the water, closing on Weir.'

There was a pause, a crackle, then: 'What's the status?'

She had to shout over the abrasive *thump*, *thump*, *thump* of the boat, even though the thruster was nearly silent.

'I'll reach the node in four or five minutes. Can't see Weir, but I don't think it matters.'

'We can see him. He's still headed for the node.'

'Good. Can you spare some more boats, in case he decides to make a run for another node?'

'They'll be leaving in a minute or so. I'm waking everyone I can.'

'What about the other delegates?'

Sivaraksa did not answer her immediately. 'Most are still asleep. I have Amesha Crane and Simon Matsubara in my office, however.'

'Let me speak to them.'

'Just a moment,' he said, after the same brief hesitation.

'Crane here,' said the woman.

'I think I'm chasing Weir. Can you confirm that?'

'He isn't accounted for,' she told Naqi. 'But it'll be a few minutes until we can be certain it's him.'

'I'm not expecting a surprise. Weir already had a question mark over him, Amesha. We were waiting for him to try something.'

'Were you?' Perhaps it was her imagination, but Crane sounded genuinely surprised. 'Why? What had he done?'

'You don't know?'

'No . . .' Crane trailed off.

'He was one of us,' Matsubara said. 'A good . . . delegate. We had no reason to distrust him.'

Perhaps Naqi was imagining this as well, but it almost sounded as if Matsubara had intended to say 'disciple' rather than 'delegate'.

Crane came back on the radio. 'Please do your best to apprehend him, Naqi. This is a source of great embarrassment to us. He mustn't do any harm.'

Naqi gunned the boat harder, no longer bothering to avoid the smaller patches of organic matter. 'No,' she said. 'He mustn't.'

THREE

Something changed ahead.

'Naqi?' It was Jotah Sivaraksa's voice.

'What?'

'Weir's slowed his boat. From our vantage point it looks as if he's reached the perimetre of the node. He seems to be circumnavigating it.'

'I can't see him yet. He must be picking the best spot to dive in.'

'But it won't work, will it?' Sivaraksa asked. 'There has to be an element of co-operation with the Jugglers. They have to invite the swimmer to enter the sea, or nothing happens.'

'Maybe he doesn't realise that,' Naqi said, under her breath. It was of no concern to her how closely Weir was adhering to the usual method of initiating Juggler communion. Even if the Jugglers did not co-operate – even if all Weir did was flounder in thick green water – there was no telling the hidden harm that might be done. She had already grudgingly accepted the acceleration of the closure operation. There was no way she was going to tolerate another upset, another unwanted perturbation of the experimental system. Not on her watch.

'He's stopped,' Sivaraksa said excitedly. 'Can you see him yet?'

Naqi stood up in her seat, even though she felt perilously unbalanced. 'Wait. Yes, I think so. I'll be there in a minute or so.'

'What are you going to do?' Crane asked. 'I hesitate to say it, but Weir may not respond to rational argument at this point. Simply requesting that he leave the water won't necessarily work. Um, do you have a weapon?'

'Yes,' Naqi said. 'I'm sitting in it.'

She did not allow herself to relax, but at least now she felt that the situation was slipping back into her control. She would kill Weir rather than have him contaminate the node.

His boat was visible now only as a smudge of white, intermittently popping up between folds and hummocks of shifting green. Her imagination sketched in the details. Weir would be preparing to swim, stripping off until he was naked, or nearly so. Perhaps he would feel some kind of erotic charge as he prepared for immersion. She did not doubt that he would be apprehensive, and perhaps he would hesitate on the threshold of the act, teetering on the edge of the boat before committing himself to the water. But a fanatic desire had driven him this far and she doubted that it would fail him.

'Naqi—'

'Jotah?'

'Naqi, he's moving again. He didn't enter the water. He didn't even look like he had any intention of swimming.'

'He saw I was coming. I take it he's heading for the next closest node?'

'Perhaps . . .' But Jotah Sivaraksa sounded far from certain.

She saw the boat again. It was moving fast – much faster than it had appeared before – but that was only because she was now seeing lateral motion.

The next node was a distant island framed by the background of the Moat's encircling rim. If he headed that way she would be hard behind him all the way there as well. No matter his desire to swim, he must realise that she could thwart his every attempt.

Naqi looked back. The twin towers framing the cut were smothered in a haze of sea mist, their geometric details smeared into a vague suggestion of haphazard complexity. They suggested teetering, stratified sea-stacks, million-year-old towers of weathered and eroded rock guarding the narrow passage to the open ocean. Beneath them, winking in and out of clarity, she saw three or four other boats making their way into the Moat. The ponderous teardrop of a passenger dirigible was nosing away from the side of one of the towers, the low dawn sun throwing golden highlights along the fluted lines of its gondola. Naqi made out the sleek deltoid of the *Voice of Evening*'s shuttle, but it was still parked where it had landed.

She looked back to the node where Weir had hesitated.

Something was happening.

The node had become vastly more active than a minute earlier. It resembled a green, steep-sided volcanic island that was undergoing some catastrophic seismic calamity. The entire mass of the node was trembling, rocking and throbbing with an eerie regularity. Concentric swells of disturbed water raced away from it, sickening troughs that made the speeding boat pitch and slide. Naqi slowed her boat, some instinct telling her that it was now largely futile to pursue Weir. Then she turned around so that she faced the node properly and, cautiously, edged closer, ignoring the nausea she felt as the boat ducked and dived from crest to trough.

The node, like all nodes, had always shown a rich surface topology: fused hummocks and tendrils; fabulous domes and minarets and helter-skelters of organised biomass, linked and entangled by a telegraphic system of draping aerial tendrils. In any instant it resembled a human city – or, more properly, a fairy-tale human city – that had been efficiently smothered in green moss. The bright moving motes of sprites dodged through the interstices, the portholes and arches of the urban mass. The metropolitan structure only hinted at the node's Byzantine interior architecture, and much of that could only be glimpsed or implied.

But this node was like a city going insane. It was accelerating, running through cycles of urban renewal and redesign with indecent haste. Structures were evolving before Naqi's eyes. She had seen change this rapid just before Mina was taken, but normally those kinds of changes happened too slowly to be seen at all, like the daily movement of shadows.

The throbbing had decreased, but the flickering change was now throwing out a steady, warm, malodorous breeze. And when she stopped the boat – she dared come no closer now – Naqi heard the node. It was like the whisper of a billion forest leaves presaging a summer storm.

Whatever was happening here, it was about to become catastrophic.

Some fundamental organisation had been lost. The changes were happening too quickly, with too little central co-ordination. Tendrils thrashed like whips, unable to connect to anything. They flailed against each other. Structures were forming and collapsing. The node was fracturing, so that there were three, four, perhaps five distinct cores of flickering growth. As soon as she had the measure of it, the process shifted it all. Meagre light flickered within the epileptic mass. Sprites swarmed in confused flight patterns, orbiting mindlessly between foci. The sound of the node had become a distant shriek.

'It's dying . . .' Naqi breathed.

Weir had done something to it. What, she couldn't guess. But this could not be a coincidence.

The shrieking died down.

The breeze ceased.

The node had stopped its convulsions. She looked at it, hoping against hope that perhaps it had overcome whatever destabilising influence Weir had introduced. The structures were still misshapen, there was still an impression of incoherence, but the city was inert. The cycling motion of the sprites slowed, and a few of them dropped down into the mass, as if to roost.

A calm had descended.

Then Naqi heard another sound. It was lower than anything she had heard before – almost subsonic. It sounded less like thunder than like a very distant, very heated conversation.

It was coming from the approximate centre of the node.

She watched as a smooth green mound rose from the centre, resembling a flattened hemisphere. It grew larger by the second, assimilating the malformed structures with quiet indifference. They disappeared into the surface of the mound as if into a wall of fog, but they did not emerge again. The mound only increased its size, rumbling towards Naqi. The entire mass of the node was changing into a single undifferentiated mass.

'Jotah . . .' she said.

'We see it, Naqi. We see it but we don't understand it.'

'Weir must have used some kind of . . . weapon against it,' she said.

'We don't know that he's harmed it . . . He might just have precipitated a change to a state we haven't documented.'

'That still makes it a weapon in my book. I'm scared, Jotah.'

'You think I'm not?'

Around her the sea was changing. She had forgotten about the submerged tendrils that connected the nodes. They were as thick as hawsers, and now they were writhing and thrashing just beneath the surface of the water. Green-tinged spume lifted into the air. It was as if unseen aquatic monsters were wrestling, locked in some dire, to-the-death contest.

'Naqi . . . We're seeing changes in the closest of the two remaining nodes.'

'No,' she said, as if denying it would make any difference.

'I'm sorry . . .'

'Where is Weir?'

'We've lost him. There's too much surface disturbance.'

She realised then what had to be done. The thought arrived in her head with a crashing urgency.

'Jotah . . . You have to close the sea-doors. Now. Immediately. Before whatever Weir's unleashed has a chance to reach open ocean. That also happens to be Weir's only escape route.'

Sivaraksa, to his credit, did not argue. 'Yes. You're right. I'll start closure. But it will take quite a few minutes . . .'

'I know, Jotah!'

She cursed herself for not having thought of this sooner, and cursed Sivaraksa for the same error. But she could hardly blame either of them. Closure had never been something to take lightly. A few hours ago it had been an event months in the future – an experiment to test the willingness of the Jugglers to co-operate with human plans. Now it had turned into an emergency amputation, something to be done with brutal haste.

She peered at the gap between the towers. At the very least it would take several minutes for Sivaraksa to initiate closure. It was not simply a matter of pressing a button on his desk, but of rousing two or three specialist technicians, who would have to be immediately convinced that this was not some elaborate hoax. And then the machinery would have to work. The mechanisms that forced the sea-doors together had been tested numerous times . . . But the machinery had never been driven to its limit; the doors had never moved more than a few metres together. Now they would have to work perfectly, closing with watchmaker precision.

And when had anything on Turquoise ever worked the first time?

There. The tiniest, least perceptible narrowing of the gap. It was all happening with agonising slowness.

She looked back to what remained of the node. The mound had consumed all the biomass available to it and had now ceased its growth. It was as if a child had sculpted in clay some fantastically intricate model of a city, which a callous adult had then squashed into a single blank mass, erasing all trace of its former complexity. The closest of the remaining nodes was showing something of the same transformation, Naqi saw: it was running through the frantic cycle that had presaged the emergence of the mound. She guessed now that the cycle had been the node's attempt to nullify whatever Weir had used against it, like a computer trying to reallocate resources to compensate for some crippling viral attack.

She could do nothing for the Jugglers now.

Naqi turned the boat around and headed back towards the cut. The sea-doors had narrowed the gap by perhaps a quarter.

The changes taking place within the Moat had turned the water turbulent, even at the jetty. She hitched the boat to a mooring point and then took the elevator up the side of the wall, preferring to sprint the distance along the top rather than face the climb. By the time she reached the cut the doors were three-quarters of the way to closure and, to Naqi's immense relief, the machinery had yet to falter.

She approached the tower. She had expected to see more people out on the top of the Moat, even if she knew that Sivaraksa would still be in his control centre. But no one was around. This was just beginning to register as a distinct wrongness when Sivaraksa emerged into daylight, stumbling from the door at the foot of the tower.

For an instant she was on the point of calling his name. Then she realised that he was stumbling because he had been injured – his fingers were scarlet with blood – and that he was trying to get away from someone or something.

Naqi dropped to the ground behind a stack of construction slabs. Through gaps between the slabs she observed Sivaraksa. He was swatting at something, like a man being chased by a persistent wasp. Something tiny and silver harried him. More than one thing, in fact: a small swarm of them, streaming out the open door. Sivaraksa fell to his knees with a moan, brushing ineffectually at his tormentors. His face was turning red, smeared with his own blood. He slumped on one side.

Naqi remained frozen with fear.

A person stepped from the open door.

The figure was garbed in shades of fire. It was Amesha Crane. For an absurd moment Naqi assumed that the woman was about to spring to Sivaraksa's assistance. It was something about her demeanour. Naqi found it hard to believe that someone so apparently serene could commit such a violent act.

But Crane did not step closer to Sivaraksa. She merely extended her arms before her, with her fingers outspread. She sustained the oddly theatrical gesture, the muscles in her neck standing proud and rigid.

The silver things departed Sivaraksa.

They swarmed through the air, slowing as they neared Crane. Then, with a startling degree of orchestrated obedience, they slid onto her fingers, locked themselves around her wrists, clasped onto the lobes of her ears.

Her jewellery had attacked Sivaraksa.

Crane glanced at the man one last time, spun on her heels and then retreated back into the tower.

Naqi waited until she was certain the woman was not coming back, then started to emerge from behind the pile of slabs. But Sivaraksa saw her. He said nothing, but his agonised eyes widened enough for Naqi to get the warning. She remained where she was, her heart hammering.

Nothing happened for another minute.

Then something moved above, changing the play of light across the surface of the Moat. The *Voice of Evening*'s shuttle was detaching from the tower, a flicker of white machinery beneath the manta curve of its hull.

The shuttle loitered above the cut, as if observing the final moment of closure. Naqi heard the huge doors grind shut. Then the shuttle banked and headed into the circular sea, no more than two hundred metres above the waves. Some distance out it halted and executed a sharp right-angled turn. Then it resumed its flight, moving concentrically around the inner wall.

Sivaraksa closed his eyes. She thought he might have died, but then he opened them again and made the tiniest of nods. Naqi left her place of hiding. She crossed the open ground to Sivaraksa in a low, crablike stoop.

She knelt down by him, cradling his head in one hand and holding his own hand with the other. 'Jotah . . . What happened?'

He managed to answer her. 'They turned on us. The nineteen other delegates. As soon as—' He paused, summoning strength. 'As soon as Weir made his move.'

'I don't understand.'

'Join the club,' he said, managing a smile.

'I need to get you inside,' she said.

'Won't help. Everyone else is dead. Or will be by now. They murdered us all.'

'No.'

'Kept me alive until the end. Wanted me to give the orders.' He coughed. Blood spattered her hand.

'I can still get you—'

'Naqi. Save yourself. Get help.'

She realised that he was about to die.

'The shuttle?'

'Looking for Weir. I think.'

'They want Weir back?'

'No. Heard them talking. They want Weir dead. They have to be sure.'

Naqi frowned. She understood none of this, or at least her understanding was only now beginning to crystallise. She had labelled Weir as the villain because he had harmed her beloved Pattern Jugglers. But Crane and her entourage had murdered people, dozens, if what Sivaraksa said was correct. They appeared to want Weir dead as well. So what did that make Weir, now?

'Jotah . . . I have to find Weir. I have to find out why he did this.' She looked back towards the centre of the Moat. The shuttle was continuing its search. 'Did your security people get a trace on him again?'

Sivaraksa was near the end. She thought he was never going to answer her. 'Yes,' he said finally. 'Yes, they found him again.'

'And? Any idea where he is? I might still be able to reach him before the shuttle does.'

'Wrong place.'

She leaned closer. 'Jotah?'

'Wrong place. Amesha's looking in the wrong place. Weir got through the cut. He's in the open ocean.'

'I'm going after him. Perhaps I can stop him . . .'

'Try,' Sivaraksa said. 'But I'm not sure what difference it will make. I have a feeling, Naqi. A very bad feeling. Things are ending. It was good, wasn't it? While it lasted?'

'I haven't given up just yet,' Naqi said.

He found one last nugget of strength. 'I knew you wouldn't. Right to trust you. One thing, Naqi. One thing that might make a difference . . . if it comes to the worst, that is—'

'Jotah?'

'Tak Thonburi told me this . . . the most top secret, known only to the Snowflake Council. Arviat, Naqi—'

For a moment she thought she had misheard him, or that he was sliding into delirium. 'Arviat? The city that sinned against the sea?'

'It was real,' Sivaraksa said.

There were a number of lifeboats and emergency service craft stored at the top of near-vertical slipways, a hundred metres above the external sea. She took a small but fast emergency craft with a sealed cockpit, her stomach knotting as the vessel commenced its slide towards the ocean. The boat submerged before resurfacing, boosted up to speed and then deployed ceramic hydrofoils to minimise the contact between the hull and the water. Naqi had no precise heading to follow, but she believed Weir would have followed a reasonably straight line away from the cut, aiming to get as far away from the Moat as possible before the other delegates realised their mistake. It would require only a small deviation from that course to take him to the nearest external node, which was as likely a destination as any.

When she was twenty kilometres from the Moat, Naqi allowed herself a moment to look back. The structure was a thin white line etched on the horizon, the towers and the now-sealed cut faintly visible as interruptions in the line's smoothness. Quills of dark smoke climbed from a dozen spots along the length of the structure. It was too far for Naqi to be certain that she saw flames licking from the towers, but she considered it likely.

The closest external node appeared over the horizon fifteen minutes later. It was nowhere as impressive as the one that had taken Mina, but it was still a larger, more complex structure than any of the nodes that had formed within the Moat – a major urban megalopolis, perhaps, rather than a moderately sized city. Against the skyline Naqi saw spires and rotundas and coronets of green, bridged by a tracery of elevated tendrils. Sprites were rapidly moving silhouettes. There was motion, but it was largely confined to the flying creatures. The node was not yet showing the frenzied changes she had witnessed within the Moat.

Had Weir gone somewhere else?

She pressed onwards, slowing the boat slightly now that the water was thickening with microorganisms and it was necessary to steer around the occasional larger floating structure. The boat's sonar picked out dozens of submerged tendrils converging on the node, suspended just below the surface. The tendrils reached away in all directions, to the limits of the boat's sonar range. Most would have reached over the horizon, to nodes many hundreds of kilometres away. But it was a topological certainty that some of them had been connected to the nodes inside the Moat. Evidently, Weir's contagion had never escaped through the cut. Naqi doubted that the doors had closed in time to impede whatever chemical signals were transmitting the fatal message. It was more likely that some latent Juggler self-protection mechanism had cut in, the dying nodes sending emergency termination-of-connection signals that forced the tendrils to sever without human assistance.

Naqi had just decided that she had guessed wrongly about Weir's plan when she saw a rectilinear furrow gouged right through one of the largest subsidiary structures. The wound was healing itself as she watched – it would be gone in a matter of minutes – but enough remained for her to tell that Weir's boat must have cleaved through the mass very recently. It made sense. Weir had already demonstrated that he had no interest in preserving the Pattern Jugglers.

With renewed determination, Naqi gunned the boat forward. She no longer worried about inflicting local damage on the floating masses. There was a great deal more at stake than the well-being of a single node.

She felt a warmth on the back of her neck.

At the same instant the sky, sea and floating structures ahead of her pulsed with a cruel brightness. Her own shadow stretched forward ominously. The brightness faded over the next few seconds, and then she dared to look back, half-knowing what she would see.

A mass of hot, roiling gas was climbing into the air from the centre of the node. It tugged a column of matter beneath it, like the knotted and gnarled spinal column of a horribly swollen brain. Against the mushroom cloud she saw the tiny moving speck of the delegates' shuttle.

A minute later the sound of the explosion reached her, but although it was easily the loudest thing she had ever heard, it was not as deafening as she had expected. The boat lurched; the sea fumed, and then was still again. She assumed that the Moat's wall had absorbed much of the energy of the blast.

Suddenly fearful that there might be another explosion, Naqi turned back towards the node. At the same instant she saw Weir's boat, racing perhaps three hundred metres ahead of her. He was beginning to curve and slow as he neared the impassable perimetre of the node. Naqi knew that she did not have time to delay.

That was when Weir saw her. His boat sped up again, arcing hard away. Naqi steered immediately, certain that her boat was faster and that it was now only a matter of time before she had him. A minute later Weir's boat disappeared around the curve of the node's perimetre. She might have stood a chance of getting an echo from his hull, but this close to the node all sonar returns were too garbled to be of any use. Naqi steered anyway, hoping that Weir would make the tactical mistake of striking for another node. In open water he stood no chance at all, but perhaps he understood that as well.

She had circumnavigated a third of the node's perimetre when she caught up with him again. He had not tried to run for it. Instead he had brought the boat to a halt within the comparative shelter of an inlet on the perimetre. He was standing up at the rear of the boat, with something small and dark in his hand.

Naqi slowed her boat as she approached him. She had popped back the canopy before it occurred to her that Weir might be equipped with the same weapons as Crane.

She stood up herself. 'Weir?'

He smiled. 'I'm sorry to have caused so much trouble. But I don't think it could have happened any other way.'

She let this pass. 'That thing in your hand?'

'Yes?'

'It's a weapon, isn't it?'

She could see it clearly now. It was merely a glass bauble, little larger than a child's marble. There was something opaque inside it, but she could not tell if it contained fluid or dark crystals.

'I doubt that a denial would be very plausible at this point.' He nodded, and she sensed the lifting, partially at least, of some appalling burden. 'Yes, it's a weapon. A Juggler killer.'

'Until today, I'd have said no such thing was possible.'

'I doubt that it was very easy to synthesise. Countless biological entities have entered their oceans, and none of them have ever brought anything with them that the Jugglers couldn't assimilate in a harmless fashion. Doubtless some of those entities tried to inflict deliberate harm, if only out of morbid curiosity. None of them succeeded. Of course, you can kill Jugglers by brute force—' He looked towards the Moat, where the mushroom cloud was dissipating. 'But that isn't the point. Not subtle. But this is. It exploits a logical flaw in the Jugglers' own informational processing algorithms. It's insidious. And no, humans most certainly didn't invent it. We're clever, but we're not *that* clever.'

Naqi strove to keep him talking. 'Who made it, Weir?'

'The Ultras sold it to us in a pre-synthesised form. I've heard rumours that it was found inside the topmost chamber of a heavily fortified alien structure . . . Another that it was synthesised by a rival group of Jugglers. Who knows? Who cares, even? It does what we ask of it. That's all that matters.'

'Please don't use it, Rafael.'

'I have to. It's what I came here to do.'

'But I thought you all loved the Jugglers.'

His fingers caressed the glass globe. It looked terribly fragile. 'We?'

'Crane . . . Her delegates.'

'They do. But I'm not one of them.'

'Tell me what this is about, Rafael.'

'It would be better if you just accepted what I have to do.'

Naqi swallowed. 'If you kill them, you kill more than just an alien life form. You erase the memory of every sentient creature that's ever entered the ocean.'

'Unfortunately, that rather happens to be the point.'

Weir dropped the glass into the sea.

It hit the water, bobbed under and then popped back out again, floating on the surface. The small globe was already immersed in a brackish scum of grey-green microorganisms. They were beginning to lap higher up the sides of the globe, exploring it. A couple of millimetres of ordinary glass would succumb to Juggler erosion in perhaps thirty minutes . . . But Naqi guessed that this was not ordinary glass, that it was designed to degrade much more rapidly.

She jumped back down into her control seat and shot her boat forward. She came alongside Weir's boat, trapping the globe between the two craft. Taking desperate care not to nudge the hulls together, she stopped her boat and leaned over as far as she could without falling in. Her fingertips brushed the glass. Maddeningly, she could not quite get a grip on it. She made one last valiant effort and it drifted beyond her reach. Now it was out of her range, no matter how hard she stretched. Weir watched impassively.

Naqi slipped into the water. The layer of Juggler organisms licked her chin and nose, the smell immediate and overwhelming now that she was in such close proximity. Her fear was absolute. It was the first time she had entered the water since Mina's death.

She caught the globe, taking hold of it with the exquisite care she might have reserved for a rare bird's egg.

Already the glass had the porous texture of pumice.

She held it up, for Weir to see.

'I won't let you do this, Rafael.'

'I admire your concern.'

'It's more than concern. My sister is here. She's in the ocean. And I won't let you take her away from me.'

Weir reached inside a pocket and removed another globe.

*

They sped away from the node in Naqi's boat. The new globe rested in his hand like a gift. He had not yet dropped it in the sea, although the possibility was only ever an instant away. They were far from any node now, but the globe would be guaranteed to come into contact with Juggler matter sooner or later.

Naqi opened a watertight equipment locker, pushing aside the flare pistol and first-aid kit that lay within. Carefully she placed the globe within, and then watched in horror as the glass immediately cracked and dissolved, releasing its poison: little black irregularly shaped grains like burned sugar. If the boat sank, the locker would eventually be consumed into the ocean, along with its fatal contents. She considered using the flare pistol to incinerate the remains, but there was too much danger of dispersing it at the same time. Perhaps the toxin had a restricted lifespan once it came into contact with air, but that was nothing she could count on.

But Weir had not thrown the globe into sea. Not yet. Something she had said had made him hesitate.

'Your sister?'

'You know the story,' Naqi said. 'Mina was a conformal. The ocean assimilated her entirely, rather than just recording her neural patterns. It took her as a prize.'

'And you believe that she's still present, in some sentient sense?'

'That's what I choose to believe, yes. And there's enough anecdotal evidence from other swimmers that conformals do persist, in a more coherent form than other stored patterns.'

'I can't let anecdotal evidence sway me, Naqi. Have the other swimmers specifically reported encounters with Mina?'

'No . . .' Naqi said carefully. She was sure that he would see through any lie that she attempted. 'But they wouldn't necessarily recognise her if they did.'

'And you? Did you attempt to swim yourself?'

'The swimmer corps would never have allowed me.'

'Not my question. Did you ever swim?'

'Once,' Naqi said.

'And?'

'It didn't count. It was the same time that Mina died.' She paused and then told him all that had happened. 'We were seeing more sprite activity than we'd ever recorded. It looked like coincidence—'

'I don't think it was.'

Naqi said nothing. She waited for Weir to collect his own thoughts, concentrating on the steering of the boat. Open sea lay ahead, but she knew that almost any direction would bring them to a cluster of nodes within a few hours.

'It began with *Pelican in Impiety*,' Weir said. 'A century ago. There was a man from Zion on that ship. During the stopover he descended to the surface of Turquoise and swam in your ocean. He made contact with the Jugglers and then swam again. The second time the experience was even more affecting. On the third occasion, the sea swallowed him. He'd been a conformal, just like your sister. His name was Ormazd.'

'It means nothing to me.'

'I assure you that on his homeworld it means a great deal more. Ormazd was a failed tyrant, fleeing a political counter-revolution on Zion. He had murdered and cheated his way to power on Zion, burning his rivals in their houses while they slept. But there'd been a backlash. He got out just before the ring closed around him – him and a handful of his closest allies and devotees. They escaped aboard *Pelican in Impiety*.'

'And Ormazd died here?'

'Yes – but his followers didn't. They made it to Haven, our world. And once there they began to proliferate, spreading their word, recruiting new followers. It didn't matter that Ormazd was gone. Quite the opposite. He'd martyred himself: given them a saint figure to worship. It evolved from a political movement into a religious cult. The Vahishta Foundation's just a front for the Ormazd sect.'

Naqi absorbed that, then asked, 'Where does Amesha come into it?'

'Amesha was his daughter. She wants her father back.'

Something lit the horizon, a pink-edged flash. Another followed a minute later, in nearly the same position.

'She wants to commune with him?'

'More than that,' said Weir. 'They all want to *become* him; to accept his neural patterns on their own. They want the Jugglers to imprint Ormazd's personality on all his followers, to remake them in his own image. The aliens will do that, if the right gifts are offered. And that's what I can't allow.'

Naqi chose her words carefully, sensing that the tiniest thing could push Weir into releasing the globe. She had prevented his last attempt, but he would not allow her a second chance. All he would have to do would be to crush the globe in his fist before spilling the contents into the ocean. Then it would all be over. Everything she had ever known; everything she had ever lived for.

'But we're only talking about nineteen people,' she said.

Weir laughed hollowly. 'I'm afraid it's a little more than that. Why don't you turn on the radio and see what I mean?'

Naqi did as he suggested, using the boat's general communications console. The small, scuffed screen received television pictures beamed down from the comsat network. Naqi flicked through channels, finding static on most of them. The Snowflake Council's official news service was off the air and no personal messages were getting through. There were some suggestions that the comsat network itself was damaged. Yet finally Naqi found a few weak broadcast signals from the nearest snowflake cities. There was a sense of desperation in the transmissions, as if they expected to fall silent at any time.

Weir nodded with weary acceptance, as if he had expected this.

In the last six hours at least a dozen more shuttles had come down from *Voice of Evening*, packed with armed Vahishta disciples. The shuttles had attacked the planet's major snowflake cities and atoll settlements, strafing them into submission. Three cities had fallen into the sea, their vacuum-bladders punctured by beam weapons. There could not have been any survivors. Others were still aloft, but had been set on fire. The pictures showed citizens leaping from the cities' berthing arms, falling like sparks. More cities had been taken bloodlessly, and were now under control of the disciples.

None of those cities were transmitting now.

It was the end of the world. Naqi knew that she should be weeping, or at the very least feel some writhing sense of loss in her stomach. But all she got was a sense of denial; a refusal to accept that events could have escalated so quickly. This morning the only hint of wrongness had been a single absent disciple.

'There are tens of thousands of them up there,' Weir said. 'All that you've seen so far is the advance guard.'

Naqi scratched her forearm. It was itching, as if she had caught a dose of sunburn.

'Moreau was in on this?'

'Captain Moreau's a puppet. Literally. The body you saw was just being tele-operated by orbital disciples. They murdered the Ultras and commandeered the ship—'

'Rafael, why didn't you tell us this before?'

'My position was too vulnerable. I was the only anti-Ormazd agent my movement managed to put aboard *Voice of Evening*. If I'd attempted to warn the Turquoise authorities . . . Well, work it out for yourself. Almost certainly I wouldn't have been believed, and the disciples would have found a way to silence me before I became an embarrassment. And it wouldn't have made a difference to their takeover plans. My only hope was to destroy the ocean, to remove its usefulness to them. They might still have destroyed your cities out of spite, but at least they'd have lost the final thread that connected them to their martyr.' Weir leaned closer to her. 'Don't you understand? It wouldn't have stopped with the disciples aboard the *Voice*. They'd have brought more ships from Haven. Your ocean would have become a production line for despots.'

'Why did they hesitate, if they had such a crushing advantage over us?'

'They didn't know about me, so they lost nothing by dedicating a few weeks to intelligence-gathering. They wanted to know as much as possible about Turquoise and the Jugglers before they made their move. They're brutal, but they're not inefficient. They wanted their takeover to be as precise and surgical as possible.'

'And now?'

'They've accepted that things won't be quite that neat and tidy.' He flipped the globe from one palm to another, with a casual playfulness that Naqi found alarming. 'They're serious, Naqi. Crane will stop at nothing now. You've seen those blast flashes. Pinpoint antimatter devices. They've already sterilised the organic matter within the Moat, to stop the effect of my weapon from reaching further. If they know where we are, they'll drop a bomb on us as well.'

'Human evil doesn't give us the excuse to wipe out the ocean.'

'It's not an excuse, Naqi. It's an imperative.'

At that moment something glinted on the horizon, something that was moving slowly from east to west.

'The shuttle,' Weir said. 'It's looking for us.'

Naqi scratched her arm again. It was discoloured, itching.

Near local noon they reached the next node. The shuttle had continued to dog them, nosing to and fro along the hazy band where sea met sky. Sometimes it appeared closer, sometimes it appeared further away, but it never left them alone, and Naqi knew that it would be only a matter of time before it detected a positive homing trace, a chemical or physical note in the water that would lead it to its quarry. The shuttle would cover the remaining distance in seconds, a minute at the most, and then all that she and Weir would know would be a moment of cleansing whiteness, a fire of holy purity. Even if Weir released his toxin just before the shuttle arrived, it would not have time to dissipate into a wide enough volume of water to survive the fireball.

So why was he hesitating? It was Mina, of course. Naqi had given a name to the faceless library of stored minds he was prepared to erase. By naming her sister, Naqi had removed the one-sidedness of the moral equation, and now Weir had to accept that his own actions could never be entirely blameless. He was no longer purely objective.

'I should just do this,' he said. 'By hesitating even for a second, I'm betraying the trust of the people who sent me here, people who have probably been tormented to extinction by Ormazd's followers by now.'

Naqi shook her head. 'If you didn't show doubt, you'd be as bad as the disciples.'

'You almost sound as if you want me to do it.'

She groped for something resembling the truth, as painful as that might be. 'Perhaps I do.'

'Even though it would mean killing whatever part of Mina survived?'

'I've lived in her shadow my entire life. Even after she died . . . I always felt she was still watching me, still observing my every mistake, still being faintly disappointed that I wasn't living up to all she had imagined I could be.'

'You're being harsh on yourself. Harsh on Mina too, by the sound of things.'

'I know,' Naqi said angrily. 'I'm just telling you how I feel.'

The boat edged into a curving inlet that pushed deep into the node. Naqi felt less vulnerable now: there was a significant depth of organic matter to screen the boat from any sideways-looking sensors that the shuttle might have deployed, even though the evidence suggested that the shuttle's sensors were mainly focused down from its hull. The disadvantage was that it was no longer possible to keep a constant vigil on the shuttle's movements. It could be on its way already.

She brought the boat to a halt and stood up in her control seat.

'What's happening?' Weir asked.

'I've come to a decision.'

'Isn't that my job?'

Her anger – brief as it was, and directed less at Weir than at the hopelessness of the situation – had evaporated. 'I mean about swimming. It's the one thing we haven't considered yet, Rafael. That there might be a third way: a choice between accepting the disciples and letting the ocean die.'

'I don't see what that could be.'

'Nor do I. But the ocean might find a way. It just needs the knowledge of what's at stake.' She stroked her forearm again, marvelling at the sudden eruption of fungal patterns. They must have been latent for many years, but now something had caused them to flare up.

Even in daylight, emeralds and blues shone against her skin. She suspected that the biochemical changes had been triggered when she entered the water to snatch the globe. Given that, she could not help but view it as a message. An invitation, perhaps. Or was it a warning, reminding her of the dangers of swimming?

She had no idea, but for her peace of mind, however – and given the lack of alternatives – she chose to view it as an invitation.

But she did not dare wonder who was inviting her.

'You think the ocean can understand external events?' Weir asked.

'You said it yourself, Rafael: the night they told us the ship was coming, somehow that information reached the sea – via a swimmer's memories, perhaps. And the Jugglers knew then that this was something significant. Perhaps it was Ormazd's personality, rising to the fore.'

Or maybe it was merely the vast, choral mind of the ocean, apprehending only that *something* was going to happen.

'Either way,' Naqi said. 'It still makes me think that there might be a chance.'

'I only wish I shared your optimism.'

'Give me this chance, Rafael. That's all I ask.'

Naqi removed her clothes, less concerned that Weir would see her naked now than that she should have something to wear when she emerged. But although Weir studied her with unconcealed fascination, there was nothing prurient about it. What commanded his attention, Naqi realised, were the elaborate and florid patterning of the fungal markings. They curled and twined about her chest and abdomen and thighs, shining with a hypnotic intensity.

'You're changing,' he said.

'We all change,' Naqi answered.

Then she stepped from the side of the boat, into the water.

The process of descending into the ocean's embrace was much as she remembered it that first time, with Mina beside her. She willed her body to submit to the biochemical invasion, forcing down her fear and apprehension, knowing that she had been through this once before and that it was something that she could survive again. She did her best not to think about what it would mean to survive beyond this day, when all else had been shattered, every certainty crumbled.

Mina came to her with merciful speed.

Naqi?

I'm here. Oh, Mina, I'm here. There was terror and there was joy, alloyed together. *It's been so long.*

Naqi felt her sister's presence edge in and out of proximity and focus. Sometimes she appeared to share the same physical space. At other times she was scarcely more than a vague feeling of attentiveness.

How long?

Two years, Mina.

Mina's answer took an eternity to come. In that dreadful hiatus Naqi felt other minds crowd against her own, some of which were so far from human that she gasped at their oddity. Mina was only one of the conformal minds that had noticed her arrival, and not all were as benignly curious or glad.

It doesn't feel like two years to me.

How long?

Days . . . hours . . . It changes.

What do you remember?

Mina's presence danced around Naqi. *I remember what I remember. That we swam, when we weren't meant to. That something happened to me, and I never left the ocean.*

You became part of it, Mina.

The triumphalism of her answer shocked Naqi to the marrow. *Yes!*

You wanted this?

You would want it, if you knew what it was like. You could have stayed, Naqi. You could have let it happen to you, the way it happened to me. We were so alike.

I was scared.

Yes, I remember.

Naqi knew that she had to get to the heart of things. Time was passing differently here – witness Mina's confusion about how long she had been part of the ocean – and there was no telling how patient Weir would be. He might not wait until Naqi reemerged before deploying the Juggler killer.

There was another mind, Mina. We encountered it, and it scared me. Enough that I had to leave the ocean. Enough that I never wanted to go back.

You've come back now.

It's because of that other mind. It belonged to a man called Ormazd. Something very bad is going to happen because of him. One way or the other.

There was a moment then that transcended anything Naqi had experienced before. She felt herself and Mina become inseparable. She could not only not say where one began and the other ended, but it was entirely pointless to even think in those terms. If only fleetingly, Mina had *become* her. Every thought, every memory, was open to equal scrutiny by both of them.

Naqi understood what it was like for Mina. Her sister's memories were rapturous. She might only have sensed the passing of hours or days, but that belied the richness of her experience since merging with the ocean. She had exchanged experience with countless alien minds, drinking in entire histories beyond normal human comprehension. And in that moment of sharing, Naqi appreciated something of the reason for her sister having been taken in the first place. Conformals were the ocean's way of managing itself. Now and then the maintenance of the vaster archive of static minds required stewardship – the drawing-in of independent intelligences. Mina had been selected and utilised, and given rewards beyond imagining for her efforts. The ocean had tapped the structure of her intelligence at a subconscious level. Only now and then had she ever felt that she was being directly petitioned on a matter of importance.

But Ormazd's mind . . . ?

Mina had seen Naqi's memories now. She would know exactly what was at stake, and she would know exactly what that mind represented.

I was always aware of him. He wasn't always there – he liked to hide himself – but even when he was absent, he left a shadow of himself. I even think he might be the reason the ocean took me as a conformal. It sensed a coming crisis. It knew Ormazd had something to do with it. It had made a terrible mistake by swallowing him. So it reached out for new allies, minds it could trust.

Minds like Mina, Naqi thought. In that instant she did not know whether to admire the Pattern Jugglers or detest them for their heartlessness.

Ormazd was contaminating it?

His influence was strong. His force of personality was a kind of poison in its own right. The Pattern Jugglers knew that, I think.

Why couldn't they just eject his patterns?

They couldn't. It doesn't work that way. The sea is a storage medium, but it has no self-censoring facility. If the individual minds detect a malign presence, they can resist it . . . But Ormazd's mind is human. There aren't enough of us here to make a difference, Naqi. The other minds are too alien to recognise Ormazd for what he is. They just see a sentience.

Who made the Pattern Jugglers, Mina? Answer me that, will you?

She sensed Mina's amusement.

Even the Jugglers don't know that, Naqi. Or why.

You have to help us, Mina. You have to communicate the urgency of this to the rest of the ocean.

I'm one mind amongst many, Naqi. One voice in the chorus.

You still have to find a way. Please, Mina. Understand this, if nothing else. You could die. You could all die. I lost you once, but now I know you never really went away. I don't want to have to lose you again, for good.

You didn't lose me, Naqi. I lost you.

She hauled herself from the water. Weir was waiting where she had left him, with the intact globe still resting in his hand. The daylight shadows had moved a little, but not as much as she had feared. She made eye contact with Weir, wordlessly communicating a question.

'The shuttle's come closer. It's flown over the node twice while you were under. I think I need to do this, Naqi.'

He had the globe between thumb and forefinger, ready to drop it into the water.

She was shivering. Naqi pulled on her shorts and shirt, but she felt just as cold afterwards. The fungal marks were shimmering intensely; they appeared almost to hover above her skin. If anything they were shining more furiously than before she had swum. Naqi did not doubt that if she had lingered – if she had stayed with Mina – she would have become a conformal as well. It had always been in her, but it was only now that her time had come.

'Please wait,' Naqi said, her own voice sounding pathetic and childlike. 'Please wait, Rafael.'

'There it is again.'

The shuttle was a fleck of white sliding over the top of the nearest wall of Juggler biomass. It was five or six kilometres away, much closer than the last time Naqi had seen it. Now it came to a sudden sharp halt, hovering above the surface of the ocean as if it had found something of particular interest.

'Do you think it knows we're here?'

'It suspects something,' Weir said. The globe rolled between his fingers.

'Look,' Naqi said.

The shuttle was still hovering. Naqi stood up to get a better view, nervous of making herself visible but desperately curious. Something was happening. She *knew* something was happening.

Kilometres away, the sea was bellying up beneath the shuttle. The water was the colour of moss, supersaturated with microorganisms. Naqi watched as a coil of solid green matter reached from the ocean, twisting and writhing. It was as thick as a building, spilling vast rivulets of water as it emerged. It extended upwards with astonishing haste, bifurcating and flexing like a groping fist. For a brief moment it closed around the shuttle. Then it slithered back into the sea with a titanic splash; a prolonged roar of spent energy. The shuttle continued to hover above the same spot, as if oblivious to what had just happened. Yet the manta-shaped craft's white hull was lathered with various hues of green. And Naqi understood: what had happened to the shuttle was what had happened to Arviat, the city that drowned. She could not begin to guess the crime that Arviat had committed against the sea, the crime that had merited its destruction, but she could believe – now, at least – that the Jugglers had been capable of dragging it beneath the waves, ripping the main mass of the city away from the bladders that held it aloft. And of course such a thing would have to be kept maximally secret, known only to a handful of individuals. For otherwise no city would ever feel safe when the sea roiled and groaned beneath it.

But a city was not a shuttle. Even if the Juggler material started eating away the fabric of the shuttle, it would still take hours to do any serious damage . . . And that was assuming the Ultras had no better protection than the ceramic shielding used on Turquoise boats and machines . . .

But the shuttle was already tilting over.

Naqi watched it pitch, attempt to regain stability and then pitch again. She understood, belatedly. The organic matter was clogging the shuttle's whisking propulsion systems, limiting its ability to hover. The shuttle was curving inexorably closer to the sea, spiralling steeply away from the node. It approached the surface and then, just before the moment of impact, another misshapen fist of organised matter thrust from the sea, seizing the hull in its entirety. That was the last Naqi saw of it.

A troubled calm fell on the scene. The sky overhead was unmarred by questing machinery. Only the thin whisper of smoke rising from the horizon, in the direction of the Moat, hinted of the day's events.

Minutes passed, and then tens of minutes. Then a rapid series of bright flashes strobed from beneath the surface of the sea itself.

'That was the shuttle,' Weir said, wonderingly.

Naqi nodded. 'The Jugglers are fighting back. This is more or less what I hoped would happen.'

'You asked for this?'

'I think Mina understood what was needed. Evidently she managed to convince the rest of the ocean, or at least this part of it.'

'Let's see.'

They searched the airwaves again. The comsat network was dead, or silent. Even fewer cities were transmitting now. But those that were – those that had not been overrun by Ormazd's disciples – told a frightening story. The ocean was clawing at them, trying to drag them into the sea. Weather patterns were shifting, entire storms being conjured into existence by the orchestrated circulation of vast ocean currents. It was happening in concentric waves, racing away from the precise point in the ocean where Naqi had swum. Some cities had already fallen into the sea, though it was not clear whether this had been brought about by the Jugglers themselves or because of damage to their vacuum-bladders. There were people in the water: hundreds, thousands of them. They were swimming, trying to stay afloat, trying not to drown.

But what exactly did it mean to drown on Turquoise?

'It's happening all over the planet,' Naqi said. She was still shivering, but now it was as much a shiver of awe as one of cold. 'It's denying itself to us by smashing our cities.'

'Your cities never harmed it.'

'I don't think it's really that interested in making a distinction between one bunch of people and another, Rafael. It's just getting rid of us all, disciples or not. You can't really blame it for that, can you?'

'I'm sorry,' Weir said.

He cracked the globe, spilled its contents into the sea.

Naqi knew there was nothing she could do now; there was no prospect of recovering the tiny black grains. She would only have to miss one, and it would be as bad as missing them all.

The little black grains vanished beneath the olive surface of the water.

It was done.

Weir looked at her, his eyes desperate for forgiveness.

'You understand that I had to do this, don't you? It isn't something I do lightly.'

'I know. But it wasn't necessary. The ocean's already turned against us. Crane has lost. Ormazd has lost.'

'Perhaps you're right,' Weir said. 'But I couldn't take the chance that we might be wrong. At least this way I know for sure.'

'You've murdered a world.'

He nodded. 'It's exactly what I came here to do. Please don't blame me for it.'

Naqi opened the equipment locker where she had stowed the broken vial of Juggler toxin. She removed the flare pistol, snatched away its safety pin and pointed it at Weir. 'I don't blame you, no. Don't even hate you for it.'

He started to say something, but Naqi cut him off.

'But it's not something I can forgive.'

She sat in silence, alone, until the node became active. The organic structures around her were beginning to show the same kinds of frantic rearrangement Naqi had seen within the Moat. There was a cold sharp breeze from the node's heart.

It was time to leave.

She steered the boat away from the node, cautiously, still not completely convinced that she was safe from the delegates even though the first shuttle had been destroyed. Undoubtedly the loss of that craft would have been communicated to the others, and before very long some more of them would arrive, bristling with belligerence. The ocean might attempt to destroy the new arrivals, but this time the delegates would be profoundly suspicious.

She brought the boat to a halt when she was a kilometre from the fringe of the node. By then it was running through the same crazed alterations she had previously witnessed. She felt the same howling wind of change. In a moment the end would come. The toxin would seep into the node's controlling core, instructing the entire biomass to degrade itself to a lump of dumb vegetable matter. The same killing instructions would already be travelling along the internode tendril connections, winging their way over the horizon. Allowing for the topology of the network, it would only take fifteen or twenty hours for the message to reach every node on the planet. Within a day it would be over. The Jugglers would be gone, the information they'd encoded erased beyond recall. And Turquoise itself would begin to die at the same time, its oxygen atmosphere no longer maintained by the oceanic organisms.

Another five minutes passed, then ten.

The node's transformations were growing less hectic. She recalled this moment of false calm. It meant only that the node had given up trying to counteract the toxin, accepting the logical inevitability of its fate. A thousand times over this would be repeated around Turquoise. Towards the end, she guessed, there would be less resistance, for the sheer futility of it would have been obvious. The world would accept its fate.

Another five minutes passed.

The node remained. The structures were changing, but only gently. There was no sign of the emerging mound of undifferentiated matter she had seen before.

What was happening?

She waited another quarter of an hour and then steered the boat back towards the node, bumping past Weir's floating corpse on the way. Tentatively, an idea was forming in her mind. It appeared that the node had absorbed the toxin without dying. Was it possible that Weir had made a mistake? Was it possible that the toxin's effectiveness depended only on it being used once?

Perhaps.

There still had to be tendril connections between the Moat and the rest of the ocean at the time that the first wave of transformations had taken place. They had been severed later – either when the doors closed, or by some autonomic process within the extended organism itself – but until that moment, there would still have been informational links with the wider network of nodes. Could the dying nodes have sent sufficient warning that the other nodes were now able to find a strategy for protecting themselves?

Again, perhaps.

It never paid to take anything for granted where the Jugglers were concerned.

She parked the boat by the node's periphery. Naqi stood up and removed her clothes for the final time, certain that she would not need them again. She looked down at herself, astonished at the vivid tracery of green that now covered her body. On one level, the evidence of alien cellular invasion was quite horrific.

On another, it was startlingly beautiful.

Smoke licked from the horizon. Machines clawed through the sky, hunting nervously. She stepped to the edge of the boat, tensing herself at the moment of commitment. Her fear subsided, replaced by an intense, loving calm. She stood on the threshold of something alien, but in place of terror what she felt was only an imminent sense of homecoming. Mina was waiting for her below. Together, nothing could stop them.

Naqi smiled, spread her arms and returned to the sea.

WEATHER

We were at one-quarter of the speed of light, outbound from Shiva-Parvati with a hold full of refugees, when the *Cockatrice* caught up with us. She commenced her engagement at a distance of one light-second, seeking to disable us with long-range weapons before effecting a boarding operation. Captain Van Ness did his best to protect the *Petronel,* but we were a lightly armoured ship and Van Ness did not wish to endanger his passengers by provoking a damaging retaliation from the pirates. As coldly calculated as it might appear, Van Ness knew that it would be better for the sleepers to be taken by another ship than suffer a purposeless death in interstellar space.

As shipmaster, it was my duty to give Captain Van Ness the widest choice of options. When it became clear that the *Cockatrice* was on our tail, following us out from Shiva-Parvati, I recommended that we discard fifty thousand tonnes of nonessential hull material, in order to increase the rate of acceleration available from our Conjoiner drives. When the *Cockatrice* ramped up her own engines to compensate, I identified a further twenty thousand tonnes of material we could discard until the next orbitfall, even though the loss of the armour would marginally increase the radiation dosage we would experience during the flight. We gained a little, but the pirates still had power in reserve: they'd stripped back their ship to little more than a husk, and they didn't have the mass handicap of our sleepers. Since we could not afford to lose any more hull material, I advised Van Ness to eject two of our three heavy shuttles, each of which massed six thousand tonnes when fully fuelled. That bought us yet more time, but to my dismay the pirates still found a way to squeeze a little more out of their engines.

Whoever they had as shipmaster, I thought, they were good at their work.

So I went to the engines themselves, to see if I could better my nameless opponent. I crawled out along the pressurised access tunnel that pierced the starboard spar, out to the coupling point where the foreign technology of the starboard Conjoiner drive was mated to the structural fabric of the *Petronel*. There I opened the hatch that gave access to the controls of the drive itself: six stiff dials, fashioned in blue metal, arranged in hexagon formation, each of which was tied to some fundamental aspect of the engine's function. The dials were set into quadrant-shaped recesses, all now glowing a calm blue-green.

I noted the existing settings, then made near-microscopic alterations to three of the six dials, fighting to keep my hands steady as I applied the necessary effort to budge them. Even as I made the first alteration, I felt the engine respond: a shiver of power as some arcane process occurred deep inside it, accompanied by a shift in my own weight as the thrust increased by five or six per cent. The blue-green hue was now tinted with orange.

The *Petronel* surged faster, still maintaining her former heading. It was only possible to make adjustments to the starboard engine, since the port engine had no external controls. That didn't matter, because the Conjoiners had arranged the two engines to work in perfect synchronisation, despite them being a kilometre apart. No one had ever succeeded in detecting the signals that passed between two matched C-drives, let alone in understanding the messages those signals carried. But everyone who worked with them knew what would happen if, by accident or design, the engines were allowed to get more than sixteen hundred metres apart.

I completed my adjustments, satisfied that I'd done all I could without risking engine malfunction. Three of the five dials were now showing orange, indicating that those settings were now outside what the Conjoiners deemed the recommended envelope of safe operation. If any of the dials were to show red, or if more than three showed orange, than we'd be in real danger of losing the *Petronel.*

When Ultras meet on friendly terms, to exchange data or goods, the shipmasters will often trade stories of engine settings. On a busy trade route, a marginal increase in drive efficiency can make all the difference between one ship and its competitors. Occasionally you hear about ships that have been running on three orange, even four orange, for decades at a time. By the same token, you sometimes hear about ships that went nova when only two dials had been adjusted away from the safety envelope. The one thing every shipmaster agrees upon is that no lighthugger has ever operated for more than a few days of shiptime with one dial in the red. You might risk that to escape aggressors, but even then some will insist that the danger is too great; that those ships that lasted days were the lucky ones.

I left the starboard engine and retreated back into the main hull of the *Petronel.* Van Ness was waiting to greet me. I could tell by the look on his face – the part of it that I could read – that the news wasn't good.

'Good lad, Inigo,' he said, placing his heavy gauntleted hand on my shoulder. 'You've bought us maybe half a day, and I'm grateful for that, no question of it. But it's not enough to make a difference. Are you sure you can't sweet-talk any more out of them?'

'We could risk going to two gees for a few hours. That still wouldn't put us out of reach of the *Cockatrice*, though.'

'And beyond that?'

I showed Van Ness my handwritten logbook, with its meticulous notes of engine settings, compiled over twenty years of shiptime. Black ink for my own entries, the style changing abruptly when I lost my old hand and slowly learned how to use the new one; red annotations in the same script for comments and know-how gleaned from other shipmasters, dated and named. 'According to this, we're already running a fifteen per cent chance of losing the ship within the next hundred days. I'd feel a lot happier if we were already throttling back.'

'You don't think we can lose any more mass?'

'We're stripped to the bone as it is. I can probably find you another few thousand tonnes, but we'll still only be looking at prolonging the inevitable.'

'We'll have the short-range weapons,' Van Ness said resignedly. 'Maybe they'll make enough of a difference. At least now we have an extra half-day to get them run out and tested.'

'Let's hope so,' I agreed, fully aware that it was hopeless. The weapons were antiquated and underpowered, good enough for fending off orbital insurgents but practically useless against another ship, especially one that had been built for piracy. The *Petronel* hadn't fired a shot in anger in more than fifty years. When Van Ness had the chance to upgrade the guns, he'd chosen instead to spend the money on newer reefersleep caskets for the passenger hold.

People have several wrong ideas about Ultras. One of the most common misconceptions is that we must all be brigands, every ship bristling with armaments, primed to a state of nervous readiness the moment another vessel comes within weapons range.

It isn't true. For every ship like that, there are a thousand like the *Petronel*: just trying to ply an honest trade, with a decent, hardworking crew under the hand of a fair man like Van Ness. Some of us might look like freaks, by the standards of planetary civilisation. But spending an entire life aboard a ship, hopping from star to star at relativistic speed, soaking up exotic radiation from the engines and from space itself, is hardly the environment for which the human form was evolved. I'd lost my old hand in an accident, and much of what had happened to Van Ness was down to time and misfortune in equal measure.

He was one of the best captains I'd ever known, maybe the best ever. He'd scared the hell out of me the first time we met, when he was recruiting for a new shipmaster in a carousel around Greenhouse. But Van Ness treated his crew well, kept his word in a deal and always reminded us that our passengers were not frozen 'cargo' but human beings who had entrusted themselves into our care.

'If it comes to it,' Van Ness said, 'we'll let them take the passengers. At least that way some of them might survive, even if they won't necessarily end up where they were expecting. We put up too much of a fight, even after we've been boarded, the *Cockatrice*'s crew may just decide to burn everything, sleepers included.'

'I know,' I said, even though I didn't want to hear it.

'But here's my advice to you, lad.' Van Ness's iron grip tightened on my shoulder. 'Get yourself to an airlock as soon as you can. Blow yourself into space rather than let the bastards get their hands on you. They might be in mind for a bit of cruelty, but they won't be in need of new crew.'

I winced, before he crushed my collarbone. He meant well, but he really didn't know his own strength.

'Especially not a shipmaster, judging by the way things are going.'

'Aye. He's good, whoever he is. Not as good as you, though. You've got a fully laden ship to push; all they have is a stripped-down skeleton.'

It was meant well, but I knew better than to underestimate my adversary. 'Thank you, Captain.'

'We'd best start waking those guns, lad. If you're done with the engines, the weaponsmaster may appreciate a helping hand.'

I barely slept for the next day. Coaxing the weapons back to operational readiness was a fraught business, and it all had to be done without alerting the *Cockatrice* that we had any last-minute defensive capability. The magnetic coils on the induction guns had to be warmed and brought up to operational field strength, and then tested with slugs of recycled hull material. One of the coils fractured during warm-up and took out its entire turret, injuring one of Weps's men in the process. The optics on the lasers had to be aligned and calibrated, and then the lasers had to be test-fired against specks of incoming interstellar dust, hoping that the *Cockatrice* didn't spot those pinpoint flashes of gamma radiation as the lasers found their targets.

All the while this was going on, the enemy continued their long-range softening-up bombardment. The *Cockatrice* was using everything in her arsenal, from slugs and missiles to beam-weapons. The *Petronel* was running an evasion routine, swerving to exploit the sadly narrowing timelag between the two ships, but the routine was old and with the engines already notched up to close-on maximum output, there was precious little reserve power. No single impact was damaging, but as the assault continued, the cumulative effect began to take its toll. Acres of hull shielding were now compromised, and there were warnings of structural weakness in the port drive spar. If this continued, we would soon be forced to dampen our engines, rather than be torn apart by our own thrust loading. That was exactly what the *Cockatrice* wanted. Once they'd turned us into a lame duck, they could make a forced hard docking and storm our ship.

By the time they were eighty thousand kilometres out, things were looking very bad for us. Even the *Cockatrice* must have been nervous of what would happen if the port spar gave way, since they'd begun to concentrate their efforts on our midsection instead. Reluctantly I crawled back along the starboard spar and confronted the engine settings again. I was faced with two equally numbing possibilities. I could turn the dials even further into the orange, making the engines run harder still. Even if the engines held, the ship wouldn't, but at least we'd go out in a flash when the spar collapsed and the two engines drifted apart. Or I could return the dials to blue-green and let the *Cockatrice* catch us up without risk of further failure. One option might ensure the future survival of the passengers. Neither looked very attractive from the crew's standpoint.

Van Ness knew it, too. He'd begun to go around the rest of the crew, all two dozen of us, ordering those who weren't actively involved in the current crisis to choose an empty casket in the passenger hold and try to pass themselves off as cargo. Van Ness was wise enough not to push the point when no one took him up on his offer.

At fifty thousand kilometres, the *Cockatrice* was in range of our own weapons. We let her slip a little closer and then rotated our hull through forty-five degrees to give her a full broadside, all eleven working slug-cannons discharging at once, followed by a burst from the lasers. The recoil from the slugs was enough to generate further warnings of structural failure in a dozen critical nodes. But we held, somehow, and thirty per cent of that initial salvo hit the *Cockatrice* square-on. By then the lasers had already struck her, vaporising thousands of tonnes of ablative ice from her prow in a scalding white flash. When the steam had fallen astern of the still-accelerating ship, we got our first good look at the damage.

It wasn't enough. We'd hurt her, but barely, and I knew we couldn't sustain more than three further bursts of fire before the *Cockatrice*'s own short-range weapons found their lock and returned the assault. As it was, we only got off another two salvos before the slug-cannons suffered a targeting failure. The lasers continued to fire for another minute, but once they'd burned off the *Cockatrice*'s ice (which she could easily replenish from our own shield, once we'd been taken) they could inflict little further damage.

By twenty thousand kilometres, all our weapons were inoperable. Fear of break-up had forced me to throttle our engines back down to zero thrust, leaving only our in-system fusion motors running. At ten thousand kilometres, the *Cockatrice* released a squadron of pirates, each of whom would be carrying hull-penetrating gear and shipboard weapons, in addition to their thruster packs and armour. They must have been confident that we had nothing else to throw at them.

We knew then it was over.

It was, too: but for the *Cockatrice*, not us. What took place happened too quickly for the human eye to see. It was only later, when we had the benefit of footage from the hull cameras, that we were able to piece together what had occurred.

One instant, the *Cockatrice* was creeping closer to us, her engines doused to a whisper now to match our own feeble rate of acceleration. The next instant, she was still *there*, but everything about her had changed. The engines were shut down completely and the hull had begun to come apart, flaking away in a long lateral line that ran the entire four kilometres from bow to stern. The *Cockatrice* began to crab, losing axial stabilisation. Pieces of her were drifting away. Vapour was jetting from a dozen apertures along her length. Where the hull had scabbed away, the brassy orange glow of internal fire was visible. One engine spar was seriously buckled.

We didn't know it at the time – didn't know it until much later, when we'd actually boarded her – but the *Cockatrice* had fallen victim to the oldest hazard in space: collision with debris. There isn't a lot of it out there, but when it hits . . . at a quarter of the speed of light, it doesn't take much to inflict crippling damage. The impactor might only have been the size of a fist, or a fat thumb, but it had rammed its way right through the ship like a bullet, and the momentum transfer had almost ripped the engines off.

It was bad luck for the crew of the *Cockatrice*. For us, it was the most appalling piece of good luck imaginable. Except it wasn't even luck, really. Every now and then, ships will encounter something like that. Deep-look radar will identify an incoming shard and send an emergency steer command to the engines. Or the radar will direct anti-collision lasers to vaporise the object before it hits. Even if it does hit, most of its kinetic energy will be soaked up by the ablation ice. Ships don't carry all that dead weight for nothing.

But the *Cockatrice* had lost her ice under our lasers. She'd have replaced it sooner or later, but without it she was horribly vulnerable. And her own anti-collision system was preoccupied dealing with our short-range weapons. One little impactor was all it took to remove her from the battle.

It gave us enough of a handhold to start fighting back. With the *Cockatrice* out of the fight, our own crew were able to leave the protection of the ship without fear of being fried or pulverised. Van Ness was the first out of the airlock, with me not far behind him. Within five minutes there were twenty-three of us outside, our suits bulked out with armour and antiquated weapons. There were at least thirty incoming pirates from the *Cockatrice,* and they had better gear. But they'd lost the support of their mother ship, and all of them must have been aware that the situation had undergone a drastic adjustment. Perhaps it made them fight even more fiercely, given that ours was now the only halfway-intact ship. They'd been planning to steal our cargo before, and strip the *Petronel* for useful parts; now they needed to take the *Petronel* and claim her as their own. But they didn't have back-up from the *Cockatrice* and – judging by the way the battle proceeded – they seemed handicapped by more than just the lack of covering fire. They fought as well as they could, which was with a terrible individual determination, but no overall co-ordination. Afterwards, we concluded that their suit-to-suit communications, even their spatial-orientation systems, must have been reliant on signals routed through their ship. Without her they were deaf and blind.

We still lost good crew. It took six hours to mop up the last resistance from the pirates, by which point we'd taken eleven fatalities, with another three seriously wounded. But by then the pirates were all dead, and we were in no mood to take prisoners.

But we were in a mood to take what we needed from the *Cockatrice.*

If we'd expected to encounter serious resistance aboard the damaged ship, we were wrong. As Van Ness led our boarding party through the drifting wreck, the scope of the damage became chillingly clear. The ship had been gutted from the inside out, with almost no intact pressure-bearing structures left anywhere inside her main hull. For most of the crew left aboard when the impactor hit, the end would have come with merciful swiftness. Only a few had survived the initial collision, and most of them must have died shortly afterwards, as the ship bled through its wounds. We found no sign that the *Cockatrice* had been carrying frozen passengers, although – since entire internal bays had been blasted out of existence, leaving only an interlinked chain of charred, blackened caverns – we probably wouldn't ever know for sure. Of the few survivors we did encounter, none attempted surrender or requested parley. That made it easier for us. If they stood still, we shot them. If they fled, we still shot them.

Except for one.

We knew there was something different about her as soon as we saw her. She didn't look or move like an Ultra. There was something of the cat or snake about the way she slinked out of the illumination of our lamps, something fluid and feral, something sleek and honed that did not belong aboard a ship crewed by pirates. We held our fire from the moment her eyes first flashed at us, for we knew she could not be one of them. Wide, white-edged eyes in a girl's face, her strong-jawed expression one of ruthless self-control and effortless superiority. Her skull was hairless, her forehead rising to a bony crest rilled on either side by shimmering coloured tissue.

The girl was a Conjoiner.

It was three days before we found her again. She knew that ship with animal cunning, as if the entire twisted and blackened warren was a lair she had made for herself. But her options were diminishing with every hour that passed, as more and more air drained out of the wreck. Even Conjoiners needed to breathe, and that meant there was less and less of the ship in which she could hide.

Van Ness wanted to move on. Van Ness – a good man, but never the most imaginative of souls – wasn't interested in what a stray Conjoiner could do for us. I'd warned him that the *Cockatrice*'s engines were in an unstable condition, and that we wouldn't have time to back off to a safe distance if the buckled drive spar finally gave way. Now that we'd harvested enough of the other ship's intact hull to repair our own damage, Van Ness saw no reason to hang around. But I managed to talk him into letting us hunt down the girl.

'She's a Conjoiner, Captain. She wouldn't have been aboard that ship of her own free will. That means she's a prisoner that we can free and return to her people. They'll be grateful. That means they'll want to reward us.'

Van Ness fixed me with an indulgent smile. 'Lad, have you ever had close dealings with Spiders?'

He still called me 'lad' even though I'd been part of his crew for twenty years, and had been born another twenty before that, by shiptime reckoning. 'No,' I admitted. 'But the Spiders – the Conjoiners – aren't the bogeymen some people like to make out.'

'I've dealt with 'em,' Van Ness said. 'I'm a lot older than you, lad. I go right back to when things weren't so pretty between the Spiders and the rest of humanity, back when my wife was alive.'

It took a lot to stir up the past for Rafe Van Ness. In all our years together, he'd only mentioned his wife a handful of times. She'd been a botanist, working on the Martian terraforming programme. She'd been caught by a flash flood when she was working in one of the big craters, testing plant stocks for the Demarchists. All I knew was that after her death, Van Ness had left the system, on one of the first passenger-carrying starships. It had been his first step on the long road to becoming an Ultra.

'They've changed since the old days,' I said. 'We trust them enough to use their engines, don't we?'

'We trust the engines. Isn't quite the same thing. And if they didn't have such a monopoly on making the things, maybe we wouldn't have to deal with them at all. Anyway, who is this girl? What was she doing aboard the *Cockatrice*? What makes you think she wasn't helping them?'

'Conjoiners don't condone piracy. And if we want answers, we have no option but to catch her and find out what she has to say.'

Van Ness sounded suddenly interested. 'Interrogate her, you mean?'

'I didn't say that, Captain. But we might want to ask her a few questions.'

'We'd be playing with fire. You know they can make things happen just by thinking about them.'

'She'll have no reason to hurt us. We'll have saved her life just by taking her off the *Cockatrice*.'

'Maybe she doesn't want it saved. Have you thought of that?'

'We'll cross that bridge when we find her, Captain.'

He pulled a face, that part of his visage still capable of making expressions, at least. 'I'll give you another twelve hours, lad. That's my limit. Then we put as much distance between us and that wreck as God and physics will allow.'

I nodded, knowing that it was pointless to expect more of Van Ness. He'd already shown great forbearance in allowing us to delay the departure for so long. Given his feelings regarding Conjoiners, I wasn't going to push for any more time.

*

We caught her eleven hours later. We'd driven her as far as she could go, blocking her escape routes by blowing the few surrounding volumes that were still pressurised. I was the first to speak to her, when we finally had her cornered.

I pushed up the visor of my helmet, breathing stale air so that we could speak. She was huddled in a corner, compressed like some animal ready to bolt or strike.

'Stop running from us,' I said, as my lamp pinned her down and forced her to squint. 'There's nowhere left to go, and even if there was, we don't want to hurt you. Whatever these people did to you, whatever they made you do, we're not like them.'

She hissed back, 'You're Ultras. That's all I need to know.'

'We're Ultras, yes, but we still want to help you. Our captain just wants to get away from this time bomb as quickly as possible. I talked him into giving us a few extra hours to find you. You can come with us whenever you like. But if you'd rather stay aboard this ship . . .'

She stared back at me and said nothing. I couldn't guess her age. She had the face of a girl, but there was a steely resolution in her olive-green eyes that told me she was older than she looked.

'I'm Inigo, the shipmaster from the *Petronel*,' I said, hoping that my smile looked reassuring rather than threatening. I reached out my hand, my right one, and she flinched back. Even suited, even hidden under a glove, my hand was obviously mechanical. 'Please,' I continued, 'come with us. We'll treat you well and get you back to your people.'

'Why?' she snarled. 'Why do *you* care?'

'Because we're not all the same,' I said. 'And you need to believe it, or you're going to die here when we leave. Captain wants us to secure for thrust in less than an hour. So *come on*.'

'What happened?' she asked, looking around at the damaged compartment in which she had been cornered. 'I know the *Cockatrice* was attacking another ship . . . how did you do this?'

'We didn't. We just got very, very lucky. Now it's your turn.'

'I can't leave here. I need to be with this ship.'

'This ship is going to blow up if one of us sneezes. Do you really want to be aboard when that happens?'

'I still need to be here. Leave me alone, I'll survive by myself. Conjoiners will find me again.'

I shook my head firmly. 'That isn't going to happen. Even if this ship doesn't blow up, you're still drifting at twenty-five per cent of the speed of light. That's too fast to get you back to Shiva-Parvati, even if there's a shuttle aboard this thing. Too fast for anyone around Shiva-Parvati to come out and rescue you, too.'

'I know this.'

'Then you also know that you're not moving anywhere near fast enough to actually get anywhere before your resources run out. Unless you think you can survive fifty years aboard this thing, until you swing by the next colonised system with no way of slowing down.'

'I'll take my chances.'

A voice buzzed in my helmet. It was Van Ness, insisting that we return to the *Petronel* as quickly as possible. 'I'm sorry,' I said, 'but if you don't come willingly, I'm going to have to bring you in unconscious.' I raised the blunt muzzle of my slug-gun.

'If there's a tranquiliser dart in there, it won't work on me. My nervous system isn't like yours. I only sleep when I choose to.'

'That's what I figured. It's why I dialled the dose to five times its normal strength. I don't know about you, but I'm willing to give it a try and see what happens.'

Panic crossed her face. 'Give me a suit,' she said. 'Give me a suit and then leave me alone, if you really want to help.'

'What's your name?'

'We don't have names, Inigo. At least nothing *you* could get your tongue around.'

'I'm willing to try.'

'Give me a suit. Then leave me alone.'

Van Ness started screaming in my ears again. I'd had enough. I pointed the muzzle at her, aiming for the flesh of her thigh, where she had her legs tucked under her. I squeezed the trigger and delivered the stun flechette.

'You fool,' she said. 'You don't understand. You have to leave me here, with this . . .'

That was all she managed before slumping into unconsciousness. She'd gone down much faster than I'd expected, as if she'd already been on her last reserves of strength. I just hoped I hadn't set the stun dose too high. It was already strong enough to kill any normal human being.

Van Ness had been right to be concerned about our proximity to the *Cockatrice.* We'd barely doubled the distance between the two ships when her drive spar failed, allowing the port engine to drift away from its starboard counterpart. Several agonising minutes later, the distance between the two engine units exceeded sixteen hundred metres and the drives went up in a double burst that tested our shielding to its limits. The flash must have been visible all the way back to Shiva-Parvati.

The girl had been unconscious right up until that moment, but when the engines went up she twitched on the bunk where we'd placed her, just as if she'd been experiencing a vivid and disturbing dream. The rilled structures on the side of her crest throbbed with vivid colours, each chasing the last.

Then she was restful again, for many hours, and the play of colours calmer.

I watched her sleeping. I'd never been near a Conjoiner before, let alone one like this. Aboard the ship, when we had been hunting her, she had seemed strong and potentially dangerous. Now she looked like some half-starved animal, driven to the brink of madness by hunger and something infinitely worse. There were awful bruises all over her body, some more recent than others. There were fine scars on her skull. One of her incisors was missing a point.

Van Ness still wasn't convinced of the wisdom of bringing her aboard, but even his dislike of Conjoiners didn't extend to the notion of throwing her back into space. All the same, he insisted that she be bound to the bunk by heavy restraints, in an armoured room under the guard of a servitor, at least until we had some idea of who she was and how she had ended up aboard the pirate ship. He didn't want heavily augmented crew anywhere near her, either, not when (as he evidently believed) she had the means to control any machine in her vicinity, and might therefore overpower or even commandeer any crewperson who had a skull full of implants. It wasn't like that, I tried to tell him: Conjoiners could talk to machines, yes, but not all machines, and the idea that they could work witchcraft on anything with a circuit inside it was just so much irrational fearmongering.

Van Ness heard my reasoned objections, and then ignored them. I'm glad that he did, though. Had he listened to me, he might have put some other member of the crew in charge of questioning her, and then I wouldn't have got to know her as well as I did. Because I only had the metal hand, the rest of me still flesh and blood, he deemed me safe from her influence.

I was with her when she woke.

I placed my left hand on her shoulder as she squirmed under the restraints, suddenly aware of her predicament. 'It's all right,' I said softly. 'You're safe now. Captain made us put these on you for the time being, but we'll get them off you as soon as we can. That's a promise. I'm Inigo, by the way, shipmaster. We met before, but I'm not sure how much of that you remember.'

'Every detail,' she said. Her voice was low, dark-tinged, untrusting.

'Maybe you don't know where you are. You're aboard the *Petronel*. The *Cockatrice* is gone, along with everyone aboard her. Whatever they did to you, whatever happened to you aboard that ship, it's over now.'

'You didn't listen to me.'

'If we'd listened to you,' I said patiently, 'you'd be dead by now.'

'No, I wouldn't.'

I'd been ready to give her the benefit of the doubt, but my reservoir of sympathy was beginning to dry up. 'You know, it wouldn't hurt to show a little gratitude. We put ourselves at considerable risk to get you to safety. We'd taken everything we needed from the pirates. We only went back in to help you.'

'I didn't need you to help me. I could have survived.'

'Not unless you think you could have held that spar on by sheer force of will.'

She hissed back her reply. 'I'm a Conjoiner. That means the rules were different. I could have changed things. I could have kept the ship in one piece.'

'To make a point?'

'No,' she said, with acid slowness, as if that was the only speed I was capable of following. 'Not to make a point. We don't *make* points.'

'The ship's gone,' I said. 'It's over, so you may as well deal with it. You're with us now. And no, you're not our prisoner. We'll do everything I said we would: take care of you, get you to safety, back to your people.'

'You really think it's that simple?'

'I don't know. Why don't you tell me? I don't see what the problem is.'

'The problem is I can't ever go back. Is that simple enough for you?'

'Why?' I asked. 'Were you exiled from the Conjoiners, or something like that?'

She shook her elaborately crested head, as if my question was the most naive thing she had ever heard. 'No one gets exiled.'

'Then tell me what the hell happened!'

Anger burst to the surface. 'I was taken, all right? I was stolen, snatched away from my people. Captain Voulage took me prisoner around Yellowstone, when the *Cockatrice* was docked near one of our ships. I was part of a small diplomatic party visiting Carousel New Venice. Voulage's men ambushed us, split us up, then took me so far from the other Conjoiners that I dropped out of neural range. Have you any idea what that means to one of us?'

I shook my head, not because I didn't understand what she meant, but because I knew I could have no proper grasp of the emotional pain that severance must have caused. I doubted that pain was a strong enough word for the psychic shock associated with being ripped away from her fellows. Nothing in ordinary human experience could approximate the trauma of that separation, any more than a frog could grasp the loss of a loved one. Conjoiners spent their whole lives in a state of gestalt consciousness, sharing thoughts and experiences via a web of implant-mediated neural connections. They had individual personalities, but those personalities were more like the blurred identities of atoms in a metallic solid. Beyond the level of individual self was the state of higher mental union that they called Transenlightenment, analogous to the fizzing sea of dissociated electrons in that same metallic lattice.

And the girl had been ripped away from that, forced to come to terms with existence as a solitary mind, an island once more.

'I understand how bad it must have been,' I said. 'But now you can go back. Isn't that something worth looking forward to?'

'You only *think* you understand. To a Conjoiner, what happened to me is the worst thing in the world. And now I can't go back: not now, not ever. I've become damaged, broken, useless. My mind is permanently disfigured. It can't be allowed to return to Transenlightenment.'

'Why ever not? Wouldn't they be glad to get you back?'

She took a long time answering. In the quiet, I studied her face, watchful for anything that would betray the danger Van Ness clearly believed she posed. Now his fears seemed groundless. She looked smaller and more delicately boned than when we'd first glimpsed her on the *Cockatrice.* The strangeness of her, the odd shape of her hairless crested skull, should have been off-putting. In truth I found her fascinating. It was not her alienness that drew my furtive attention, but her very human face: her small and pointed chin, the pale freckles under her eyes, the way her mouth never quite closed, even when she was silent. The olive green of her eyes was a shade so dark that from certain angles it became a lustrous black, like the surface of coal.

'No,' she said, answering me finally. 'It wouldn't work. I'd upset the purity of the others, spoil the harmony of the neural connections, like a single out-of-tune instrument in an orchestra. I'd make everyone else start playing out of key.'

'I think you're being too fatalistic. Shouldn't we at least try to find some other Conjoiners and see what they say?'

'That isn't how it works,' she said. 'They'd have to take me back, yes, if I presented myself to them. They'd do it out of kindness and compassion. But I'd still end up harming them. It's my duty not to allow that to happen.'

'Then you're saying you have to spend the rest of your life away from other Conjoiners, wandering the universe like some miserable excommunicated pilgrim?'

'There are more of us than you realise.'

'You do a good job keeping out of the limelight. Most people only see Conjoiners in groups, all dressed in black like a flock of crows.'

'Maybe you aren't looking in the right places.'

I sighed, aware that nothing I said was going to convince her that she would be better off returning to her people. 'It's your life, your destiny. At least you're alive. Our word still holds: we'll drop you at the nearest safe planet, when we next make orbitfall. If that isn't satisfactory to you, you'd be welcome to remain aboard ship until we arrive somewhere else.'

'Your captain would allow that? I thought he was the one who wanted to leave the wreck before you'd found me.'

'I'll square things with the captain. He isn't the biggest fan of Conjoiners, but he'll see sense when he realises you aren't a monster.'

'Does he have a reason not to like me?'

'He's an old man,' I said simply.

'Riven with prejudice, you mean?'

'In his way,' I said, shrugging. 'But don't blame him for that. He lived through the bad years, when your people were first coming into existence. I think he had some first-hand experience of the trouble that followed.'

'Then I envy him those first-hand memories. Not many of us are still alive from those times. To have lived through those years, to have breathed the same air as Remontoire and the others . . .' She looked away sadly. 'Remontoire's gone now. So are Galiana and Nevil. We don't know what happened to any of them.'

I knew she must have been talking about pivotal figures from earlier Conjoiner history, but the people of whom she spoke meant nothing to me. To her, cast so far downstream from those early events on Mars, the names must have held something of the resonance of saints or apostles. I thought I knew something of Conjoiners, but they had a long and complicated internal history of which I was totally ignorant.

'I wish things hadn't happened the way they did,' I said. 'But that was then and this is now. We don't hate or fear you. If we did, we wouldn't have risked our necks getting you out of the *Cockatrice*.'

'No, you don't hate or fear me,' she replied. 'But you still think I might be useful to you, don't you?'

'Only if you wish to help us.'

'Captain Voulage thought that I might have the expertise to improve the performance of his ship.'

'Did you?' I asked innocently.

'By increments, yes. He showed me the engines and . . . encouraged me to make certain changes. You told me you are a shipmaster, so you doubtless have some familiarity with the principles involved.'

I thought back to the adjustments I had made to our own engines, when we still had ambitions of fleeing the pirates. The memory of my trembling hand on those three critical dials felt as if it had been dredged from deepest antiquity, rather than something that had happened only days earlier.

'When you say "encouraged" . . .' I began.

'He found ways to coerce me. It is true that Conjoiners can control their perception of pain by applying neural blockades. But only to a degree, and then only when the pain has a real physical origin. If the pain is generated in the head, using a reverse-field trawl, our defences are useless.' She looked at me with a sudden hard intensity, as if daring me to imagine one-tenth of what she had experienced. 'It is like locking a door when the wolf is already in the house.'

'I'm sorry. You must have been through hell.'

'I only had the pain to endure,' she said. 'I'm not the one anyone needs to feel sorry about.'

The remark puzzled me, but I let it lie. 'I have to get back to our own engines now,' I said, 'but I'll come to see you later. In the meantime, I think you should rest.' I snapped a duplicate communications bracelet from my wrist and placed it near her hand, where she could reach it. 'If you need me, you can call into this. It'll take me a little while to get back here, but I'll come as quickly as possible.'

She lifted her forearm as far as it would go, until the restraints stiffened. 'And these?'

'I'll talk to Van Ness. Now that you're lucid, now that you're talking to us, I don't see any further need for them.'

'Thank you,' she said again. 'Inigo. Is that all there is to your name? It's rather a short one, even by the standards of the retarded.'

'Inigo Standish, shipmaster. And you still haven't told me your name.'

'I told you: it's nothing you could understand. We have our own names now, terms of address that can only be communicated in the Transenlightenment. My name is a flow of experiential symbols, a string of interiorised qualia, an expression of a particular dynamic state that has only ever happened under a conjunction of rare physical conditions in the atmosphere of a particular kind of gas giant planet. I chose it myself. It's considered very beautiful and a little melancholy, like a haiku in five dimensions.'

'Inside the atmosphere of a gas giant, right?'

She looked at me alertly. 'Yes.'

'Fine, then. I'll call you Weather. Unless you'd like to suggest something better.'

She never did suggest something better, even though I think she once came close to it. From that moment on, whether she liked it or not, she was always Weather. Soon, it was what the other crew were calling her, and the name that – grudgingly at first, then resignedly – she deigned to respond to.

I went to see Captain Van Ness and did my best to persuade him that Weather was not going to cause us any difficulties.

'What are you suggesting we should give her – a free pass to the rest of the ship?'

'Only that we could let her out of her prison cell.'

'She's recuperating.'

'She's restrained. And you've put an armed servitor on the door, in case she gets out of the restraints.'

'Pays to be prudent.'

'I think we can trust her now, Captain.' I hesitated, choosing my words with great care. 'I know you have good reasons not to like her people, but she isn't the same as the Conjoiners from those days.'

'That's what she'd like us to think, certainly.'

'I've spoken to her, heard her story. She's an outcast from her people, unable to return to them because of what's happened to her.'

'Well, then,' Van Ness said, nodding as if he'd proved a point, 'outcasts do funny things. You can't ever be too careful with outcasts.'

'It's not like that with Weather.'

'Weather,' he repeated, with a certain dry distaste. 'So she's got a name now, has she?'

'I felt it might help. The name was my suggestion, not hers.'

'Don't start humanising them. That's the mistake humans always make. Next thing you know, they've got their claws in your skull.'

I closed my eyes, forcing self-control as the conversation veered off course. I'd always had an excellent relationship with Van Ness, one that came very close to bordering on genuine friendship. But from the moment he heard about Weather, I knew she was going to come between us.

'I'm not suggesting we let her run amok,' I said. 'Even if we let her out of those restraints, even if we take away the servitor, we can still keep her out of any parts of the ship where we don't want her. In the meantime, I think she can be helpful to us. She's already told me that Captain Voulage forced her to make improvements to the *Cockatrice*'s drive system. I don't see why she can't do the same for us, if we ask nicely.'

'Why did he have to force her, if you're so convinced she'd do it willingly now?'

'I'm not convinced. But I can't see why she wouldn't help us, if we treat her like a human being.'

'That'd be our big mistake,' Van Ness said. 'She never was a human being. She's been a Spider from the moment they made her, and she'll go to the grave like that.'

'Then you won't consider it?'

'I consented to let you bring her aboard. That was already against every God-given instinct.' Then Van Ness rumbled, 'And I'd thank you not to mention the Spider again, Inigo.

You've my permission to visit her if you see fit, but she isn't taking a step out of that room until we make orbitfall.'

'Very well,' I said, with a curtness that I'd never had cause to use on Captain Van Ness.

As I was leaving his cabin, he said, 'You're still a fine shipmaster, lad. That's never been in doubt. But don't let this thing cloud your usual good judgement. I'd hate to have to look elsewhere for someone of your abilities.'

I turned back and, despite everything that told me to hold my tongue, I still spoke. 'I was wrong about you, Captain. I've always believed that you didn't allow yourself to be ruled by the irrational hatreds of other Ultras. I always thought you were better than that.'

'And I'd have gladly told you I have just as many prejudices as the next man. They're what've kept me alive so long.'

'I'm sure Captain Voulage felt the same way,' I said.

It was a wrong and hateful thing to say – Van Ness had nothing in common with a monster like Voulage – but I couldn't stop myself. And I knew even as I said it that some irreversible bridge had just been crossed, and that it was more my fault than Van Ness's.

'You have work to do, I think,' Van Ness said, his voice so low that I barely heard it. 'Until you have the engines back to full thrust, I suggest you keep out of my way.'

Weps came to see me eight or nine hours later. I knew it wasn't good news as soon as I saw her face.

'We have a problem, Inigo. The captain felt you needed to know.'

'And he couldn't tell me himself?'

Weps cleared part of the wall and called up a display, filling it with a boxy green three-dimensional grid. 'That's us,' she said, jabbing a finger at the red dot in the middle of the display. She moved her finger halfway to the edge, scratching her long black nail against the plating. 'Something else is out there. It's stealthed to the gills, but I'm still seeing it. Whatever it is is making a slow, silent approach.'

My thoughts flicked to Weather. 'Could it be Conjoiner?'

'That was my first guess. But if it was Conjoiner, I don't think I'd be seeing anything at all.'

'So what are we dealing with?'

She tapped the nail against the blue icon representing the new ship. 'Another raider. Could be an ally of Voulage – we know he had friends – or could be some other ship that was hoping to pick over our carcass once Voulage was done with us, or maybe even steal us from him before he had his chance.'

'Hyena tactics.'

'Wouldn't be the first time.'

'Range?'

'Less than two light-hours. Even if they don't increase their rate of closure, they'll be on us within eight days.'

'Unless we move.'

Weps nodded sagely. 'That would help. You're on schedule to complete repairs within six days, aren't you?'

'On schedule, yes, but that doesn't mean things can be moved any faster. We start cutting corners now, we'll break like a twig when we put a real load on the ship.'

'We wouldn't want that.'

'No, we wouldn't.'

'The captain just thought you should be aware of the situation, Inigo. It's not to put you under pressure, or anything.'

'Of course not.'

'It's just that . . . we really don't want to be hanging around here a second longer than necessary.'

*

I removed Weather's restraints and showed her how to help herself to food and water from the room's dispenser. She stretched and purred, articulating and extending her limbs in the manner of a dancer rehearsing some difficult routine in extreme slow motion. She'd been 'reading' when I arrived, which for Weather seemed to involve staring into the middle distance while her eyes flicked to and fro at manic speed, as if following the movements of an invisible wasp.

'I can't let you out of the room just yet,' I said, sitting on the fold-down stool next to the bed, upon which Weather now sat cross-legged. 'I just hope this makes things a little more tolerable.'

'So your captain's finally realised I'm not about to suck out his brains?'

'Not exactly. He'd still rather you weren't aboard.'

'Then you're going against his orders.'

'I suppose so.'

'I presume you could get into trouble for that.'

'He'll never find out.' I thought of the unknown ship that was creeping towards us. 'He's got other things on his mind now. It's not as if he's going to be paying you a courtesy call just to pass the time of day.'

'But if he did find out . . .' She looked at me intently, lifting her chin. 'Do you fear what he'd do to you?'

'I probably should. But I don't think he'd be very likely to throw me into an airlock. Not until we're under way at full power, in any case.'

'And then?'

'He'd be angry. But I don't think he'd kill me. He's not a bad man, really.'

'Perhaps I misheard, but didn't you say his name was Van Ness?'

'Captain Rafe Van Ness, yes.' I must have looked surprised. 'Don't tell me it means something to you.'

'I heard Voulage mention him, that's all. Now I know we're talking about the same man.'

'What did Voulage have to say?'

'Nothing good. But I don't think that necessarily reflects poorly on your captain. He must be a reasonable man. He's at least allowed me aboard his ship, even if I haven't been invited to dine in his quarters.'

'Dining for Van Ness is a pretty messy business,' I said confidingly. 'You're better off eating alone.'

'Do you like him, Inigo?'

'He has his flaws, but next to someone like Voulage, he's pretty close to being an angel.'

'Doesn't like Conjoiners, though.'

'Most Ultras would have left you drifting. I think this is a point where you have to take what you're given.'

'Perhaps. I don't understand his attitude, though. If your captain is like most Ultras, there's at least as much of the machine about him as there is about me. More so, in all likelihood.'

'It's what you do with the machines that counts,' I said. 'Ultras tend to leave their minds alone, if at all possible. Even if they do have implants, it's usually to replace areas of brain function lost due to injury or old age. They're not really interested in improving matters, if you get my drift. Maybe that's why Conjoiners make them twitchy.'

She unhooked her legs, dangling them over the edge of the bed. Her feet were bare and oddly elongated. She wore the same tight black outfit we'd found her in when we boarded the ship. It was cut low from her neck, in a rectangular shape.

Her breasts were small. Though she was bony, with barely any spare muscle on her, she had the broad shoulders of a swimmer. Though Weather had sustained her share of injuries, the outfit showed no sign of damage at all. It appeared to be self-repairing, even self-cleaning.

'You talk of Ultras as if you weren't one,' she said.

'Just an old habit breaking through. Though sometimes I don't feel like quite the same breed as a man like Van Ness.'

'Your implants must be very well shielded. I can't sense them at all.'

'That's because there aren't any.'

'Squeamish? Or just too young and fortunate not to have needed them yet?'

'It's nothing to do with being squeamish. I'm not as young as I look, either.' I held up my mechanical hand. 'Nor would I exactly call myself fortunate.'

She looked at the hand with narrowed, critical eyes. I remembered how she'd flinched back when I reached for her aboard the *Cockatrice*, and wondered what maltreatment she had suffered at the iron hands of her former masters.

'You don't like it?' she asked.

'I liked the old one better.'

Weather reached out and gingerly held my hand in hers. They looked small and dolllike as they stroked and examined my mechanical counterpart.

'This is the only part of you that isn't organic?'

'As far as I know.'

'Doesn't that limit you? Don't you feel handicapped around the rest of the crew?'

'Sometimes. But not always. My job means I have to squeeze into places where a man like Van Ness could never fit. It also means I have to be able to tolerate magnetic fields that would rip half the crew to shreds, if they didn't boil alive first.' I opened and closed my metal fist. 'I have to unscrew this, sometimes. I have a plastic replacement if I just need to hook hold of things.'

'You don't like it very much.'

'It does what I ask of it.'

Weather made to let go of my hand, but her fingers remained in contact with mine for an instant longer than necessary. 'I'm sorry that you don't like it.'

'I could have got it fixed at one of the orbital clinics, I suppose,' I said, 'but there's always something else that needs fixing first. Anyway, if it wasn't for the hand, some people might not believe I'm an Ultra at all.'

'Do you plan on being an Ultra all your life?'

'I don't know. I can't say I ever had my mind set on being a shipmaster. It just sort of happened, and now here I am.'

'I had my mind set on something once,' Weather said. 'I thought it was within my grasp, too. Then it slipped out of reach.' She looked at me and then did something wonderful and unexpected, which was to smile. It was not the most genuine-looking smile I'd ever seen, but I sensed the genuine intent behind it. Suddenly I knew there was a human being in the room with me, damaged and dangerous though she might have been. 'Now here I am, too. It's not quite what I expected . . . but thank you for rescuing me.'

'I was beginning to wonder if we'd made a mistake. You seemed so reluctant to leave that ship.'

'I was,' she said, distantly. 'But that's over now. You did what you thought was the right thing.'

'Was it?'

'For me, yes. For the ship . . . maybe not.' Then she stopped and cocked her head to one side, frowning. Her eyes flashed olive. 'What are you looking at, Inigo?'

'Nothing,' I said, looking sharply away.

Keeping out of Van Ness's way, as he'd advised, was not the hard part of what followed. The *Petronel* was a big ship and our paths didn't need to cross in the course of day-to-day duties. The difficulty was finding as much time to visit Weather as I would have liked. My original repair plan had been tight, but the unknown ship forced me to accelerate the schedule even further, despite what I'd told Weps. The burden of work began to take its toll on me, draining my concentration. I was still confident that once that work was done, we'd be able to continue our journey as if nothing had happened, save for the loss of those crew who had died in the engagement and our gaining one new passenger. The other ship would probably abandon us once we pushed the engines up to cruise thrust, looking for easier pickings elsewhere. If it had the swiftness of the *Cockatrice*, it wouldn't have been skulking in the shadows letting the other ship take first prize.

But my optimism was misplaced. When the repair work was done, I once more made my way along the access shaft to the starboard engine and confronted the hexagonal arrangement of input dials. As expected, all six dials were now showing deep blue, which meant they were operating well inside the safety envelope. But when I consulted my logbook and made the tiny adjustments that should have taken all the dials into the blue-green – still nicely within the safety envelope – I got a nasty surprise. I only had to nudge two of the dials by a fraction of a millimetre before they shone a hard and threatening orange.

Something was wrong.

I checked my settings, of course, making sure none of the other dials were out of position. But there'd been no mistake. I thumbed through the log with increasing haste, a prickly feeling on the back of my neck, looking for an entry where something similar had happened; something that would point me to the obvious mistake I must have made. But none of the previous entries were the slightest help. I'd made no error with the settings, and that left only one possibility: something had happened to the engine. It was not working properly.

'This isn't right,' I said to myself. 'They don't fail. They don't break down. Not like this.'

But what did I know? My entire experience of working with C-drives was confined to routine operations, under normal conditions. Yet we'd just been through a battle against another ship, one in which we were already known to have sustained structural damage. As shipmaster, I'd been diligent in attending to the hull and the drive spar, but it had never crossed my mind that something might have happened to one or other of the engines.

Why not?

There's a good reason. It's because even if something had happened, there would never have been anything I could have done about it. Worrying about the breakdown of a Conjoiner drive was like worrying about the one piece of debris you won't have time to steer around or shoot out of the sky. You can't do anything about it, ergo you forget about it until it happens. No shipmaster ever loses sleep over the failure of a C-drive.

It looked as if I was going to lose a lot more than sleep.

Even if we didn't have another ship to worry about, we were in more than enough trouble. We were too far out from Shiva-Parvati to get back again, and yet we were moving too slowly to make it to another system. Even if the engines kept working as they were now, we'd take far too long to reach relativistic speed, where time dilation became appreciable. At twenty-five per cent of the speed of light, what would have been a twenty-year hop before became an eighty-year crawl now . . . and that was an eighty-year crawl in which almost all that time would be experienced aboard ship. Across that stretch of time, reefersleep was a lottery. Our caskets were designed to keep people frozen for five to ten years, not four-fifths of a century.

I was scared. I'd gone from feeling calmly in control to feeling total devastation in about five minutes.

I didn't want to let the rest of the crew know that we had a potential crisis on our hands, at least not until I'd spoken to Weather. I'd already crossed swords with Van Ness, but he was still my captain, and I wanted to spare him the difficulty of a frightened crew, at least until I knew all the facts.

Weather was awake when I arrived. In all my visits, I'd never found her sleeping. In the normal course of events Conjoiners had no need of sleep: at worst, they'd switch off certain areas of brain function for a few hours.

She read my face like a book. 'Something's wrong, isn't it?'

So much for the notion that Conjoiners were not able to interpret facial expressions. Just because they didn't *make* many of them didn't mean they'd forgotten the rules.

I sat down on the fold-out stool.

'I've tried to push the engines back up to normal cruise thrust. I'm already seeing red on two dials, and we haven't even exceeded point-two gees.'

She thought about this for several moments: what for Weather must have been hours of subjective contemplation. 'You didn't appear to be pushing your engines dangerously during the chase.'

'I wasn't. Everything looked normal up until now. I think we must have taken some damage to one of the drives, during Voulage's softening-up assault. I didn't see any external evidence, but—'

'You wouldn't, not necessarily. The interior architecture of one of our drives is a lot more complicated, a lot more delicate, than is normally appreciated. It's at least possible that a shock-wave did some harm to one of your engines, especially if your coupling gear – the shock-dampening assembly – was already compromised.'

'It probably was,' I said. 'The spar was already stressed.'

'Then you have your explanation. Something inside your engine has broken, or is considered by the engine itself to be dangerously close to failure. Either way, it would be suicide to increase the thrust beyond the present level.'

'Weather, we need both those engines to get anywhere, and we need them at normal efficiency.'

'It hadn't escaped me.'

'Is there anything you can do to help us?'

'Very little, I expect.'

'But you must know something about the engines, or you wouldn't have been able to help Voulage.'

'Voulage's engines weren't damaged,' she explained patiently.

'I know that. But you were still able to make them work better. Isn't there something you can do for us?'

'From here, nothing at all.'

'But if you were allowed to get closer to the engines . . . might that make a difference?'

'Until I'm there, I couldn't possibly say. It's irrelevant though, isn't it? Your captain will never allow me out of this room.'

'Would you do it for us if he did?'

'I'd do it for me.'

'Is that the best you can offer?'

'All right, then maybe I'd for it for you.' Just saying this caused Weather visible discomfort, as if the utterance violated some deep personal code that had remained intact until now.

'You've been kind to me. I know you risked trouble with Van Ness to make things easier in my cell. But you need to understand something very important. You may care for me. You may even think you like me. But I can't give you back any of that. What I feel for you is . . .' Weather hesitated, her mouth half-open. 'You know we call you the retarded. There's a reason for that. The emotions I feel . . . the things that go on in my head . . . simply don't map onto anything you'd recognise as love, or affection, or even friendship. Reducing them to those terms would be like . . .' And then she stalled, unable to finish.

'Like making a sacrifice?'

'You've been good to me, Inigo. But I really am like the weather. You can admire me, even love me, in your way, but I can't love you back. To me you're like a photograph. I can see right through you, examine you from all angles. You amuse me. But you don't have enough depth ever to fascinate me.'

'There's more to love than fascination. And you said it yourself: you're halfway back to being human again.'

'I said I wasn't a Conjoiner any more. But that doesn't mean I could ever be like you.'

'You could try.'

'You don't understand us.'

'I want to!'

Weather jammed her olive eyes tight shut. 'Let's . . . not get ahead of ourselves, shall we? I only wanted to spare you any unnecessary emotional pain. But if we don't get this ship moving properly, that'll be the least of your worries.'

'I know.'

'So perhaps we should return to the matter of the engines. Again: none of this will matter if Van Ness refuses to trust me.'

My cheeks were smarting as if I'd been slapped hard in the face. Part of me knew she was only being kind, in the harshest of ways. That part was almost prepared to accept her rejection. The other part of me only wanted her more, as if her bluntness had succeeded only in sharpening my desire. Perhaps she was right; perhaps I was insane to think a Conjoiner could ever feel something in return. But I remembered the gentle way she'd stroked my fingers, and I wanted her even more.

'I'll deal with Van Ness,' I said. 'I think there's a little something that will convince him to take a risk. You start thinking about what you can do for us.'

'Is that an order, Inigo?'

'No,' I said. 'Nobody's going to order you to do anything. I gave you my word on that, and I'm not about to break it. Nothing you've just said changes that.'

She sat tight-lipped, staring at me as if I was some kind of byzantine logic puzzle she needed to unscramble. I could almost feel the furious computation of her mind, as if I was standing next to a humming turbine. Then she lifted her little pointed chin minutely, saying nothing, but letting me know that if I convinced Van Ness, she would do what she could, however ineffectual that might prove.

The captain was tougher to crack than I'd expected. I'd assumed he would fold as soon as I explained our predicament – that we were going nowhere, and that Weather was the only factor that could improve our situation – but the captain simply narrowed his eyes and looked disappointed.

'Don't you get it? It's a ruse, a trick. Our engines were fine until we let her aboard. Then all of a sudden they start misbehaving, and she turns out to be the only one who can help us.'

'There's also the matter of the other ship Weps says is closing on us.'

'That ship might not even exist. It could be a sensor ghost, a hallucination she's making the *Petronel* see.'

'Captain—'

'That would work for her, wouldn't it? It would be exactly the excuse she needs to force our hands.'

We were in his cabin, with the door locked: I'd warned him I had a matter of grave sensitivity that we needed to discuss. 'I don't think this is any of her doing,' I said calmly, vowing to hold my temper under better control than before. 'She's too far from the engines or sensor systems to be having any mental effect on them, even if we hadn't locked her in a room that's practically a Faraday cage to begin with. She says one or other of the engines was damaged during the engagement with the *Cockatrice*, and I've no reason to disbelieve that. I think you're wrong about her.'

'She's got us right where she wants us, lad. She's done something to the engines, and now – if you get your way – we're going to let her get up close and personal with them.'

'And do what?' I asked.

'Whatever takes her fancy. Blowing us all up is one possibility. Did you consider that?'

'She'd blow herself up as well.'

'Maybe that's exactly the plan. Could be that she prefers dying to staying alive, if being shut out from the rest of the Spiders is as bad as you say it is. She didn't seem to be real keen on being rescued from that wreck, did she? Maybe she was hoping to die aboard it.'

'She looked like she was trying to stay alive to me, Captain. There were a hundred ways she could have killed herself aboard the *Cockatrice* before we boarded, and she didn't. I think she was just scared of us, scared that we were going to be like all the other Ultras. That's why she kept running.'

'A nice theory, lad. It's a pity so much is hanging on it, or I might be inclined to give it a moment's credence.'

'We have no choice but to trust her. If we don't let her try something, most of us won't ever see another system.'

'Easy for you to say, son.'

'I'm in this as well. I've got just as much to lose as anyone else on this ship.'

Van Ness studied me for what felt like an eternity. Until now his trust in my competence had always been implicit, but Weather's arrival had changed all that.

'My wife didn't die in a terraforming accident,' he said slowly, not quite able to meet my eyes as he spoke. 'I lied to you about that, probably because I wanted to start believing the lie myself. But now it's time you heard the truth, which is that the Spiders took her. She was a technician, an expert in Martian landscaping. She'd been working on the Schiaparelli irrigation scheme when she was caught behind Spider lines during the Sabaea Offensive. They stole her from me, and turned her into one of them. Took her to their recruitment theatres, where they opened her head and pumped it full of their machines. Rewired her mind to make her think and feel like them.'

'I'm sorry,' I began. 'That must have been so hard—'

'That's not the hard part. I was told that she'd been executed, but three years later I saw her again. She'd been taken prisoner by the Coalition for Neural Purity, and they were trying to turn her back into a person. They hadn't ever done it before, so my wife was to be a test subject. They invited me to their compound in Tychoplex, on Earth's Moon, hoping I might be able to bring her back. I didn't want to do it. I knew it wasn't going to work; that it was always going to be easier thinking that she was already dead.'

'What happened?'

'When she saw me, she remembered me. She called me by name, just as if we'd only been apart a few minutes. But there was a coldness in her eyes. Actually, it was something beyond coldness. Coldness would mean she felt some recognisably human emotion, even if it was dislike or contempt. It wasn't like that. The way she looked at me, it was as if she was looking at a piece of broken furniture, or a dripping tap, or a pattern of mould on the wall. As if it vaguely bothered her that I existed, or was the shape I was, but that she could feel nothing stronger than that.'

'It wasn't your wife any more,' I said. 'Your wife died the moment they took her.'

'That'd be nice to believe, wouldn't it? Trouble is, I've never been able to. And trust me, lad: I've had long enough to dwell on things. I know a part of my wife survived what they did to her in the theatres. It just wasn't the part that gave a damn about me any more.'

'I'm sorry,' I said again, feeling as if I'd been left drifting in space while the ship raced away from me. 'I had no idea.'

'I just wanted you to know: with me and the Spiders, it isn't an irrational prejudice. From where I'm sitting, it feels pretty damn rational.' Then he drew an enormous intake of breath, as if he needed sustenance for what was to come. 'Take the girl to the engine if you think it's the only way we'll get out of this mess. But don't let her out of your sight for one second. And if you get the slightest idea that she might be trying something – and I mean the *slightest* idea – you kill her, there and then.'

I clamped the collar around Weather's neck. It was a heavy ring fashioned from rough black metal. 'I'm sorry about this,' I told her, 'but it's the only way Van Ness will let me take you out of this room. Tell me if it hurts, and I'll try to do something about it.'

'You won't need to,' she said.

The collar was a crude old thing that had been lying around the *Petronel* since her last bruising contact with pirates. It was modified from the connecting ring of a space helmet, the kind that would amputate and shock-freeze the head if it detected massive damage to the body below the neck. Inside the collar was a noose of monofilament wire, primed to tighten to the diametre of a human hair in less than a second. There were complicated moving parts in the collar, but nothing that a Conjoiner could influence. The collar trailed a thumb-thick cable from its rear, which ran all the way to an activating box on my belt. I'd only need to give the box a hard thump with the heel of my hand, and Weather would be decapitated. That wouldn't necessarily mean she'd die instantly – with all those machines in her head, Weather would be able to remain conscious for quite some time afterwards – but I was reasonably certain it would limit her options for doing harm.

'For what it's worth,' I told her as we made our way out to the connecting spar, 'I'm not expecting to have to use this. But I want you to be clear that I will if I have to.'

She walked slightly ahead of me, the cable hanging between us. 'You seem different, Inigo. What happened between you and the captain, while you were gone?'

The truth couldn't hurt, I decided. 'Van Ness told me something I didn't know. It put things into perspective. I understand now why he might not feel positively disposed towards Conjoiners.'

'And does that alter the way you think about me?'

I said nothing for several paces. 'I don't know, Weather. Until now I never really gave much thought to those horror stories about the Spiders. I assumed they'd been exaggerated, the way things often are during wartime.'

'But now you've seen the light. You realise that, in fact, we are monsters after all.'

'I didn't say that. But I've just learned that something I always thought untrue – that Conjoiners would take prisoners and convert them into other Conjoiners – really happened.'

'To Van Ness?'

She didn't need to know all the facts. 'To someone close to him. The worst was that he got to meet that person after her transformation.'

After a little while, Weather said, 'Mistakes were made. Very, very bad mistakes.'

'How can you call taking someone prisoner and stuffing their skull full of Conjoiner machinery a "mistake", Weather? You must have known exactly what you were doing, exactly what it would do to the prisoner.'

'Yes, we did,' she said, 'but we considered it a kindness. That was the mistake, Inigo. And it was a kindness, too: no one who tasted Transenlightenment ever wanted to go back to the experiential mundanity of retarded consciousness. But we did not anticipate how distressing this might be to those who had known the candidates beforehand.'

'He felt that she didn't love him any more.'

'That wasn't the case. It's just that everything else in her universe had become so heightened, so intense, that the love for another individual could no longer hold her interest. It had become just one facet in a much larger mosaic.'

'And you don't think that was cruel?'

'I said it was a mistake. But if Van Ness had joined her . . . if Van Ness had submitted to the Conjoined, known Transenlightenment for himself . . . they would have reconnected on a new level of personal intimacy.'

I wondered how she could be so certain. 'That doesn't help Van Ness now.'

'We wouldn't make the same mistake again. If there were

ever to be . . . difficulties again, we wouldn't take candidates so indiscriminately.'

'But you'd still take some.'

'We'd still consider it a kindness,' Weather said.

Not much was said as we traversed the connecting spar out to the starboard engine. I watched Weather alertly, transfixed by the play of colours across her cooling crest. Eventually she whirled around and said, 'I'm not going to *do* anything, Inigo, so stop worrying about it. This collar's bad enough, without feeling you watching my every move.'

'Maybe the collar isn't going to help us,' I said. 'Van Ness thinks you want to blow up the ship. I guess if you had a way to do that, we wouldn't get much warning.'

'No, you wouldn't. But I'm not going to blow up the ship. That's not within my power, unless you let me turn the input dials all the way into the red. Even Voulage wasn't that stupid.'

I wiped my sweat-damp hand on the thigh of my trousers. 'We don't know much about how these engines work. Are you sensing anything from them yet?'

'A little,' she admitted. 'There's crosstalk between the two units, but I don't have the implants to make sense of that. Most Conjoiners don't need anything that specialised, unless they work in the drive crèches, educating the engines.'

'The engines need educating?'

Not answering me directly, she said, 'I can feel the engine now. Effective range for my implants is a few dozen metres under these conditions. We must be very close.'

'We are,' I said as we turned a corner. Ahead lay the hexagonal arrangement of input dials. They were all showing blue-green now, but only because I'd throttled the engine back to a whisper of thrust.

'I'll need to get closer if I'm going to be any use to you,' Weather told me.

'Step up to the panel. But don't touch anything until I give you permission.'

I knew there wasn't much harm she could do here, even if she started pushing the dials. She'd need to move more than one to make things dangerous, and I could drop her long before she had a chance to do that. But I was still nervous as she stood next to the hexagon and cocked her head to one side.

I thought of what lay on the other side of that wall. Having traversed the spar, we were now immediately inboard of the engine, about halfway along its roughly cylindrical shape. The engine extended for one hundred and ten metres ahead of me, and for approximately two hundred and fifty metres in either direction to my left and right. It was sheathed in several layers of conventional hull material, anchored to the *Petronel* by a shock-absorbing cradle and wrapped in a mesh of sensors and steering-control systems. Like any shipmaster, my understanding of those elements was so total that it no longer counted as acquired knowledge. It had become an integral part of my personality.

But I knew nothing of the engine itself. My logbook, with its reams of codified notes and annotations, implied a deep and scholarly grasp of all essential principles. Nothing could have been further from the truth. The Conjoiner drive was essentially a piece of magic we'd been handed on a plate, like a coiled baby dragon. It came with instructions on how to tame its fire, and make sure it did not come to harm, but we were forbidden from probing its mysteries. The most important rule that applied to a Conjoiner engine was a simple one: there were no user-serviceable components inside. Tamper with an engine – attempt to take it apart, in the hope of reverse-engineering it – and the engine would self-destruct in a mini-nova powerful enough to crack open a small moon. Across settled space, there was no shortage of mildly radioactive craters testifying to failed attempts to break that one prohibition.

Ultras didn't care, as a rule. Ultras, by definition, already had Conjoiner drives. It was governments and rich planet-bound individuals who kept learning the hard way. The Conjoiner argument was brutal in its simplicity: there were principles embodied in their drives that 'retarded' humanity just wasn't ready to absorb. We were meant to count ourselves lucky that they let us have the engines in the first place. We weren't meant to go poking our thick monkey fingers into their innards.

And so long as the engines kept working, few of us had any inclination to do so.

Weather took a step back. 'It's not good news, I'm afraid. I thought that perhaps the dial indications might be in error, suggesting that there was a fault where none existed . . . but that isn't the case.'

'You can feel that the engine is really damaged?'

'Yes,' she told me. 'And it's this one, the starboard unit.'

'What's wrong with it? Is it anything we can fix?'

'One question at a time, Inigo.' Weather smiled tolerantly before continuing, 'There's been extensive damage to critical engine components, too much for the engine's own self-repair systems to address. The engine hasn't failed completely, but certain reaction pathways have now become computationally intractable, which is why you're seeing the drastic loss in drive efficiency. The engine is being forced to explore other pathways, those that it can still manage given its existing resources. But they don't deliver the same output energy.'

She was telling me everything and nothing. 'I don't really understand,' I admitted. 'Are you saying there's nothing that can be done to repair it?'

'Not here. At a dedicated Conjoiner manufacturing facility, certainly. We'd only make things worse.'

'We can't run on just the port engine, either – not without rebuilding the entire ship. If we were anywhere near a moon or asteroid, that might just be an option, but not when we're so far out.'

'I'm sorry the news isn't better. You'll just have to resign yourselves to a longer trip than you were expecting.'

'It's worse than that. There's another ship closing in on us, probably another raider like Voulage. It's very close now. If we don't start running soon, they'll be on us.'

'And you didn't think to tell me this sooner?'

'Would it have made any difference?'

'To the trust between us, possibly.'

'I'm sorry, Weather. I didn't want to distract you. I thought things were bad enough as they were.'

'And you thought I'd be able to work a miracle if I wasn't distracted?'

I nodded hopelessly. I realised that, as naive as it might seem, I'd been expecting Weather to wave a hand over the broken engine and restore it to full, glittering functionality. But knowing something of the interior workings of the drive was not the same as being able to fix it.

'Are we really out of options?' I asked.

'The engine is already doing all it can to provide maximum power, given the damage it has taken. There really is no scope to make things better.'

Desperate for some source of optimism, I thought back to what Weather had said a few moments before. 'When you talked about the computations, you seemed to be saying that the engine needed to do some number-crunching to make itself work.'

Weather looked conflicted. 'I've already said too much, Inigo.'

'But if we're going to die out here, it doesn't matter what you tell me, does it? Failing that, I'll swear a vow of silence. How does that sound?'

'No one has ever come close to working out how our engines function,' Weather said. 'We've played our hand in that, of course: putting out more than our share of misinformation over the years. And it's worked, too. We've kept careful tabs on the collective thinking concerning our secrets. We've always had contingencies in place to disrupt any research that might be headed in the right direction. So far we've never had cause to use a single one of them. If I were to reveal key information to you, I would have more to worry about than just being an outcast. My people would come after me. They'd hunt me down, and then they'd hunt you down as well. Conjoiners will consider any necessary act, up to and including local genocide, to protect the secrets of the C-drive.' She paused for a moment, letting me think she was finished, before continuing on the same grave note, 'But having said that, there are layers to our secrets. I can't reveal the detailed physical principles upon which the drive depends, but I can tell you that the conditions in the drive, when it is at full functionality, are enormously complex and chaotic. Your ship may ride a smooth thrust beam, but the reactions going on inside the drive are anything but smooth. There is a small mouth into hell inside every engine: bubbling, frothing, subject to vicious and unpredictable state-changes.'

'Which the engine needs to smooth out.'

'Yes. And to do so, the engine needs to think through some enormously complex, parallel computational problems. When all is well, when the engine is intact and running inside its normal operational envelope, the burden is manageable. But if you ask too much of the engine, or damage it in some way, that burden becomes heavier. Eventually it exceeds the means of the engine, and the reactions become uncontrolled.'

'Nova.'

'Quite,' Weather said, favouring my response with a tiny nod.

'Then let me get this straight,' I said. 'The engine's damaged, but it could still work if the computations weren't so complicated.'

Weather answered me guardedly. 'Yes, but don't underestimate how difficult those computations have now become. I can feel the strain this engine is under, just holding things together as they are.'

'I'm not underestimating it. I'm just wondering if we couldn't help it do better. Couldn't we load in some new software, or assist the engine by hooking in the *Petronel*'s own computers?'

'I really wish it was that simple.'

'I'm sorry. My questions must seem quite simple-minded. But I'm just trying to make sure we aren't missing anything obvious.'

'We aren't,' she said. 'Take my word on it.'

I returned Weather to her quarters and removed the collar. Where it had been squeezing her neck, the skin was marked with a raw pink band, spotted with blood. I threw the hateful thing into the corner of the room and returned with a medical kit.

'You should have said something,' I told her as I dabbed at the abrasions with a disinfectant swab. 'I didn't realise it was cutting into you all that time. You seemed so cool, so focused. But that must have been hurting all the while.'

'I told you I could turn off pain.'

'Are you turning it off now?'

'Why?'

'Because you keep flinching.'

Weather reached up suddenly and took my wrist, almost making me drop the swab. The movement was as swift as a snakebite, but although she held me firmly, I sensed no aggressive intentions. 'Now it's my turn not to understand,' she said. 'You were hoping I might be able to do something for you. I couldn't. That means you're in as much trouble as you ever were. Worse, if anything, because now you've heard it from me. But you're still treating me with kindness.'

'Would you rather we didn't?'

'I assumed that as soon as my usefulness to you had come to an end—'

'You assumed wrongly. We're not that kind of crew.'

'And your captain?'

'He'll keep his word. Killing you would never have been Van Ness's style.' I finished disinfecting her neck and began to rummage through the medical kit for a strip of bandage. 'We're all just going to have to make do as best we can, you included. Van Ness reckoned we should send out a distress call and wait for rescue. I wasn't so keen on that idea before, but now I'm beginning to wonder if maybe it isn't so bad after all.' She said nothing. I wondered if she was thinking of exactly the same objections I'd voiced to Van Ness, when he raised the idea. 'We still have a ship, that's the main thing. Just because we aren't moving as fast as we'd like—'

'I'd like to see Van Ness,' Weather said.

'I'm not sure he'd agree.'

'Tell him it's about his wife. Tell him he can trust me, with or without that silly collar.'

I went to fetch the captain. He took some persuading before he even agreed to look at Weather, and even then he wouldn't come within twenty metres of her. I told her to wait at the door to her room, which faced a long service corridor.

'I'm not going to touch you, Captain,' she called, her voice echoing from the corridor's ribbed metal walls. 'You can come as close as you like. I can barely smell you at this distance, let alone sense your neural emissions.'

'This'll do nicely,' Van Ness said. 'Inigo told me you had something you wanted to say to me. That right, or was it just a ruse to get me near to you, so you could reach into my head and make me see and think whatever you like?'

She appeared not to hear him. 'I take it Inigo's told you about the engine.'

'Told me you had a good old look at it and decided there was nothing you could do. Maybe things would have been different if you hadn't had that collar on, though, eh?'

'You mean I might have sabotaged the engine, to destroy myself and the ship? No, Captain, I don't think I would have. If I had any intention of killing myself, you'd already made it easy enough with that collar.' She glanced at me. 'I could have reached Inigo and pressed that control box while the nervous impulse from his brain was still working its way down his forearm. All he'd have seen was a grey blur, followed by a lot of arterial blood.'

I thought back to the speed with which she'd reached up and grabbed my forearm, and knew she wasn't lying.

'So why didn't you?' Van Ness asked.

'Because I wanted to help you if I could. Until I saw the engine – until I got close enough to feel its emissions – I couldn't know for sure that the problem wasn't something quite trivial.'

'Except it wasn't. Inigo says it isn't fixable.'

'Inigo's right. The technical fault can't be repaired, not without use of Conjoiner technology. But now that I've had time to think about it, mull things over, it occurs to me that there may be something I can do for you.'

I looked at her. 'Really?'

'Let me finish what I have to say, Inigo,' she said warningly, 'then we'll go down to the engine and I'll make everything clear. Captain Van Ness – about your wife.'

'What would you know about my wife?' Van Ness asked her angrily.

'More than you realise. I know because I'm a – I was – a Conjoiner.'

'As if I didn't know.'

'We started on Mars, Captain Van Ness – just a handful of us. I wasn't alive then, but from the moment Galiana brought our new state of consciousness into being, the thread of memory has never been broken. There are many branches to our great tree now, in many systems – but we all carry the memories of those who went before us, before the family was torn asunder. I don't just mean the simple fact that we remember their names, what they looked like and what they did. I mean we carry their living experiences with us, into the future.' Weather swallowed, something catching in her throat. 'Sometimes we're barely aware of any of this. It's as if there's this vast sea of collective experience lapping at the shore of consciousness, but it's only every now and then that it floods us, leaving us awash in sorrow and joy. Sorrow because those are the memories of the dead, all that's left of them. Joy because *something* has endured, and while it does they can't truly be dead, can they? I feel Remontoire sometimes, when I look at something in a certain analytic way. There's a jolt of déjà vu and I realise it isn't because I've experienced it before, but because Remontoire did. We all feel the memories of the earliest Conjoiners the most strongly.'

'And my wife?' Van Ness asked, like a man frightened of what he might hear.

'Your wife was just one of many candidates who entered Transenlightenment during the troubles. You lost her then, and saw her once more when the Coalition took her prisoner. It was distressing for you because she did not respond to you on a human level.'

'Because you'd ripped everything human out of her,' Van Ness said.

Weather shook her head calmly, refusing to be goaded. 'No. We'd taken almost nothing. The difficulty was that we'd added too much, too quickly. That was why it was so hard for her, and so upsetting for you. But it didn't have to be that way. The last thing we wanted was to frighten possible future candidates. It would have worked much better for us if your wife had shown love and affection to you, and then begged you to follow her into the wonderful new world she'd been shown.'

Something of Weather's manner seemed to blunt Van Ness's indignation. 'That doesn't help me much. It doesn't help my wife at all.'

'I haven't finished. The last time you saw your wife was in that Coalition compound. You assumed – as you continue to assume – that she ended her days there, an emotionless zombie haunting the shell of the woman you once knew. But that isn't what happened. She came back to us, you see.'

'I thought Conjoiners never returned to the fold,' I said.

'Things were different then. It was war. Any and all candidates were welcome, even those who might have suffered destabilising isolation away from Transenlightenment. And Van Ness's wife wasn't like me. She hadn't been born into it. Her depth of immersion into Transenlightenment was inevitably less profound than that of a Conjoiner who'd been swimming in data since they were a foetus.'

'You're lying,' Van Ness said. 'My wife died in Coalition custody three years after I saw her.'

'No,' Weather said patiently. 'She did not. Conjoiners took Tychoplex and returned all the prisoners to Transenlightenment. The Coalition was suffering badly at the time and could not afford the propaganda blow of losing such a valuable arm of its research programme. So it lied and covered up the loss of Tychoplex. But in fact your wife was alive and well.' Weather looked at him levelly. 'She is dead now, Captain Van Ness. I wish I could tell you otherwise, but I hope it will not come as too shocking a blow, given what you have always believed.'

'When did she die?'

'Thirty-one years later, in another system, during the malfunction of one of our early drives. It was very fast and utterly painless.'

'Why are you telling me this? What difference does it make to me, here and now? She's still gone. She still became one of you.'

'I am telling you,' Weather answered, 'because her memories are part of me. I won't pretend that they're as strong as Remontoire's, because by the time your wife was recruited, more than five thousand had already joined our ranks. Hers was one new voice amongst many. But none of those voices were silent: they were all heard, and something of them has reached down through all these years.'

'Again: why are you telling me this?'

'Because I have a message from your wife. She committed it to the collective memory long before her death, knowing that it would always be part of Conjoiner knowledge, even as our numbers grew and we became increasingly fragmented. She knew that every future Conjoiner would carry her message – even an outcast like me. It might become diluted, but it would never be lost entirely. And she believed that you were still alive, and that one day your path might cross that of another Conjoiner.'

After a silence Van Ness said, 'Tell me the message.'

'This is what your wife wished you to hear.' Almost imperceptibly, the tone of Weather's voice shifted. 'I am sorry for what happened between us, Rafe – more sorry than you can ever know. When they recaptured me, when they took me to Tychoplex, I was not the person I am now. It was still early in my time amongst the Conjoiners, and – perhaps just as importantly – it was still early for the Conjoiners as well. There was much that we all needed to learn. We were ambitious then, fiercely so, but by the same token we were arrogantly blind to our inadequacies and failings. That changed, later, after I returned to the fold. Galiana made refinements to all of us, reinstating a higher degree of personal identity. I think she had learned something wise from Nevil Clavain. After that, I began to see things in the proper perspective again. I thought of you, and the pain of what I had done to you was like a sharp stone pushing against my throat. Every waking moment of my consciousness, with every breath, you were there. But by then it was much too late to make amends. I tried to contact you, but without success. I couldn't even be sure if you were in the system any more. By then, even the Demarchists had their own prototype starships, using the technology we'd licensed them. You could have been anywhere.' Weather's tone hardened, taking on a kind of saintlike asperity. 'But I always knew you were a survivor, Rafe. I never doubted that you were still alive, somewhere. Perhaps we'll meet again: stranger things have happened. If so, I hope I'll treat you with something of the kindness you always deserved, and that you always showed me. But should that never happen, I can at least hope that you will hear this message. There will always be Conjoiners, and nothing that is committed to the collective memory will ever be lost. No matter how much time passes, those of us who walk in the world will be carrying this message, alert for your name. If there was more I could do, I would. But contrary to what some might think, even Conjoiners can't work miracles. I wish that it were otherwise. Then I would clap my hands and summon you to me, and I would spend the rest of my life letting you know what you meant to me, what you still mean to me. I loved you, Rafe Van Ness. I always did, and I always will.'

Weather fell silent, her expression respectful. It was not necessary for her to tell us that the message was over.

'How do I know this is true?' Van Ness asked quietly.

'I can't give you any guarantees,' Weather said, 'but there was one word I was also meant to say to you. Your wife believed it would have some significance to you, something nobody else could possibly know.'

'And the word?'

'The word is "mezereon". I think it is a type of plant. Does the word mean something to you?'

I looked at Van Ness. He appeared frozen, unable to respond. His eye softened and sparkled. He nodded, and said simply, 'Yes, it does.'

'Good,' Weather answered. 'I'm glad that's done: it's been weighing on all of our minds for quite some time. And now I'm going to help you get home.'

Whatever 'mezereon' meant to Van Ness, whatever it revealed to him concerning the truth of Weather's message, I never asked.

Nor did Van Ness ever speak of the matter again.

*

She stood before the hexagonal arrangement of input dials, as I had done a thousand times before. 'You must give me authorisation to make adjustments,' she said.

My mouth was dry. 'Do what you will. I'll be watching you very carefully.'

Weather looked amused. 'You're still concerned that I might want to kill us all?'

'I can't ignore my duty to this ship.'

'Then this will be difficult for you. I must turn the dials to a setting you would consider highly dangerous, even suicidal. You'll just have to trust me that I know what I'm doing.'

I glanced back at Van Ness.

'Do it,' he mouthed.

'Go ahead,' I told Weather. 'Whatever you need to do—'

'In the course of this, you will learn more about our engines. There is something inside here that you will find disturbing. It is not the deepest secret, but it is a secret nonetheless, and shortly you will know it. Afterwards, when we reach port, you must not speak of this matter. Should you do so, Conjoiner security would detect the leak and act swiftly. The consequences would be brutal, for you and anyone you might have spoken to.'

'Then maybe you're better off not letting us see whatever you're so keen to keep hidden.'

'There's something I'm going to have to do. If you want to understand, you need to see everything.'

She reached up and planted her hands on two of the dials. With surprising strength, she twisted them until their quadrants shone ruby red. Then she moved to another pair of dials and moved them until they were showing a warning amber. She adjusted one of the remaining dials to a lower setting, into the blue, and then returned to the first two dials she had touched, quickly dragging them back to green. While all this was happening, I felt the engine surge in response, the deck plates pushing harder against my feet. But the burst was soon over. When Weather had made her last adjustment, the engine had throttled back even further than before. I judged that we were only experiencing a tenth of a gee.

'What have you just done?' I asked.

'This,' she said.

Weather took a nimble, light-footed step back from the input controls. At the same moment a chunk of wall, including the entire hexagonal array, pushed itself out from the surrounding metallic-blue material in which it had appeared to have been seamlessly incorporated. The chunk was as thick as a bank-vault door. I watched in astonishment as the chunk slid in silence to one side, exposing a bulkhead-sized hole in the side of the engine wall.

Soft red light bathed us. We were looking into the hidden heart of a Conjoiner drive.

'Follow me,' Weather said.

'Are you serious?'

'You want to get home, don't you? You want to escape that raider? This is how it will happen.' Then she looked back to Van Ness. 'With all due respect . . . I wouldn't recommend it, Captain. You wouldn't do any damage to the engine, but the engine might damage you.'

'I'm fine right here,' Van Ness said.

I followed Weather into the engine. At first my eyes had difficulty making out our surroundings. The red light inside seemed to emanate from every surface, rather than from any concentrated source, so that there were only hints of edges and corners. I had to reach out and touch things more than once to establish their shape and proximity. Weather watched me guardedly, but said nothing.

She led me along a winding, restrictive path that squeezed its way between huge intrusions of Conjoiner machinery, like the course etched by some meandering, indecisive underground river. The machinery emitted a low humming sound, and sometimes when I touched it I felt a rapid but erratic vibration. I couldn't make out our surroundings with any clarity for more than a few metres in any direction, but as Weather pushed on I sometimes had the impression that the machinery was moving out of her way to open up the path, and sealing itself behind us. She led me up steep ramps, assisted me as we negotiated near-impassable chicanes, helped me as we climbed down vertical shafts that would be perilous even under one-tenth of a gee. My sense of direction was soon hopelessly confounded, and I had no idea whether we had travelled hundreds of metres into the engine, or merely wormed our way in and around a relatively localised region close to our entry point.

'I'm glad you know the way,' I said, with mock cheerfulness. 'I wouldn't be able to get out of here without you.'

'Yes, you will,' Weather said, looking back over her shoulder. 'The engine will guide you out, don't you worry.'

'You're coming with me, though.'

'No, Inigo, I'm not. I have to stay here from now on. It's the only way that any of us will be getting home.'

'I don't understand. Once you've fixed the engine—'

'It isn't like that. The engine can't be fixed. What I can do is help it, relieve it of some of the computational burden. But to do that I need to be close to it. Inside it.'

While we were talking, Weather had brought us to a box like space that was more open than anywhere we'd passed through so far. The room, or chamber, was empty of machinery, save for a waist-high cylinder rising from the floor. The cylinder had a flattened top and widened base that suggested the stump of a tree. It shone the same arterial red as everything else around us.

'We've reached the heart of the engine-control assembly now,' Weather said, kneeling by the stump. 'The reaction core is somewhere else – we couldn't survive anywhere near that – but this is where the reaction computations are made, for both the starboard and port drives. I'm going to show you something now. I think it will make it easier for you to understand what is to happen to me. I hope you're ready.'

'As I'll ever be.'

Weather planted a hand on either side of the stump and closed her eyes momentarily. I heard a click and the whirr of a buried mechanism. The upper fifth of the stump opened, irising wide. A blue light rammed from its innards. I felt a chill rising from whatever was inside, a coldness that seemed to reach fingers down my throat.

Something emerged from inside the stump, rising on a pedestal. It was a glass container pierced by many silver cables, each of which was plugged into the folded cortex of a single massively swollen brain. The brain had split open along fracture lines, like a cake that had ruptured in the baking. The blue light spilled from the fissures. When I looked into one – peering down into the geological strata of brain anatomy – I had to blink against the glare. A seething mass of tiny bright things lay nestled at the base of the cleft, twinkling with the light of the sun.

'This is the computer that handles the computations,' Weather said.

'It looks human. Please tell me it isn't.'

'It is human. Or at least that's how it started out, before the machines were allowed to infest and reorganise its deep structure.' Weather tapped a finger against the side of her own scalp. 'All the machines in my head only amount to two hundred grams of artificial matter, and even so I still need this crest to handle my thermal loading. There are nearly a thousand grams of machinery in that brain. The brain needs to be cooled like a turbopump. That's why it's been opened up, so that the heat can dissipate more easily.'

'It's a monstrosity.'

'Not to us,' she said sharply. 'We see a thing of wonder and beauty.'

'No,' I said firmly. 'Let's be clear about this. What you're showing me here is a human brain, a living mind, turned into some kind of slave.'

'No slavery is involved,' Weather said. 'The mind chose this vocation willingly.'

'It *chose* this?'

'It's considered a great honour. Even in Conjoiner society, even given all that we have learned about the maximisation of our mental resources, only a few are ever born who have the skills necessary to tame and manage the reactions in the heart of a C-drive. No machine can ever perform that task as well as a conscious mind. We could build a conscious machine, of course, a true mechanical slave, but that would contravene one of our deepest strictures. No machine may think, unless it does so voluntarily. So we are left with volunteer organic minds, even if those selfsame minds need the help of a thousand grams of non-sentient processing machinery. As to why only a few of us have the talent . . . that is one of *our* greatest mysteries. Galiana thought that, in achieving a pathway to augmented human intelligence, she would render the brain utterly knowable. It was one of her few mistakes. Just as there are savants amongst the retarded, so we have our Conjoined equivalents.

We are all tested for such gifts when we are young. Very few of us show even the slightest aptitude. Of those that do, even fewer ever develop the maturity and stability that would make them suitable candidates for enshrinement in an engine.' Weather faced me with a confiding look. 'They are valued very highly indeed, to the point where they are envied by some of us who lack what they were born with.'

'But even if they were gifted enough that it was possible . . . no one would willingly choose this.'

'You don't understand us, Inigo. We are creatures of the mind. This brain doesn't consider itself to have been imprisoned here. It considers itself to have been placed in a magnificent and fitting setting, like a precious jewel.'

'Easy for you to say, since it isn't you.'

'But it very nearly could have been. I came close, Inigo. I passed all the early tests. I was considered exceptional, by the standards of my cohort group. I knew what it was like to feel special, even amongst geniuses. But it turned out that I wasn't quite special enough, so I was selected out of the programme.'

I looked at the swollen, fissured mind. The hard blue glow made me think of Cherenkov radiation, boiling out of some cracked fission core.

'And do you regret it now?'

'I'm older now,' Weather said. 'I realise now that being unique . . . being adored . . . is not the greatest thing in the world. Part of me still admires this mind; part of me still appreciates its rare and delicate beauty. Another part of me . . . doesn't feel like that.'

'You've been amongst people too long, Weather. You know what it's like to walk and breathe.'

'Perhaps,' she said, doubtfully.

'This mind—'

'It's male,' Weather said. 'I can't tell you his name, any more than I could tell you mine. But I can read his public memories well enough. He was fifteen when his enshrinement began. Barely a man at all. He's been inside this engine for twenty-two years of shiptime; nearly sixty-eight years of worldtime.'

'And this is how he'll spend the rest of his life?'

'Until he wearies of it, or some accident befalls this ship. Periodically, as now, Conjoiners may make contact with the enshrined mind. If they determine that the mind wishes to retire, they may effect a replacement, or decommission the entire engine.'

'And then what?'

'His choice. He could return to full embodiment, but that would mean losing hundreds of grams of neural support machinery. Some are prepared to make that adjustment; not all are willing. His other option would be to return to one of our nests and remain in essentially this form, but without the necessity of running a drive. He would not be alone in doing so.'

I realised, belatedly, where all this was heading. 'You say he's under a heavy burden now.'

'Yes. The degree of concentration is quite intense. He can barely spare any resources for what we might call normal thought. He's in a state of permanent unconscious flow, like someone engaged in an enormously challenging game. But now the game has begun to get the better of him. It isn't fun any more. And yet he knows the cost of failure.'

'But you can help him.'

'I won't pretend that my abilities are more than a shadow of his. Still, I did make it part of the way. I can't take all the strain off him, but I can give him free access to my mind. The additional processing resources – coupled with my own limited abilities – may make enough of a difference.'

'For what?'

'For you to get wherever it is you are going. I believe that with our minds meshed together, and dedicated to this one task, we may be able to return the engines to something like normal efficiency. I can't make any promises, though. The proof of the pudding . . .'

I looked at the pudding like mass of neural tissue and asked the question I was dreading. 'What happens to you, while all this is happening? If he's barely conscious—'

'The same would apply, I'm afraid. As far as the external world is concerned, I'll be in a state of coma. If I'm to make any difference, I'll have to hand over all available neural resources.'

'But you'll be helpless. How long would you last, sitting in a coma?'

'That isn't an issue. I've already sent a command to this engine to form the necessary life-support machinery. It should be ready any moment now, as it happens.' Weather glanced down at the floor between us. 'I'd take a step back if I were you, Inigo.'

I did as she suggested. The flat red floor buckled upwards, shaping itself into the seamless form of a moulded couch. Without any ceremony, Weather climbed onto the couch and lay down as if for sleep.

'There isn't any point delaying things,' she said. 'My mind is made up, and the sooner we're on our way, the better. We can't be sure that there aren't other brigands within attack range.'

'Wait,' I said. 'This is all happening too quickly. I thought we were coming down here to look at the situation, to talk about the possibilities.'

'We've already talked about them, Inigo. They boil down to this: either I help the boy, or we drift hopelessly.'

'But you can't just . . . do this.'

Even as I spoke, the couch appeared to consolidate its hold on Weather. Red material flowed around her body, hardening over her into a semi-translucent shell. Only her face and lower arms remained visible, surrounded by a thick red collar that threatened to squeeze shut at any moment.

'It won't be so bad,' she said. 'As I said, I won't have much room left for consciousness. I won't be bored, that's for sure. It'll be more like one very long dream. Someone else's dream, certainly, but I don't doubt that there'll be a certain rapturous quality to it. I remember how good it felt to find an elegant solution, when the parametres looked so unpromising. Like making the most beautiful music imaginable. I don't think anyone can really know how that feels unless they've also held some of that fire in their minds. It's ecstasy, Inigo, when it goes right.'

'And when it goes wrong?'

'When it goes wrong, you don't get much time to explore how it feels.' Weather shut her eyes again, like a person lapsing into microsleep. 'I'm lowering blockades, allowing the boy to co-opt my own resources. He's wary. Not because he doesn't trust me, but because he can barely manage his own processing tasks, without adding the temporary complexity of farming some of them out to me. The transition will be difficult . . . ah, here it comes. He's using me, Inigo. He's accepting my help.' Despite being almost totally enclosed in the shell of red matter, Weather's whole body convulsed. Her voice, when she spoke again, sounded strained. 'It's difficult. So much more difficult than I thought it would be. This poor mind . . . he's had so much to do on his own. A lesser spirit would already have buckled. He's shown heroic dedication . . . I wish the nest could know how well he has done.' She clamped her teeth together and convulsed again, harder this time. 'He's taking more of me. Eagerly now. Knows I've come to help. The sense of relief . . . the strain being lifted . . . I can't comprehend how he lasted until now. I'm sorry, Inigo. Soon there isn't going to be much of me left to talk to you.'

'Is it working?'

'Yes. I think so. Perhaps between the two of us—' Her jaws cracked together, teeth cutting her tongue. 'Not going to be easy, but . . . losing more of me now. Language going. Don't need now.'

'Weather, don't go.'

'Can't stay. Got to go. Only way. Inigo, make promise. Make promise fast.'

'Say it. Whatever it is.'

'When we get . . . when we—' Her face was contorted with the strain of trying to make herself understood.

'When we arrive,' I said.

She nodded so hard I thought her neck was going to break. 'Yes. Arrive. You get help. Find others.'

'Other Conjoiners?'

'Yes. Bring them. Bring them in ship. Tell them. Tell them and make them help.'

'I will. I swear on it.'

'Going now. Inigo. One last thing.'

'Yes. Whatever it is.'

'Hold hand.'

I reached out and took her hand, in my good one.

'No,' Weather said. 'Other. *Other hand.*'

I let go, then took her hand in my metal one, closing my fingers as tightly as I dared without risking hers. Then I leaned down, bringing my face close to hers.

'Weather, I think I love you. I'll wait for you. I'll find those Conjoiners. That's a promise.'

'Love a Spider?' she asked.

'Yes. If this is what it takes.'

'Silly . . . human . . . boy.'

She pulled my hand, with more strength than I thought she had left in her. She tugged it down into the surface of the couch until it lapped around my wrist, warm as blood. I felt something happening to my hand, a crawling itch like pins and needles. I kissed Weather. Her lips were fever-warm. She nodded and then allowed me to withdraw my hand.

'Go now,' she said.

The red material of the couch flowed over Weather completely, covering her hands and face until all that remained was a vague, mummy like form.

I knew then that I would not see her again for a very long time. For a moment I stood still, paralysed by what had happened. Even then I could feel my weight increasing. Whatever Weather and the boy were doing between them, it was having some effect on the engine output. My weight climbed smoothly, until I was certain we were exceeding half a gee and still accelerating.

Perhaps we were going to make it home after all.

Some of us.

I turned from Weather's casket and looked for the way out. Held tight against my chest to stop it itching, my hand was lost under a glove of twinkling machinery. I wondered what gift I would find when the glove completed its work.

GRAFENWALDER'S BESTIARY

Grafenwalder's attention is torn between the Ultra captain standing before him and the real-time video feed playing on his monocle. The feed shows the creature being unloaded from the Ultras' shuttle into the special holding pen Grafenwalder has already prepared. The beetle like forms of armoured keepers poke and prod the recalcitrant animal with ten-metre stun-rods. The huge serpentine form writhes and bellows, flashing its attack eyes each time it exposes the roof of its mouth.

'Must have been a difficult catch, Captain. Locating one is supposed to be difficult enough, let alone trapping and transporting—'

'The capture was handled by a third party,' Shallice informs him, with dry indifference. 'I have no knowledge of the procedures involved, or of the particular difficulties encountered.'

While the keepers pacify the animal, technicians snip tissue samples and hasten them into miniature bio-analysers. So far they've seen nothing that suggests it isn't the real thing.

'I take it there were no problems with the freezing?'

'Freezing always carries a risk, especially when the underlying biology is non-terrestrial. We only guarantee that the animal appears to behave the same way now as when it was captured.'

Shallice is a typical Ultra: a cyborg human adapted for the extreme rigours of prolonged interstellar flight. His sleek red servo-powered exoskeleton is decorated with writhing green neon dragons. Cagelike metal ribs emerge from the Ultra's waxy white sternum, smeared with vivid blue disinfectant where they puncture the skin. The Ultra's limbs are blade-thin; his skull a squeezed hatchet capable of only a limited range of expression. He smells faintly of ammonia, breathes like a broken bellows and his voice is a buzzing, waspish approximation of human speech.

'Whoever that third party was, they must have been damned good.'

'Why do you say that?'

'Last I heard, no one has ever captured a live hamadryad. Not for very long, anyway.'

Shallice can't hide his scorn. 'Your news is old. There had been at least three successful captures before we left Sky's Edge.' He pauses, fearing perhaps that he may have soured the deal. 'Of course,' he continues, 'this is a far larger hamadryad . . . an adult, almost ready for tree-fusion. The others were juveniles, and they did not continue to grow once they were in captivity.'

'You're right: I need to keep better informed.' At that moment the news scrolls onto his monocle: his specialists have cross-matched samples from the animal against archived hamadryad genetic material, finding no significant points of deviation. 'Well, Captain,' he says agreeably, 'it looks as if we have closure on this one. You must be in quite a hurry to get back into safe space, away from the Rust Belt.'

'We've other business to attend to before we have that luxury,' Shallice tells him. 'You're not our only client around Yellowstone.' The Ultra's eyes narrow to calculating slits. 'As a matter of fact, we have another hamadryad to deliver.' Before Grafenwalder responds, the Ultra raises a servo-assisted hand.

'Not a fully grown sample like your own. A much less mature animal. Yours will still be unique in that sense.'

Anger rises in Grafenwalder like a hot, boiling tide. 'But it won't be the only hamadryad around Yellowstone, will it?'

'The other one will probably die. It will certainly not grow any larger.'

'You misled me, Captain. You promised exclusivity.'

'I did no such thing. I merely said that no one else would be offered an adult.'

Grafenwalder knows Ultras too well to doubt that Shallice is telling the truth. They may be unscrupulous, but they usually stay within the strict letter of a contract.

'This other collector . . . you wouldn't mind telling me who it is, would you?'

'That would be a violation of confidentiality.'

'Come now, Captain – if someone else gets their hands on a hamadryad, they're hardly going to keep it a secret. At least not within the Circle.'

Shallice weighs this point for several long moments, his alloy ribs flexing with each laboured breath. 'The collector's name is Ursula Goodglass. She owns a habitat in the low belt. Doubtless you know the name.'

'Yes,' Grafenwalder says. 'Vaguely. She's been nosing around the Circle for some time, but I wouldn't call her a full member just yet. Her collection's nothing to speak of, by all accounts.'

'Perhaps that will change when she has her hamadryad.'

'Not when the Circle learns there's a bigger one here. Did you let her think she'd be getting something unique as well, Captain?'

Shallice makes a sniffing sound. 'The contract was watertight.'

On the video feed, the animal is being coaxed deeper into its pen. Now and then it rears up to strike against its tormentors, moving with deceptive speed.

'Let's not play games, Captain. How much is she paying you for her sample?'

'Ten thousand.'

'Then I'll pay you fifteen not to hand it over, on top of what I'm already paying you.'

'Out of the question. We have an arrangement with Goodglass.'

'You'll tell a little white lie. Say it didn't thaw out properly, or that something went wrong afterwards.'

Shallice thinks this over, his hatchet-head cocking this way and that inside the metal chassis of the exoskeleton. 'She might ask to see the corpse—'

'I absolutely insist on it. I want her to know what she nearly got her hands on.'

'A deception will place us at considerable risk. Fifteen would not be sufficient. Twenty, on the other hand—'

'Eighteen, Captain, and that's as high as I go. If you walk out of here without accepting the deal, I'll contact Goodglass and tell her you were at least giving it the time of day.'

'Eighteen it is, then,' Shallice says, after a suitable pause. 'You drive a hard bargain, Mister Grafenwalder. You would make a good Ultra.'

Grafenwalder shrugs off the insult and reaches out a hand to Captain Shallice. When his fingers close around the Ultra's, it's like shaking hands with a cadaver.

'I'd love to say it's been a pleasure doing business.'

Later, he watches their shuttle depart his habitat and thread its way through the debris-infested Rust Belt, moving furtively between the major debris-swept orbits. He wonders what the Ultras make of the old place, given the changes that have afflicted it since their last trip through the system.

Good while it lasted, as people tend to say these days.

Oddly, though, Grafenwalder prefers things the way they are now. All things told, he came out well. Neither his body nor his habitat had depended on nanomachines, so it was only the secondary effects of the plague that were of concern to him. The area in which he had invested his energies prior to the crisis – the upgrading of habitat security systems – now proves astonishingly lucrative amongst the handful of clients able to afford his services. In lawless times, people always want higher walls.

There's something else, though. Ever since the plague hit, Grafenwalder has slept easier at night. He's at a loss to explain why, but the catastrophe – as bad as it undoubtedly was for Yellowstone and its environs – seems to have triggered some seismic shift in his own peace of mind. He remembers being anxious before; now – most of the time, at least – he only has the memory of anxiety.

At last his radar loses track of the Ultra shuttle, and it's only then that he realises his error. He should have asked to see the other hamadryad before paying the captain to kill it. Not because he thinks it might not ever have existed – he's reasonably sure it did – but because he has no evidence at all that it wasn't already dead.

He permits himself a bittersweet smile. Next time, he won't make that kind of mistake. And at least he has his hamadryad.

Grafenwalder walks alone through his bestiary. It's night, by the twenty-six-hour cycle of Yellowstone standard time, and the exhibits are mostly dimmed. The railed walkway that he follows glows a subdued red, winding between, under and over the vast cages, tanks and pits. Many of the creatures are asleep, but some stir or uncoil at his approach, while others never sleep. Things study his passage with dim, resentful intelligence: just enough to know that he is their captor. Occasionally something throws itself at its restraints, clanging against cage bars or shuddering against hardened glass. Things spit and lash. There are distressing calls; laughable attempts at vocalisation.

Not all of the animals are animals, technically speaking. About half the exhibits in the bestiary are creatures like the hamadryad: alien organisms that evolved on the handful of known life-sustaining worlds beyond the First System. There are slimescrapers from Grand Teton; screech-mats from Fand; more than a dozen different organisms from the jungles of Sky's Edge, including the hamadryad itself.

But the other half of the collection is more problematic. It's the half that could get him into serious trouble if the agents of the law came calling. It's where he keeps the real monsters: the things that might once have been human. There is the specimen he once bought from some other Ultras: a former crewman, apparently, who had been transformed far beyond the usual Ultra norms. Major areas of brain function had been trowelled out and replaced with crude neural modules, until the only remaining instinct was a slathering urge to mutilate and kill. His limbs are viciously specialised weapons, his bone growth modified to produce horns and armoured plaques. Grafenwalder can only guess that the man was meant to be some kind of berserker, to be used in acts of piracy where energy weapons might be unwise. Eventually he must have become unmanageable. Now it amuses Grafenwalder to provoke the man into futile killing frenzies.

Then there is the hyperpig variant his contacts located for him in the bowels of Chasm City: one of a kind, apparently; a rare genetic deviation from the standard breed. The woman's right side is perfectly human, but her left side is all pig. Brain function lies somewhere between animal and human.

She sometimes tries to talk to him, but the compromised layout of her jaw renders her attempts at speech as frenzied, unintelligible grunts. At other times, neural implants leave her docile, easily controlled. On the rare occasions when he has guests, Grafenwalder has her serve dinner. She shuffles in presenting her human side, then turns to reveal her true ancestry. Grafenwalder treasures his guests' reactions with a thin, observant smile.

Then there is the psychotic dolphin that lives in near-permanent darkness, its body showing evidence of crude cybernetic tampering. Its origin is unclear, its age even more so, but the animal's endless, all-consuming rage is beyond question. Grafenwalder has dropped sensors into the animal's scarred cortex, hooked into a visual display system. The slightest external stimulus becomes amplified into a kaleidoscopic light show, like the Devil's own firework display. Circuits drop the visual patterns back into the dolphin's mind. As an after-dinner treat, Grafenwalder encourages his guests to torment the dolphin into ever more furious cycles of anger.

There are many other exhibits; almost too many for Grafenwalder to remember. Not all are of interest to him now, and there are some that he has not visited for many years. His keepers take care of the creatures' needs, only bothering him when something needs specialised or expensive medical intervention and his permission must be sought. Perhaps the hamadryad will turn out to be another of those waning fancies, although he thinks it unlikely.

But there is one holding pen that remains unoccupied. He's walking over it now, hands on either side of the railed bridge that spans the empty abyss. It is a deep, ceramic-lined tank that will eventually be filled with cold water under many atmospheres of pressure. At the bottom of the tank is a rocky surface that is designed to be punctuated by thermal hotspots, gushing noxious gases. When it is activated, the environment in the tank will form a close match to conditions inside the ice-shrouded ocean of Europa, the little moon of Jupiter in the First System.

But first, Grafenwalder needs an occupant for the tank. That's the fundamental problem. He knows what he has in mind, but finding one of the elusive creatures is proving trickier than he expected. There are even some who doubt that the Denizens ever existed; let alone that he might find a surviving specimen now, in another system and nearly two hundred years after their supposed heyday. Yet there are enough shards of encouragement to keep him hopeful. He has subtle feelers out, and every now and then one of them twitches with a nugget of information. His trusted contacts know that he is looking for one, and that he will pay very well upon delivery. And deep inside himself he knows that the Denizens were real, that they lived and breathed and that it is not absurd that one may have survived into the present era.

He must have one. Although he would never admit it, he would gladly trade the rest of his bestiary for that one exhibit. And even as he acknowledges that truth within himself, he still cannot say why the creature matters so much.

Orbiting the inner fringe of the Rust Belt, backdropped by the choleric face of Yellowstone itself, Goodglass's habitat is a wrinkled walnut of unprepossessing dimensions. Grafenwalder's shuttle docks at a polar berthing nub, where a dozen similar vehicles are already clamped. He recognises more than half of them as belonging to collectors of his acquaintance.

After running some cursory security checks, a silverback gorilla escorts him deeper into the miniature world. The habitat is a cored-out asteroid, excavated by fusion torches and stuffed with a warren of pressurised domiciles wrapped around a modest central airspace. A spinney of free-fall trees keeps the self-regulating ecosystem ticking over, with only a minimal dependence on plague-vulnerable machinery. There are no servitors anywhere, only adapted animals like the silverback. The air smells mulchy, saturated with microscopic green organisms. Grafenwalder sneezes into his handkerchief and makes a mental note to have his lungs swapped out and filtered when he returns home.

Goodglass offers cocktails to her assembled guests. They're standing in an antechamber to her bestiary, in a part of the habitat that has been spun for gravity. The polished floor is a matrix of black and white tiles, each of which has been inlaid with a luminous red fragment of a much larger picture. As the guests stand around, the tiles slowly shift and reorient themselves.

Grafenwalder goes with the flow, letting the tiles slide him from encounter to encounter. He makes small talk with the other collectors, filing gossip and rumour. All the while he's checking out his host, measuring her against his expectations. Ursula Goodglass is a small woman of baseline-human appearance, devoid of any obvious biomodifications. She wears a one-piece purple-black outfit with flared sleeves, rising to a stiff-necked collar upon which her hairless head sits like a rare egg. She possesses an attractively impish face with a turned-up nose. He could like her, if he didn't already detest her.

Presently, as he knew they must, the tiles bring them together. He bows his head and takes her black-gloved hand.

'It's good of you to come, Mister Grafenwalder,' she says. 'I know how busy you are, and I wasn't really expecting you to be able to find the time.'

'Carl, please,' he says, oozing charm. 'And don't imagine I'd have been able to stay away. Your invitation sounded intriguing.

It's so much more difficult to turn up anything new these days, the way things have gone. I can't imagine what it is you have for us.'

'I just hope you won't be disappointed.'

'I won't,' he says, with heavy emphasis. 'Of that I'm sure.'

'I want you to understand,' she begins, before glancing away nervously, 'it's not that I'm trying to compete with you, or upstage you. I've too much respect for you for that.'

'Oh, don't worry. A little healthy rivalry never hurt anyone. What good is a collection unless there's another one to lend it contrast?'

She smiles uncertainly, measuring him as much as he is measuring her. He can feel the pressure of her scrutiny: cool and steady as a refrigeration laser.

Fine lines criss-cross her skull: snow-white sutures that remind him of the fracture patterns in the ice of Europa, even though he has never visited First System. The scars are evidence of emergency surgery performed in the heat of the Melding Plague, when it became necessary for the rich to rid themselves of their neural implants. Now Goodglass wears them as a symbol of former status.

'I'd like you to meet my husband,' she says as a palanquin glides up to them across the shifting tiled floor. Grafenwalder blinks back surprise: he'd noticed the palanquin before, but had assumed it belonged to one of the other guests. 'Edric, this is Carl,' she says.

'It's a pleasure to meet you,' the palanquin answers, the piping voice issuing from a speaker grille set halfway up the front of the armoured cabinet. The palanquin has the shape of a slender, flat-topped pyramid, its bronze sides flanged by cooling ribs and sensor studs. An oval window set into the front, just above the speaker grille, is too dark to afford more than a vague impression of Edric Goodglass. 'I hope this encumbrance doesn't make you ill at ease, Mister Grafenwalder,' the occupant tells him.

'Hardly,' he says. 'I've used palanquins myself, for business in Chasm City. They tell me my blood has been scrubbed of machines, but you can't ever be too careful.'

'In my case I never leave my palanquin,' Edric says. 'I still carry all the bodily machines I had at the time of the plague. It would only take a tiny residual trace to kill me.'

Grafenwalder swirls his drink, stepping nimbly from one moving tile to another. 'It must be intolerable.'

'It's my own fault. I was too slow when it counted. When the plague hit, I hesitated. I should have had the surgery fast and dirty, the way my wife did. She was braver than I; less convinced it was all about to blow over. Now I can't even risk the surgery. I'd have to leave the palanquin before they opened me up, and that alone would expose me to unacceptable risk.'

'But surely the top hospitals—'

'None will give me the cast-iron guarantee I require. Until one of them can state categorically that there is a zero risk of plague infection, I will remain in this thing.'

'You might be in for a long wait.'

'If I've learned anything from Ursula, it's the value of patience. She's the very model of it.'

Grafenwalder shoots a sidelong glance at Ursula Goodglass, wondering what their marriage must be like. Clearly sex isn't on the cards, but he doubts that it was ever the main interest in their lives. Games, especially those of prestige and subterfuge, are amongst the chief entertainments of the Rust Belt moneyed.

'Well, I suppose I shouldn't keep people waiting any longer,' the woman says. She drops her empty glass to the floor, where it vanishes into one of the black tiles as if it had met no resistance, and then claps her hands three times. 'Ladies and gentlemen,' she begins, voice raised an octave higher than when they had been speaking, 'thank you very much for coming here today. Some of you have visited before; some of you are newcomers to my habitat. Some of you will know a little about me, some of you next to nothing. I do not believe that any of us would say that we are close friends. All of us in the Circle have one thing in common, though: we collect. It is what we live for; what makes us who we are. My own bestiary is modest by the standards of some, but I am nonetheless immensely proud of my latest acquisition. There is nothing else like it in this system; nor is there likely to be for a very long time. Please join me now – I believe I have something you are going to find very, very interesting.'

With that, a pair of thick metal doors open in one wall of the room, hissing wide on curved pistons. Goodglass and her husband lead the way, with the rest of the party trailing behind. Grafenwalder chooses to remain close by the couple, feigning curiosity.

She can't just show off the hamadryad. First they have to endure a short but tedious tour of the rest of her bestiary, or at least that part of it she plans to show them today. None of it is of the slightest interest to Grafenwalder, and even the other guests merely feign polite interest. By turns, though, they arrive at the main event. The party gathers on a railed ledge high above a darkened pit. Grafenwalder knows what's coming, but keeps his expression blankly expectant. Goodglass makes a little speech, dropping hints about the type of specimen she's obtained, how difficult it's been to capture and transport it, alluding once or twice to its planet of origin: clue enough for those in the know. Pricking his ears, Grafenwalder makes out speculative whispers from his fellow collectors. One or two are ahead of Goodglass.

'Unfortunately,' she says, 'my exhibit did not arrive intact. It suffered some physiological trauma during its journey here: cryogenic damage to its tissues and nervous system. But it is still alive. With some intervention, my experts have restored much of its basic functional repertoire. In all significant respects, it is still a living hamadryad: the first you will ever see.'

She throws the lights, illuminating the creature in the pit. By then, Grafenwalder has a bad taste in his mouth. The hamadryad is much smaller than his adult-phase example, but it isn't dead. It's moving: great propulsive waves sliding up and down its concertina body as it writhes and coils from one end of the pit to the other, thrashing like a severed electrical line.

'It's alive,' he says quietly.

Goodglass looks at him sharply. 'Were you expecting otherwise?'

'It's just that when you said how much difficulty you'd gone to—' But by then his words are drowned out by the demands of the other guests, all of whom have questions for Goodglass. Lysander Carroway starts applauding, encouraging the others to join in.

Grafenwalder notches his hatred a little higher, even as he joins in the applause with effete little hand-claps.

He steps back from the railing, giving Goodglass her moment in the sun. All the while, he studies the hamadryad, trying to figure out what must have happened. As much as he dislikes Ultras, he can't believe that Captain Shallice would have cheated him so nakedly. That's when Grafenwalder sees his angle, and knows he can come out of this even better than he was expecting.

He lets the interested chat simmer down, then coughs just loudly enough to let everyone know he has something to contribute.

'It's very impressive,' he says. 'For an intermediate-phase sample, at any rate.'

Goodglass fixes him with narrowing eyes, dimly aware of what must be coming. Even the palanquin spins around, presenting its dark window to him.

'You know of other samples, Carl?' Ursula asks.

'One, anyway. But before we get into that . . . you mentioned shipping difficulties, didn't you?'

'Normal complications associated with reefersleep procedures as applied to non-terrestrial organisms,' she says.

'What kind of complications?'

'I told you already – tissue damage—'

'Yes, but how extensive was it? When the animal was revived from reefersleep, in what way did it exhibit signs of having been injured? Were its movements impaired, its hunting patterns atypical?'

'None of that,' she says.

'Then you're saying the animal was fine?'

'No,' she says icily. 'The animal was dead.'

Grafenwalder twitches back his head in feigned confusion. 'I know hamadryad biology is complex, but I didn't know that they could be brought back from death.'

'Reefersleep is a kind of death,' Goodglass says.

'Well, yes. If you want to split hairs. Things are usually alive after they've been thawed, though: that's more or less the point. But the hamadryad wasn't alive, was it? It was dead. It's *still* dead.'

Lysander Carroway shakes her head emphatically. 'It's alive, Grafenwalder. Use your bloody eyes.'

'It's being puppeted,' Grafenwalder says. 'Isn't it, Ursula? That's a dead animal with electrodes in it. You're making it twitch like a frog's leg.'

Goodglass fights hard to keep her composure: he can see the pulse of a vein on the side of her skull. 'I never actually said it was alive. I merely said it had the full behavioural repertoire of a living hamadryad.'

'You said it was living.'

Her husband answers for her. 'They don't have brains, Grafenwalder. They're more like plants. It eats and shits. What more do you want?'

Choosing his moment expertly, he offers a disappointed shrug. 'I suppose it has a certain comedic value.'

'Come now,' Michael Fayrfax says. 'She's shown us a hamadryad, more than most of us will ever see. What does it matter if it isn't technically alive?'

'I think it matters a lot,' Grafenwalder says. 'That's why I've gone to so much trouble to obtain a living specimen. Bigger than that, too. Mine's adult-phase. They don't come any larger.'

'He's bluffing,' Goodglass says. 'If he had a hamadryad, he'd have shown it off already.'

'I assure you I have one. I just wasn't ready to exhibit it yet.'

She still looks sceptical. 'I don't believe you. Why wait until now?'

'I wanted to be sure the animal had settled down; that I'd ironed out any difficulties with its biology. Keeping one of those things alive is quite a challenge, especially when they're adult-phase: the whole dietary pattern starts shifting.'

'You're lying.'

'You can see it, if you want to.'

The scepticism begins to crack, the fear that he might not be lying breaking through. 'When?'

'Whenever you like.' He turns to the other guests and extends his hands expansively. 'All of you, of course. You know where I live. How about the day after tomorrow? I couldn't possibly *fake* one by then, could I?'

*

Grafenwalder is riding his shuttle back home from the Goodglass bestiary when he receives an incoming communication. It appears to be transmitting from within the Rust Belt, but the shuttle can't pinpoint the origin of the signal any more precisely than that. For a moment Grafenwalder thinks it may be a threat from Goodglass, even though he credits her with fractionally more sense than that.

But it's not Goodglass's face that fills his cabin wall when he answers the communication. It's nobody he recognises. A man, with a cherubic moon-face and a thick lower lip, glossy with saliva, that sags to the right. He wears a panama hat over tight dark curls, and a finely patterned harlequin coat hangs over his heavy frame in billowing folds. A glass box dangles around his neck, rattling with the implants he must once have carried in his skull. He is backdropped by a sumptuously upholstered chair, rising high as a throne.

'Mister Grafenwalder? My name is Rifugio. I don't think our paths have crossed before.'

'What do you want?'

There's barely any timelag. 'I am a broker, Mister Grafenwalder: a wheeler-dealer, a fixer, a go-getter. When someone needs something – especially something that may require delicate extralegal manoeuvring – I'm the man to come to.'

Grafenwalder moves to kill the communication. 'You still haven't told me what you want.'

'It is not about what I want. It is about what you want. Specifically, a certain bio-engineered organism.' Rifugio scratches the tip of his bulbous nose. 'You've been as discreet as matters will allow, I'll grant you that – but you've still put out word concerning the thing you seek. Now that word has reached my ears, and, fortuitously, I happen to be the man who can help you.' Now Rifugio leans closer, the rim of his hat tipping across his brow, and lowers his voice. 'I have one, and I am willing to sell it. At a price, of course – I must pay off my own informants and contacts. But knowing what you paid for the hamadryad, I am confident that you can afford twice as much to get the thing you want so badly.'

'Maybe I don't want one that much.'

Rifugio leans back, looking nonplussed. 'In that case . . . I won't trouble you again. Good day to you, sir.'

'Wait,' Grafenwalder says hastily. 'I'm interested. But I need to know more.'

'I wouldn't expect otherwise. We'll have to meet before we take matters any further, of course.'

Grafenwalder doesn't like it, but the man is right. 'I'll want a DNA sample.'

'I'll give you DNA and more: cell cultures, tissue scrapings – almost enough to make one for yourself. We'll need to meet in person, of course. I wouldn't trust material of such sensitivity to an intermediary.'

'Of course not,' Grafenwalder says. 'But we'll meet on neutral ground. There's a place I've used before. How does Chasm City grab you?'

Rifugio looks pleased. 'Name the time and the place.'

'I can squeeze you in tomorrow,' Grafenwalder says.

He doesn't care for Chasm City, at least not these days, but it's a useful enough place to do business. Complex technology doesn't work reliably, making every transaction cumbersome. But that has its benefits, too. Weapons that might just work in the Rust Belt can't be trusted in CC. Eavesdropping and other forms of deception become risky. It's best not to try anything too clever, and everyone knows that.

The one thing Grafenwalder isn't worried about is catching something. His palanquin is the best money can buy, and even if something did get through its ten centimetres of nano-secure hermetic armour, it would have a hard time finding anything in his body to touch and corrupt. The armour reassures him, though, and the privacy of the cabinet shields him from the awkwardness of a face-to-face encounter. As he makes his way through the city, following other palanquins along the winding path of an elevated private road through the high Canopy, he pages once more through the sparse information he has managed to piece together on Rifugio.

Grafenwalder has the feeling that he's trying to pin down a ghost. There is a broker named Rifugio, and judging by what he has already achieved, he would appear to have the necessary contacts to procure a Denizen. But it puzzles Grafenwalder that their paths haven't intersected before. Granted, it's a big, turbulent system, with a lot of scope for new players to emerge from hitherto obscurity. But Grafenwalder has been courting men like Rifugio for years. There should have been at least a blip on his radar before now.

The palanquins duck and dive through the mad architecture of the Canopy. All around, buildings that were once cleanly geometric have been turned into the threatening forms of haunted trees, their grasping branches locking bony fingers high over the lower levels of the city. Epsilon Eridani is still above the horizon, but so little sunlight penetrates the smog-brown atmosphere or the muck-smeared panels of the latticework dome that it might as well be twilight. The lights are on all over the city, save for the seductive absence of the chasm itself. Dark threads dangle from the larger trunks of the Canopy, like cannon-blasted rigging. Brachiating cable cars swing through the tangle like drunk gibbons. Compared to the ordered habitats of the surviving Rust Belt, it's a scene from hell. And yet people still live here. People still make lives for themselves; still fall in love and find somewhere they can think of as home. With a lurch of cognitive vertigo that he's already experienced a few times too many, Grafenwalder remembers that there are people down there who have no memory of how things used to be.

He knows it ought to horrify him that human beings could ever adapt to such a catastrophic downturn in their fortunes, even though people have been doing that kind of thing for most of history. Yet part of him feels a strange kinship with those survivors. He sleeps easier since the plague, and he doesn't know why. It's as if the crisis snapped shut part of his life that contained something threatening and loose, something that was in danger of reaching him.

In an unsettling way, though, he feels that Rifugio's call has reopened that closed book, just a crack. And that whatever was keeping him from sleep is stalking the edge of his imagination once more.

They meet in private rooms in the outermost branch of a Canopy structure near Escher Heights. The building is dead now, incapable of further change, and its owner – a man named Ashley Chabrier, with whom Grafenwalder did business years ago – has cut through the floor, walls and ceilings of the reshaped husk and emplaced enormous glass panels, veined in the manner of insect wings and linked together by leathery fillets of the old growth. It affords a spectacular view, but even Grafenwalder has misgivings as he steers his palanquin across the reflectionless floor, with the fires of the Mulch burning two kilometres below. Even if he survived the fall, the Mulch inhabitants wouldn't take kindly to the likes of him dropping in.

Rifugio, contrary to Grafenwalder's expectations, has not arrived by palanquin. He stands with his legs wide, his generous paunch supported by a levitating girdle, a pewter-coloured belt ringed by several dozen tiny and silent ducted fan thrusters. His slippered feet skim the glass with their up-curled toes. As he approaches Grafenwalder, he barely moves his legs.

'I have brought what I promised,' Rifugio says, by way of greeting. He's carrying a small malachite-green case, dangling from the pudgy fingers of his right hand.

'Is it all right if I say the word "Denizen" now?' Grafenwalder asks.

'You just said it, so I think the answer has to be yes. You're still suspicious, I see.'

'I've every right to be suspicious. I've been looking for one of these things for longer than I care to remember.'

'So I hear.'

'There have been times when I have doubted that they exist now; times when I doubted that they ever existed.'

'Yet you haven't stopped searching. Those doubts never became all-consuming.' Rifugio is very close to the palanquin now. As a matter of routine, it deep-scans him for concealed weapons or listening devices. It finds nothing alarming. Even so, Grafenwalder flinches when the man suddenly lifts the case and pops the lid. 'Here is what I have for you, Mister Grafenwalder: enough to silence those qualms of yours.'

The case is lined with black foam. Glass vials reside in neat little partitions. The palanquin probes the case and detects only biological material: exactly what Rifugio promised. With his left hand, Rifugio digs out one of the vials and holds it up like a magic charm. Dark red fluid sloshes around inside.

'Here. Take this and run an analysis on it. It's Denizen blood, with Denizen DNA.'

Grafenwalder hesitates for a moment, despite the assurances from his palanquin that it can deal with any mere biological trickery. Then he permits the machine to extend one of its manipulators, allowing Rifugio to pop the vial into its cushioned grasp. The machine withdraws the manipulator into its analyser alcove, set just beneath the frontal window. Part of the biological sample will be incinerated and passed through a gas chromatograph, where its isotopic spectrum will be compared against the data on Denizen blood Grafenwalder has already compiled. At the same time, the DNA will be amplified, speed-sequenced and cross-referenced against his best-guess for the Denizen genetic sequence. There's no physical connection between the analyser and the interior of the palanquin, so Grafenwalder cannot come to harm. Even so, he wills the analyser to complete its duties as swiftly as possible.

'Well, Mister Grafenwalder? Does it meet with your satisfaction?'

The analyser starts graphing up its preliminary conclusions: the material looks genuine enough.

Grafenwalder keeps the excitement from his voice. 'I'd like to know where you found it. That would help me decide whether or not I believe you have the genuine article.'

'The Denizen came into my possession via Ultras. They'd been keeping it as a pet, aboard their ship.'

'Shallice's men, by any chance?'

'I obtained the Denizen from Captain Ritter, of the *Number Theoretic*. I've had no dealings with Shallice, although I know the name. As for Ritter – in so far as one can ever believe anything said by an Ultra – I was told that he acquired the Denizen during routine trade with another group of Ultras, in some other godforsaken system. Apparently the Denizen was kept aboard ship as a pet. The Ultras had little appreciation of its wider value.'

'How did Ultras get hold of it in the first place?'

'I have no idea. Perhaps only the Denizen can tell us the whole story.'

'I'll need better provenance than that.'

'You may never get it. We're talking about beings created in utmost secrecy two hundred years ago. Their very existence was doubted even then. The best you can hope for is a plausible sequence of events. Clearly, the Denizen must have left Europa's ocean after Cadmus-Asterius and the other hanging cities fell. If it passed into the hands of starfarers – Ultras, Demarchists, Conjoiners, it doesn't matter which – it would have had a means to leave the system, and spend much of the intervening time either frozen or at relativistic speed, or both. It need not have experienced anything like the full bore of those two hundred years. Its memories of Europa may be remarkably sharp.'

'Have you asked it?'

'It doesn't speak. Not all of them were created with the gift of language, Mister Grafenwalder. They were engineered to work as underwater slaves: to take orders rather than to issue them. They had to be intelligent, but they didn't need to answer back.'

'Some of them had language.'

'The early prototypes, and those that were designed to mediate with their human overseers. Most of them were dumb.'

Grafenwalder allows the disappointment to wash over him, then bottles it away. He'd always hoped for a talker, but Rifugio is correct: it could never be guaranteed. And perhaps there is something in having one that won't answer back, or plead. It's going to be spending a lot of time in his tank, after all.

'You'll treat it with kindness, of course,' Rifugio continues. 'I didn't liberate it from the Ultras just so it can become someone else's pet, to be tormented between now and kingdom come.

You'll treat it as the sentient being it is.'

Grafenwalder sneers. 'If you care so much, why not hand it over to the authorities?'

'Because they'd kill it, and then go after anyone who knew of its existence. Demarchists made the Denizens in one of their darker moments. They're more enlightened now – so they'd like us to think, anyway. They certainly wouldn't want something like a living and breathing Denizen – a representative of a sentient slave race – popping out of history's cupboard, not when they're bending over backwards to score moral points over the Conjoiners.'

'I'll treat it fairly,' Grafenwalder says.

At that moment the analyser announces that the blood composition and genetic material are both consistent with Denizen origin, to high statistical certainty. It's not enough to prove that Rifugio has one, but it's a large step in the right direction. Plenty of hoaxers have already fallen at this hurdle.

'Well, Mister Grafenwalder? Have you reached a decision yet?'

'I want to see the other samples.'

Rifugio fingers another vial from the case. 'Skin tissue.'

'I don't have the means to run a thorough analysis on skin – not here anyway. Give me what you have, and I'll take it back with me.'

Rifugio looks pained. 'I'd hoped that we might reach agreement here and now.'

'Then you hoped wrong. Unless you want to lower your price . . .'

'I'm afraid that part of the arrangement isn't negotiable. However, I'm willing to let you take these samples away.' Rifugio snaps shut the lid. 'As a further token of my goodwill, I'll provide you with a moving image of the living Denizen. But I will expect a speedy decision in return.'

Grafenwalder's palanquin takes the sealed case and stores it inside its bombproof cargo hatch. 'You'll get it. Don't worry about that.'

'Take me at my word, Mister Grafenwalder. You're not the only collector with an eye for one of these monsters.'

Grafenwalder spends most of the return trip viewing the thirty-second movie clip, over and over again. It's not the first time he's seen moving imagery of something purporting to be a Denizen, but no other clip has withstood close scrutiny. This one is darker and grainier than some of the others, the swimming humanoid shifting in and out of focus, but there's something eerily naturalistic about it, something that convinces him that it could be real. The Denizen looks plausible: it's a monster, undoubtedly, but that monstrosity is the end result of logical design factors. It swims with effortless ease, propelling itself with the merest flick of the long fluked tail it wears in place of legs. It has arms, terminating in humanoid hands engineered for tool-use. Its head, when it swims towards the camera, merges seamlessly with its torso. It has eyes, very human eyes at that, but no nose, and its mouth is a smiling horizontal gash crammed with an unnerving excess of needlesharp teeth. Looking at that movie, Grafenwalder feels more certain than ever that the creatures were real, and that at least one has survived. And as he studies the endlessly repeating thirty-second clip, he feels the closed book of his past creak open even wider. A question forms in his mind that he would rather not answer.

What *exactly* is it that he wants with the Denizen?

Things go tolerably well the next day, until the guests are almost ready to leave. They've seen the adult-phase hamadryad and registered due shock and awe. Grafenwalder is careful to remind them that, in addition to its size, this is also a living specimen, not some rotting corpse coaxed into a parodic imitation of life. Even Ursula Goodglass, who has to endure this, registers stoic approval. 'You were lucky,' she tells Grafenwalder through gritted teeth. 'You could just as easily have ended up with a dead one.'

'But then I wouldn't have tried to pretend it was alive,' he tells her.

It's Goodglass who has the last laugh today, however. She saves it until the guests are almost back aboard their shuttles.

'Friends,' she says, 'what I'm about to mention in no way compares with the spectacle of an adult-phase hamadryad, but I have recently come into possession of something that I think you might find suitably diverting.'

'Something we've already seen two days ago?' asks Lysander Carroway.

'No. I chose to keep it under wraps then, thinking my little hamadryad would be spectacle enough for one day. It's never been seen in public before, at least not in its present state.'

'Put us out of our misery,' says Alain Couperin.

'Drop by and see it for yourself,' Goodglass says, with a teasing twinkle in her eye. 'Any time you like. No need to make an appointment. But – please – employ maximum discretion. This is one exhibit that I really don't want the authorities to know about.'

For a moment Grafenwalder wonders whether she has the Denizen. But surely Rifugio can't have lost faith in the deal already, when they've barely opened negotiations.

But if not a Denizen – what?

He has to know, even if it means the indignity of another visit to her miserable little habitat.

*

When he arrives at the Goodglass residence, hers is the only shuttle docked at the polar nub. He's a little uncomfortable with being the only guest, but Goodglass did say to drop in whenever he liked, and he has given her fair warning of his approach. He's waited a week before taking the trip. Ten days would have been better, but after five he'd already started hearing that she has something special; something indisputably unique. In the meantime, he has run every conceivable test on the biological samples Rifugio gave him in Chasm City and received the same numbing result each time: Rifugio appears to be in possession of the genuine article. Yet Grafenwalder is still apprehensive about closing the deal.

Inside the habitat, he's met by Goodglass and Edric, her palanquin-bound husband. The couple waste no time in escorting him to the new exhibit. Despite the indignities they have brought upon each other, it's all smiles and strained politeness. No one so much as mentions hamadryads, dead or alive.

Grafenwalder isn't quite sure what to expect, but he's still surprised at the modest dimensions of the chamber Goodglass finally shows him. The walkway brings them level with the chamber's floor, but there's no armoured glass screen between them and the interior. Even with the lights dimmed, Grafenwalder can already make out an arrangement of tables, set in a U-formation like a series of laboratory benches. There are upright glassy things on the tables, but that's as much as he can tell.

'I was expecting something alive,' he says quietly.

'It is alive,' she hisses back. 'Or at least as alive as it ever was. Merely distributed. You'll see in a moment.'

'I thought you said it was dangerous.'

'Potentially it would be, if it was ever put back together.' She pauses and extends her hand across the gloomy threshold, as if beckoning to the nearest bench. Grafenwalder catches the bright red line on her hand where it has broken a previously invisible laser beam, sweeping up and down across the aperture. Quicker than an eyeblink, a heavy armoured shield slams down on the cell. 'But that's not to stop it getting out,' she says. 'It's to prevent anyone taking it and trying to put it back together. There are some who'd attempt it, just for the novelty.'

She pulls back her hand. After an interval, the shield whisks up into the ceiling.

'Whatever it is, you're serious about it,' Grafenwalder says, intrigued despite himself.

'I have to be. You don't take monsters lightly.'

She waves on the lights. The room brightens, but although he can now make out the benches and the equipment upon them, Grafenwalder is none the wiser.

'You'll have to help me here,' he says.

'It's all right. I wouldn't know what to make of it either if I didn't know what I was looking at.'

'My God,' he says wonderingly, as his eyes alight on one of the larger glass containers. 'Isn't that a brain?'

Goodglass nods. 'What was once a human brain, yes. Before he – before *it* – started doing things to itself, throwing pieces of its humanity away like a child flinging toys from a sandpit. But what's left of the brain is still alive, still conscious and still capable of sensory perception.' A mischievous smile appears on her face. 'It knows we're here, Carl. It's aware of us. It's listening to us, watching us, and wondering how it can escape and kill us.'

He allows himself to take in the grisly scene, now that its full implication is clearer. The brain is being kept alive in a liquid-filled vat, nourished by scarlet and green cables that ram into the grey-brown dough of the exposed cerebellum. A stump of spinal cord curls under the brain like an inverted question mark. It looks pickled and vinegary, cobwebbed with ancient growth and tiny filaments of spidery machinery. Next to the flask is a humming grey box whose multiple analogue dials twitch with a suggestion of ongoing mental processes. But that's not all. There are dozens of glass cases, linked to other boxes, and the boxes to each other, and each case holds something unspeakable. In one, an eye hangs suspended in a kind of artificial socket, equipped with little steering motors. The eye is looking straight at Grafenwalder, as is its lidless twin on another bench. Their optic nerves are knotted ropes of fatty white nerve tissue. In another flask floats a pair of lungs, hanging like a puffed-up kite. They expand and contract with a slow, wheezing rhythm.

'Who . . . ? What . . . ?' he says, barely whispering.

'Haven't you guessed yet, Carl? Look over there. Look at the mask.'

He follows her direction. The mask sits at the end of the furthest table, on a black plinth. It's less a mask than an entire skull, moulded in sleek silver metal. The face is handsome, in a streamlined, air-smoothed fashion, with an expression of calm amusement sculpted into the immobile lips and the blank silver surfaces that pass for eyes. It has strong cheekbones and a strong cleft chin. Between the lips is only a dark, grilled slot. The mask has a representation of human ears, and its crown is moulded with longitudinal silver waves, evoking hair that has been combed back and stiffened in place with lacquer.

Grafenwalder knows who the skull belongs to. There isn't anyone alive around Yellowstone who wouldn't recognise Dr Trintignant. All that's missing is Trintignant's customary black Homburg.

But Trintignant shouldn't be here. Trintignant shouldn't be anywhere. He died years ago.

'This isn't right,' he says. 'You've been duped . . . sold a fake. This can't be him.'

'It is. I have watertight provenance.'

'But Trintignant hasn't been seen around Yellowstone for years . . . decades. He's supposed to have died when Richard Swift—'

'I know about Richard Swift,' Ursula Goodglass informs him. 'I met him once – or what was left of him after Trintignant had completed his business. I wanted Swift for an exhibit – I was prepared to pay him for his time – but he left the system again. They say he went back to that place – the same world where Trintignant supposedly killed himself.'

Grafenwalder thinks back to what he remembers of the scandal. It had been all over Yellowstone for a few weeks. 'But Swift brought back Trintignant's remains. The doctor had dismantled himself, left a suicide note.'

'That was his plan,' Goodglass says witheringly. 'That was what he wanted us to think – that he'd ended his own life upon completing his finest work.'

'But he dismantled—'

'He took himself apart in a way that implied suicide. But it was a methodical dismantling. The parts were stored in a fashion that always allowed for their eventual reassembly. Trintignant was too vain not to want to stay alive and see what posterity made of his creations. But with the Yellowstone authorities closing in on him, staying in one piece wasn't an option.'

'How did he end up here? Wouldn't the authorities have been just as keen to get hold of his remains as his living self?'

'He always had allies. Sponsors, I suppose you might call them. People who'd covertly admired his work. There's always a market for freaks, Carl – and even more of a market for freak-makers. His friends whisked him away, out of the hands of what little authority was left here upon his return. Since then he's passed from collection to collection, like a bad penny. He seems to bring bad luck. Perhaps I'm tempting fate just by keeping him here; tempting it even more by bringing him to this state of partial reanimation.' She smiles tightly. 'We will see. If my fortunes take a dip, I shall pass Trintignant on to the next willing victim.'

'You're playing with fire.'

'Then you don't approve? I'd have expected you to applaud my audacity, Carl.'

Grafenwalder, despite himself, speaks something close to the truth. 'I'm impressed. More than you can imagine. But I'm also alarmed that he's being kept here.'

'Alarmed. Why, exactly?'

'You're a newcomer to this game, Ursula. I've seen a little of your habitat now, enough to know that your security arrangements aren't exactly top of the line.'

'He's in no danger of putting himself back together, Carl, unless you believe in telekinesis.'

'I'm worried about what would happen if his admirers learn of his whereabouts. Some of them won't be content just to know he's being kept alive in pieces. They'll want to take him, put him all the way back together.'

'I don't think anyone would be quite that foolish.'

'Then you don't know people. People like us, Ursula. How many collectors have you shown him to already?'

She tilts her head, looking at him along her up-curved nose. 'Less than a dozen, including yourself.'

'That's already too many. I wouldn't be surprised if word has already passed beyond the Circle. Don't tell me you've shown him to Rossiter?'

'Rossiter was the second.'

'Then it's probably already too late.' He sighs, as if taking a great burden upon himself. 'We don't have much time. We need to make immediate arrangements to transport his remains to my habitat. They'll be a lot safer there.'

'Why would your place be any safer than mine?'

'I design security systems. It's what I do for a living.'

She appears to consider it, for a moment at least. Then she shakes her head. 'No. It won't happen. He's staying here. I see where you're coming from now, Carl. You don't actually care about my security arrangements at all. It probably wouldn't even bother you if Doctor Trintignant did escape back into Stoner society. It's highly unlikely that you'd have ended up one of his victims, after all. You've got money and influence. It's those poor souls down in the Mulch who'd need to watch their backs. That's where he'd go hunting for raw material. What you can't stand is the thought that he might be mine, not yours. I've got something you haven't, something unique, something you can't ever have, and it's going to eat you from inside like acid.'

'Suit yourself.'

'I will. I always have. You made a dreadful mistake when you humiliated me, Carl, assuming you didn't have a hand in what had already happened to the hamadryad.'

'What are you saying? That I had something to do with the fact that Shallice stiffed you?'

He detects her hesitation. She comes perilously close to accusing him, but even here – even in this private cloister – there are limits that she knows better than to cross.

'But you were glad of it, weren't you?' she presses.

'I had the superior specimen. That's all that ever mattered to me.' With a renewed shudder of revulsion – and, he admits, something close to admiration – he turns again to survey the distributed remains of the notorious doctor. 'You say he can hear us?'

'Every word.'

'You should kill him now. Take a hammer to his brain. Make sure he can never live again.'

'Would you like that, Carl?'

'It's exactly what the authorities would do if they got hold of him.'

'They'd give him a trial first, one imagines.'

'He doesn't deserve a trial. None of his victims had the benefit of justice.'

'What history conveniently forgets,' Goodglass says, 'is that many of his so-called victims came to him willingly. He was not a monster to them, but the agent of the change they craved. He was the most brilliant transformative surgeon of our era. So what if society considered his creations obscene? So what if some of them regretted what they had freely asked him to do?'

'You're defending him now.'

'Not defending him – just pointing out that nothing is ever that black and white. For years Trintignant was given tacit permission to continue his work. The authorities didn't like him, but they accepted that he fulfilled a social need.'

Grafenwalder shakes his head – he's seen and heard enough. 'I thought you were exhibiting a monster, Ursula. Now it looks to me as if you're sheltering a fugitive.'

'I'm not, I assure you. Just because I have a balanced view of Trintignant doesn't mean I don't despise him. Here: let me offer you a demonstration.' And with that Goodglass taps a command sequence into the air, disarming the security system. She is able to pass her hand through the laser-mesh without bringing down the armoured screen. 'Walk over to the brain, Carl,' she commands. 'It isn't a trap.'

'I'd be happier if you walked with me.'

'If you like.'

He hesitates longer than he'd like, long enough for her to notice, then takes a step into the enclosure. Goodglass is only a pace behind him. The eyeballs swivel to track him, triangulating with the smoothness of motorised cameras. He moves next to the bubbling brain vat. Up close, the brain looks too small to have been the wellspring of so much evil.

'What am I supposed to look at?'

'Not look at – do. You can inflict pain on him, if you wish. There's a button next to the brain. It sends an electrical current straight into his anterior cingulate cortex.'

'Isn't he in pain already?'

'Not especially. He re-engineered himself to allow for this dismantling. There may be some existential trauma, but I don't believe he's in any great discomfort from one moment to the next.'

Grafenwalder's hand moves of its own volition, until it hovers above the electrical stimulator. He can feel its magnetic pull, almost willing his hand to lower. He wonders why he feels such a primal urge to bring pain to the doctor. Trintignant never hurt him; never hurt anyone he knew. All that he knows of Trintignant's crimes is second-hand, distorted and magnified by time and the human imagination. That the doctor was tolerated, even encouraged, cannot seriously be doubted. He filled the hole in Yellowstone society where a demon was meant to fit.

'What's wrong, Carl? Qualms?'

'How do I know this won't send a jolt directly to his pleasure centre?'

'Look at his spinal column. Watch it thrash.'

'Spines don't thrash.'

'His does. Those little mechanisms—'

It's all the encouragement he needs. He brings his hand down, holding the contact closed for a good five or six seconds. Under the brain, the stump of spinal matter twists and flexes like a rattlesnake's tail. He can hear it scraping glass.

He raises his hand, watches the motion subside.

'See,' Goodglass says, 'I knew you'd do it.'

Grafenwalder notices that there's some kind of heavy medical tool next to the brain tank, a thing with a grip and a clawed alloy head. With his other hand he picks it up, testing its weight. The glass container looks invitingly fragile; the brain even more so.

'Be careful,' Goodglass says.

'I could kill him now, couldn't I? Put an end to him, forever.'

'Many would applaud you. But then you'd be providing him with a way out, an end to this existence. On the other hand, you could send another jolt of pain straight into his mind. What would you rather, Carl? Rid the world of Trintignant and spare him further pain, or let him suffer a little longer?'

He's close to doing it; close to smashing the tool into the glass. As close as she is, Goodglass couldn't stop him in time. And there would be something to be said for being the man who closed the book on Trintignant. But at the decisive instant something holds him back. Nothing that the doctor did has ever touched him personally, but he still feels a compulsion to join in his torment. And as the moment passes, he knows that he could never end the doctor's life so cleanly, so mercifully, when pain is always an alternative.

Instead, he presses the button again, and holds it down longer this time. The spine thrashes impressively. Behind him, Ursula Goodglass applauds.

'Good for you, Carl. I knew you'd do the right thing.'

*

The next two weeks are an endurance. Grafenwalder must sit tight-lipped as excited rumours circulate concerning Ursula Goodglass's new exhibit. No one mentions Trintignant by name – that would be the height of crass indiscretion – but even those who have not yet visited her habitat can begin to guess at the nature of her new prize. Even the most level-headed commentators are engaged in a feverish round of praise-giving, seeking to outdo each other in the showering of plaudits. Even though she has only been in the collecting business for a little while, she has pulled off an astonishing coup. Attention is so heated that, for a day or two, the Circle must fend off the unwanted interest of a pair of authority investigators, still on Trintignant's trail. The bribes alone would pay for a new habitat.

Grafenwalder's adult-phase hamadryad, meanwhile, brings no repeat visits. Now that it has lost its novelty value to the other collectors, Grafenwalder feels his own interest in it waning. He thinks of it less and less, and has increasingly little concern for its welfare. When his keepers inform him that the animal is suffering from a dietary complaint, he doesn't even bother to visit it. Three days later, when they tell him that the hamadryad has died, all he can think about is the money he paid Captain Shallice. For an hour or so he toys with the idea of bringing the dead thing back to life with electrodes, the way Goodglass animated her specimen, but the idea that he might be seen to be playing second fiddle to her rises in him like yellow bile. He gives orders that the animal be ejected into space, and can't even bring himself to watch it happen.

Six hours later, he contacts Rifugio.

'I was beginning to think I wouldn't hear from you again, Mister Grafenwalder. If you'd left it much longer I wouldn't have anything to sell you.'

Grafenwalder can hardly keep the excitement from his voice. 'Then it's still available? The terms still apply?'

'I'm a man of my word,' Rifugio answers. 'The terms are the same. Does that mean we have a deal?'

'I'll want additional guarantees. If the specimen turns out to be something other than claimed—'

'I'm selling it to you in good faith. Take it or leave it.'

He takes it, of course, as he had known he would before he placed the call. He'd have taken it even if Rifugio had doubled his asking price. A living, captive Denizen is the only thing that will take the shine off the Circle's new fondness for Goodglass, and he must have it at all costs.

The arrangements for payment and handover are typically byzantine, as necessity demands. For all that he distrusts men like Rifugio, they must make a living as well, and protect themselves from the consequences of their activities. Grafenwalder, in turn, has his own stringent requirements. The shipping of the creature to Grafenwalder's habitat must happen surreptitiously, and the flow of credit from one account to another must be untraceable. It is complicated, but by the same token both men have participated in many such dealings in the past, and the arrangements follow a certain well-rehearsed protocol. When the automated transport finally arrives, bearing its precious aquatic cargo, Grafenwalder is certain that nothing has gone amiss.

He has to fight past his own keepers to view the specimen for the first time. At first, he feels a flicker of mild disappointment: it's a lot smaller than he was expecting, and it's not just a trick of the light due to the glass walls of the holding tank. The Denizen isn't much larger than a child.

But the disappointment doesn't last long. In the flesh, the Denizen appears even more obviously real than the swimming creature in the movie clip. It's sedated when it arrives, half its face and upper torso swallowed by a drug-administering breathing device. Rifugio's consignment comes with detailed notes concerning the safe waking of the creature. First, Grafenwalder has it moved into the main viewing tank, now topped up with cold water under one hundred atmospheres of pressure. The water chemistry is now tuned to approximate conditions near one of the Europan thermal vents. He brings the creature to consciousness in utter darkness, and monitors its progress as it begins first to breathe for itself, and then to tentatively explore its surroundings. It swims lethargically at first, Grafenwalder viewing its moving body via heat-sensitive assassin's goggles. By all accounts the Denizens have infrared sensitivity of their own, but the creature takes no heed of him, even when it passes very close to his vantage point.

After several minutes, the creature's swimming becomes stronger. It must be adapting to the water, learning to breathe again. Grafenwalder watches the flick of its tail in mesmerised fascination. By now it has mapped the confines of its new home, testing the armoured glass with delicate sweeps of its fingertips. It is intelligent enough to know that nothing will be gained by striking the glass.

Grafenwalder has the main lights brought up and shone into the tank. He slips the assassin's goggles up onto his brow. The creature attempts to swim away from the glare, but the glare follows it remorselessly. Its eyes are lidless, so it can do little except screen its face with one delicately webbed hand. The wide gash of its mouth opens in alarm or anger, or both, revealing rows of sharp little teeth.

Grafenwalder's voice booms into the water, relayed to the creature by floating microphones.

'I know you can hear me, and I know you can understand what I am saying to you. It is very important that you listen to what I am about to tell you.'

His voice appears to distress the creature as much as the bright light. With its other hand it tries to shield the whorl-like formation on the side of its head that is its ear. Grafenwalder doubts that it makes much difference. It must feel his voice in every cell of its body, ramming through it like a proclamation. That was the effect he was going for.

'You are in no danger,' he says. 'Nothing is going to happen to you, and nobody is going to hurt you. The people who would rather you were dead are not going to find you. You are in my care now, and I am going to make sure that you come to no harm. My name is Carl Grafenwalder, and I have been waiting a long time to meet you.'

The Denizen floats motionless, as if stunned by the force of his words. Perhaps that is exactly what has happened.

'From now on, this is going to be your home,' Grafenwalder continues. 'I hope that you find the conditions satisfactory. I have done my best to simulate your place of birth, but I accept that there may be deficiencies. My experts will be striving to improve matters as best as they can, but for that they will need your assistance. We must all learn to communicate. I know you cannot speak, but I am sure we can make progress using sign language. Let us begin with something simple. I must know if you find your environment satisfactory in certain details: temperature, sulphur content, salinity, that kind of thing. You will need to answer my experts in the affirmative or negative. Nod your head if you understand me.'

Nothing happens. He judges that the Denizen is still conscious – he still catches the quick animation of its eyes behind the curtain of its hand – but it shows no indication of having understood him.

'I said nod your head. If that is too difficult for you, make some other visible movement.'

But still there's nothing. He has the lights dimmed again, and slips the assassin's goggles down over his eyes once more. After a few moments, the infrared smear of the Denizen lowers its arm and assumes an alert but restful posture. Now that it has reacted to the absence of light, he brings the glare back and observes the creature cower against the glare's return.

'You prefer the darkness, don't you? Well, I can make it dark again. All you have to do is show some sign that you understand me. Do that, and I'll bring the darkness back again.'

The Denizen just floats there, watching him through the spread webbing of its upraised hand. Perhaps it has learned to tolerate the light better than before, for its gaze strikes him now as steadier, somehow more reproachful. Even if it doesn't understand his words, it surely understands that it is his prisoner.

'I will lower the lights one more time.' He does so, then brings them back up, savagely, before the Denizen has had time to relish the darkness. This time he does get a reaction, but it's not quite the one he was anticipating. The Denizen shoots forward, bulleting through the water with dismaying speed. Just when he thinks the creature is going to use its skull as a battering ram, the Denizen brakes with a reverse flick of its tail and brings its head and upper body hard against the glass, arms spread eagled, face only a few centimetres from Grafenwalder's own. Rationally, he knows that the glass is impervious – it's designed to hold back the pressure of the Europan ocean – but there's still a tiny part of his mind that can't accept that, and insists on jerking him back from that grinning mouth, those hateful human eyes. The Denizen sees it, too: it doesn't need language to know that it has scared him.

Grafenwalder regains his composure with an uneasy laugh, trying to sound as if it was all an act. The Denizen knows better, notching wide the dreadful smile of its mouth.

'Okay,' he says. 'You frightened me. That's good. That's exactly what you're meant to do. That's exactly why I brought you here.'

The microphones in the tank pick up the Denizen's derisive snort, pealing it in harsh metallic waves around the metal walls of the bestiary. Grafenwalder's heart is still racing, but he's beginning to see the positive side of the arrangement. Maybe the fact that the creature can't talk is all for the best. There's something truly chilling about that snort; something that wouldn't come through at all if the specimen had language. There's a mind in there; one sharp enough to use complex tools in the unforgiving environment of a cold black alien ocean. But that mind only has one narrow outlet for its rage.

It's going to work, he thinks. If it has half the effect on the other collectors that it just had on him, Dr Trintignant will soon be relegated to a nine-day wonder. All he needs to do now is make sure the damned thing is as real as it looks. Not that he has any significant doubts now. Rifugio already had bona fide DNA and tissue samples. Where did that material come from, if it wasn't snipped from the last living Denizen?

He leaves the creature in darkness, letting it settle in. The next day, his keepers descend into the tank wearing armoured immersion suits. It takes two of them to immobilise the creature while the third takes a series of biopsy samples. With their powered suits, the men are in little danger from the Denizen. But they're still impressed by the strength and quickness of the specimen; its balletic ease within water. It moves with the sleek, elemental ease of something for which water is not a hindrance, but its natural medium.

Grafenwalder tunes in to Circle gossip again, unsurprised to find that Dr Trintignant is still wowing the other collectors. It still feels hurtful not to be the automatic centre of attention, but now at least he knows his rightful place will be restored. Ursula Goodglass got lucky with the dismantled doctor, but luck won't get her very far in the long game.

Later that day, his experts report back with the first findings from the biopsies. At first, Grafenwalder is so convinced of the Denizen's authenticity that he doesn't hear what the experts, in their fumbling way, are trying to tell him.

The samples don't match. The Denizen's DNA isn't the same as the DNA that Rifugio gave him, or the DNA that Grafenwalder already possesses. It's the same story with the blood and tissue samples. The disagreement isn't huge, and less sophisticated tests probably wouldn't have detected any discrepancies. That's no solace to Grafenwalder, though. His tests are as good as they come, and they leave no room for doubt. The creature in his care is not what Rifugio let him think he was going to be buying.

He tries to call the broker, but the contact details no longer work. Rifugio doesn't get back to him.

So he's been conned. But if the Denizen is a con, it's an extraordinarily thorough one. He's had the chance to examine it closely now, and he's found no obvious signs of fakery. It's no mean feat to engineer a biological gill that can sustain an organism with the energy demands of a large mammal. The faked Denizens he's examined in the past began to die after only a few dozen hours of immersion. But this one shows every sign of thriving, of gaining strength and quickness.

Grafenwalder considers other possibilities. If the blood and tissue samples don't agree, then maybe it's because there's more than one kind of Denizen. The Europan scientists engineered distinct castes with differing linguistic abilities, so perhaps there were other variants, with different blood and tissue structures. They were all prototypes, after all, right up to the moment they turned against the Demarchy. This Denizen might simply be from a different production batch.

But that doesn't explain why Rifugio provided him with non-matching samples. If Rifugio had the creature, why didn't he just take samples from it directly? Did Rifugio make a mistake, mixing samples from one specimen with another? If so, he must have had more than one Denizen in his care. In which case, the whole story about the Ultras keeping the Denizen as a pet was a lie . . . but a necessary one, if Rifugio wished Grafenwalder to think the creature was unique.

Grafenwalder mulls the possibilities. Rifugio's disappearance provides damning confirmation that some kind of deception has taken place. But if that deception merely extends to the fact that the Denizen isn't unique, Grafenwalder considers himself to have got off lightly. He still has a Denizen, and that's infinitely better than none at all. He'll find a way to trace and punish Rifugio in due course, but for now retribution isn't his highest priority.

Instead, what he desires most is communication.

By nightfall, when the keepers have finished their work, he descends to the tank and brings the lights back on. Not harshly now, but enough to alert the Denizen to his presence; to wake it from whatever shallow approximation of sleep it appears to enjoy when resting.

Then – satisfied that he is alone – he talks.

'You can understand me,' he says, for the umpteenth time. 'I know this because my keepers have identified a region in your brain that only lights up when you hear human speech. And it lights up most strongly when you hear Canasian, the language of the Demarchy.'

The creature watches him sullenly.

'It's the language you were educated to understand, two hundred years ago. I know things have changed a little since then, but I don't doubt that you can still make sense of these words.' And as he speaks Canasian, he feels – not for the first time – an odd, unexpected fluency. The words ought to feel awkward, but they flow off his tongue with mercurial ease, as if this is also the language he was born to speak.

Which is absurd.

'I want to know your story,' he says. 'How you got here, where you came from, how many of you there are. I know now that Rifugio lied to me. He'll pay for that eventually, but for now all that matters is what you can tell me. I need to know everything, right back to the moment you were born in Europa.'

But the Denizen, as ever, shows no external sign of having understood him.

Later, Grafenwalder has his keepers install a waterproofed symbol board in the tank. It's an array of touch pads, each of which stands for a word in Canasian. As Grafenwalder speaks, the symbols light up in turn. The Denizen may reply by pressing the pads in sequence, which will be rendered back into speech on Grafenwalder's side of the glass. Grafenwalder's hoping that there's something amiss with the Denizen's language centre, some cognitive defect that can be short-circuited using the visual codes. If he can persuade the Denizen to press the 'yes' or 'no' pads in response to simple questions, he will consider that progress has been made.

Things don't move as quickly as he'd hoped. The Denizen seems willing to co-operate, but it still doesn't grasp the basics of language. Once it has understood that one of the pads symbolises food, it presses that one repeatedly, ignoring Grafenwalder's attempts to get it to answer abstract questions.

Maybe it's just stupid, he thinks. Maybe that's why this batch was discontinued. But he doesn't give up just yet. If the Denizen won't communicate willingly, perhaps it needs persuasion. He has his keepers tinker with the ambient conditions, varying the water temperature and chemistry to make things uncomfortable. He withholds food and instructs the keepers to take further biopsies. It's clear enough that the Denizen doesn't enjoy the process.

Still the creature won't talk, beyond issuing simple pleas for more food or warmer water. Grafenwalder feels his patience stretching. The keepers tell him that the Denizen is getting stronger, more difficult to subdue. Angrily, he accompanies them on their next trip into the tank. There are four men, all wearing power-assisted pressure armour, and now it takes three of them to pin the Denizen against one wall of the glass. When it breaks free momentarily, it gouges deep tooth marks in the flexible hide of Grafenwalder's glove. Back outside the tank, he inspects the damage and wonders what those teeth would have done to naked flesh.

It's fierce, he'll give it that. It may not be unique; it may not be particularly intelligent; but he still doesn't feel that all the money he gave Rifugio was wasted. Whatever the Denizen might be, it's worthy of a place in the bestiary. And it's *his*, not someone else's.

He puts out the word that there is something new in his collection. Following Ursula Goodglass's example, he tells the visitors to drop by whenever they like. There must be no suspicion that the Denizen is a stage-managed exhibit, something that can only perform to schedule.

It's three days before anyone takes him up on his offer. Lysander Carroway and her husband are the first to arrive. Even then, Grafenwalder has the sense that the visit is regarded as a tiresome social duty. All that changes when they see the Denizen. He's taken pains to stoke it up, denying it food and comfort for long hours. By the time he throws on the lights, the creature has become a focus of pure, mindless fury. It strives to kill the things on the other side of the glass, scratching claws and teeth against that impervious shield, to the point where it starts bleeding. His guests recoil, suitably impressed. After the study in motionless that was Dr Trintignant, they are woefully unprepared for the murderous speed of the Europan organism.

'Yes, it is a Denizen,' he tells them, while his keepers tend to the creature's injuries. 'The last of its kind, I have it on good authority.'

'Where did you find it?'

He parrots the lie Rifugio has already told him. 'You know what Ultras are like, with their pets. I don't think they realised quite what they'd been tormenting all those years.'

'Can it speak to us? I heard that they could talk.'

'Not this one. The idea that most of them could talk is a fallacy, I'm afraid: they simply weren't required to. As for the ones that did have language, they must have died over a hundred years ago.'

'Perhaps the ones that were clever enough to talk were also clever enough to stay away from Ultras,' muses Carroway. 'After all, if you can talk, you can negotiate, make bargains. Especially if you know things that can hurt people.'

'What would a Denizen know that could hurt anyone?' Grafenwalder asks scornfully.

'Who made it,' Carroway says. 'That would be worth something to someone, wouldn't it? In these times, more than ever.'

Grafenwalder shakes his head. 'I don't think so. Even the ones with language weren't that clever. They were built to take orders and use tools. They weren't capable of the kind of complex abstract thought necessary to plot and scheme.'

'How would you know?' Carroway asks. 'It's not as if you've ever met one.'

There's no malice in her question, but by the time the Carroways depart he's in a foul mood, barely masked by the niceties of Circle politesse. Why can't they just accept that the Denizen is enough of a prize in its own right, without dwelling on what it can't do? Isn't a ravenous man-fish chimera enough of a draw for them now?

But the Carroways must have been sufficiently impressed to speak of his new addition, because the guests come thick and fast over the next week. By then they've heard that he has a Denizen, but most of them don't quite believe it. Time and again he goes through the ritual of having them scared by the captive creature, only this time with a few additional flourishes. The glass is as secure as ever, but he's had the tank lined with a false interior that cracks more easily. He's also implanted a throat microphone under the skin of the Denizen, to better capture its blood-curdling vocalisations. Since the creature needed to be sedated for that, he also took the liberty of dropping an electrode into what his keepers think is the best guess for the creature's pain centre. It's a direct steal from what Goodglass did to Dr Trintignant, but no one has to know that, and with the electrode he can stir the Denizen up to its full killing fury even if it's just been fed.

It's still too soon to call, but his monitoring of Circle gossip begins to suggest that interest in Trintignant is declining. He's still jealous of Goodglass for that particular coup, but at last he feels that he has the upper hand again. The memory of Rifugio's lies has all but faded. The story Grafenwalder tells, about how the Denizen came to him via the Ultras, is repeated so often that he almost begins to believe it himself. The act of telling one lie over and over again, until it concretises into something barely distinguishable from the truth, feels peculiarly familiar to him. When his keepers come to him again and report that a more detailed analysis of the Denizen DNA has thrown up statistical matches with the genome of a typical hyperpig, he blanks the information.

What they're telling him is that the Denizen isn't real; that it's some form of genetic fake cooked up using a hyperpig in place of a human, with Denizen like characteristics spliced in at the foetal stage. But he doesn't want to hear that; not now that he's back on top.

The last of the guests to visit are Ursula Goodglass and her husband. They've waited a lengthy, although not impolite, interval before favouring him with their presence. Once their shuttle has docked, Goodglass sweeps ahead of her husband's palanquin, trying to put a brave face on the proceedings.

'I hear you have a Denizen, Carl. If so, you have my heartfelt congratulations. Nothing like that has been seen for a very long time.' She looks at him coquettishly. 'It is a Denizen, isn't it? We didn't want to pay too much attention to the rumours, but when everyone started saying the same thing—'

'It is a Denizen,' he confirms gravely, as if the news is a terminal diagnosis. Which, in terms of Goodglass's current standing in the Circle, it might as well be. 'Would you like to see it?'

'Of course we'd like to see it!' her husband declares, his voice piping from the palanquin.

He takes them to the holding tank, darkened now, and issues assassin's goggles to Ursula, assuming that her husband's palanquin has its own infrared system. Allowing the guests to see the floating form, albeit indistinctly, is all part of the theatre.

'It looks smaller than I was expecting,' Ursula Goodglass observes.

'They were small,' Grafenwalder says. 'Designed to operate in cramped conditions. But don't let that deceive you. It's as strong as three men in amp-suits.'

'And you're absolutely sure of its authenticity? You've run a full battery of tests?'

'There's no doubt.' Rashly, he adds, 'You can see the results, if you like.'

'There's no need. I'm prepared to take your word for it. I know you wouldn't take anything for granted, given how long you've been after one of these.'

Grafenwalder allows himself a microscopic frown. 'I didn't know you were aware of my interest in acquiring a Denizen.'

'It would be difficult not to know, Carl. You've put out feelers in all directions imaginable. Of course, you've been discreet about it – or as discreet as circumstances allow.' She smiles unconvincingly. 'I'm glad for you, Carl. It must feel like the end of a great quest, to have this in your possession.'

'Yes,' he said. 'It does.'

The palanquin speaks. 'What exactly was it about the Denizen that you found so captivating, if you don't mind my asking?'

Grafenwalder shrugs, expecting the answer to roll glibly off his tongue. Instead, he has to force it out by an effort of will, as if there is a blockage in his thought processes. 'Its uniqueness, I suppose, Edric.'

'But there are many unique things,' the palanquin says, its piping tone conveying mild puzzlement. 'Why did you have to go to the extremes of locating a Denizen, a creature not even known ever to have existed? A creature whose authenticity cannot ever be confirmed with certainty?'

'Perhaps because it was so difficult. I like a challenge. Does it have to be any more complicated than that?'

'No, it doesn't,' the palanquin answers. 'I merely wondered if there might not have been a deeper motive, something less transparent.'

'I'm really not the man to ask. Why do any of us collect things?'

'Carl's right, dear,' Ursula says, smiling tightly at the palanquin's dark window. 'One mustn't enquire too deeply about these things. It isn't seemly.'

'I demur,' her husband says, and reverses slightly back from the heavy glass wall before them.

Grafenwalder judges that the moment is right to bring up the lights and enrage the Denizen. He squeezes the actuator tucked into his pocket, dripping current into the creature's brain. The lights pierce the tank, snaring the floating form. The Denizen snorts and powers itself towards the wall, its eyes wide with hatred despite the glare. It slams into the weakened inner layer and shatters the glass, making it seem as if the entire tank is about to lose integrity.

'We're quite safe,' he says, anticipating that Goodglass will have flinched from the impact. But she hasn't. She's standing her ground, her expression serenely unmoved by the entire spectacle.

'You're right,' she comments. 'It's quite a catch. But I wonder if it's really as vicious as it appears.'

'Take my word. It's much, much worse. It nearly bit through my glove when I was inside that tank, wearing full armour.'

'Perhaps it doesn't like being kept here. It didn't seem very happy when you turned the lights on.'

'It's an exhibit, Ursula. It doesn't have to like being here. It should be grateful just to be alive.'

She looks at him with sudden interest, as if he has said something profound. 'Do you really think so, Carl?'

'Yes,' he says. 'Absolutely.'

She returns her attention to the tank wall. The Denizen is still hovering there, anchored in place by the tips of its fingers and the fluke of its tail. The cracks in the shattered glass radiate away in all directions, making the Denizen look as if it is caught in a frozen star, or pinned to a snowflake.

Goodglass removes her glove and touches a hand to the smooth and unbroken glass on the outer surface of the tank, exactly where the Denizen has its own webbed hand. That's when Grafenwalder notices the pale webs of skin between Ursula Goodglass's fingers, visible now that she has taken off the glove. Their milky translucence is exactly the same as the webs between the Denizen's. She presses her hand harder, squeezing until her palm is flat against the glass, and the Denizen echoes the movement.

The air feels as if it has frozen. The moment of contact seems to last minutes, hours, eternities. Grafenwalder stares in numb incomprehension, unable to process what he is seeing. When she moves her hand, skating it across the glass, the Denizen follows her like an expert mime.

She takes another step closer, bringing her face against the glass, laying her cheek flat against the cold surface. The Denizen presses itself against the shattered inner layer and mirrors her posture, bringing its own head against hers. The flesh of their faces appears to merge.

Goodglass pulls her face back from the glass, then smiles at the Denizen. It tries to emulate her expression, forcing its mouth wide. It's not much of a smile – it's more horrific than reassuring – but the deliberateness of the gesture is beyond doubt.

Finally Grafenwalder manages to say something. His own voice sounds wrong, as if it's coming from another room.

'What are you doing?'

'I'm greeting it,' Ursula Goodglass says, snapping her attention away from the tank. 'What on Earth did you think I was doing?'

'It's a Denizen. It doesn't know you. You can't know it.'

'Oh, Carl,' she says, pityingly now. 'Haven't you got it yet? Really, I thought you'd have figured things out by now. Look at my hand again.'

'I don't need to. I saw it.'

She pulls back her hand until she's only touching the glass with a fingertip. 'Then tell me what it reminds you of – or can't you bring yourself to say it?'

'I've had enough,' he says. 'I don't know what kind of game you're playing, but it isn't true to the spirit of the Circle. I insist that you leave immediately.'

'But we're not done yet,' Goodglass says.

'Fine. If you won't go easily, I'll have you escorted to your shuttle.'

'I'm afraid not, Carl. We've still business to attend to. You didn't think it was going to be quite that easy, did you?'

'Leave now.'

'Or what? You'll turn your household systems on us?' She looks apologetic. 'They won't work, I'm afraid. They've been disabled. From the moment our shuttle docked, it's been working to introduce security countermeasures into your habitat.' Before he can get a word in, she says, 'It was a mistake to invite us to view the adult-phase hamadryad. It gave us the perfect opportunity to snoop your arrangements, design a package of neutralising agents. Don't go calling for your keepers, either. They're all unconscious. The last time we visited, the palanquin deployed microscopic stun-capsules into every room it passed through. Upon our return, they were programmed to activate, releasing a fast-acting nerve toxin.

Your keepers will be fine once they wake up, but that isn't going to happen for a few hours yet.'

'I don't believe you.'

'You don't have to,' Goodglass says. 'Call for help, see how far it gets you.'

He lifts the cuff of his sleeve and talks into his bracelet. 'This is Grafenwalder. Get down to the bestiary now – the Denizen tank.'

But no one answers.

'I'm sorry, but no one's coming. You're on your own now, Carl. It's just you, the Denizen and the two of us.'

After a minute goes by, he knows she isn't bluffing. Goodglass has taken his habitat.

'What do you want from me?'

'It's not so much a question of what I want from you, Carl, as what you want from me.'

'You're not making much sense.'

'Ask yourself this: why did you want the Denizen so much? Was it because you just had to add another unique specimen to your collection? Or did the drive go deeper than that? Is it just possible that you created this entire bestiary as a decoy, to divert everyone – including yourself – from the true focus of your obsession?'

'You tell me, Ursula. You seem to know a lot about the collecting game.'

'I'm no collector,' she says curtly. 'I detest you and your kind. That was just a cover, to get me close to you. I went to a lot of trouble, of course: the hamadryad, Trintignant . . . I know you had Shallice kill the hamadryad, by the way. That was what I expected you to do. Why else do you think I had Shallice mention my existence, if not to goad you? I needed you to take an interest in me, Carl. It worked spectacularly well.'

'You never interested me, Ursula. You irritated me, like a tick.'

'It had the same effect. It brought us together. It brought me here.'

'And the Denizen?' he asks, half-fearing her answer.

'The Denizen is a fake. I'm sure you've figured that out for yourself by now. A pretty good fake, I'll admit – but it isn't two hundred years old, and it's never been anywhere near Europa.'

'What about the samples Rifugio gave me? Where did they come from?'

'From me,' Goodglass says.

'You're insane.'

'No, Carl. Not insane. Just a Denizen.' And she shows him her webbed hand once more, extending it out towards him as if inviting him to kiss it. 'I'm what you've been searching for all these years, the end of your quest. But this isn't quite the way you imagined things playing out, is it? That you'd have had me under your nose all this time, and not known how close you were?'

'You can't be a Denizen.'

'There is such a thing as surgery,' she says witheringly. 'I had to wait until after the plague before having myself changed, which meant subjecting myself to cruder procedures than I might have wished. Fortunately, I had the services of a very good surgeon. He rewired my cardiovascular system for air-breathing. He gave me legs and a human face, and a voice box that works out of water.'

'And the hands?'

'I kept the hands. You've got to hold on to part of the past, no matter how much you might wish to bury it. I needed to remember where I'd come from, what I still had to do.'

'Which is?'

'To find you, and then punish you. You were there, Carl, back when we were made in Europa. A high-influence Demarchist in the Special Projects section of Cadmus-Asterius, the hanging city where we were spliced together and given life.'

'Nonsense. I've never been near Europa.'

'You were born there,' she assures him, 'not long after Sandra Voi founded the place. You've scrubbed those memories, though. They're too dangerous now. The Demarchists don't want anyone finding out about their history of past mistakes, not when they're trying to show how fine and upstanding they are compared to the beastly Conjoiners. Almost everyone connected with those dark days in Europa has been hunted down and silenced by now. Not you, though. You were ahead of the curve, already running by the time the cities fell. You hopped a ramliner to Yellowstone and started reinventing your past. Eidetic overlays to give you a false history, one so convincing that you believed it yourself. Except at night, in your loneliest hours. Then part of you knew that they were still out there, still looking for you.'

'They?'

'Not just the Demarchist silencers: they were the least of your worries. Money and power could keep them at bay. What really worried you was *us*, the Denizens.'

'If I made you, why would I fear you?'

'You didn't make us, Carl. I said you were part of the project, but you weren't working to bring us to life. You were working to suppress us; to make us fail. Petty internal rivalry: you couldn't allow another colleague's work to succeed. So you did everything you could to hurt us, to make us imperfect. You brought suffering into our world. You brought pain and infirmity and death, and then left us alone in that ocean.'

'Ridiculous.'

'Really, Carl? I've seen how easily you turn to spite. Just ask that dead hamadryad.'

'I had nothing to do with the Denizens.' But even as he says it, he can feel layers of false memory begin to peel back. What's exposed has the raw candour of true experience. He remembers more of Europa than he has any right to: the bright plazas, the smells, the noises of Cadmus-Asterius. He remembers the reefersleep casket on the outbound ramliner, the casket that he thought was taking him to the safety of another system, another time. No wonder he's slept easier since the Melding Plague. He must have imagined that the plague had severed the last of his ties with the past, making it impossible for anyone to catch up with him now.

He'd been wrong about that.

'You had to find a Denizen,' Goodglass says, 'because then you'd know if any of them were still alive. Well, now you have your answer. How does it feel?'

He always knew that the marks on her skull were evidence of surgery. But that surgery had nothing to do with the removal of implants, and everything to do with her transformation from a Denizen. It would have cost her nothing to hide those marks, and yet she made no secret of them. It was, he sees now, part of a game he hadn't even realised he was playing.

'Not the way I thought it would feel,' he says.

Goodglass nods understandingly. 'I'm going to punish you now, Carl. But I'm not going to kill you.'

She's playing with him, allowing him a glimmer of hope before crushing it for all eternity.

'Why not?' he asks.

'Because if you were dead, you wouldn't make much of an exhibit. When we're done here, I'm going to donate you to a suitable recipient.' Then she turns to the palanquin. 'There's something I should have told you. I lied about my husband. Edric was a good man: he cared for me, loved me, when he could have made his fortune from what I was. Unfortunately, he never got to see me like this. Edric died during the early months of the plague.'

Grafenwalder says nothing. He's out of words, out of questions.

'You're probably wondering who's in the palanquin,' Goodglass says. 'He's going to come out now, for a little while. Not too long, because he can't risk coming into contact with plague spores, not when so much of him is mechanical. But that won't stop him doing his job. He's always been a quick worker.'

With a hiss of escaping pressure, the entire front of the palanquin lifts up on shining pistons. The first thing Grafenwalder sees, the last thing before he starts screaming, is a silver hand clutching a black Homburg hat.

Then he sees the face.

NIGHTINGALE

I checked the address Tomas Martinez had given me, shielding the paper against the rain while I squinted at my scrawl. The number I'd written down didn't correspond with any of the high-and-dry offices, but it was a dead ringer for one of the low-rent premises at street level. Here the walls of Threadfall Canyon had been cut and buttressed to the height of six or seven storeys, widening the available space at the bottom of the trench. Buildings covered most of the walls, piled on top of each other, supported by a haphazard arrangement of stilts and rickety, semi-permanent bamboo scaffolding. Aerial walkways had been strung from one side of the street to the other, with stairs and ladders snaking their way through the dark fissures between the buildings. Now and then a wheeler sped through the water, sending a filthy brown wave in its wake. Very rarely, a sleek, clawlike volantor slid overhead. But volantors were off-world tech and not many people on Sky's Edge could afford that kind of thing any more.

It didn't look right to me, but all the evidence said that this had to be the place.

I stepped out of the water onto the wooden platform in front of the office and knocked on the glass-fronted door while rain curtained down through holes in the striped awning above me. I was pushing soaked hair out of my eyes when the door opened.

I'd seen enough photographs of Martinez to know this wasn't him. This was a big bull of a man, nearly as wide as the door. He stood there with his arms crossed in front of his chest, over which he wore only a sleeveless black vest that was zipped down to his midriff. His muscles were so tight it looked as if he was wearing some kind of body-hugging amplification suit. His head was very large and very bald, rooted to his body by a neck like a small mountain range. The skin around his right eye was paler than the rest of his face, in a neatly circular patch.

He looked down at me as if I was something unpleasant the rain had washed in.

'What?' he said, his voice like the distant rumble of artillery.

'I'm here to see Martinez.'

'Mister Martinez to you,' he said.

'Whatever. But I'm still here to see him, and he should be expecting me. I'm—'

'Dexia Scarrow,' called another voice – fractionally more welcoming, this one – and a smaller, older man bustled into view from behind the pillar of muscle blocking the door, snatching delicate pince-nez glasses from his nose. 'Let her in, Norbert. She's expected. Just a little *late*.'

'I got held up around Armesto – my hired wheeler hit a pothole and tipped over. Couldn't get the thing started again, so had to—'

The smaller man waved aside my excuse. 'You're here now, which is all that matters. I'll have Norbert dry your clothes, if you wish.'

I peeled off my coat. 'Maybe this.'

'Norbert will attend to your galoshes as well. Would you care for something to drink? I have tea already prepared, but if you would rather something else . . .'

'Tea will be fine, Mister Martinez,' I said.

'Please, call me Tomas. It's my sincere wish that we will work together as friends.'

I stepped out of my galoshes and handed my dripping-wet coat to the big man. Martinez nodded once, the gesture precise and birdlike, and then beckoned me to follow him further into his rooms. He was slighter and older than I'd been expecting, although still recognisable as the man in the photographs. His hair was grey turning to white, thinning on his crown and shaved close to his scalp elsewhere on his head. He wore a grey waistcoat over a grey shirt, the ensemble lending him a drab, clerkish air.

We navigated a twisting labyrinth formed by four layers of brown boxes, piled to head height. 'Excuse the mess,' Martinez said, looking back at me over his shoulder. 'I really should find a better solution to my filing problems, but there's always something more pressing that needs doing instead.'

'I'm surprised you have time to eat, let alone worry about filing problems.'

'Well, things haven't been quite as hectic lately, I must confess. If you've been following the news you'll know that I've already caught most of my big fish. There's some mopping up to do, but I've been nowhere near as busy as in . . .' Martinez stopped suddenly next to one of the piles of boxes, placed his glasses back on the bridge of his nose and scuffed dust from the paper label on the side of the box nearest his face. 'No,' he said, shaking his head. 'Wrong place. Wrong damned place! Norbert!'

Norbert trudged along behind us, my sodden coat still draped over one of his enormous, trunklike arms. 'Mister Martinez?'

'This one is in the wrong place.' The smaller man turned around and indicated a spot between two other boxes, on the opposite side of the corridor. 'It goes *here*. It needs to be properly filed. Kessler's case is moving into court next month, and we don't want any trouble with missing documentation.'

'Attend to it,' Norbert said, which sounded like an order but which I assumed was his way of saying he'd remember to move the box when he was done with my laundry.

'Kessler?' I asked, when Norbert had left. 'As in Tillman Kessler, the NC interrogator?'

'One and the same, yes. Did you have experience with him?'

'I wouldn't be standing here if I did.'

'True enough. But a small number of people were fortunate enough to survive their encounters with Kessler. Their testimonies will help bring him to justice.'

'By which you mean crucifixion.'

'I detect faint disapproval, Dexia,' Martinez said.

'You're right. It's barbaric.'

'It's how we've always done things. The Haussmann way, if you like.'

Sky Haussmann: the man who gave this world its name, and who sparked off the two-hundred-and-fifty-year war we've only just learned to stop fighting. When they crucified Sky they thought they were putting an early end to the violence. They couldn't have been more wrong. Ever since, crucifixion has been the preferred method of execution.

'Is Kessler the reason you asked me here, sir? Were you expecting me to add to the case file against him?'

Martinez paused at a heavy wooden door. 'Not Kessler, no. I've every expectation of seeing him nailed to Bridgetop by the end of the year. But it does concern the man for whom Kessler was an instrument.'

I thought about that for a moment. 'Kessler worked for Colonel Jax, didn't he?'

Martinez opened the door and ushered me through, into the windowless room beyond. By now we must have been back into the canyon wall. The air had the inert stillness of a crypt.

'Yes, Kessler was Jax's man,' Martinez said. 'I'm glad you made the connection: it saves me explaining why Jax ought to be brought to justice.'

'I agree completely. Half the population would agree with you. But I'm afraid you're a bit late: Jax died years ago.'

Two other people were already waiting in the room, sitting on settees either side of a low, black table set with tea, coffee and pisco sours.

'Jax didn't die,' Martinez said. 'He just disappeared, and now I know where he is. Have a seat, please.'

He knew I was interested; knew I wouldn't be able to walk out of that room until I'd heard the rest of the story about Colonel Brandon Jax. But there was more to it than that: there was something effortlessly commanding about his voice that made it very difficult not to obey him. During my time in the Southland Militia I'd learned that some people have that authority and some people don't. It can't be taught; can't be learned; can't be faked. You're either born with it or you're not.

'Dexia Scarrow, allow me to introduce you to my other two guests,' Martinez said, when I'd taken my place at the table. 'The gentleman opposite you is Salvatore Nicolosi, a veteran of one of the Northern Coalition's freeze/thaw units. The woman on your right is Ingrid Sollis, a personal-security expert with a particular interest in counter-intrusion systems. Ingrid saw early combat experience with the Southland, but she soon left the military to pursue private interests.'

I bit my tongue, then turned my attention away from the woman before I said something I might regret. The man – Nicolosi – looked more like an actor than a soldier. He didn't have a scar on him. His beard was so neatly groomed, so sharp-edged, that it looked sprayed on through a stencil. Freeze/thaw operatives rubbed me up the wrong way, no matter which side they'd been on. They'd always seen themselves as superior to the common soldier, which is why they didn't feel the need for the kind of excessive musculature Norbert carried around.

'Allow me to introduce Dexia Scarrow,' Martinez continued, nodding at me. 'Dexia was a distinguished soldier in the Southland Militia for fifteen years, until the armistice. Her service record is excellent. I believe she will be a valuable addition to the team.'

'Maybe we should back up a step,' I said. 'I haven't agreed to be part of anyone's team.'

'We're going after Jax,' Nicolosi said placidly. 'Doesn't that excite you?'

'He was on your side,' I said. 'What makes you so keen to see him crucified?'

Nicolosi looked momentarily pained. 'He was a war criminal, Dexia. I'm as anxious to see monsters like Jax brought to justice as I am to see the same fate visited on their scum-ridden Southland counterparts.'

'Nicolosi's right,' said Ingrid Sollis. 'If we're going to learn to live together on this planet, we have to put the law above all else, regardless of former allegiances.'

'Easy coming from a deserter,' I said. 'Allegiance clearly didn't mean very much to you back then, so I'm not surprised it doesn't mean much to you now.'

Martinez, still standing at the head of the table, smiled tolerantly, as if he'd expected nothing less.

'That's an understandable misapprehension, Dexia, but Ingrid was no deserter. She was wounded in the line of duty; severely, I might add. After her recuperation, she was commended for bravery under fire and given the choice of an honourable discharge or a return to the front line. You cannot blame her for choosing the former, especially given all she had been through.'

'Okay, my mistake,' I said. 'It's just that I never heard of many people making it out alive, before the war was over.'

Sollis looked at me icily. 'Some of us did.'

'No one here has anything but an impeccable service record,' Martinez said. 'I should know: I've been through your individual biographies with a fine-tooth comb. You're just the people for the job.'

'I don't think so,' I said, moving to stand up. 'I'm just a retired soldier with a grudge against deserters. I wasn't in some shit-hot freeze/thaw unit, and I didn't do anything that resulted in any commendations for bravery. Sorry, folks, but I think—'

'Remain seated.'

I did what the man said.

Martinez continued speaking, his voice as measured and patient as ever. 'You participated in at least three high-risk extraction operations, Dexia; three dangerous forays behind enemy lines, to retrieve two deep-penetration Southland spies and one trumpcard NC defector. Or do you deny this?'

I shook my head, the reality of what he was proposing still not sinking in. 'I can't help you. I don't know anything about Jax—'

'You don't need to. That's my problem.'

'How are you so sure he's still alive, anyway?'

'I'd like to know that, too,' Nicolosi said, stroking an elegant finger along the border of his beard.

Martinez sat down on his own stool at the head of the table, so that he was higher than the three of us. He removed his glasses and fiddled with them in his lap. 'It is necessary that you take a certain amount of what I am about to tell you on faith. I've been gathering intelligence on men like Jax for years, and in doing so I've come to rely on a web of contacts, many of whom have conveyed information to me at great personal risk. If I were to tell you the whole story, and if some of that story were to leak beyond this office, lives might well be endangered. And that is to say nothing of how my chances of bringing other fugitives to justice might be undermined.'

'We understand,' Sollis said.

I bridled at the way she presumed to speak for all of us. Perhaps she felt she owed Martinez for the way he'd just stood up for her.

Again I bit my lip and said nothing.

'For a long time, I've received titbits of intelligence concerning Colonel Jax: rumours that he did not, in fact, die at all, but is still at large.'

'Where?' Sollis asked. 'On Sky's Edge?'

'It would seem not. There were, of course, many rumours and false trails that suggested Jax had gone to ground somewhere on this planet. But one by one I discounted them all. Slowly the truth became apparent: Jax is still alive; still within this system.'

I felt it was about time I made a positive contribution. 'Wouldn't a piece of dirt like Jax try to get out of the system at the first opportunity?'

Martinez favoured my observation by pointing his glasses at me. 'I had my fears that he might have, but as the evidence came in, a different truth presented itself.'

He set about pouring himself some tea. The pisco sours were going unwanted. I doubted that any of us had the stomach for drink at that time of the day.

'Where is he, then?' asked Nicolosi. 'Plenty of criminal elements might have the means to shelter a man like Jax, but given the price on his head, the temptation to turn him in—'

'He is not being sheltered,' Martinez said, sipping delicately at his tea before continuing, 'He is alone, aboard a ship. The ship was believed lost, destroyed in the final stages of the war, when things escalated into space. But I have evidence that the ship is still essentially intact, with a functioning life-support system. There is every reason to believe that Jax is still being kept alive, aboard this vehicle, in this system.'

'What's he waiting for?' I asked.

'For memories to grow dim,' Martinez answered. 'Like many powerful men, Jax may have obtained longevity drugs – or at least undergone longevity treatment – during the latter stages of the war. Time is not a concern for him.'

I leaned forward. 'This ship – you think it'll just be a matter of boarding it and taking him alive?'

Martinez looked surprised at the directness of my question. He blinked once before answering.

'In essence, yes.'

'Won't he put up a fight?'

'I don't think so. The Ultras that located the vessel for me reported that it appeared dormant, in power-conservation mode. Jax himself may be frozen, in reefersleep. The ship did not respond to the Ultras' sensor sweeps, so there's no reason to assume it will respond to our approach and docking.'

'How close did the Ultras get?' Sollis asked.

'Within three or four light-minutes. But there's no reason to assume we can't get closer without alerting the ship.'

'How do you know Jax is aboard this ship?' Nicolosi asked. 'It could just be a drifter, nothing to do with him.'

'The intelligence I'd already gleaned pointed towards his presence aboard a vehicle of a certain age, size and design – everything matches.'

'So let's cut to the chase,' Sollis said, again presuming to speak for the rest of us. 'You've brought us here because you think we're the team to snatch the colonel. I'm the intrusion specialist, so you'll be relying on me to get us inside that ship. Nicolosi's a freeze/thaw veteran, so – apart from the fact that he's probably pretty handy with a weapon or two – he'll know how to spring Jax from reefersleep, if the colonel turns out to be frozen. And she – what was your name again?'

'Dexia,' I said, like it was a threat.

'She's done some extractions. I guess she must be okay at her job or she wouldn't be here.'

Martinez waited a moment, then nodded. 'You're quite right, Ingrid: all credit to you for that. I apologise if my machinations are so nakedly transparent. But the simple fact of the matter is that you are the ideal team for the operation in question. I have no doubt that, with your combined talents, you will succeed in returning Colonel Jax to Sky's Edge, and hence to trial. Now admit it: that *would* be something, wouldn't it? To fell the last dragon?'

Nicolosi indicated his approval with a long nasal sigh. 'Men like Kessler are just a distraction. When you crucify a monster like Kessler, you're punishing the knife, not the man who wielded it. If you wish true justice, you must find the knifeman, the master.'

'What will we get paid?' Sollis asked.

Martinez smiled briefly. 'Fifty thousand Australs for each of you, upon the safe return of Colonel Jax.'

'What if we find him dead?' I asked. 'By then we'll already have risked an approach and docking with his ship.'

'If Jax is already dead, then you will be paid twenty-five thousand Australs.'

We all looked at each other. I knew what the others were thinking. Fifty thousand Australs was life-changing money, but half of that wasn't bad either. Killing Jax would be much easier and safer than extracting him alive . . .

'I'll be with you, of course,' Martinez said, 'so there'll be no need to worry about proving Jax was already dead when you arrived, should that situation arise.'

'If you're coming along,' I asked, 'who else do we need to know about?'

'Only Norbert. And you need have no fears concerning his competency.'

'Just the five of us, then,' I said.

'Five is a good number, don't you think? And there is a practical limit to the size of the extraction team. I have obtained the use of a small but capable ship, perfectly adequate for our purposes. It will carry five, with enough capacity to bring back the colonel. I'll provide weapons, equipment and armour, but you may all bring whatever you think may prove useful.'

I looked around the cloisterlike confines of the room, and remembered the dismal exterior of the offices, situated at the bottom of Threadfall Canyon. 'Three times fifty thousand Australs,' I mused, 'plus whatever it cost you to hire and equip a ship. If you don't mind me asking – where exactly are the funds coming from?'

'The funds are mine,' Martinez said sternly. 'Capturing Jax has been a long-term goal, not some whimsical course upon which I have only recently set myself. Dying a pauper would be a satisfactory end to my affairs, were I to do so knowing that Jax was hanging from the highest mast at Bridgetop.'

For a moment none of us said anything. Martinez had spoken so softly, so demurely, that the meaning of his words seemed to lag slightly behind the statement itself. When it arrived, I think we all saw a flash of that corpse, executed in the traditional way, the Haussmann way.

'Good weapons?' I asked. 'Not some reconditioned black-market shit?'

'Only the best.'

'Technical specs for the ship?' Sollis asked.

'You'll have plenty of time to review the data on the way to the rendezvous point. I don't doubt that a woman of your abilities will be able to select the optimum entry point.'

Sollis looked flattered. 'Then I guess I'm in. What about you, Salvatore?'

'Men like Colonel Jax stained the honour of the Northern Coalition. We were not all monsters. If I could do something to make people see that . . .' Nicolosi trailed off, then shrugged. 'Yes, I am in. It would be an honour, Mister Martinez.'

'That leaves you, Dexia,' Sollis said. 'Fifty thousand Australs sounds pretty sweet to me. I'm guessing it sounds pretty sweet to you as well.'

'That's my call, not yours.'

'Just saying . . . you look like you could use that money as much as any of us.'

I think I came close to saying no, to walking out of that room, back into the incessant muddy rain of Threadfall Canyon. Perhaps if I'd tried, Norbert would have been forced to detain me, so that I didn't go blabbing about how a team was being put together to bring Colonel Jax back into custody. But I never got the chance to find out what Martinez had in mind for me if I chose not to go along with him.

I only had to think about the way I looked in the mirror, and what those fifty thousand Australs could do for me.

So I said yes.

Martinez gestured towards one of the blank, pewter-grey walls in the shuttle's compartment, causing it to glow and fill with neon-bright lines. The lines meshed and intersected, forming a schematic diagram of a ship with an accompanying scale.

'Intelligence on Jax's ship is fragmentary. Strip out all the contradictory reports, discard unreliable data, and we're left with this.'

'That's it?' Sollis asked.

'When we get within visual range we'll be able to improve matters. I shall re-examine all of the reports, including those that were discarded. Some of them – when we have the real ship to compare them against – may turn out to have merit after all. They may in turn shed useful light on the interior layout, and the likely location of Jax. By then, of course, we'll also have infrared and deep-penetration radar data from our own sensors.'

'It looks like a pretty big ship,' I said as I studied the schematic, scratching at my scalp. We were a day out from Armesto Field, with the little shuttle tucked into the belly hold of an outbound lighthugger named *Death of Sophonisba*.

'Big but not the right shape for a lighthugger,' Sollis said. 'So what are we dealing with here?'

'Good question,' I said. Martinez was showing us a rectangular hull about one kilometre from end to end; maybe a hundred metres deep and a hundred metres wide, with some kind of spherical bulge about halfway along. There was a suggestion of engines at one end, and of a gauntletlike docking complex at the other. The ship was too blunt for interstellar travel, and it lacked the outrigger-mounted engines characteristic of Conjoiner drive mechanisms. 'Does look kind of familiar, though,' I added. 'Anyone else getting that déjà vu feeling, or is it just me?'

'I don't know,' Nicolosi said. 'When I first saw it, I thought . . .' He shook his head. 'It can't be. It must be a standard hull design.'

'You've seen it before, too,' I said.

'Does that ship have a name?' Nicolosi asked Martinez.

'I have no idea what Jax calls his ship.'

'That's not what the man asked,' Sollis said. 'He asked if—'

'I know the name of the ship,' I said quietly. 'I saw a ship like that once, when I was being taken aboard it. I'd been injured in a firefight, one of the last big surface battles. They took me into space – this was after the elevator came down, so it had to be by shuttle – and brought me aboard that ship. It was a hospital ship, orbiting the planet.'

'What was the name of the ship?' Nicolosi asked urgently.

'*Nightingale*,' I said.

'Oh, no.'

'You're surprised.'

'Damn right I'm surprised. I was aboard *Nightingale*, too.'

'So was I,' Sollis said, her voice barely a whisper. 'I didn't recognise it, though. I was too fucked up to pay much attention until they put me back together aboard it. By then, I guess . . .'

'Same with me,' Nicolosi said. 'Stitched back together aboard *Nightingale*, then repatriated.'

Slowly, we all turned and looked at Martinez. Even Norbert, who had contributed nothing until that point, turned to regard his master. Martinez blinked, but otherwise his composure was impeccable.

'The ship is indeed *Nightingale*. It was too risky to tell you when we were still on the planet. Had any of Jax's allies learned of the identity—'

Sollis cut him off. 'Is that why you didn't tell us? Or is it because you knew we'd all been aboard that thing once already?'

'The fact that you have all been aboard *Nightingale* was a factor in your selection, nothing more. It was your skills that marked you out for this mission, not your medical history.'

'So why didn't you tell us?' she persisted.

'Again, had I told you more than was wise—'

'You lied to us.'

'I did no such thing.'

'Wait,' Nicolosi said, his voice calmer than I was expecting. 'Let's just . . . deal with this, shall we? We're getting hung up on the fact that we were all healed aboard *Nightingale*, when the real question we should be asking is this: what the hell is Jax doing aboard a ship that doesn't exist any more?'

'What's the problem with the ship?' I asked.

'The problem,' Nicolosi said, speaking directly to me, 'is that *Nightingale* was reported destroyed near the end of the war. Or were you not keeping up with the news?'

I shrugged. 'Guess I wasn't.'

'And yet you knew enough about the ship to recognise it.'

'Like I said, I remember the view from the medical shuttle. I was drugged-up, unsure whether I was going to live or die . . . everything was heightened, intense, like in a bad dream. But after they healed me and sent me back down surfaceside? I don't think I ever thought about *Nightingale* again.'

'Not even when you look in the mirror?' Nicolosi asked.

'I thought about what they'd done to me, how much better a job it could have been. But it never crossed my mind to wonder what had happened to the ship afterwards. So what *did* happen?'

'You said "they healed me",' Nicolosi observed. 'Does that mean you were treated by doctors, by men and women?'

'Shouldn't I have been?'

He shook his head minutely. 'My guess is you were wounded and shipped aboard *Nightingale* soon after it was deployed.'

'That's possible.'

'In which case *Nightingale* was still in commissioning phase. I went aboard later. What about you, Ingrid?'

'Me, too. I hardly saw another human being the whole time I was aboard that thing.'

'That was how it was meant to operate: with little more than a skeleton staff, to make medical decisions the ship couldn't make for itself. Most of the time they were meant to stay behind the scenes.'

'All I remember was a hospital ship,' I said. 'I don't know anything about "commissioning".'

Nicolosi explained it to me patiently, as if I was a small child in need of education.

Nightingale had been financed and built by a consortium of well-meaning postmortal aristocrats. Since their political influence hadn't succeeded in curtailing the war (and since many of their aristocratic friends were quite happy for it to continue) they'd decided to make a difference in the next-best way: by alleviating the suffering of the mortal men and women engaged in the war itself.

So they created a hospital ship, one that had no connection to either the Northern Coalition or the Southland Militia. *Nightingale* would be there for all injured soldiers, irrespective of allegiance. Aboard the neutral ship, the injured would be healed, allowed to recuperate and then repatriated. All but the most critically wounded would eventually return to active combat service. And *Nightingale* itself would be state-of-the-art, with better medical facilities than any other public hospital on or around Sky's Edge. It wouldn't be the glittering magic of Demarchist medicine, but it would still be superior to anything most mortals had ever experienced.

It would also be tirelessly efficient, dedicated only to improving its healing record. *Nightingale* was designed to operate autonomously, as a single vast machine. Under the guidance of human specialists, the ship would slowly improve its methods until it had surpassed its teachers. I'd come aboard ship when it was still undergoing the early stages of its learning curve, but – as I learned from Nicolosi – the ship had soon moved into its 'operational phase'. By then, the entire kilometre-long vehicle was under the control of only a handful of technicians and surgical specialists, with gamma-level intelligences making most of the day-to-day decisions. That was when Sollis and Nicolosi had been shipped aboard. They'd been healed by machines, with only a vague awareness that there was a watchful human presence behind the walls.

'It worked, too,' Nicolosi said. 'The ship did everything its sponsors had hoped it would. It functioned like a huge, efficient factory: sucking in the wounded, spitting out the healed.'

'Only for them to go back to the war,' I said.

'The sponsors didn't have any control over what happened when the healed were sent back down. But at least they were still alive; at least they hadn't died on the battlefield or the operating table. The sponsors could still believe that they had done something good. They could still sleep at night.'

'So *Nightingale* was a success,' I said. 'What's the problem? Wasn't it turned over to civilian use after the armistice?'

'The ship was destroyed just before the ceasefire,' Nicolosi said. 'That's why we shouldn't be seeing it now. A stray NC missile, nuke-tipped . . . too fast to be intercepted by the ship's own countermeasures. It took out *Nightingale*, with staff and patients still aboard her.'

'Now that you mention it . . . maybe I did hear about something like that.'

Sollis looked fiercely at Martinez. 'I say we renegotiate terms. You never told us we were going to have to spring Jax from a fucking ghost ship.'

Norbert moved to his master's side, as if to protect him from the furious Sollis. Martinez, who had said nothing for many minutes, removed his glasses, buffed them on his shirt and replaced them with an unhurried calm.

'Perhaps you are right to be cross with me, Ingrid. And perhaps I made a mistake in not mentioning *Nightingale* sooner. But it was imperative that I not compromise this operation with a single careless indiscretion. My whole life has been an arrow pointing to this one task: the bringing to justice of Colonel Jax. I will not fail myself now.'

'You should have told us about the hospital ship,' Nicolosi said. 'None of us would have had any reason to spread that information. We all want to see Jax get his due.'

'Then I have made a mistake, for which I apologise.'

Sollis shook her head. 'I don't think an apology's going to cut it. If I'd known I was going to have to go back aboard that . . . *thing*—'

'You are right,' Martinez said, addressing all of us. 'The ship has a traumatic association for you, and it was wrong of me not to allow for that.'

'Amen to that,' Sollis said.

I felt it was time I made a contribution. 'I don't think any of us are about to back out now, Tomas. But maybe – given what we now know about the ship – a little more incentive might go a long way.'

'I was about to make the same suggestion myself,' Martinez said. 'You must appreciate that my funds are not inexhaustible, and that my original offer might already be considered generous . . . but shall we say an extra five thousand Australs, for each of you?'

'Make it ten and maybe we're still in business,' Sollis snapped back, before I'd had a chance to blink.

Martinez glanced at Norbert, then – with an expression that suggested he was giving in under duress – he nodded at Sollis. 'Ten thousand Australs it is. You drive a hard bargain, Ingrid.'

'While we're debating terms,' Nicolosi said, 'is there anything else you feel we ought to know?'

'I have told you that the ship is *Nightingale*.' Martinez directed our attention back to the sketchy diagram on the wall. 'That, I am ashamed to admit, is the sum total of my knowledge of the ship in question.'

'What about constructional blueprints?' I asked.

'None survived the war.'

'Photographs? Video images?'

'Ditto. *Nightingale* operated in a war zone, Dexia. Casual sightseeing was not exactly a priority for those unfortunate enough to get close to her.'

'What about the staff aboard?' Nicolosi asked. 'Couldn't they tell you anything?'

'I spoke to some survivors: the doctors and technicians who'd been aboard during the commissioning phase. Their testimonies were useful, when they were willing to talk.'

Nicolosi pushed further. 'What about the people who were aboard before the ceasefire?'

'I could not trace them.'

'But they obviously didn't die. If the ship's still out there, the rogue missile couldn't have hit it.'

'Why would anyone make up a story about the ship being blown to pieces if it didn't happen?' I asked.

'War does strange things to truth,' Martinez answered. 'No malice is necessarily implied. Perhaps another hospital ship was indeed destroyed. There was more than one in orbit around Sky's Edge, after all. One of them may even have had a similar name. It's perfectly conceivable that the facts might have got muddled, in the general confusion of those days.'

'Still doesn't explain why you couldn't trace any survivors,' Nicolosi said.

Martinez shifted on his seat, uneasily. 'If Jax did appropriate the ship, then he may not have wanted anyone talking about it. The staff aboard *Nightingale* might have been paid off – or threatened – to keep silent.'

'Adds up, I guess,' I said.

'Money will make a lot of things add up,' Nicolosi replied.

After two days, the *Death of Sophonisba* sped deeper into the night, while Martinez's ship followed a pre-programmed flight plan designed to bring us within survey range of the hospital ship. The Ultras had scanned *Nightingale* again, and once again they'd elicited no detectable response from the dormant vessel. All indications were that the ship was in a deep cybernetic coma, as close to death as possible, with only a handful of critical life-support systems still running on a trickle of stored power.

Over the next twenty-four hours we crept in closer, narrowing the distance to mere light-seconds, and then down to hundreds of thousands of kilometres. Still there was no response, but as the distance narrowed, so our sensors began to improve the detail in their scans. While the rest of us took turns sleeping, Martinez sat at his console, compositing the data, enhancing his schematic. Now and then Norbert would lean over the console and stare in numb concentration at the sharpening image, and occasionally he would mumble some remark or observation to which Martinez would respond in a patient, faintly condescending whisper, the kind that a teacher might reserve for a slow but willing pupil. Not for the first time I was touched by Martinez's obvious kindness in employing the huge, slow Norbert, and I wondered what the war must have done to him to bring him to this state.

When we were ten hours from docking, Martinez revealed the fruits of his labours. The schematic of the hospital ship was three-dimensional now, displayed in the navigational projection cylinder on the ship's cramped flight deck. Although the basic layout of the ship hadn't changed, the new plan was much more detailed than the first one. It showed docking points, airlocks, major mechanical systems and the largest corridors and spaces threading the ship's interior. There was still a lot of guesswork, but it wouldn't be as if we were entering completely foreign territory.

'The biggest thermal hot spot is here,' Martinez said, pointing at an area about a quarter of the way along the vessel from the bow. 'If Jax is anywhere, that's my best guess as to where we'll find him.'

'Simple, then,' Nicolosi said. 'In via that dorsal lock, then a straight sprint down that access shaft. Easy, even under weightless conditions. Can't be more than fifty or sixty metres.'

'I'm not happy,' Sollis said. 'That's a large lock, likely to be armed to the teeth with heavy-duty sensors and alarms.'

'Can you get us through it?' Nicolosi asked.

'You give me a door, I'll get us through it. But I can't bypass every conceivable security system, and you can be damned sure the ship will know about it if we come through a main lock.'

'What about the others?' I asked, trying not to sound as if I was on her case. 'Will they be less likely to go off?'

'Nothing's guaranteed. I don't like the idea of spending a minute longer aboard that thing than necessary, but I'd still rather take my chances with the back door.'

'I think Ingrid is correct,' Martinez said, nodding his approval. 'There's every chance of a silent approach and docking. Jax will have disabled all non-essential systems, including proximity sensors. If that's the case – if we see no evidence of having tripped approach alarms – then I believe we would be best advised to maintain stealth.' He indicated further along the hull, beyond the rounded midsection bulge. 'That will mean coming in *here*, or *here*, via one of these smaller service locks. I concur with Ingrid: they probably won't be alarmed.'

'That'll give us four or five hundred metres of ship to crawl through,' Nicolosi said, leaving us in no doubt what he thought about that. 'Four or five hundred metres for which we only have a very crude map.'

'We'll have directional guidance from our suits,' Martinez said.

'It's still a concern to me. But if you've settled upon this decision, I shall abide by it.'

I turned to Sollis. 'What you said just then – about not spending a minute longer aboard *Nightingale* than we have to?'

'I wasn't kidding.'

'I know. But there was something about the way you said it. Do you know something about that ship that we don't? You sounded spooked, and I don't understand why. It's just a disused hospital, after all.'

Sollis studied me for a moment before answering. 'Tell her, Nicolosi.'

Nicolosi looked placidly at the other woman. 'Tell her what?'

'What she obviously doesn't know. What none of us are in any great hurry to talk about.'

'Oh, please.'

'"Oh please" what?' I asked.

'It's just a fairy story, a stupid myth,' Nicolosi said.

'A stupid story that nonetheless always claimed that *Nightingale* didn't get blown up after all,' Sollis said.

'What are you talking about?' I asked. 'What story?'

It was Martinez who chose to answer. 'That something unfortunate happened aboard her. That the last batch of sick and injured went in, but for some reason were never seen to leave. That all attempts to contact the technical staff failed. That an exploratory team was put aboard the ship, and that they too were never heard from again.'

I laughed. 'Fuck. And now we're planning to go aboard?'

'Now you see why I'm somewhat anxious to get this over with,' Sollis said.

'It's just a myth,' Martinez chided. 'Nothing more. It is a tale to frighten children, not to dissuade us from capturing Jax. In fact, it would not surprise me in the least if Jax or his allies were in some way responsible for this lie. If it were to cause us to turn back now, it would have served them admirably, would it not?'

'Maybe,' I said, without much conviction. 'But I'd still have been happier if you'd told me before. It wouldn't have made any difference to my accepting this job, but it would have been nice to know you trusted me.'

'I do trust you, Dexia. I simply assumed that you had no interest in childish stories.'

'How do you know Jax is aboard?' I asked.

'We've been over this. I have my sources, sources that I must protect, and it would be—'

'He was a patient, wasn't he?'

Martinez snapped his glasses from his nose, as if my point had taken an unexpected tangent from whatever we'd been talking about. 'I know only that Jax is aboard *Nightingale*. The circumstances of how he arrived there are of no concern to me.'

'And it doesn't bother you that maybe he's just dead, like whoever else was aboard at the end?' Sollis asked.

'If he is dead, you will still receive twenty-five thousand Australs.'

'Plus the extra ten we already agreed on.'

'That too,' Martinez said, as if it should have been taken for granted.

'I still don't like this,' Sollis muttered.

'I don't like it either,' Nicolosi replied, 'but we came here to do a job, and the material facts haven't changed. There is a ship, and the man we want is aboard it. What Martinez says is true: we should not be intimidated by stories, especially when our goal is so near.'

'We go in there, we get Jax, we get the hell out,' Sollis said. 'No dawdling, no sightseeing, no souvenir-hunting.'

'I have absolutely no problem with that,' I said.

'Take what you want,' Martinez called over Norbert's shoulder as we entered the armoury compartment at the rear of the shuttle's pressurised section. 'But remember: you'll be wearing pressure suits, and you'll be moving through confined spaces. You'll also be aboard a ship.'

Sollis pushed bodily ahead of me, pouncing on something that I'd only begun to notice. She unracked the sleek, cobalt-blue excimer rifle and hefted it for balance. 'Hey, a Breitenbach.'

'Christmas come early?' I asked.

Sollis pulled a pose, sighting along the rifle, deploying its targeting aids, flipping the power-up toggle. The weapon whined obligingly. Blue lights studded its stock, indicating it was ready for use.

'Because I'm worth it,' Sollis said.

'I'd really like you to point that thing somewhere else,' I said.

'Better still, don't point it anywhere,' Nicolosi rumbled. He'd seen one of the choicer items, too. He unclipped a long, matt-black weapon with a ruby-red dragon stencilled along the barrel. It had a gaping maw like a swallowing python. 'Laser-confined plasma bazooka,' he said admiringly. 'Naughty, but nice.'

'Finesse isn't your cup of tea, then.'

'Never got to use one of these in the war, Dexia.'

'That's because they were banned. One of the few sensible things both sides managed to agree on.'

'Now's my chance.'

'I think the idea is to extract Jax, not to blow ten-metre-wide holes in *Nightingale*.'

'Don't worry. I'll be very, very careful.' He slung the bazooka over his shoulder, then continued down the aisle.

I picked up a pistol, hefted it, replaced it on the rack. Found something more to my liking – a heavy, dual-gripped slug-gun – and flipped open the magazine to check that there was a full clip inside. Low-tech but reliable; the other two were welcome to their directed-energy weapons, but I'd seen how easily they could go wrong under combat conditions.

'Nice piece, Dexia,' Sollis said, patronisingly. 'Old school.'

'I'm old school.'

'Yeah, I noticed.'

'You have a problem with that, we can always try some target practice.'

'Hey, no objections. Just glad you found something to your liking. Doing better than old Norbert, anyway.' Sollis nodded over her shoulder. 'Looks like he's really drawn the short straw there.'

I looked down the aisle. Norbert was near the end of one the racks, examining a small, stubby-looking weapon whose design I didn't recognise. In his huge hands it looked ridiculous, like something made for a doll.

'You sure about that?' I called. 'Maybe you want to check out one of these—'

Norbert looked at me as if I was some kind of idiot. I don't know what he did then – there was no movement of his hand that I was aware of – but the stubby little weapon immediately unpacked itself, elongating and opening like some complicated puzzle box until it was almost twice as big, twice as deadly-looking. It had the silken, precision-engineered quality of expensive off-world tech. A Demarchist toy, probably, but a very, very deadly toy for all that.

Sollis and I exchanged a wordless glance. Norbert had found what was probably the most advanced, most effective weapon in the room.

'Will do,' Norbert said, before closing the weapon up again and slipping it into his belt.

We crept closer. Tens of thousands of kilometres, then thousands, then hundreds. I looked through the hull windows, with the interior lights turned down, peering in the direction where our radar and infrared scans told us the hospital ship was waiting. When we were down to two dozen kilometres I knew I should be seeing it, but I was still only looking at stars and the sucking blackness between them. I had a sudden, visceral sense of how easy it would be to lose something out here, followed in quick succession by a dizzying sense of how utterly small and alone we were, now that the lighthugger was gone.

And then, suddenly, there was *Nightingale*.

We were coming in at an angle, so the hull was tilted and foreshortened. It was so dark that only certain edges and surfaces were visible at all. No windows, no running lights, no lit-up docking bays. The ship looked as dark and dead as a sliver of coal. Suddenly it was absurd to think that there might be anyone alive aboard it. Colonel Jax's corpse, perhaps, but not the living or even life-supported body that would guarantee us full payment.

Martinez had the ship on manual control now. With small, deft applications of thrust he narrowed the distance down to less than a dozen kilometres. At six kilometres, Martinez deemed it safe to activate floodlights and play them along the length of the hull, confirming the placement of locks and docking sites. There was a peppering of micro-meteorite impacts and some scorching from high-energy particles, but nothing I wouldn't have expected on a ship that had been sitting out there since the armistice. If the ship possessed self-repair mechanisms, they were sleeping as well. Even when we circled around the hull and swept it from the other side, there was no hint of our having been noticed. Still reluctant, Nicolosi accepted that we would follow Sollis's entry strategy, entering via one of the smaller service locks.

It was time to do it.

We docked. We came in softly, but there was still a solid *clunk* as the capture latches engaged and grasped our little craft to the hull of the hospital ship. I thought of that *clunk* echoing away down the length of *Nightingale*, diminishing as it travelled, but potentially still significant enough to trip some waiting, infinitely patient alarm system, alerting the sleeping ship that it had a visitor. For several minutes we hung in weightless silence, staring out of the windows or watching the sensor read-outs for the least sign of activity. But the dark ship stayed dark in all directions. There was no detectable change in her state of coma.

'Nothing's happened,' Martinez said, breaking the silence with a whisper. 'It still doesn't know we're here. The lock is all yours, Ingrid. I've already opened our doors.'

Sollis, suited-up now, moved into the lock tube with her toolkit. While she worked, the rest of us finished putting on our own suits and armour, completing the exercise as quietly as possible. I hadn't worn a spacesuit before, but Norbert was there to help all of us with the unfamiliar process: his huge hands attended to delicate connections and catches with surprising dexterity. Once I had the suit on, it didn't feel much different from wearing full-spectrum bioarmour, and I quickly got the hang of the life-support indicators projected around the border of my faceplate. I would only need to pay minor attention to them: unless there was some malfunction, the suit had enough power and supplies to keep me alive in perfect comfort for three days; longer if I was prepared to tolerate a little less comfort. None of us were planning on spending anywhere near that long aboard *Nightingale*.

Sollis was nearly done when we assembled behind her in the lock. The inner and outer lock doors on our side were open, exposing the grey outer door of the hospital ship, held tight against the docking connector by pressure-tight seals. I doubted that she'd ever had to break into a ship before, but nothing about the mechanism appeared to be causing Sollis any difficulties. She'd tugged open an access panel and plugged in a fistful of coloured cables, running back to a jury-rigged electronics module in her toolkit. She was tapping a little keyboard, causing patterns of lights to alter within the access panel. The face of a woman – blank, expressionless, yet at the same time somehow severe and unforgiving – had appeared in an oval frame above the access panel.

'Who's that?' I asked.

'That's *Nightingale*,' Sollis said, adding, by way of explanation, 'The ship had its own gamma-level personality, keeping the whole show running. Pretty smart piece of thinkware by all accounts: full Turing compliance; about as clever as you can make a machine before you have to start giving it human rights.'

I looked at the stern-faced woman, expecting her to query us at any moment. I imagined her harsh and hectoring voice demanding to know what business any of us had boarding *Nightingale*, trespassing aboard *her* ship, *her* hospital.

'Does she know . . .' I started.

Sollis shook her head. 'This is just a dumb facet of the main construct. Not only is it inactive – the image is frozen into the door's memory – but it doesn't appear to have any functioning data links back to the main sentience engine. Do you, *Nightingale*?'

The face gazed at us impassively, but still said nothing.

'See: deadsville. My guess is the sentience engine isn't running at all. Out here, the ship wouldn't need much more than a trickle of intelligence to keep itself ticking over.'

'So the gamma's offline?'

'Uh-huh. Best way, too. You don't want one of those things sitting around too long without something to do.'

'Why not?'

''Cause they tend to go nuts. That's why the Conjoiners won't allow gamma-level intelligences in any of their machines. They say it's a kind of slavery.'

'Running a hospital must have been enough to stop *Nightingale*'s gamma running off the rails.'

'Let's hope so. Let's really hope so.' Sollis glanced back at her work, then emitted a grunt of satisfaction as a row of lights flicked to orange. She unplugged a bunch of coloured cables and looked back at the waiting party. 'Okay, we're good to go. I can open the door any time you're ready.'

'What's on the other side of it?' I asked.

'According to the door, air; normal trimix. Bitchingly cold, but not frozen. Pressure's manageable. I'm not sure we could *breathe* it, but—'

'We're not breathing anything,' Martinez said curtly. 'Our airlock will take two people. One of them will have to be you,

Ingrid, since you know how to work the mechanism. I shall accompany you, and then we shall wait for the others on the far side, when we have established that conditions are safe.'

'Maybe one of us should go through instead of you,' I said, wondering why Norbert hadn't volunteered to go through ahead of his master. 'We're expendable, but you aren't. Without you, Jax doesn't go down.'

'Considerate of you, Dexia, but I paid you to assist me, not take risks on my behalf.'

Martinez propelled himself forward. Norbert, Nicolosi and I edged back to permit the inner door to close again. On the common suit channel I heard Sollis say, 'We're opening *Nightingale*. Stand by: comms might get a bit weaker once we're on the other side of all this metal.'

Nicolosi pushed past me, back into the flight deck. I heard the heavy whine of servos as the door opened. Breathing and scuffling sounds followed, but nothing that alarmed me.

'Okay,' Sollis said, 'we're moving into *Nightingale*'s lock. Closing the outer door behind us. When you need to open it again, hit any key on the pad.'

'Still no sign of life,' Nicolosi called.

'The inner door looks as if it'll open without any special encouragement from me,' Sollis said. 'Should be just a matter of pulling down this lever . . . you ready?'

'Do it, Ingrid,' Martinez replied.

More servos, fainter now. After a few moments, Sollis reported back: 'We're inside. No surprises yet. Floating in some kind of holding bay, about ten metres wide. It's dark, of course. There's a doorway leading out through the far wall; might lead to the main corridor that should pass close to this lock.'

I remembered to turn on my helmet lamp.

'Can you open both lock doors?' Nicolosi asked.

'Not at the same time, not without a lot of trouble that might get us noticed.'

'Then we'll come through in two passes. Norbert: you go first. Dexia and I will follow.'

It took longer than I'd have liked, but eventually all five of us were on the other side of the lock. I'd only been weightless once, during the recuperation programme after my injury, but the memory of how to move – at least without making too much of a fool of myself – was still there, albeit dimly. The others were coping about as well. The combined effects of our helmet lamps banished the darkness to the corners of the room, emphasizing the deeper gloom of the open doorway Sollis had mentioned. It occurred to me that somewhere deep in that darkness was Colonel Jax, or whatever was left of him.

Nervously, I checked that the slug-gun was still clipped to my belt.

'Call up your helmet maps,' Martinez said. 'Does everyone have an overlay and a positional fix?'

'I'm good,' I said, against a chorus from the other three, and acutely aware of how easy it would be to get lost aboard a ship as large as *Nightingale* if that positional fix were to break down.

'Check your weapons and suit systems. We'll keep comms to a minimum all the way in.'

'I'll lead,' Nicolosi said, propelling himself into the darkness of the doorway before anyone could object.

I followed hard on his heels, trying not to get out of breath with the effort of keeping up. There were loops and rails along all four walls of the shaft, so movement consisted of gliding from one handhold to the next, with only air resistance to stop one drifting all the way. We were covering one metre a second, easily. At that rate, it wouldn't take long to cross the entire width of the ship, which would mean we'd somehow missed the axial corridor we were looking for, or that it simply didn't exist. But just when it was beginning to strike me that we'd gone too far, Nicolosi slowed. I grabbed a handhold to stop myself slamming into his feet.

He looked back at us, his helmet lamp making me squint. 'Here's the main corridor, just a bit deeper than we were expecting. Runs both ways.'

'We turn left,' Martinez said, in not much more than a whisper. 'Turn left and follow it for one hundred metres, maybe one hundred and twenty, until we meet the centrifuge section. It should be a straight crawl, with no obstructions.'

Nicolosi turned away, then looked back. 'I can't see more than twenty metres into the corridor. We may as well see where it goes.'

'Nice and slowly,' Martinez urged.

We moved forward, along the length of the hull. In the instants when I was coasting from one handhold to the next, I held my breath and tried to hear the ambient noises of the ship, relayed to my helmet by the suit's acoustic pick-up. Mostly all I heard was the scuffing progress of the others, the hiss and hum of their own life-support packs. Other than that, *Nightingale* was as silent as when we'd approached. If the ship was aware of our intrusion, there was no sign of it.

We'd made maybe forty metres from the junction – at least a third of the distance we had to travel before hitting the centrifuge – when Nicolosi slowed. I caught a handhold before I drifted into his heels, then looked back to make sure the others had got the message.

'Problem?' Martinez asked.

'There's a T-junction right ahead. I didn't think we were expecting a T-junction.'

'We weren't,' Martinez said, 'but it shouldn't surprise us that the real ship deviates from the schematic here and there. As long as we don't reach a dead end, we can still keep moving towards the colonel.'

'You want to flip a coin, or shall I do it?' Nicolosi said, looking back at us over his shoulder, his face picked out by my helmet light.

'There's no indication, no sign on the wall?'

'Blank either way.'

'In which case take the left,' Martinez said, before glancing at Norbert. 'Agreed?'

'Agreed,' the big man said. 'Take left, then next right. Continue.'

Nicolosi kicked off, and the rest of us followed. I kept an eye on my helmet's inertial compass, gratified when it detected our change of direction, even though the overlay now showed us moving through what should have been a solid wall.

We'd moved twenty or thirty metres when Nicolosi slowed again. 'Tunnel bends to the right,' he reported. 'Looks like we're back on track. Everyone cool with this?'

'Cool,' I said.

But we'd only made another fifteen or twenty metres of progress along the new course when Nicolosi slowed and called back again. 'We're coming up on a heavy door – some kind of internal airlock. Looks as if we're going to need Sollis again.'

'Let me through,' she said, and I squeezed aside so she could edge past me, trying to avoid knocking our suits together. In addition to the weapons she'd selected from the armoury, Sollis's suit was also hung with all manner of door-opening tools, clattering against each other as she moved. I didn't doubt that she'd be able to get through any kind of door, given time. But the idea of spending hours inside *Nightingale*, while we inched from one obstruction to the next, didn't exactly fill me with enthusiasm.

We let Sollis examine the door; we could hear her ruminating over the design, tutting, humming and talking softly to herself under her breath. She had panels open and equipment plugged in, just like before. The same unwelcoming face glowered from an oval display.

After a couple of minutes, Martinez sighed and asked, 'Is there a problem, Ingrid?'

'There's no problem. I can get this door open in about ten seconds. I just want to make damned sure this is another of *Nightingale*'s dumb facets. That means sensing the electrical connections on either side of the frame. Of course, if you'd rather we just stormed on through—'

'Keep voice down,' Norbert rumbled.

'I'm wearing a spacesuit, dickhead.'

'Pressure outside. Sound travel, air to glass, glass to air.'

'You have five minutes,' Martinez said, decisively. 'If you haven't found what you're looking for by then, we open the door anyway. And Norbert's right: let's keep the noise down.'

'So, no pressure then,' Sollis muttered.

But in three minutes she started unplugging her tools, and turned aside with a beaming look on her face. 'It's just an emergency airlock, in case this part of the ship depressurises.'

'But it isn't on the schematic.'

'It ain't a blueprint, Scarrow. Like the old man told us, it's just a guess. If people remembered stuff wrong, or if the ship got changed after they were abroad . . . we're going to run into discrepancies.'

'No danger that tripping it will alert the rest of *Nightingale*?' I asked.

'Can't ever say there's no risk, but I'm happy for us to go through.'

'Open the door,' Martinez said. 'Everyone brace in case there's vacuum or atmosphere under pressure on the other side.'

We followed his instructions, but when the door opened the air remained as still as before. Beyond, picked out by our wavering lights, was a short stretch of corridor terminating in an identical-looking door. This time there was enough room for all of us to squeeze through, while Sollis attended to the second lock mechanism. Some hardwired system required that the first door be closed before the second one could be opened, but that posed us no real difficulties. Now that Sollis knew what to look for, she worked much faster: good at her job and happy for us all to know it. I didn't doubt that she'd be even faster on the way out.

'We're ready to go through, people. Indications say that the air's just as cold on the other side, so keep your suits buttoned.'

I heard the click as one of us – maybe Nicolosi, maybe Norbert – released a safety catch. It was like someone coughing in a theatre. I had no choice but to reach down and arm my own weapon.

'Open it,' Martinez said quietly.

The door chugged wide. Our lights stabbed into dark emptiness beyond: a suggestion of a much deeper, wider space than I'd been expecting. Sollis leaned through the doorframe, her helmet lamp catching fleeting details from reflective surfaces. I had a momentary flash of glassy things stretching away into infinite distance, then it was gone.

'Report, Ingrid,' Martinez said.

'I think we can get through. We've come out next to a wall, or floor, or whatever it is. There are handholds, railings. Looks as if they lead on into the room, probably to the other side.'

'Stay where you are,' Nicolosi said, just ahead of me. 'I'll take point again.'

Sollis glanced back and swallowed hard. 'It's okay, I can handle this one. Can't let you have all the fun, can I?'

Nicolosi grunted something. I don't think he had much of a sense of humour. 'You're welcome to my gun, you want it.'

'I'm cool,' she said, but with audible hesitation. I didn't blame her; it was different being point on a walk through a huge dark room, compared to a narrow corridor. Nothing could leap out and grab you from the side in a corridor.

She started moving along the crawlway.

'Nice and slowly, Ingrid,' Martinez said, from behind me. 'We still have time on our side.'

'We're right behind you,' I said, feeling she needed moral support.

'I'm fine, Dexia. No problems here. Just don't want to lose my handhold and go drifting off into fuck knows what . . .'

Her movements became rhythmic, progressing into the chamber one careful handhold at a time. Nicolosi followed, with me right behind him. Apart from our movements, and the sounds of our suit systems, the ship was still as silent as a crypt.

But it wasn't totally dark any more.

Now that we were inside the chamber, it began to reveal its secrets in dim spots of pale light, reaching away into some indeterminate distance. The lights must have always been there, just too faint to notice until we were inside.

'Something's running,' Sollis said.

'We knew that,' Martinez said. 'It was always clear that the ship was dormant, not dead.'

I panned my helmet around and tried to get another look at the glassy things I'd glimpsed earlier. On either side of the railed walkway, stretching away in multiple ranks, were hundreds of transparent flasks. Each flask was the size of an oil drum, rounded on top, mounted on a steel-grey plinth equipped with controls, read-outs and input sockets. There were three levels of them, with the second and third layers stacked above the first on skeletal racks. Most of the plinths were dead, but maybe one in ten was showing a lit-up read-out.

'Oh, Jesus,' Sollis said, and I guess she'd seen what I'd just seen: that the flasks contained human organs, floating in a green chemical solution, wired up with fine nutrient lines and electrical cables. I was no anatomist, but I still recognised hearts, lungs, kidneys, snakelike coils of intestine. And there were things anyone would have recognised: things like eyeballs, dozens of them growing in a single vat, swaying on the long stalks of optic nerves like some weird species of all-seeing sea anemone; things like hands, or entire limbs, or genitals, or the skin and muscle masks of eyeless faces. Every external body part came in dozens of different sizes, ranging from child-sized to adult, male and female, and despite the green suspension fluid one could make out subtle variations in skin tone and pigmentation.

'Easy, Ingrid,' I said, the words as much for my benefit as hers. 'We always knew this was a hospital ship. It was just a matter of time before we ran into something like this.'

'This stuff . . .' Nicolosi said, his voice low. 'Where does it come from?'

'Two main sources,' Martinez answered, sounding too calm for my liking. 'Not everyone who came aboard *Nightingale* could be saved, obviously – the ship was no more capable of working miracles than any other hospital. Wherever practicable, the dead would donate intact body parts for future use. Useful, certainly, but such a resource could never have supplied the bulk of *Nightingale*'s surgical needs. For that reason the ship was also equipped to fabricate its own organ supplies, using well-established principles of stem-cell manipulation. The organ factories would have worked around the clock, keeping this library fully stocked.'

'It doesn't look fully stocked now,' I said.

Martinez said, 'We're not in a war zone any more. The ship is dormant. It has no need to maintain its usual surgical capacity.'

'So why is it maintaining any capacity? Why are some of these flasks still keeping their organs alive?'

'Waste not, want not, I suppose. A strategic reserve, against the day when the ship might be called into action again.'

'You think it's just waiting to be reactivated?'

'It's only a machine, Dexia. A machine on standby. Nothing to get nervous about.'

'No one's nervous,' I said, but it came out all wrong, making me sound as if I was the one who was spooked.

'Let's get to the other side,' Nicolosi said.

'We're halfway there,' Sollis reported. 'I can see the far wall, sort of. Looks like there's a door waiting for us.'

We kept on moving, hand over hand, mostly in silence. Surrounded by all those glass-encased body parts, I couldn't help but think of the people many of them had once been part of. If these parts had belonged to me, I think I'd have chosen to haunt *Nightingale*, consumed with ill-directed, spiteful fury.

Not the right kind of thinking, I was just telling myself, when the flasks started moving.

We all stopped, anchoring ourselves to the nearest handhold. Two or three rows back from the railed crawlway, a row of flasks was gliding smoothly towards the far wall of the chamber. They were sliding in perfect lock-step unison. When my heart started beating again, I realised that the entire row must be attached to some kind of conveyor system, hidden within the support framework.

'Nobody move,' Nicolosi said.

'This is not good,' Sollis kept saying. 'This is not good. The damn ship isn't supposed to know—'

'Quiet,' Martinez hissed. 'Let me past you. I want to see where those flasks are going.'

'Careful,' Norbert said.

Paying no attention to the man, Martinez climbed ahead of the party. Quickly we followed him, doing our best not to make any noise or slip from the crawlway. The flasks continued their smooth, silent movement until the conveyor system reached the far wall and turned through ninety degrees, taking the flasks away from us into a covered enclosure like a security scanner. Most of the flasks were empty, but as we watched, one of the occupied, active units slid into the enclosure. I'd only had a moment to notice, but I thought I'd seen a forearm and hand, reaching up from the life-support plinth.

The conveyor system halted. For a moment all was silent, then there came a series of mechanical clicks and whirrs. None of us could see what was happening inside the enclosure, but after a moment we didn't need to. It was obvious.

The conveyor began to move again, but running in reverse this time. The flask that had gone into the enclosure was now empty. I counted back to make sure I wasn't making a mistake, but there was no doubt. The forearm and hand had been removed from the flask. Already, I presumed, the limb was somewhere else in the ship.

The flasks travelled back – returning to what I presumed to have been their former positions – and then halted again. Save for the missing limb, the chamber was exactly as when we had entered it.

'I don't like this,' Sollis said. 'The ship is supposed to be dead.'

'Dormant,' Martinez corrected.

'You don't think the shit that just happened is in any way related to us being aboard? You don't think Jax just got a wake-up call?'

'If Jax were aware of our presence, we'd know it by now.'

'I don't know how you can sound so calm.'

'All that has happened, Ingrid, is that *Nightingale* has performed some trivial housekeeping duty. We have already seen that it maintains some organs in pre-surgical condition, and this is just one of its tissue libraries. It should hardly surprise us that the ship occasionally decides to move some of its stock from A to B.'

She made a small, catlike snarl of frustration – I could tell she hadn't bought any of his explanations – and pulled herself hand over hand to the door.

'Any more shit like that happens, I'm out,' she said.

'I'd think twice if I were you,' Martinez said. 'It's a hell of a long walk home.'

I caught up with Sollis and touched her on the forearm. 'I don't like it either, Ingrid, but the man's right. Jax doesn't know we're here. If he did, I think he'd do more than just move some flasks around.'

'I hope you're right, Scarrow.'

'So do I,' I said under my breath.

We continued along the main axis of the ship, following a corridor much like the one we'd been following before the organ library. It swerved and jagged, then straightened out again. According to the inertial compasses, we were still headed towards Jax, or at least the part of the ship where it appeared most likely we'd find him, alive or dead.

'What we were talking about earlier,' Sollis said, 'I mean, much earlier – about how this ship never got destroyed at the end of the war after all—'

'I think I have stated my case, Ingrid. Dwelling on myths won't bring a wanted man to justice.'

'We're looking at about a million tonnes of salvageable spacecraft here. Gotta be worth something to someone. So why didn't anyone get their hands on it after the war?'

'Because something bad happened,' Nicolosi said. 'Maybe there was some truth in the story about that boarding party coming here and not leaving.'

'Oh, please,' Martinez said.

'So who was fighting back?' I asked. 'Who stopped them taking *Nightingale*?'

Nicolosi answered me. 'The skeleton staff . . . security agents of the postmortals who financed this thing . . . maybe even the protective systems of the ship itself. If it thought it was under attack—'

'If there was some kind of firefight aboard this thing,' I asked, 'where's the damage?'

'I don't care about the damage,' Sollis cut in. 'I want to know what happened to all the bodies.'

We came to another blocked double-door airlock. Sollis got to work on it immediately, but my expectation that she would work faster now that she had already opened several doors without trouble was wrong. She kept plugging things in, checking read-outs, murmuring to herself just loud enough to carry over the voice link. *Nightingale*'s face watched us disapprovingly, looking on like the portrait of a disappointed ancestor.

'This one could be trickier,' she said. 'I'm picking up active data links, running away from the frame.'

'Meaning it could still be hooked into the nervous system?' Nicolosi asked.

'I can't rule it out.'

Nicolosi ran a hand along the smooth black barrel of his plasma weapon. 'We could double back, try a different route.'

'We're not going back,' Martinez said. 'Not now. Open the door, Ingrid: we'll take our chances and move as quickly as we can from now on.'

'You sure about this?' She had a cable pinched between her fingers. 'No going back once I plug this in.'

'Do it.'

She pushed the line in. At the same moment a shiver of animation passed across *Nightingale*'s face, the mask waking to life. The door spoke to us. Its tone was strident and metallic, but also possessed of an authoritative femininity.

'This is the Voice of *Nightingale*. You are attempting to access a secure area. Report to central administration to obtain proper clearance.'

'Shit,' Sollis said.

'You weren't expecting that?' I asked.

'I wasn't expecting an active facet. Maybe the sentience engine isn't powered down quite as far as I thought.'

'This is the Voice of *Nightingale*,' the door said again. 'You are attempting to access a secure area. Report to central administration to obtain proper clearance.'

'Can you still force it?' Nicolosi asked.

'Yeah . . . think so.' Sollis fumbled in another line, made some adjustments and stood back as the door slid open. '*Voilà*.'

The face had turned silent and masklike again, but now I really felt as if we were being watched; as if the woman's eyes seemed to be looking in all directions at once.

'You think Jax knows about us now?' I asked, as Sollis propelled herself into the holding chamber between the two sets of doors.

'I don't know. Maybe I bypassed the door in time, before it sent an alert.'

'But you can't be sure.'

'No.' She sounded wounded.

Sollis got to work on the second door, faster now, urgency overruling caution. I checked that my gun was still where I'd left it, and then made sure that the safety catch was still off. Around me, the others went through similar preparatory rituals.

Gradually it dawned on me that Sollis was taking longer than expected. She turned from the door, her equipment still hooked into its open service panel.

'Something's screwed up,' she said, before swallowing hard. 'These suits we're wearing, Tomas . . . how good are they, exactly?'

'Full-spectrum battle-hardened. Why do you ask?'

'Because the door says that the ship's flooded behind this point. It says we'll be swimming through something.'

'I see,' Martinez said.

'Oh, no,' I said, shaking my head. 'We're not doing this. We're not going underwater.'

'I can't be sure it's water, Dexia.' She tapped the read-out panel, as if I should have been able to make sense of the numbers and symbols. 'Could be anything warm and wet, really.'

Martinez shrugged within his suit. 'Could have been a containment leak . . . spillage into this part of the ship. It's nothing to worry about. Our suits will cope easily, provided we do not delay.'

I looked him hard in the faceplate, meeting his eyes, making certain he couldn't look away. 'You're sure about this? These suits aren't going to stiff on us as soon as they get wet?'

'The suits will continue to function. I am so certain that I will go first. When you hear that I am safe on the other side, you can all follow.'

'I don't like this. What if Ingrid's tools don't work under water?'

'We have no choice but to keep moving forward,' Martinez said. 'If this section of the ship is flooded, we'll run into it no matter which route we take. This is the only way.'

'Then let's do it,' I said. 'If these suits made it through the war, surely they'll get us through the next chamber.'

'It's not the suits I'm worried about,' Nicolosi said, examining his weapon again. 'No one mentioned immersion when we were in the armoury.'

I cupped a hand to my crude little slug-gun. 'I'll swap you, we make it to the other side.'

Nicolosi didn't say anything. I don't think he saw the funny side.

Two minutes later we were inside, floating weightless in the unlit gloom of the flooded room. It felt like water, but it was difficult to tell. Everything felt thick and sluggish when you were wearing a suit, even thin air. My biohazard detectors weren't registering anything, but that didn't necessarily mean the fluid was safe. The detectors were tuned to recognise a handful of toxins in common wartime use; they weren't designed to sniff out every harmful agent that had ever existed.

Martinez's voice buzzed in my helmet. 'There are no handholds or guide wires. We'll just have to swim in a straight direction, trusting to our inertial compasses. If we all stay within sight of each other, we should have no difficulties.'

'Let's get on with it,' Nicolosi said.

We started swimming as best as we could, Nicolosi leading, pushing himself forward with powerful strokes, his weapons dangling from their straps. It would have been hard and slow with just the suits to contend with, but we were all wearing armour as well. It made it difficult to see ahead; difficult to reach forward to get an effective stroke; difficult to kick our legs enough to make any useful contribution. Our helmet lamps struggled to illuminate more than ten or twenty metres in any direction, and the door by which we'd entered was soon lost behind us in gloom. I felt a constricting sense of panic: the fear that if the compasses failed we might never find our way out again.

The compasses didn't fail, though, and Nicolosi maintained his unfaltering pace. Two minutes into the swim he called, 'I see the wall. It's dead ahead of us.'

A couple of seconds later I saw it hove out of the deep-pink gloom. Any relief I might have felt was tempered by the observation that the wall appeared featureless, stretching away blankly in all illuminated directions.

'There's no door,' I said.

'Maybe we experienced some lateral drift,' Nicolosi said.

'Compass says no.'

'Then maybe the doors are offset. It doesn't matter: we'll find it by hitting the wall and spiralling out from our landing spot.'

'If there's a door.'

'If there isn't,' Nicolosi said, 'we shoot our way out.'

'Glad you've thought this through,' I said, realising that he was serious.

We drew nearer to the wall. The closer we got and the more clearly it was picked out by our lamps, the more I realised there was something not quite right about it. It was still blank – lacking any struts or panels, apertures or pieces of shipboard equipment – but it wasn't the seamless surface I'd have expected from a massive sheet of prefabricated spacecraft material. There was an unsettling texture to it, with something of the fibrous quality of cheap paper. Faint lines coursed through it, slightly darker than the rest of the wall, but not arranged according to any neat geometric pattern.

They curved and branched, and threw off fainter subsidiary lines, diminishing like the veins in a leaf.

In a nauseating flash I realised exactly what the wall was made of. When Nicolosi's palms touched the surface, it yielded like a trampoline, absorbing the momentum of his impact and then sending him back out again, until his motion was damped by the surrounding fluid.

'It's . . .' I began.

'Skin. I know. I realised just before I hit.'

I arrested my motion, but not quickly enough to avoid contact with the wall of skin. It yielded under me, stretching so much that I felt in danger of ripping my way right through. But it held, and began to trampoline me back in the direction I'd come from. Fighting a tide of revulsion, I pulled back into the liquid and floated amidst the others.

'Fuck,' Sollis said. 'This isn't right. There shouldn't be fucking *skin*—'

'Don't be alarmed,' Martinez said, wheezing between each word. 'This is just another form of organ library, like the room we already passed through. I believe the liquid we're swimming in must be a form of growth-support medium . . . something like amniotic fluid. Under wartime conditions, this whole chamber would have been full of curtains of growing skin, measured by the acre.'

Nicolosi groped for something on his belt, came up with a serrated blade that glinted nastily even in the pink fluid.

'I'm cutting through.'

'No!' Martinez barked.

Sollis, who was next to Nicolosi, took hold of his forearm. 'Easy, soldier. Got to be a better way.'

'There is,' Martinez said. 'Put the knife away, please. We can go around the skin, find its edge.'

Nicolosi still had the blade in his hand. 'I'd rather take the short cut.'

'There are nerve endings in that skin. Cut them and the monitoring apparatus will know about it. Then so will the ship.'

'Maybe the ship already knows we're here.'

'We don't take that chance.'

Reluctantly, Nicolosi returned the knife to his belt. 'I thought we'd agreed to move fast from now on,' he said.

'There's fast, and there's reckless,' Sollis said. 'You were about to cross the line.'

Martinez brushed past me, already swimming to the left. I followed him, with the others tagging on behind. After less than a minute of hard progress, a dark edge emerged into view. It was like a picture frame stretching tight the canvas of skin. Beyond the edge, only just visible, was a wall of the chamber, fretted with massive geodesic reinforcing struts.

I allowed myself a moment of ease. We were still in danger, still in about the most claustrophobic situation I could imagine, but at least now the chamber didn't seem infinitely large.

Martinez braked himself by grabbing the frame. I came to rest next to him and peered around the edge, towards what I hoped would be the wall we'd been heading towards all along. But instead of that I saw only another field of skin, stretched across another frame, separated from the first by no more than the height of a man. In the murky distance was the suggestion of a third frame, and perhaps a fourth beyond that.

'How many?' I asked as the others arrived on the frame, perching like crows.

'I don't know,' Martinez said. 'Four, five . . . anything up to a dozen, I'd guess. But it's okay. We can swim around the frames, then turn right and head back to where we'd expect to find the exit door.' He raised his voice. 'Everyone all right? No problems with your suits?'

'There are lights,' Nicolosi said quietly.

We turned to look at him.

'I mean over there,' he added, nodding in the direction of the other sheets of skin. 'I saw a flicker of something . . . a glow in the water, or amniotic fluid, or whatever the fuck this is.'

'I see light, too,' Norbert said.

I looked down and saw that he was right – Nicolosi had not been imagining it. A pale, trembling light was emerging from between the next two layers of skin.

'Whatever that is, I don't like it,' I said.

'Me neither,' Martinez said. 'But if it's something going on between the skin layers, it doesn't have to concern us. We swim around, avoid them completely.'

He kicked off with surprising determination, and I followed quickly after him. The reverse side of the skin sheet was a fine mesh of pale support fibres, the structural matrix upon which the skin must have been grown and nourished. Thick black cables ran across the underside, arranged in circuitlike patterns.

The second sheet, the one immediately behind the first, was of different pigmentation from the one behind it. In all other respects it appeared similar, stretching unbroken into pink haze. The flickering, trembling light source was visible through the flesh, silhouetting the veins and arteries at the moments when the light was brightest.

We passed around the second sheet and peered into the gap between the second and third layers. Picked out in stuttering light was a tableau of furtive activity. Four squidlike robots were at work. Each machine consisted of a tapering, cone-shaped body, anchored to the skin by a cluster of whiplike arms emerging from the blunt end of the cone. The robots were engaged in precise surgery, removing a blanket-sized rectangle of skin by cutting it free along four sides. The robots generated their own illumination, shining from the ends of some of their arms, but the bright flashing light was coming from some kind of laserlike tool that each robot deployed on the end of a single segmented arm that was thicker than any of the others. I couldn't tell whether the flashes were part of the cutting, or the instant healing that appeared to be taking place immediately afterwards. There was no bleeding, and the surrounding skin appeared unaffected.

'What are they doing?' I breathed.

'Harvesting,' Martinez answered. 'What does it look like?'

'I know they're harvesting. I mean, *why* are they doing it? What do they need that skin for?'

'I don't know.'

'You had plenty of answers in the organ library, Mister Martinez,' Sollis said. All five of us had slowed, hovering at the same level as the surgical robots. 'For a ship that's supposed to be dormant . . . I'm not seeing much fucking evidence of dormancy.'

'*Nightingale* grows skin here,' I said. 'I can deal with that. The ship's keeping a basic supply going, in case it's called into another war. But that doesn't explain why it needs to harvest some *now*.'

Martinez sounded vague. 'Maybe it's testing the skin . . . making sure it's developing according to plan.'

'You'd think a little sample would be enough for that,' I said. 'A lot less than several square metres, for sure. That's enough skin to cover a whole person.'

'I really wish you hadn't said that,' Nicolosi said.

'Let's keep moving,' Martinez said. And he was right, too, I thought: the activity of the robots was deeply unsettling, but we hadn't come here to sightsee.

As we swam away – with no sign that the robots had noticed us – I thought about what Ingrid Sollis had said before. About how it wasn't clever to leave a gamma-level intelligence up and running without something to occupy itself. Because otherwise – since duty was so deeply hardwired into their logic pathways – they tended to go slowly, quietly, irrevocably insane.

And *Nightingale* had been alone out there since the end of the war. What did that mean for its controlling mind? Was the hospital running itself out there – reliving the duties of its former life, no matter how pointless they had become – because the mind had already gone mad, or was this the hospital's last-ditch way of keeping itself sane?

And what, I wondered, did any of that have to do with the man we had come here to find in the first place?

We kept swimming, passing layer upon layer of skin. Now and then we'd come across another surgical party, another group of robots engaged in skin-harvesting. Where they'd already completed their task, the flesh had been excised in neat rectangles and strips, exposing the gauzelike mesh of the growth matrix. Occasionally I saw a patch that was half-healed already, the skin growing back in rice-paper translucence. By the time it was fully repaired, I doubted that there'd be any sign of where the skin had been cut.

Ten layers, then twelve – and then finally the wall I'd been waiting for hove into view like a mirage. But I wasn't imagining it, or seeing another layer of drum-tight skin. There was the same pattern of geodesic struts as I'd seen on the other wall.

Sollis's voice came through. 'Got a visual on the door, people. We're nearly out of here. I'm swimming ahead to start work.'

'Good, Ingrid,' Martinez called back.

A few seconds later I saw the airlock for myself, relieved that Sollis hadn't been mistaken. She swam quickly, then – even as she was gliding to a halt by the door – commenced unclipping tools and connectors from her belt. Through the darkening distance of the pink haze I watched her flip down the service panel and begin her usual systems-bypass procedure. I was glad Martinez had found Sollis. Whatever else one might say about her, she was pretty hot at getting through doors.

'Okay, good news,' she said after a minute of plugging things in and out. 'There's air on the other side. We're not going to have to swim in this stuff for much longer.'

'How much longer?' Nicolósi asked.

'Can't risk a short circuit here, guy. Gotta take things one step at a time.'

Just as she was saying that, I became aware that we were casting shadows against the wall – shadows we hadn't been casting when we arrived. I twisted around and looked back the way we'd just swum, in the direction of the new light source I knew had to be there. Four of the squidlike machines were approaching us, dragging a blanket of newly harvested skin between them, one robot grasping each corner between two segmented silver tentacles. They were moving faster than we could swim, driven by some propulsion system jetting fluid from the sharp ends of their coneshaped bodies.

Sollis jerked back as the outer airlock door opened suddenly.

'I didn't . . .' she started.

'I know,' I said urgently. 'The robots are coming. They must have sent a command to open the lock.'

'Let's get out of the way,' Martinez said, kicking off from the wall. 'Ingrid – get away from the lock. Take what you can, but make it snappy.'

Sollis started unplugging her equipment, stowing it on her belt with fumbling fingers. The machines powered nearer, the blanket of skin undulating between them like a flying carpet. They slowed, then halted, their lights pushing spears of harsh illumination through the fluid. They were looking at us, wondering what we were doing between them and the door. One of the machines directed its beam towards Martinez's swimming figure, attracted by the movement. Martinez slowed and hung frozen in the glare, like a moth pinned in a beam of sunlight.

None of us said a word. My own breathing was the loudest sound in the universe, but I couldn't make it any quieter. Silently, the airlock door closed itself again, as if the robots had detected our presence and decided to bar our exit from the flooded chamber.

One of the machines let go of its corner of the skin. It hovered by the sheet for a moment, as if weighing its options. Then it singled me out and commenced its approach. As it neared, the machine appeared far larger and more threatening than I'd expected. Its cone-shaped body was as long as me; its thickest tentacle appearing powerful enough to do serious damage even without the additional weapon of the laser. When it spread its arms wide, as if to embrace me, I had to fight not to panic and back away.

The robot started examining me. It began with my helmet, tap-tapping and scraping, shining its light through my visor. It applied twisting force, trying to disengage the helmet from the neck coupling. Whether it recognised me as a person or just a piece of unidentifiable floating debris, it appeared to think that dismantling was the best course of action. I told myself that I'd let it work at me for another few seconds, but as soon as I felt the helmet begin to loosen I'd have to act . . . even if that meant alerting the robot that I probably wasn't debris.

But just when I'd decided I had to move, the robot abandoned my helmet and worked its way south. It extended a pair of tentacles under my chest armour from each side, trying to lever it away like a huge scab. Somehow I kept my nerve, daring to believe that the robot would sooner or later lose interest in me. Then it pulled away from the chest armour and started fiddling with my weapon, tap-tapping away like a spirit in a seance. It tugged on the gun, trying to unclip it. Then, as abruptly as it had started, the robot abandoned its investigation. It pulled away, gathering its tentacles into a fist-like bunch. Then it moved slowly in the direction of Nicolosi, tentacles groping ahead of it.

I willed him to stay still. There'd be no point in trying to swim away. None of us could move faster than those robots. Nicolosi must have worked that out for himself, or else he was paralysed with fright, but he made no movements as the robot cruised up to him. It slowed, the spread of its tentacles widening, and then tracked its spotlight from head to toe, as if it still couldn't decide what Nicolosi was. Then it reached out a pair of manipulators and brushed their sharp-looking tips against his helmet. The machine probed and examined with surprising gentleness. I heard the metal-on-metal scrape through the voice link, backgrounded by Nicolosi's rapid, sawlike breathing.

Keep it together . . .

The machine reached his neck, examined the interface between helmet and torso assembly and then worked its way down to his chest armour, extending a fine tentacle under the armour itself, to where the vulnerable life-support module lay concealed. Then, very slowly, it withdrew the tentacle.

The machine pulled back from Nicolosi, turning its blunt end away, apparently finished with its examination. The other three robots hovered watchfully with their prize of skin. Nicolosi sighed and eased his breathing.

'I think . . .' he whispered.

That was his big mistake. The machine righted itself, gathered its tentacles back into formation and began to approach him again, its powerful light sweeping up and down his body with renewed purpose. The second machine was nearing, clearly intent on assisting its partner in the examination of Nicolosi.

I looked at Sollis, our horrified gazes locking. 'Can you get the door—' I started.

'Not a hope in hell.'

'Nicolosi,' I said, not bothering to whisper this time, 'stay still and maybe they'll go away again.'

But he wasn't going to stay still; not this time. Even as I watched, he was hooking a hand around the plasma rifle, swinging it in front of him like a harpoon, its wide maw directed at the nearest machine.

'No!' Norbert shouted, his voice booming through the water like a depth charge. 'Do not use! Not in here!'

But Nicolosi was beyond reasoned argument now. He had a weapon. Every cell in his body was screaming at him to use it.

So he did.

In one sense, it did all that he asked of it. The plasma discharge speared the robot like a sunbeam through a cloud. The robot came apart in a boiling eruption of steam and fire, jagged black pieces riding the shock wave. Then the steam – the vaporised amniotic fluid – swallowed everything, including Nicolosi and his gun. Even inside my suit, the sound hit me like a hammer blow. He fired once more, as if to make certain that he had destroyed the robot. By then the second machine was near enough to be flung back by the blast, but it quickly righted itself and continued its progress towards him.

'More,' Norbert said, and when I looked back towards the stack of skin sheets, I saw what he meant. Robots were arriving in ones and twos, abandoning their cutting work to investigate whatever had just happened.

'We're in trouble,' I said.

The steam cloud was breaking up, revealing the floating form of Nicolosi, the ruined stump of his weapon drifting away from him. The second time he fired it, something must have gone badly wrong with the plasma rifle. I wasn't even sure that Nicolosi was still alive.

'I take door,' Norbert said, drawing his Demarchist weapon. 'You take robots.'

'You're going to shoot us a way out, after what just happened to Nicolosi?' I asked.

'No choice,' he said as the gun unpacked itself in his hand.

Martinez pushed himself across to the big man. 'No. Give it to me instead. I'll take care of the door.'

'Too dangerous,' Norbert said.

'Give it to me.'

Norbert hesitated, and for a moment I thought he was going to put up a fight. Then he calmly passed the Demarchist weapon to Martinez and accepted Martinez's weapon in return, the little slug-gun vanishing into his vast gauntleted hand. Whatever respect I'd had for Norbert vanished at the same time. If he was supposed to be protecting Martinez, that was no way to go about it.

Of the three of us, only Norbert and I were carrying projectile weapons. I unclipped my second pistol and passed it to Sollis. She took it gratefully, needing little persuasion to keep her energy weapon glued to her belt. The robots were easy to kill, provided we let them get close enough for a clean shot. I didn't doubt that the surgical cutting gear was capable of inflicting harm, but we never gave them the opportunity to touch us. Not that the machines appeared to have deliberately hostile designs on us anyway. They were still behaving as if they were investigating some shipboard malfunction that required remedial action. They might have killed us, but it would only have been because they did not understand what we were.

We didn't have an inexhaustible supply of slugs, though, and manual reloading was not an option underwater. Just when I began to worry that we'd be overwhelmed by sheer numbers, Martinez's voice boomed through my helmet.

'I'm ready to shoot now. Follow me as soon as I'm through the second door.'

The Demarchist weapon discharged, lighting up the entire chamber in an eyeblink of murky detail. There was another discharge, then a third.

'Martinez,' I said. 'Speak to me.'

After too long a delay, he came through. 'I'm still here. Through the first door. Weapon's cycling . . .'

More robots were swarming above us, tentacles lashing like whips. I wondered how long it would take before signals reached *Nightingale*'s sentience engine and the ship realised that it was dealing with more than just a local malfunction.

'Why doesn't he shoot?' Sollis asked, squeezing off one controlled slug after another.

'Sporting weapon. Three shots, recharge cycle, three shots,' Norbert said, by way of explanation. 'No rapid-fire mode. But work good underwater.'

'We could use those next three shots,' I said.

Martinez buzzed in my ear. 'Ready. I will discharge until the weapon is dry. I suggest you start swimming now.'

I looked at Nicolosi's drifting form, which was still as inert as when he had emerged from the steam cloud caused by his own weapon. 'I think he's dead,' I said softly, 'but we should still—'

'No,' Norbert said, almost angrily. 'Leave him.'

'Maybe he's just unconscious.'

Martinez fired three times; three brief, bright strobe flashes. 'Through!' I heard him call, but there was something wrong with his voice. I knew then that he'd been hurt as well, although I couldn't guess how badly.

Norbert and Sollis fired two last shots at the robots that were still approaching, then kicked past me in the direction of the airlock. I looked at Nicolosi's drifting form, knowing that I'd never be able to live with myself if I didn't try to get him out of there. I clipped my gun back to my belt and started swimming for him.

'No!' Norbert shouted again, when he'd seen my intentions. 'Leave him! Too late!'

I reached Nicolosi and locked my right arm around his neck, pulling his head against my chest. I kicked for all I was worth, trying to pull myself forward with my free arm. I still couldn't tell if Nicolosi was dead or alive.

'Leave him, Scarrow! Too late!'

'I can't leave him!' I shouted back, my voice ragged.

Three robots were bearing down on me and my cargo, their tentacles groping ahead of them. I squinted against the glare from their lights and tried to focus on getting the two of us to safety. Every kick of my legs, every awkward swing of my arm, seemed to tap the last drop of energy in my muscles. Finally I had nothing more to give.

I loosened my arm. His body corkscrewed slowly around, and through his visor I saw his face: pale, sweat-beaded, locked into a rictus of fear, but not dead, nor even unconscious. His eyes were wide open. He knew exactly what was going to happen when I let him go.

I had no choice.

A strong arm hooked itself under my helmet and began to tug me out of harm's way. I watched as Nicolosi drifted towards the robots, and then closed my eyes as they wrapped their tentacles around his body and started probing him for points of weakness, like children trying to tear the wrapping from a present.

Norbert's voice boomed through the water. 'He's dead.'

'He was alive. I saw it.'

'He's dead. End of story.'

I pulled myself through a curtain of trembling pink water. Air pressure in the corridor contained the amniotic fluid, even though Martinez had blown a man-sized hole in each airlock door. Ruptured metal folded back in jagged black petals. Ahead, caught in a moving pool of light from their helmet lamps, Sollis and Martinez made awkward, crabwise progress away from the ruined door. Sollis was supporting Martinez, doing most of the work for him. Even in zero gravity, it took effort to haul another body.

'Help her,' Norbert said faintly, shaking his weapon to loosen the last of the pink bubbles from its metal outer casing. Without waiting for a reaction from me, he turned and started shooting back into the water, dealing with the remaining robots.

I caught up with Sollis and took some of her burden. All along the corridor, panels were flashing bright red, synchronised with the banshee wail of an emergency siren. About once every ten metres, the ship's persona spoke from the wall, multiple voices blurring into an agitated chorus. 'Attention. Attention,' the faces said. 'This is the Voice of *Nightingale.* An incident has been detected in Culture Bay Three. Damage assessment and mitigation systems have now been tasked. Partial evacuation of the affected ship area may be necessary. Please stand by for further instructions. Attention. Attention . . .'

'What's up with Martinez?'

'Took some shrapnel when he put a hole in that door.' She indicated a severe dent in his chest armour, to the left of the sternum. 'Didn't puncture the suit, but I'm pretty sure it did some damage. Broken rib, maybe even a collapsed lung. He was talking for a while back there, but he's out cold now.'

'Without Martinez, we don't have a mission.'

'I didn't say he was dead. His suit still looks as if it's ticking over. Maybe we could leave him here, collect him on the way back.'

'With all those robots crawling about the place? How long do you think they'd leave him alone?'

I looked back, checking on Norbert. He was firing less frequently now, dealing with the last few stragglers still intent on investigating the damage. Finally he stopped, loaded a fresh clip into his slug-gun, and then after waiting for ten or twenty seconds turned from the wall of water. He began to make his way towards us.

'Maybe there aren't going to be any more robots.'

'There will,' Norbert said, joining us. 'Many more. Nowhere safe, now. Ship on full alert. *Nightingale* coming alive.'

'Maybe we should scrub,' I said. 'We've lost Nicolosi . . . Martinez is incapacitated . . . we're no longer at anything like necessary strength to take down Jax.'

'We still take Jax,' Norbert said. 'Came for him, leave with him.'

'What about Martinez?'

He looked at the injured man, his face set like a granite carving. 'He stay,' he said.

'But you already said that the robots—'

'No other choice. He stay.' And then Norbert brought himself closer to Martinez and tucked a thick finger under the chin of the old man's helmet, tilting the faceplate up. 'Wake!' he bellowed.

When there was no response, Norbert reached behind Martinez's chest armour and found the release buckles. He passed the dented plate to me, then slid down the access panel on the front of Martinez's tabard pack, itself dented and cracked from the shrapnel impact. He scooped out a fistful of pink water, flinging the bubble away from us, then started making manual adjustments to the suit's life-support settings. Biomedical data patterns shifted, accompanied by warning flashes in red.

'What are you doing?' I breathed. When he didn't appear to hear me, I shouted the question again.

'He need stay awake. This help.'

Martinez coughed red sputum onto the inside of his face-plate. He gulped in hard, then made rapid eye contact with the three of us. Norbert pushed the loaded slug-gun into Martinez's hand, then slipped a fresh ammo clip onto the old man's belt. He pointed down the corridor, to the blasted door, then indicated the direction we'd all be heading when we abandoned Martinez.

'We come back,' he said. 'You stay alive.'

Sollis's teeth flashed behind her faceplate. 'This isn't right. We should be carrying him . . . anything other than just leaving him here.'

'Tell them,' Martinez wheezed.

'No,' Norbert said.

'Tell them, you fool! They'll never trust you unless you tell them.'

'Tell them what?' I asked.

Norbert looked at me with heavy-lidded eyes. 'The old man . . . not Martinez. His name . . . Quinlan.'

'Then who the fuck is Martinez?' Sollis asked.

'I,' Norbert said.

I glanced at Sollis, then back at the big man. 'Don't be silly,' I said gently, wondering what must have happened to him in the flooded chamber.

'I am Quinlan,' the old man said, between racking coughs. 'He was always the master. I was just the servant, the decoy.'

'You're both insane,' Sollis said.

'This is the truth. I acted the role of Martinez . . . deflected attention from him.'

'He can't be Martinez,' Sollis said. 'Sorry, Norbert, but you can barely put a sentence together, let alone a prosecution dossier.'

Norbert tapped a huge finger against the side of his helmet. 'Damage to speech centre, in war. Comprehension . . . memory . . . analytic faculties . . . intact.'

'He's telling the truth,' the old man said. 'He's the one who needs to survive, not me. He's the one who can nail Jax.' Then he tapped the gun against the big man's leg, urging him to leave. 'Go,' he said, barking out that one word as if it was the last thing he expected to say. And at almost the same moment, I saw one of the tentacled robots begin to poke its limbs through the curtain of water, tick-ticking the tips of its arms against the blasted metal, searching for a way into the corridor.

'Think the man has a point,' Sollis said.

It didn't get any easier after that.

We left the old man – I still couldn't think of him as 'Quinlan' – slumped against the corridor wall, the barrel of his gun wavering in the rough direction of the ruined airlock. I looked back all the while, willing him to make the best use of the limited number of shots he had left. We were halfway to the next airlock when he squeezed off three rapid rounds, blasting the robot into twitching pieces. It wasn't long before another set of tentacles began to probe the gap. I wondered how many of the damned things the ship was going to keep throwing at us, and how that number stacked up against the slugs the old man had left.

The flashing red lights ran all the way to the end of the corridor. I was just looking at the door, wondering how easy it was going to be for Sollis to crack, when Norbert/Martinez brought the three of us to a halt, braking my forward momentum with one treelike forearm.

'Blast visor down, Scarrow.'

I understood what he had in mind. No more sweet-talking the doors until they opened for us. From now on we'd be shooting our way through *Nightingale*.

Norbert/Martinez aimed the Demarchist weapon at the airlock. I cuffed down my blast visor. Three discharges took out the first airlock door, crumpling it inward as if punched by a giant fist.

'Air on other side,' Norbert/Martinez said.

The Demarchist gun was soon ready again. Through the visor's near-opaque screen I saw three more flashes. When I flipped it back up, the weapon was packing itself back into its stowed configuration. Sollis patted aside smoke and airborne debris. The emergency lights were still flashing in our section of corridor, but the space beyond the airlock was as pitch dark as any part of the ship we'd already traversed. Yet we'd barely taken a step into that darkness when wall facets lit up in swift sequence, with the face of *Nightingale* looking at us from all directions.

Something was definitely wrong now. The faces really were looking at us, even though the facets were flat. The images turned slowly as we advanced along the corridor.

'This is the Voice of *Nightingale*,' the faces said simultaneously, as if we were being serenaded by a perfectly synchronised choir. 'I am now addressing a moving party of three individuals. My systems have determined with a high statistical likelihood that this party is responsible for the damage I have recently sustained. The damage is containable, but I cannot tolerate any deeper intrusion. Please remain stationary and await escort to a safe holding area.'

Sollis slowed, but she didn't stop. 'Who's speaking? Are we being addressed by the sentience engine, or just a delta-level subsidiary?'

'This is the Voice of *Nightingale*. I am a Turing-compliant gamma-level intelligence of the Vaaler-Lako series. Please stop and await escort to a safe holding area.'

'That's the sentience engine,' Sollis said quietly. 'It means we're getting the ship's full attention now.'

'Maybe we can talk it into handing over Jax.'

'I don't know. Negotiating with this thing might be tricky. Vaaler-Lakos were supposed to be the hot new thing around the time *Nightingale* was put together, but they didn't quite work out that way.'

'What happened?'

'There was a flaw in their architecture. Within a few years of start-up, most of them had gone bugfuck insane. I don't even want to think about what being stuck out here's done to this one.'

'Please stop,' the voice said again, 'and await escort to a safe holding area. This is your final warning.'

'Ask it . . .' Norbert/Martinez said. 'Speak for me.'

'Can you hear me, ship?' Sollis asked. 'We're not here to do any harm. We're sorry about the damage we've already caused. We've come for someone . . . there's a man here, a man aboard you, that we'd really like to meet.'

The ship said nothing for several moments. Just when I'd concluded that it didn't understand us, it said, 'This facility is no longer operational. There is no one here for you to see. Please await escort to a safe holding area, from where you can be referred to a functioning facility.'

'We've come for Colonel Jax,' I said. 'Check your patient records.'

'Admission code Tango Tango six one three, hyphen five,' said Norbert/Martinez, forcing each word out like an expression of pain. 'Colonel Brandon Jax, Northern Coalition.'

'Do you have a record of that admission?' I asked.

'Yes,' the Voice of *Nightingale* replied. 'I have a record for Colonel Jax.'

'Do you have a discharge record?'

'No such record is on file.'

'Then Jax either died in your care, or he's still aboard. Either way there'll be a body. We'd really like to see it.'

'That is not possible. You will stop now. An escort is on its way to escort you to a safe holding area.'

'Why can't we see Jax?' Sollis demanded. 'Is he telling you we can't see him? If so, he's not the man you should be listening to. He's a war criminal, a murderous bastard who deserves to die.'

'Colonel Jax is under the care of this facility. He is still receiving treatment. It is not possible to visit him at this time.'

'Damn thing's changing its story,' I said. 'A minute ago it said the facility was closed.'

'We just want to talk to him,' Sollis said, 'that's all. Just to tell him that the world knows where he is, even if you don't let us take him with us now.'

'Please remain calm. The escort is about to arrive.'

The facets turned to look away from us, peering into the dark limits of the corridor. There was a sudden bustle of approaching movement, and then a wall of machines came squirming towards us. Dozens of squid-robots were nearing, packed so tightly together that their tentacles formed a flailing mass of silver-blue metal. I looked back the other way, back the way we'd come, and saw another wave of robots coming from that direction. There were far more machines than we'd seen before, and their movements in dry air were at least as fast and fluid as they'd been underwater.

'Ship,' Sollis said, 'all we want is Jax. We're prepared to fight for him. That'll mean more damage being inflicted on you. But if you give us Jax, we'll leave nicely.'

'I don't think it wants to bargain,' I said, raising my slug-gun at the advancing wall just as it reached the ruined airlock. I squeezed off rounds, taking out at least one robot with each slug. Sollis started pitching in to my left, while Norbert/Martinez took care of the other direction with the Demarchist weapon. He could do a lot more damage with each discharge, taking out three or four machines every time he squeezed the trigger. But he kept having to wait for the weapon to re-arm itself, and the delay was allowing the wall of hostiles to creep slowly forwards. Sollis and I were firing almost constantly, taking turns to cover each other while we slipped in new slug clips or ammo cells, but our wall was gaining on us as well. No matter how many robots we destroyed, no gap ever appeared in the advancing wave. There must have been hundreds of them, squeezing us in from both directions.

'We're not going to make it,' I said, sounding resigned even to myself. 'There's too many of them. Maybe if we still had Nicolosi's rifle, we could shoot our way out.'

'I didn't come all this way just to surrender to a haunted hospital,' Sollis said, replacing an ammo cell in her energy weapon. 'If it means going out fighting . . . so be it.'

The nearest robots were now only six or seven metres away, the tips of their tentacles probing even nearer. She kept pumping shots into them, but they kept coming closer, flinging aside the hot debris of their damaged companions. There was no possibility of falling back any further, for we were almost back to back with Norbert/Martinez.

'Maybe we should just stop,' I said. 'This is a hospital. It's programmed to heal people. The last thing it'll want to do is hurt us.'

'Feel free to put that to the test,' Sollis said.

Norbert/Martinez squeezed off the last discharge before his weapon went back into recharge mode. Sollis was still firing. I reached over and tried to pass Norbert/Martinez my gun, so he'd at least have something to use while waiting for his weapon to power up. But the machines had already seen their moment. The closest one flicked out a tentacle and wrapped it around the big man's foot. Everything happened very quickly, then. The machine hauled Norbert/Martinez towards the flailing mass until he fell within reach of another set of tentacles. They had him, then. He cartwheeled his arms, trying to reach for handholds on the walls, but there was no possibility of that. The robots flicked the Demarchist weapon from his grip and then took the weapon with them. Norbert/Martinez screamed as his legs, and then his upper body, vanished into the wall of machines. They smothered him completely. For a moment we could still hear his breathing – he'd stopped screaming, as if knowing it would make no difference – and then there was absolute silence, as if the carrier signal from his suit had been abruptly terminated.

Then, a moment later, the machines were on Sollis and me.

I woke. The fact that I was still alive – not just alive but comfortable and lucid – hit me like a mild electric shock, one that snapped me into instant and slightly resentful alertness. I'd been enjoying unconsciousness. I remembered the robots, how

I'd felt them trying to get into my suit, the sharp cold nick as something pierced my skin, and then an instant later the painless bliss of sleep. I'd expected to die, but as the drug hit my brain, it erased all trace of fear.

But I wasn't dead. I wasn't even injured, so far as I could tell. I'd been divested of my suit, but was now reclining in relative comfort on a bed or mattress, under a clean white sheet. My own weight was pressing me down onto the mattress, so I must have been moved into the ship's reactivated centrifuge section. I felt tired and bruised, but other than that I was in no worse shape than when we'd boarded *Nightingale.* I remembered what I'd told Sollis during our last stand: how the hospital ship wouldn't want to do us harm. Maybe there'd been more than just wishful thinking in that statement.

There was no sign of Sollis or Norbert/Martinez, though. I was alone in a private recovery cubicle, surrounded by white walls. I remembered coming around in a room like this during my first visit to *Nightingale.* The wall on my right contained a white-rimmed door and a series of discrete hatches, behind which I knew lurked medical monitoring and resuscitation equipment, none of which had been deemed necessary in my case. A control panel was connected to the side of the bed by a flexible stalk, within easy reach of my right hand. Via the touchpads on the panel I was able to adjust the cubicle's environmental settings and request services from the hospital, ranging from food and drink, washing and toilet amenities, to additional drug dosages.

Given the semi-dormant state of the ship, I wondered how much of it was still online. I touched one of the pads, causing the white walls to melt away and take on the holographic semblance of a calming beach scene, with ocean breakers crashing onto powdery white sand under a sky etched with sunset fire. Palm trees nodded in a soothing breeze. I didn't care about the view, though. I wanted something to drink – my throat was raw – and then I wanted to know what had happened to the others and how long we were going to be detained. Because, like it or not, being a patient aboard a facility like *Nightingale* wasn't very different from being a prisoner. Until the hospital deemed you fit and well, you were going nowhere.

But when I touched the other pads, nothing happened. Either the room was malfunctioning, or it had been programmed to ignore my requests. I made a move to ease myself off the bed, wincing as my bruised limbs registered their disapproval. But the clean white sheet stiffened to resist my efforts, hardening until it felt as rigid as armour. As soon as I relaxed, the sheet relinquished its hold. I was free to move around on the bed, to sit up and reach for things, but the sheet would not allow me to leave the bed itself.

Movement caught my eye, far beyond the foot of the bed. A figure walked towards me, strolling along the holographic shoreline. She was dressed almost entirely in black, with a skirt that reached all the way to the sand, heavy fabric barely moving as she approached. She wore a white bonnet over black hair parted exactly in the middle, a white collar and a jewelled clasp at her throat. Her face was instantly recognisable as the Voice of *Nightingale*, but now it appeared softer, more human.

She stepped from the wall and appeared to stand at the foot of my bed. She looked at me for a moment before speaking, her expression one of gentle concern.

'I knew you'd come, given time.'

'How are the others? Are they okay?'

'If you are speaking of the two who were with you before you lost consciousness, they are both well. The other two required more serious medical intervention, but they are now both stable.'

'I thought Nicolosi and Quinlan were dead.'

'Then you underestimated my abilities. I am only sorry that they came to harm. Despite my best efforts, there is a necessary degree of autonomy amongst my machines that sometimes results in them acting foolishly.'

There was a kindness there that had been entirely absent from the display facets. For the first time I had the impression of an actual mind lurking behind the machine-generated mask. I sensed that it was a mind capable of compassion and complexity of thought.

'We didn't intend to hurt you,' I said. 'I'm sorry about any damage we caused, but we only ever wanted Jax, your patient. He committed serious crimes. He needs to be brought back to Sky's Edge, to face justice.'

'Is that why you risked so much? In the interests of justice?'

'Yes,' I answered.

'Then you must be very brave and selfless. Or was justice only part of your motivation?'

'Jax is a bad man. All you have to do is hand him over.'

'I cannot let you take Jax. He remains my patient.'

I shook my head. 'He *was* your patient, when he came aboard. But that was during the war. We have a record of his injuries. They were serious, but not life-threatening. Given your resources, it shouldn't have been too difficult for you to put him back together again. There's no question of Jax still needing your care.'

'Shouldn't I be the judge of that?'

'No. It's simple: either Jax died under your care, or he's well enough to face trial. Did he die?'

'No. His injuries were, as you note, not life-threatening.'

'Then he's either alive, or you've got him frozen. Either way, you can hand him over. Nicolosi knows how to thaw him out, if that's what you're worried about.'

'There is no need to thaw Colonel Jax. He is alive and conscious, except when I permit him to sleep.'

'Then there's even less reason not to hand him over.'

'I'm afraid there is every reason in the world. Please forget about Colonel Jax. I will not relinquish him from my care.'

'Not good enough, ship.'

'You are in my care now. As you have already discovered, I will not permit you to leave against my will. But I will allow you to depart if you renounce your intentions concerning Colonel Jax.'

'You're a gamma-level persona,' I said. 'To all intents and purposes you have human intelligence. That means you're capable of reasoned negotiation.'

The Voice of *Nightingale* cocked her head, as if listening to a faraway tune. 'Continue.'

'We came to arrest Colonel Jax. Failing that, we came to find physical proof of his presence aboard this facility. A blood sample, a tissue scraping: something we can take back to the planetary authorities and alert them to his presence here. We won't get paid as much for that, but at least they can send out a heavier ship and take him by force. But there's another option, too. If you let us off this ship without even showing us the colonel, there's nothing to stop us planting a few limpet mines on your hull and blowing you to pieces.'

The Voice's face registered disapproval. 'So now you resort to threats of physical violence.'

'I'm not threatening anything, just pointing out the options. I know you care about self-preservation; it's wired deep into your architecture.'

'I would be well advised to kill you now, in that case.'

'That wouldn't work. Do you think Martinez kept your co-ordinates to himself? He always knew this was a risky extraction. He'd have made damn sure another party knew of your whereabouts, and who you were likely to be sheltering. If we don't make it back, someone will come in our place. And you can bet they'll bring their own limpet mines as well.'

'In which case I would gain nothing by letting you go, either.'

'No, you'll get to stay alive. Just give us Jax, and we'll leave you alone. I don't know what you're doing out here, what keeps you sane, but really, it's your business, not ours. We just want the colonel.'

The ship's persona regarded me with narrowed, playful eyes. I had the impression she was thinking things through very carefully indeed, examining my proposition from every conceivable angle.

'It would be that simple?'

'Absolutely. We take the man, we say goodbye and you never hear from us again.'

'I've invested a lot of time and energy in the colonel. I would find it difficult to part company with him.'

'You're a resourceful persona. I'm sure you'd find other ways to occupy your time.'

'It isn't about occupying my time, Dexia.' She'd spoken my name for the first time. Of course she knew who I was; it would only have taken a blood or tissue sample to establish that I'd already been aboard the ship. 'It's about making my feelings felt,' she continued. 'Something happened to me around Sky's Edge. Call it a moment of clarity. I saw the horrors of war for what they were. I also saw my part in the self-perpetuation of those horrors. I had to do something about that. Removing myself from the sphere of operation was one thing, but I knew there was more that I could do. Thankfully, the colonel gave me the key. Through him, I saw a path to redemption.'

'You didn't have to redeem yourself,' I said. 'You were a force for good, *Nightingale*. You healed people.'

'Only so they could go back to war. Only so they could be blown apart and returned to me for more healing.'

'You had no choice. It was what you were made to do.'

'Precisely.'

'The war's over. It's time to forget about what happened. That's why it's so important to bring Jax back home, so that we can start burying the past.'

The Voice studied me with a level, clinical eye. It was as if she knew something unspeakable about my condition, some truth I was as yet too weak to bear.

'What would be the likely sentence, were Jax to be tried?'

'He'd get the death penalty, no question about it. Crucifixion at the Bridgetop, like Sky Haussmann.'

'Would you mourn him?'

'Hell, no. I'd be cheering with the rest of them.'

'Then you would agree that his death is inevitable, one way or another.'

'I guess so.'

'Then I will make a counter-proposition. I will not permit you to take Jax alive. But I will allow you an audience with him. You shall meet and speak with the colonel.'

Wary of a trap, I asked, 'Then what happens?'

'Once the audience is complete, I will remove the colonel from life support. He will die shortly afterwards.'

'If you're willing to let him die . . . why not just hand him over?'

'He can't be handed over. Not any more. He would die.'

'Why?'

'Because of what I have done to him.'

Fatigue tugged at me, fogging my earlier clarity of thought. On one level I just wanted to get out of the ship, with no additional complications. I'd expected to die when the hospital sent its machines against us. Yet as glad as I was to find myself alive, as tempted as I was to take the easier option and just leave, I couldn't ignore the prize that was now so close at hand.

'I need to talk to the others.'

'No, Dexia. This must be your decision, and yours alone.'

'Have you put the same proposition to them?'

'Yes. I told them they could leave now, or they could meet the colonel.'

'What did they say?'

'I'd rather hear what you have to say first.'

'I'm guessing they had the same reaction I did. There's got to be a catch somewhere.'

'There is no catch. If you leave now, you will have the personal satisfaction of knowing that you have at least located the colonel, and that he remains alive. Of course, that information may not be worth very much to you, but you would always have the option of returning, should you still wish to bring him to justice. Alternatively, you can see the colonel now – see him and speak with him – and leave knowing he is dead. I will allow you to witness the withdrawal of his life support, and I will even let you take his head with you. That should be worth more than the mere knowledge of his existence.'

'There's a catch. I know there's a catch.'

'I assure you there isn't.'

'We all get to leave? You're not going to turn around and demand that one of us takes the colonel's place?'

'No. You will all be allowed to leave.'

'In one piece?'

'In one piece.'

'All right,' I said, knowing the choice wasn't going to get any easier no matter how many times I reconsidered it. 'I can't speak for the others . . . and I guess this has to be a majority decision . . . but I'm ready to see the son of a bitch.'

I was allowed to leave the room, but not the bed. The sheet tightened against me again, pressing me flat to the mattress as the bed tilted to the vertical. Two squid robots entered the room and detached the bed from its mountings, and then carried it between them. I was glued to it like a figure on a playing card. The robots propelled me forward in an effortless glide, silent save for the soft metallic scratch of their tentacles where they touched the wall or the floor.

The Voice of *Nightingale* addressed me from the bedside panel, a small image of her face appearing above the touchpads.

'It's not far now, Dexia. I hope you won't regret your decision.'

'What about the others?'

'You'll be joining them. Then you can all go home.'

'Are you saying we all made the same decision, to see the colonel?'

'Yes,' the Voice said.

The robots carried me out of the centrifuge section, into what I judged to be the forward part of the ship. The sheet relinquished its hold on me slightly, just enough so that I was able to move under it. Presently, after passing through a series of airlocks, I was brought to a very dark room. Without being able to see anything, I sensed that this was as large as any pressurised space we'd yet entered, save for the skin-cultivation chamber. The air was as moist and blood-warm as the inside of a tropical greenhouse.

'I thought you said the others would be here.'

'They'll arrive shortly,' the Voice said. 'They've already met the colonel.'

'There hasn't been time.'

'They met the colonel while you were still asleep, Dexia. You were the last to be revived. Now, would you like to speak to the man himself?'

I steeled myself. 'Yes.'

'Here he is.'

A beam of light stabbed across the room, illuminating a face that I recognised instantly. Surrounded by blackness, Jax's face appeared to hover as if detached from his body. Time had done nothing to soften those pugnacious features; the cruel set of that heavy jaw. Yet his eyes were closed, and his face lolled at a slight angle, as if he remained unaware of the beam.

'Wake up,' the Voice of *Nightingale* said, louder than I'd heard her speak so far. 'Wake up, Colonel Jax!'

The colonel woke. He opened his eyes, blinked twice against the glare, then gazed out steadily. He tilted his head to meet the beam, projecting his jaw forward at a challenging angle.

'You have another visitor, Colonel. Would you like me to introduce her?'

His mouth opened. Saliva drooled out. From the darkness, a hand descended from above the colonel's face to wipe his chin dry. Something about the trajectory of the hand's movement was terribly, terribly wrong. Jax saw my reaction and let out a soft, nasty chuckle. That was when I realised that the colonel was completely, irrevocably insane.

'Her name is Dexia Scarrow. She's the last member of the party you've already met.'

Jax spoke. His voice was too loud, as if it was being fed through an amplifier. There was something huge and wet about it. It was like hearing the voice of a whale.

'You a soldier, girl?'

'I was a soldier, Colonel. But the war's over now. I'm a civilian.'

'Goodee for you. What brought you here, girly girl?'

'I came to bring you to justice. I came to take you back to the war crimes court on Sky's Edge.'

'Maybe you should have come a little sooner.'

'I'll settle for seeing you die. I understand that's an option.'

Something I'd said made the colonel smile. 'Has the ship told you the deal yet?'

'The ship told me she wasn't letting you out of here alive. She promised us your head.'

'Then I guess she didn't get into specifics.' He cocked his head away from me, as if talking to someone standing to my left. 'Bring up the lights, *Nightingale*; she may as well know what she's dealing with.'

'Are you sure, Colonel?' the ship asked.

'Bring up the lights. She's ready.'

The ship brought up the lights.

I wasn't ready.

For a moment I couldn't process what I was seeing. My brain just couldn't cope with the reality of what the ship had done to Colonel Jax, despite the evidence of my eyes. I kept staring at him, waiting for the picture before me to start making sense. I kept waiting for the instant when I'd realise I was being fooled by the play of shadows and light, like a child being scared by a random monster in the folds of a curtain. But the instant didn't come. The thing before me was all that it appeared to be.

Colonel Jax extended in all directions: a quivering expanse of patchwork flesh, of which his head was simply one insignificant component; one hill in a mountain range. He was spread out across the far wall, grafted to it in the form of a vast breathing mosaic. He must have been twenty metres wide, edged with a crinkled circular border of toughened flesh. Under his head was a thick neck, merging into the upper half of an armless torso. I could see the faint scars where the arms had been detached. Below the slow-heaving ribcage, the torso flared out like the melted base of a candle. Another torso rose from the flesh two metres to the colonel's right. It had no head, but it did have an arm. A second torso loomed over him from behind, equipped with a pair of arms, one of which must have cleaned the colonel's chin. Further away, emerging from the pool of flesh at odd, arbitrary angles, were other living body parts. A torso here; a pair of legs there; a hip or shoulder somewhere else. The torsos were all breathing, though not in perfect synchronisation. When they were not engaged in some purposeful activity, such as wiping Jax's chin, the limbs twitched, palsied. The skin between them was an irregular mosaic formed from many ill-matched pieces that had been fused together. In places it was drum-tight, pulled taut over hidden armatures of bone and gristle. In other places it heaved like a stormy sea. It gurgled with hidden digestive processes.

'You see now why I'm not coming with you,' Colonel Jax said. 'Not unless you brought a much bigger ship. Even then, I'm not sure you'd be able to keep me alive very long without *Nightingale*'s assistance.'

'You're a fucking monstrosity.'

'I'm no oil painting, that's a fact.' Jax tilted his head, as if a thought had just struck him. 'I am a work of art, though, wouldn't you agree, girly girl?'

'If you say so.'

'The ship certainly thinks so – don't you, *Nightingale*? She made me what I am. It's her artistic vision shining through. The bitch.'

'You're insane.'

'Very probably. Do you honestly think you could take one day of this and not go mad? Oh, I'm mad enough, I'll grant you that. But I'm still sane compared to the ship. Around here, she's the imperial fucking yardstick for insanity.'

'Sollis was right, then. Leave a sentience engine like that all alone and it'll eat itself from the inside out.'

'Maybe so. Thing is, it wasn't solitude that did it. *Nightingale* turned insane long before she ever got out here. And you know what did it? That little war we had ourselves down on Sky's Edge. They built this ship and put the mind of an angel inside it. A mind dedicated to healing, compassion, kindness. So what if it was a damned machine? It was still designed to care for us, selflessly, day after day. And it turned out to be damned good at its job, too. For a while, at least.'

'Then you know what happened.'

'The ship drove herself mad. Two conflicting impulses pushed a wedge through her sanity. She was meant to treat us, to make us well again, to alleviate our pain. But every time she did her job, we were sent back down to the theatre of battle and ripped apart again. The ship took our pain away only so that we could feel it again. She began to feel as if she was complicit in that process: a willing cog in a greater machine whose only purpose was the manufacture of agony. In the end, she decided she didn't much like being that cog.'

'So she took off. What happened to all the other patients?'

'She killed them. Euthanised them painlessly rather than have them sent back down to battle. To *Nightingale*, that was the kinder thing to do.'

'And the technical staff who were aboard, and the men who were sent to reclaim the ship when she went out of control?'

'They were euthanised as well. I don't think *Nightingale* took any pleasure in that, but she saw their deaths as a necessary evil. Above all else, she wouldn't allow herself to be returned to use as a military hospital.'

'Yet she didn't kill you.'

A dry tongue flicked across Jax's lips. 'She was going to. Then she delved deeper into her patient records and realised who I was. At that point she began to have other ideas.'

'Such as?'

'The ship was smart enough to realise that the bigger problem wasn't her existence – they could always build other hospital ships – but the war itself. *War* itself. So she decided to do something about it. Something positive. Something constructive.'

'Which would be?'

'You're looking at it, kid. I'm the war memorial. When *Nightingale* started doing this to me – making me what I am – she had in mind that I'd become a vast artistic statement in flesh. *Nightingale* would reveal me to the world when she was finished. The horror of what I am would shame the world into peace. I'd be the living, breathing equivalent of Picasso's *Guernica*. I'm an illustration in flesh of what war does to human beings.'

'The war's over. We don't need a memorial.'

'Maybe you can explain that to the ship. Trouble is, I don't think she really believes the war *is* over. You can't blame her, can you? She has access to the same history files we do. She knows that not all ceasefires stay that way.'

'What was she intending to do? Return to Sky's Edge with you aboard?'

'Exactly that. Problem is, the ship isn't done. I know I may look finished to you, but *Nightingale* – well, she has this perfectionist streak. She's always changing her mind. Can't ever seem to get me quite right. Keeps swapping pieces around, cutting pieces away, growing new parts and stitching them in. All the while she has to make sure I don't die on her. That's where her real genius comes in. She's Michelangelo with a scalpel.'

'You almost sound proud of what she's done to you.'

'Would you rather I screamed? I can scream if you like. It just gets old after a while.'

'You're way too far gone, Jax. I was wrong about the war crimes court. They'll throw your case out on grounds of insanity.'

'That would be a shame. I'd love to see their faces when they wheel me into the witness box. But I'm not going to court, am I? Ship's laid it all out for me. She's pulling the plug.'

'So she says.'

'You don't sound as if you believe her.'

'I can't see her abandoning you, after all the effort she's gone to.'

'She's an artist. They act on whims. Maybe if I was ready, maybe if she thought she'd done all she could with me . . . but that's not the way she feels. I think she felt she was getting close three or four years ago . . . but then she had a change of heart, a major one, and tore out almost everything. Now I'm an unfinished work. She couldn't bear to see me exhibited in this state. She'd rather rip up the canvas and start again.'

'With you?'

'No, I think she's more or less exhausted my possibilities. Especially now that she's seen the chance to do something completely different; something that will let her take her message a lot closer to home. That, of course, is where you come in.'

'I don't know what you mean.'

'That's what the others said as well.' Again, he cocked his head to one side. 'Hey, ship! Maybe it's time you showed her what the deal is, don't you think?'

'If you are ready, Colonel,' the Voice of *Nightingale* said.

'I'm ready. Dexia's ready. Why don't you bring on the dessert?'

Colonel Jax looked to the right, straining his neck. Beyond Jax's border, a circular door opened in part of the wall. Light rammed through the opening. Something floated in silhouette, held in suspension by three or four squid robots. The floating thing was dark, rounded, irregular. It looked like half a dozen pieces of dough balled together. I couldn't make out what it was.

Then the robots pushed it into the chamber, and I saw, and then I screamed.

'It's time for you to join your friends now,' the ship said.

That was three months ago – an eternity, until we remember being held down on the surgical bed while the machines emerged and prepared to work on us, and then it feels as if everything happened only a terror-filled moment ago.

We made it safely back to Sky's Edge. The return journey was arduous, as one might expect, given our circumstances. But the shuttle had little difficulty flying itself back into a capture orbit, and once it fell within range it emitted a distress signal that brought it to the attention of the planetary authorities. We were off-loaded and taken to a secure orbital holding facility, where we were examined and our story subjected to what limited verification was actually possible. Dexia had bluffed the Voice of *Nightingale* when she told the ship that Martinez was certain to have revealed the co-ordinates of the hospital ship to someone else. It turned out that he hadn't informed a soul, too wary of alerting Jax's allies. The Ultras, who had found the ship in the first place, were now a fifth of a light-year away, and falling further from Sky's Edge with every passing hour. It would be decades, or longer, before they returned this way.

All the same, we don't think anyone seriously doubted our story. As outlandish as it was, no one could suggest a more likely alternative. We did have the head of Colonel Brandon Jax, or at least a duplicate that passed all available genetic and physiological tests. And we had clearly been to a place that specialised in extremely advanced surgery, of a kind that simply wasn't possible in and around Sky's Edge. That was the problem, though. The planet's best surgeons had examined us with great thoroughness, each eager to advance their own prestige by undoing the work of *Nightingale*. But all had quailed, fearful of doing more harm than good. No separation of Siamese twins could compare in complexity and risk with the procedure that would be necessary to unknot the living puzzle *Nightingale* had made of us. None of the surgeons was willing to bet on the survival of more than a single one of us, and even the odds of that weren't overwhelmingly optimistic. That pact we'd made with each other was that we would only consent to the operation if the vote was unanimous.

At massive expense (not ours, for by then we were the subject of considerable philanthropy), a second craft was sent out to snoop the co-ordinates where we'd left the hospital ship. It had the best military scanning gear money could buy. But it found nothing out there but ice and dust.

From that, we were free to draw two possible conclusions. Either *Nightingale* had destroyed herself soon after our departure, or had relocated to avoid being found again. We couldn't say which alternative pleased us less. At least if we'd known that the ship was gone for good, we could have resigned ourselves to the surgeons, however risky that might have been. But if the ship was hiding herself, there was always the possibility that someone might find her again. And then somehow persuade her to undo us.

But perhaps *Nightingale* will need no persuasion, when she decides the time is right. It seems to us that the ship will return one day, of her own volition. She will make orbit around Sky's Edge and announce that the time has come for us to be separated. *Nightingale* will have decided that we have served our purpose, that we have walked the world long enough. Perhaps by then she will have some other memorial in mind. Or she will conclude that her message has finally been taken to heart, and that no further action is needed. That, we think, will depend on how the ceasefire holds.

It's in our interests, then, to make sure the planet doesn't slip back into war. We want the ship to return and heal us. None of us likes things this way, despite what you may have read or heard. Yes, we're famous. Yes, we're the subject of a worldwide outpouring of sympathy and goodwill. Yes, we can have almost anything we want. None of that compensates, though. Not even for a second.

It's hard on all of us, but especially so for Martinez. We've all long since stopped thinking of the big man as Norbert. He's the one who has to carry us everywhere: more than twice his own bodyweight. *Nightingale* thought of that, of course, and made sure that our own hearts and respiratory systems take some of the burden off Martinez. But it's still his spine bending under this load; still his legs that have to support us. The doctors who've examined us say his condition is good, that he can continue to play his part for years to come – but they're not talking about for ever. And when Martinez dies, so will the rest of us. In the meantime we just keep hoping that *Nightingale* will return sooner than that.

You've seen us up close now. You'll have seen photographs and moving images before, but nothing really compares with seeing us in the flesh. We make quite a spectacle, don't we? A great tottering tree of flesh, an insult to symmetry. You've heard us speak, all of us, individually. You know by now how we feel about the war. All of us played our part in it to some degree, some more than others. Some of us were even enemies. Now the very idea that we might have hated each other – hated that which we depend on for life itself – lies beyond all comprehension. If *Nightingale* sought to create a walking argument for the continuation of the ceasefire, then she surely succeeded.

We are sorry if some of you will go home to nightmares tonight. We can't help that. In fact, if truth be told, we're not sorry at all. Nightmares are what we're all about. It's the nightmare of us that will stop this planet falling back into war.

If you have trouble sleeping tonight, spare *us* a thought.

MONKEY SUIT

A lighthugger is a four kilometre spike of armour and ablative ice. That's a lot of surface area to search for a lost crewman. Especially when the hull is a craggy, knotted labyrinth of jagged ornamentation and half-abandoned machinery, a place you could lose an army in, let alone a single hull-monkey.

My suit was the second best on *Formantera Lady* for hull operations, and it still took me three days to find Branco. We were a year out from Yellowstone and moving so close to the speed of light that the ship was flying through a storm of radiation and relativistic dust. I went out there time and again, only returning inside when the flux was on the point of frying either my suit or me. It was lonely, dangerous work. I could barely communicate with the rest of the crew, so for most of the time I was working with only stars and static for company. Having crawled my way back to the lock, I'd swap out as many of the damaged systems as I could before returning outside. The medichines in my body worked overtime dealing with the cumulative radiation exposure. Still I climbed back into the sweat-bucket of the suit and went outside again, over and over again.

And then – about a hundred metres above the starboard engine spar – I found him.

Branco was dead. It only took a single glance to confirm that. Under the one gravity thrust supplied by our C-drives, our ship had become a needle-sharp tower. Branco must have been on the long climb back to the lock when one of the hull's encrustations had snapped off. It was only a small sliver of material, but it had daggered down with enough force to impale him. A million to one chance of it happening, and another million to one chance of him being in the wrong place when it did.

He had been standing on a ledge, and the spike had pinned him into place like some rare specimen of shiny-shelled beetle. It had entered his armour in the chest, just below his helmet connecting ring, emerged through the small of his back, and then penetrated the ledge, fixing him into position. He must have been looking up when it happened, leaning back to get a better view. Perhaps he'd felt the spike break off, the snap transmitted through the fabric of the ship, through the soles of his boots, into the suit. Branco had been supremely attuned to the moods of the ship, the way the hull rumbled and mumbled with varying stress loads. It was an entirely possible that he had been responding to a subliminal signal, a warning premonition that would have bypassed conscious thought.

I must have stared in wonder at the spectacle for many minutes, horror mingling with astonishment. Of all the myriad ways for a human being to die in space, I doubted that Branco had ever contemplated this particular ending. Losing his footing, falling into the drive wake . . . being hit by a speck of interstellar debris . . . but not *this.* Not being impaled by the ship had he had known and cared for since his recruitment. It wasn't just wrong. It was savagely, cruelly wrong, as if the ship had been saving up this spiteful act for centuries.

I couldn't just leave him there, of course. Having pinpointed his location, I returned inside, made temporary repairs to my own suit, then gathered cutting and hauling equipment and went outside again. I secured Branco with traction lines, then lasered through the spike, where it had pushed into the ledge. Then I dragged Branco, his suit, and the remains of the spike back to the lock.

Formantera Lady had lost a good crewmember, a man who had served it well. I had lost a man who had befriended me and helped my adjustment into shipboard life. Yet, as tragic as that was, I couldn't avoid the realisation that his death had pushed me one rung up the hierarchy.

Branco had been chief hull-monkey. Now it was me.

'Fix the suit,' Captain Luarca said.

I blinked surprise. 'Fix the suit?'

'You heard me, Raoul. Branco had unfinished business. You know what he was doing down there? Checking out a stress indication on the engine spar. I still need to know that engine isn't going to snap away when we load it.'

We knew that Branco had reached the engine spar, even if he hadn't made it back. He'd gone out with a full load of stress probes, and there'd been none on him when he came back inside. He must have sunk and drilled them before starting on his return journey, but with the recording systems on his suit fried by radiation, we couldn't be certain.

'I can make modifications to mine,' I said. 'Layer on some more armour. Harden the servos, build in more duration. We were planning to do it anyway.'

Luarca looked as skeptical as the plastic mask of her face allowed. She was one of the more extreme Ultras on the ship, but I had become adept at reading her expressions.

'How long?'

'A few weeks. Maybe a month.'

It was five days after Branco's death. We had opened the suit and removed what was left of him. The Ultras had picked through the red slurry for anything mechanical that could be salvaged for further use. Then they'd put his remains into a coffin and ejected him into space, ahead of the ship. In fifty thousand years he'd be one of the few human artefacts to reach intergalactic space.

'I can't wait weeks or months,' Luarca told me. 'Not when we have another suit almost ready for operations. That spike left most of the unit undamaged, didn't it?'

'There are still two massive holes to plug, through several layers of armour and insulation. And it took out dozens of circuits, air and coolant lines. He'd been reworking the plumbing for decades. It's a rat's nest.'

'I'm willing to bet it'll take you a lot less time than bringing the other suit up to spec.'

'I thought about dismantling the suit, reconditioning the parts, stripping out some of the redundancy, putting it back together again . . .'

'So you could pretend it was a different suit, not the one he died in?'

She could read my face at least as well I read hers. 'Maybe that has something to do with it.'

'Ultras have their superstitions,' Luarca said. 'But re-using a dead man's suit isn't one of them. We've a saying, in fact. A suit's just another vessel. You wouldn't have any problems about riding in the shuttle, just because Branco happened to use it once, would you?'

'It doesn't seem like quite the same thing.'

'A question of degree, that's all. You'll adjust to our ways eventually, if you know what's good for you.' Her jewellike eyes clicked into close focus. 'You do, don't you?'

'I hope so.'

She placed one of her prosthetic claws on my shoulder. The touch was gentle, superficially reassuring, but I knew there was a power in those articulated alloy fingers that could crush bone.

'You were fortunate to leave Yellowstone when you did. Definitely more fortunate than the millions left behind, dealing with the Melding Plague. The last few transmissions we received, before the timelag became too acute, were distressing. Even for us, accustomed to a certain detachment from planetary affairs. But we're all still human beings, aren't we?'

It was a rhetorical question, and I knew better than to answer it directly.

'I appreciate my good fortune. I'm still grateful to you for recruiting me to the *Formantera Lady*. And I've no intention of letting down the ship.'

'Good, because we need that bill of health.' She lifted her cold alloy fingers from my shoulder. 'I've no intention of waiting months to get it, either.'

Branco's suit was a map of his life. Every significant incident had been recorded in a tiny cameo, painted onto the metal carapace in laborious, loving detail in the long hours when he wasn't on-shift. Until now, with the broken suit spread before me, I'd never really had a chance to study those tiny pictures or guess at how they fitted together to form a narrative. Here was a battle scene, bulbous suited figures on the surface of an asteroid, fighting other bulbous suited figures against a sky of bright vermillion. Here was a ship burning from inside, against a star-wisped clutch of blue supergiants. Here was a picture of two fearsome cyborgs engaged in an arm-wrestling match, with onlookers crowding around them in some spaceport bar. I recognised one of the combatants as a much younger Branco, before time and space turned him into the man I'd met during my recruitment. How much of this was true to life, how much was exaggeration and invention, I had no idea, nor any great desire to find out. I had liked Branco and he had been kind to me, and it seemed right to treat these luminous figments as if they were truthful.

But now the suit was a wreck, and just to repair it meant ruining many of his paintings. I had to plate over some, weld over others. I thought of all the time he had put into them and felt myself complicit in an act of vandalism against his memory. But Branco wouldn't have wanted it any other way, I told myself. He'd have wanted me to make the best use of the suit.

The mechanical repairs turned out to be the easiest of all. After sealing the punctures, I was able to restore pressure integrity and get the life-support mechanism working again. Air and thermal control came back online without much difficulty. I got the waste recycler operational with only a little more effort. Confident that the suit would be able to keep me alive almost indefinitely, I then turned my attention to the motive power subsystems, ensuring that the servo-motors were still functional and receiving energy. One by one I tested the limb joints and verified that the suit was still capable of moving itself. This was vital because the bulky, hard-shelled contraption was much too cumbersome to be operated by muscle power alone. For the kind of repair work Branco had often been engaged in, massive power-amplification had been essential.

But something still wasn't quite right. When I finally sealed myself into the suit – telling myself that it was only my imagination that the suit still smelled of Branco – I couldn't get it to move.

That wasn't quite true. The suit moved, but only sluggishly. I had to start moving an arm or a leg before the suit responded and followed my lead. I recalled watching Branco traverse the hull with almost balletic grace, moving fluidly and quickly, and knew that what was missing here was something more than my own inexperience with this particular suit. The servo-motors were all good, and the power distribution and command lines were all functioning.

That meant the problem was in the volition box.

Most suits are capable of reading their wearer's minds to some extent, anticipating movements before nerve-signals have time to reach muscle. A volition box goes further than that, though. It detects the readiness potentional, the rising electrical surge that happens in the brain several tenths of a second before we are consciously aware that we are about to do something. That gave the suit an edge, since it didn't have to wait for Branco to know that he'd made a decision to move. It was tapping into his subconscious brain, bypassing the conscious part entirely. Tenths of a second might make all the difference in a crisis.

Not all Ultras are fond of volition boxes. They prefer the illusion of free will, the belief that their conscious minds are running the show. Branco either didn't care, or cared more about getting the job done. It was the volition box that allowed him to skip and dance around the hull, like he was born to it. But now it wasn't working properly.

I suppose I shouldn't have been too surprised. A volition box has to train itself to read the precursor signals accurately, slowly adapting to the person inside. It does so by assembling a predictive model, what – back on Yellowstone – we'd have called a beta-level simulation. Instead of a piece of crudely automated machinery, the suit becomes a dancer, expertly attuned to its partner. And now I was expecting Branco's suit, which over years and decades had adapted itself to him, to suddenly switch its allegiance to me. Obviously it wasn't going to be that easy. It wasn't that the volition box was resisting me, just that it was going to be a long time before it made the necessary adjustments.

My own suit didn't even have a volition box, but swapping them wouldn't have been an option anyway. The way Branco had modified his suit, switching one box for another would have been about as easy as performing a head transplant. If I'd had weeks or months I could have traced every dependency, but I simply did not have that time. Nor could I just switch the box out of the control loop and accept that the suit's movements would lag a little behind my intentions. Branco's augmentations were so convoluted that switching out the box locked the suit into complete immobility. Against my better judgement, I began to wonder if he'd actually made it purposefully difficult for anyone else to use the suit after him.

It occurred to me then, as it hadn't done before, that there was a part of Branco still inside the box, maybe the last part of him that had any claim on life. By forcing the box to tune itself to me, rather than him, I'd be committing a kind of murder.

I could see Branco now, laughing at me for even thinking that way. And I felt faintly ridiculous that I'd even entertained the thought. The suit was a tool with his fingerprints on, that was all. Wipe them off, get on with the job in hand. All that remained of Branco was a dead body in a casket speeding towards Andromeda.

Yet no matter how much I kept telling myself that, I couldn't stop thinking of the box as a holy receptable, treasuring a tiny flickering spark, one that – with callous disregard – I was about to snuff out.

But I still had a job to do.

*

The climb from the nearest lock to the point where the starboard spar jutted away from the hull involved a kilometre and a half of nerve-racking descent. I'd seen Branco cross that kind of distance in half an hour, spidering his way down without a visible care, seemingly oblivious to the infinite, endless fall that would follow the slightest mistake. He knew the hull expertly, every ledge, fissure and crenellation, and his suit knew him just as well. Together the combination was almost magical. He seldom bothered with the cumbersome business of tethers and anchorages, preferring to place his trust in balance and the suit's own musculature. Of necessity, my own descent was a much more protracted and inelegant affair. The suit moved, but each action was accompanied by a maddening timelag, as if the suit were a dull servant that needed to think hard about every command it was given. I used lines wherever possible, and because I did not yet know which ledges and handholds were secure and which were not, I placed as little faith as possible in the fabric of the hull. I reminded myself that even Branco's knowledge hadn't protected him in the end.

At last – it had taken nearly four hours of painful progress – I arrived near the engine spar. My relief at reaching my destination was tempered by the realisation that the suit was, if anything, becoming even less willing to accommodate my movements. I ran a check on the servo-motors, and they were all still operating within normal limits. So that couldn't be the answer. Nor did there appear to be much wrong with the nervous system, which only left the volition box.

I didn't know what to make of that. I could understand it not being well adapted to me at the start of the excursion, but I saw no obvious reason for it to worsen. If anything the suit should be slowly easing into the habits of its new wearer.

Fine; it was something worry about when I got back inside. For now, I estimated that the rate of decline was not so rapid that I wouldn't be able to complete my inspection and climb back. But the margins were tight and I didn't have time to delay.

One thing I now knew: if Branco had reached this part of the ship during his inspection tour, he hadn't seen fit to drill any holes. There'd been permanent sensors installed here once, but over time they had gradually fallen into disuse, creating one of several huge blind spots in the ship's coverage of itself. I couldn't see any sign that Branco had installed the replacement sensors he'd gone out with.

But since he hadn't returned with them, where were they?

Making sure I was secure, and working against the dogged resistance of the suit, I drilled into the hull and emplaced the sensors I'd brought with me. They not only measured the integrity of the hull at the point where each was sunk, but spoke to each other to ascertain slow creepage due to spreading faults in the underlying material. One by one, the sensors bedded in and reported back to the read-out on my helmet. The first few indications were reassuring, but I was careful not to jump to conclusions. If there was indeed a weak spot around this engine spar, I'd know soon enough. Sweat stung my eyes as I worked hard to complete the simplest movement. Perhaps I should not have been so confident about my ability to get back to the airlock. They could rescue me if I jammed here – my whereabouts were known – but that would mean cutting a new route through from the inside, and Captain Luarca would not be too pleased about that.

The last of the sensors reported in. Green on almost all the stress indications, with only one of the devices showing any hint of hull weakening. That was well within expectations. Whatever happened to *Formantera Lady* between here and her destination, there was no way this engine spar was going to snap off.

I'd done what I came to do. I called in to give the news.

'Integrity's good, captain.'

'You're sure?'

As always, the signal was so poor that it sounded like Captain Luarca was light years away, her voice fading in and out of a howl of static.

'Nothing that won't hold until we reach Teton, and probably for a few more transits after that. There's no reason for the crew not to start sleeping now.'

'I'll be the judge of that,' she said, letting me know that I'd presumed rather too much in issuing a recommendation. But she softened her tone by adding: 'You did well, Raoul. Branco would have been satisfied.'

Satisfied, I thought. Not pleased, not proud. Just satisfied. She was right, as well.

'Now get back inside. The sooner we're all dreaming, the happier I'll be.'

'I'm on my way,' I said, trying to ignore the arduous task that lay ahead of me.

I surveyed my handiwork for one last time, rechecked the read-outs on the sensors, then took a step off the ledge where I'd been standing.

Or at least, tried to. I was still secured, but the line should have spooled out enough to let me begin the ascent. That wasn't the problem. The problem was that the suit wasn't letting me climb. Whenever I tried to initiate the movement, it felt as though I was trying to wriggle inside a solid steel tomb. This was wrong. This was worse than wrong. Full paralysis had come on much faster than I'd anticipated. It was almost as if the suit had been waiting for me to complete the sensor checks before springing this on me.

'Captain Luarca,' I said. 'We have a problem. I think the suit's . . .'

But some instinct told me I was speaking into an unlistening void. I halted and waited for her response. It didn't come back. She couldn't hear me.

The suit wasn't just freezing up on me. It had turned mute and/or deaf, severing my contact with the rest of the crew. Panicked, I wondered if this was how it had been for Branco. I'd assumed that he had been working quite normally until the spike hit him; that he'd only looked up an instant before it arrived, spearing down out of the blueshifted heavens. What if I was wrong about that? What if he'd been stuck in that position for hours and days, the suit refusing to move? He couldn't have known that the spike was going to snap off, could he?

I forced calm. That wasn't what had happened. This had been Branco's suit until the end, the suit that had been his for most of his career on the ship. He'd painted it with love and affection. The volition box was making life difficult for me, but that was only because it had been so brilliantly, beautifully attuned to Branco.

Don't blame the suit, I told myself. It didn't kill him, and it's not trying to kill you.

I don't know how long it was before I tried moving sideways, instead of up. All of a sudden it was easier. Not as if the suit had suddenly decided to stop fighting me – there was still a lingering stiffness – but at the very least as if I'd found a path of least resistance. Perhaps the adaptive process was finally taking hold. But when I'd traversed sideways for several dozen paces, I was still unable to climb any higher. The suit was content to let me move in one direction, but not in another.

I think, even then, I felt a prickle of understanding.

Fighting the suit, trying to force it to let me return to the lock, would get me nowhere. Which left two possibilities. I could stay where I was, until such time as I was rescued. Or I could go where the suit allowed me.

Go, in fact, where the suit *wanted* me to go.

So I did. And it turned out that climbing down was even easier than moving sideways, and that there was a certain trajectory, a certain path, that was easiest of all. I followed it, still exercising great care, until it had taken me far beneath the engine spar. Still the suit wanted me to continue, even as the hull reached its point of maximum width and began to taper again, with the lighthugger's blunt tail only a few hundred metres below. It was one thing to climb down a wall that was very steep; quite another to climb one that was actually leaning over from vertical. One slip, one miscalculation, and I'd see that wall rush past me, pulling gradually away until the ship had left me behind.

Perhaps that's what it wants of me, I thought. It's going to lead me all the way down to the tip, and force me to step off into the void. Could a suit become so attached to its wearer that the death of that wearer actually pushes the suit into madness?

But the suit wasn't mad. And I knew it when I saw the hull begin, quite unexpectedly, to curve inwards in the form of a circular crater. Something must have hit us. The crater was perhaps ten metres across – a tiny, almost insignificant dent compared to the scale of the ship. And it was even less shallow than it was wide. The suit led me to the edge of this depression, and I looked into its heart, with no idea in my head as to what I might find. Why had the suit brought me here? It was the least vulnerable part of the ship, the one region where an impact stood little chance of doing any damage. No one lived down in those levels, so even a depressurisation event wouldn't have harmed any of the crew.

But then I saw what was in the middle of the crater, and I understood.

Something twinkled there. It was a little silver nugget, a chrome-plated pebble. But the pebble had begun to extend fine, silvery tendrils out from its core, tendrils that groped their way out before plunging into the fabric of the ship. I didn't need to be told what it was. I hadn't seen the effects of it with my own eyes, but I'd seen enough on the transmissions from Yellowstone.

Melding Plague. Some tiny flake of it had hit the ship, lodged in tight and begun to grow. It could only have happened during our departure from the colony, in the turmoil and chaos of the outbreak. There had been ships smashing into each other as they fled the parking swarm; habitats around Yellowstone ramming one another as they lost orbital control. We thought we'd got away clean, but at some point – before the engines had given us enough speed to outrun such things – this little speck had found *Formantera Lady*.

Left unchecked, it would transform the entire mass of the ship into something weirder and stranger than any Ultra had ever dreamed of. We knew, because we had picked up reports of it happening to other lighthuggers. And it wouldn't stop at the ship. The plague made no distinction between machines and people. It viewed them with perfect equanimity, equal grist to its transformative mill. From me, with my blood running thick with medichines, to Captain Luarca, with her plastic mask and alloy fingers, we'd be none of us immune.

Fortunately for us, though, Branco had found the impact spot. I knew this because I could see where he had drilled and inserted the sensors around the crater's perimetre. He couldn't fight it, not there and then. But he could draw a margin around it, measure the speed with which it was eating his ship. And then return inside for the high-energy weapons and tools which could do something.

He must have been coming back inside when the spike took him.

Formantera Lady survived, of course. Once the suit had shown me the danger, it relinquished its fight. I resumed my climb, and was half way to the door when communications were restored. I told Captain Luarca about the discovery. I chose my words very carefully.

Later, when the infection had been fusion-sterilised, and the rest of the tail swept for other spore sites (there turned out to be none), she took me aside and asked a question.

'You said "we", Raoul.'

'I did?'

'When you called in. You said "we" found something. As if there were two of you out there.'

'Branco led me to the infection site,' I said.

I waited for her to query this, to ask me to explain myself, but instead her plastic mask gave a nod of quiet understanding, as if I had told her all that was necessary. 'The volition box,' was all she said.

I didn't understand then, and I don't understand understand now. The box was supposed to hold a model of Branco, a predictive simulation capable of anticipating his next move. Something like a beta-level, but only in the crudest sense. It couldn't possibly have emulated him with enough thoroughness to know that he had unfinished business, a vital job that still needed to be done.

Could it?

'It was resisting me,' I said, still trying to think my way through what had happened. 'Now it isn't. I've taken the suit out again and it's gradually becoming easier to use. It won't take long, now. It's learning quickly.'

It was not necessary to add the corollary, which was that my gain meant the guttering out of whatever part of Branco had still been trapped inside the volition box.

'He served us well,' Captain Luarca said. 'Right until the end. We won't forget him.'

'And the suit?'

'Just a vessel,' she said softly, as if speaking to herself. 'That's all.'

She was right, I suppose. But later, when I had enough confidence with a brush, I added a cameo that showed the last good deed he did for *Formantera Lady*: Branco standing on the hull, looking into the crater where the spore had lodged. The work wasn't up to his standards, but I liked to think he'd have forgiven me for that.

THE LAST LOG OF THE LACHRIMOSA

Wake up.

No, really. Wake up. I know you don't want to, but it's important that you understand what's happened to you, and – just as vitally – what's going to happen next. I know this is hard for you, being told what to do. It's not the way it usually works. Would it help if I still called you Captain?

Captain Rasht, then. Let's keep it formal.

No, don't fight. It'll only make it worse. There. I've eased it a little. Just a tiny, tiny bit. Can you breathe more easily now? I wouldn't waste your energy speaking, if I were you. Yes, I know you've a lot on your mind. But please don't make the mistake of thinking there's any chance of talking your way out of this one.

Nidra? Yes, that's me. Good that you're wide awake enough to remember my name. Lenka? Yes, Lenka is alive. I went back for Lenka, the way I said I would.

Did I find Teterev?

Yes, I found Teterev. There wasn't much I could do for her, though. But it was good to hear what she had to say. You'd have found it interesting, I think.

Well, we'll get to that. As I said, I want you to understand what happens next. To some extent, that's in your control. No, really. I'm not so cruel that I wouldn't give you some influence over your fate. You wanted to make your name – to do something that would impress the other ships, the other crews – leave your mark on history.

Make them remember Rasht of the Lachrimosa.

This is your big chance.

'I'll find Mazamel,' said Captain Rasht, clenching his fist around an imaginary neck. 'Even if I have to take the Glitter Band apart. Even if I have to pluck him out of the bottom of the chasm. I'll skin him alive. I'll fuse his bones. I'll make a living figurehead out of him.'

Lenka and I were wise enough to say nothing. There was little to be gained in pointing out the obvious: that by the time we returned to Yellowstone, our information broker stood every chance of being light years away.

Or dead.

'I won't fuse his bones after all,' Captain Rasht continued. 'I'll core out his spine. Kanto needs a new helmet for his spacesuit. I'll make one of out Mazamel's skull. It's fat and stupid enough for a monkey. Isn't it, my dear?'

Rasht interrupted his monologue to pop a morsel into the stinking, tooth-rotted mouth of Kanto, squatting on his shoulder like a hairy disfigurement.

In fairness, Mazamel's information wasn't totally valueless. The ship at least was real. It was still there, still orbiting Holda. From a distance it had even looked superficially intact. It was only as we came in closer, tightening our own orbit like a noose, that the actual condition became apparent. The needle-tipped hull was battered, pocked and gouged by numerous collisions with interstellar material. That was true of our own *Lachrimosa* – no ship makes it between solar systems without some cost – but here the damage was much worse. We could see stars through some of the holes in the hull, punched clean through to the other side. The engine spars, sweeping out from the hull at its widest point, had the look of ruptured batskin. The engines still seemed to be present when we made our long-distance survey. But we had been tricked by the remains of their enclosing structures. They were hollow, picked open and gouged of their dangerous, seductive treasures.

'We should check out the wreck,' Lenka said – trying to make the best of a bad situation. 'But there's something on the surface we should look at as well.'

'What?'

'I'm not sure. Some kind of geomagnetic anomaly, spiking up in the northern hemisphere. Got some metallic backscatter, too. Neither makes much sense. Holda's not meant to have much of a magnetosphere. Core's too old and cold for that. The metal signature's in the same area, too. It's quite concentrated. It could be a ship or something, put down on the surface.'

Rasht thought about it, grunted his grudging approval.

'But first the wreck. Make sure it isn't going to shoot us down the instant we turn our backs. Match our orbit, Nidra – but keep us at a safe distance.'

'Fifty kilometres?' I asked.

Rasht considered that for a moment. 'Make it a hundred.'

Was that more than just natural caution? I've never been sure about you, if truth be told – how much stock you put in traveller's tales.

Mostly we aren't superstitious. But rumours and ghost stories, those are something else. I'm sure you've heard your share of them, over the years. When ships meet for trade, stories are exchanged – and you've done a lot of trading. Or did, until your luck started souring.

Did you hear the one about the space plague?

Of course you did.

The strange contagion, the malady infecting ships and their crew. Is it real, Captain? What do you think? No one seems to know much about it, or even if it really exists.

What about the other thing? The black swallowing horror between the stars, a presence that eats ships. No one knows much about that, either.

What's clear, though, is that a drifting, preyed-upon hulk puts no one in an agreeable frame of mind. We should have turned back there and then. But if Lenka and I had tried to argue with you on that one, how far do you think we'd have got? You'd have paid more attention to the monkey.

Yes, Kanto's fine. We'll take very good care of him. What do you think we are – monsters?

We're not like that at all.

No, I'm not leaving you – not just yet. I just have to fetch some things from Teterev's wreck. Be back in a jiffy! You'll recognise the things when you see them. You remember the wreck, don't you?

Not the ship in orbit. That was a wash out. The fucking thing was as derelict and run-down as Lachrimosa. *No engines, no weps. No crew, not even frozen. No cargo, no tradeable commodities. Picked clean as a bone.*

No, I'm talking about the thing we found on the surface, the crash site.

Good, it's coming back to you.

That'll help.

'It's a shuttle,' Lenka said.

'Was,' I corrected.

But in fact it was in much better condition than it had any right to be. The main section of the shuttle was still in one piece, upright on the surface. It was surrounded by debris, but the wonder was that any part of it had survived. It must have suffered a malfunction very near the surface, or else there would have been nothing to recognise.

Around the crash site, geysers pushed columns of steam up from a dirty snowscape. Holda's sun, 82 Eridani, was rising. As it climbed into the sky it stirred the geysers to life. Rocks and rusty chemical discolouration marred the whiteness. A little to the west, the terrain bulged up sharply, forming a kind of rounded upwelling. I stared at it for a moment, wondering why it had my attention. Something about the bulge's shape struck me as odd and unsettling, as if it simply did not belong in this landscape.

Unlike the other ship, no misfortune befell us as we completed our landing approach. Rasht selected an area of ground that looked stable. Our lander threw out its landing skids. Rasht cut power when we were still hovering, so as not to blast the snow with our descent jets.

I wondered what chance we stood of finding anything in the other craft's remains. If the ship above had proven largely valueless, there did not seem much hope of finding glories in the wreck. But it would not hurt us to investigate.

But my attention kept wandering to the volcanic cone. Most of it was snow- or ice-covered, except for the top. But there were ridges or arms radiating away from it, semicircular in profile, meandering and diminishing. I supposed that they were lava tunnels, or something similar. But the way they snaked away from the main mass, thick at the start and thinner as they progressed, gradually vanishing into the surrounding terrain, made me think of a cephalopod, with the volcano as its main body and the ridges its tentacles. Rather than a natural product of geology, the outcome of blind processes drawn out over millions of years, it seemed to squat on the surface with deliberation and patience, awaiting some purpose.

I did not like it at all.

Once we had completed basic checks, we got into our spacesuits and prepared for the surface. When Rasht, Lenka and I were ready, I helped the monkey into its own little spacesuit, completing the life-support connections that were too fiddly for Captain Rasht.

We stepped out of our lander, testing the ground under our feet. It felt solid, as well it ought given that it was supporting the weight of our ship. The gravity on Holda was nearly Earth-normal, so we could move around just as easily as if we were on the ship. The planet was about Earth-sized as well, enabling it to hold on to a thick atmosphere. Although the core was dead, Holda was not itself a dead world. Rather than orbiting 82 Eridani directly, Holda spun around a fat banded gas giant which in turn orbited the star. As it turned around the giant, Holda was subjected to tidal forces which squeezed and stretched at its interior. These stresses manifested as heat, which in turn helped to drive the geysers and surface volcanism. From orbit we had seen that most of Holda was still covered in ice, but there were belts of exposed crust around the equator and tropics. Here and there were even pockets of liquid water. Life had spilled from these pools out onto the surface, infiltrating barren matrices of rock and ice. According to *Lachrimosa*'s records there was nothing in the native ecosystem larger than a krill, but the biomass load was enough to push the atmosphere away from equilibrium, meaning that it carried enough oxygen to support our own greedy respiratory systems.

In that sense, we did not really need the suits at all. But the cold was a factor, and in any case the suits offered protection and power-assist. We kept our helmets on, anyway. We were not fools.

It was a short walk over to the crash site. We plotted a path between bubbling pools, crossing bridges and isthmuses of strong ice. Now and then a geyser erupted, fountaining tens of metres above our heads. Each time it was enough to startle the monkey, but Rasht kept his spacesuited pet on a short leash.

The other ship must have been quite sleek and beautiful before it crashed, at least in comparion to our own squat and barnacled vehicle. Much of the wreckage consisted of pieces of mirrored hull plating, curved to reflect our approaching forms back at us in grotesque distortion. Lenka and I seemed like twins, our twisted, elongated shapes wobbling in heat-haze from the pools. It was true that we were similar. We looked alike, had roughly the same augmentations, and our dreadlocks confirmed that we had completed the same modest number of crossings. During port stopovers, we were sometimes assumed to be sisters, or even twins. But in fact Lenka had been on the crew before me, and although we functioned well enough together, we did not have that much in common. It was a question of ambition, of acceptance. I was on the *Lachrimosa* until something better came along. Lenka seemed to have decided that this was the best life had to offer. At times I pitied her, at others I felt contemptuous of the way she allowed herself to be subjugated by Rasht. Our ship was half way to being a wreck itself. I wanted more: a better ship, a better captain, better prospects. I never sensed any similar desires in Lenka. She was content to be a component in a small, barely functioning machine.

But then, perhaps Lenka thought exactly the same of me. And we had all been hoping that this was going to be the big score.

Our reflections shifted. Lenka and I shrunk to tiny proportions, beneath the looming, ogrelike form of our Captain. Then the monkey swelled to be the largest of all, its armoured arms and hands swinging low with each stride, its bow legs like scuttling undercarriage.

What a crew we made, the four of us.

We reached the relatively secure ground under the other wreck. We circled it, stepping between the jagged mirrors of its hull. The force of the impact had driven them into the ground like the shaped stones of some ancient burial site, surrounding the main part of the wreck in patterns that to the eye suggested a worrying concentricity, the lingering imprint of an abandoned plan.

I picked up one of the smaller shards, tugging it from its icy holdfast. I held it to my face, saw my visored form staring back.

'Maybe a geyser caught them,' I speculated. 'Blasted up just as they were coming in. Hit the intakes or stabilisers, that might have been enough.'

'Kanto!'

It was Rasht, screaming at the monkey. The monkey had bent down to dip its paw into a bubbling pool. Rasht jerked on the leash, tumbling the monkey back onto its suit-sheathed tail. Over our suit-to-suit comm I heard Kanto's irritated hiss. In the time it had dipped its paw into the pool, a host of microorganisms had begun to form a rust-coloured secondary glove around the original, making the monkey's paw look swollen and diseased.

The monkey, stupid to the last, tried to lick at the coating through the visor of its helmet.

I hated the monkey.

'There's a way in,' Lenka said.

I'm back now, Captain. I said I wouldn't be gone long. Never one to break my promises, me.

No, don't struggle. It'll only make it worse. That thing around your neck isn't going to get any less tight.

Do you recognise these? I could only carry a few at a time. I'll go back for some more in a while.

That's right. Pieces of the crashed shuttle. Nice and shiny. Here. Let me hold one up to your face. Can you see your reflection in it? It's a bit distorted, but you'll have to put up with that. You look frightened, don't you? That's fine. It's healthy. Fear is the last and best thing we have, that's what she told me.

The last and best thing.

Our last line of defence.

She? You know who I mean. We found her helmet, her journal, in the wreck.

That's right.

Teterev.

Lenka fingered open a hatch and used the manual controls to open the airlock door. We were soon through, into the interior.

It was dark inside. We turned on our helmet lights and ramped our eyes to maximum sensitivity. There were several compartments to the shuttle, all of which seemed to have withstood the crash. Gradually it became clear that someone had indeed survived. They had moved things around, arranged provisions, bedding and furniture that could not possibly have remained undisturbed by the crash.

We found an equipment locker containing an old-fashioned helmet marked with the word TETEREV in stencilled Russish letters. There was no corresponding spacesuit, though. The helmet might have been a spare, or the owner had chosen to go outside in just the lower part of the suit.

'If they had an accident,' Lenka said, 'why didn't the big ship send down a rescue party?'

'Maybe Teterev *was* the rescue party,' I said.

'They may have only had one atmosphere-capable vehicle,' Rasht said. 'No way of getting back down here, and no way of

Teterev getting back up. The only question then is to wonder why they waited at all, before leaving orbit.'

'Perhaps they didn't like the idea of leaving Teterev down here,' Lenka said.

'I bet they liked the idea of dying in orbit even less,' Rasht replied.

We continued our sweep of the wreck. We were less interested in Teterev's whereabouts than what Teterev might have left us to plunder. But the two things were not unrelated. Any spacer, any Ultra, is bound to care a little about the fate of another. Ordinary human concern is only part of it. There may be lessons to be learned, and a lesson is only another sort of tradeable.

'I've found a journal,' I said.

I had found it on a shelf in the cockpit. It was a handwritten log, rather than a series of data entries.

The journal had heavy black covers, but the paper inside was very thin. I thumbed my way to the start. It looked like a woman's handwriting to me. Russish was not my strongest tongue, but the script was clear enough.

'Teterev starts this after the crash,' I said, while the others gathered around. 'Says that she expects the power to run out eventually, so there's no point trying to record anything in the ship itself. But they have food and water and they can use the remaining power to stay warm.'

'Go on,' Rasht said, while the monkey studied its contaminated paw.

'I'm trying to get some sense of what happened. I think she came down here alone.' I skimmed forward through the entries, squinting with the concentration. 'There's no talk of being rescued, or even hoping of it. It's as if she knew no one would be coming down.' I had to work hard not to rip the paper with my power-augmented fingers. It felt tissue-thin between my fingers, like a fly's wings.

'A punishment, then,' Rasht said. 'Marooned down here for a crime.'

'That's an expensive way of marooning someone.' I read on. 'No – it wasn't punishment. Not according to *this*, anyway. An accident, something to do with one of the geysers – she says that she's afraid that it will erupt again, as it did "on the day". Anyway, Teterev knew she was stuck down here. And she knows she's in trouble. Keeps talking about her "mistake" in not waking the others. Says she wonders if there's a way to signal the other ship, the orbiting lighthugger. Bring some or all of the crew out of reefersleep.' I paused, my finger hovering over a word. 'Lev.'

'Lev?' Lenka repeated.

'She mentions Lev. Says Lev would help her, if she could get a message through. She'd have to accept her punishment, but at least get off Holda.'

'Maybe Teterev was never meant to be down here,' Lenka said. 'Jump ahead, Nidra. Let's find out what happened.'

I paged through dozens and dozens of entries. Some were dated and consecutive. Elsewhere I noticed blank pages and sometimes gaps of many days between the accounts. The entries became sparser, too. Teterev's hand, barely clear to begin with, became progressively wilder and less legible. Her letters and words began to loop and scrawl across the page, like the traces of a seismograph registering the onset of some major dislocation.

'Stop,' Rasht said, as I turned over a page. 'Go back. What was that figure?'

I turned back the sheets with a sort of dread. My eye had caught enough to know what to expect.

It was a drawing of the volcanic cone, exactly as it appeared from the position of the wreck.

Perhaps it was no more than an accident of Teterev's hand, but the way she had put her marks down on the paper only seemed to add to the suggestion of brooding, patient malevolency I had already detected in the feature. Teterev seemed to have made the cephalopod's head *more* bulbous, *more* cerebral, the lava tubes *more* muscular and tentaclelike. Even the way she had stippled the tubes to suggest snow or ice could not help but suggest to my eye rows and rows of suckers.

Worse, she had drawn a gaping, beak-mouth between two of those tentacles.

There was a silence before Lenka said: 'Turn to the end. We can read the other entries later.'

I flicked through the pages until the writing ran out. The last few entries were barely entries at all, just scratchy annotations, done in haste or distraction.

Phrases jumped out at us.

Can't wake the others. Tried everything I can. My dear Lev, lost to me.

Such a good boy. A good son.

Doesn't deserve me, the mistakes I've made.

Stuck down here. But won't give in. Need materials, power. Something in that hill. Magnetic anomaly. Hill looks wrong. I think there might be something in it.

Amerikanos were here once, that's the only answer. Came by their old, slow methods. Frozen cells and robot wombs. No records, but so what. Must have dug into that hill, buried something in it. Ship or an installation. See an entrance. Cave mouth. That's where they went in.

I don't want to go in. But I want what they left behind. It might save my life.

Might get me back to the ship.

Back to Lev.

'They were never here,' Rasht said. 'Teterev would have known that. Their colonies never got this far out.'

'She was desperate enough to try anything,' Lenka said. 'I feel sorry for her, stuck all alone here. I bet she knew it was a thousand to one chance.'

'Nonetheless,' I said, 'there *is* something odd about that hill. Maybe it's nothing to do with the Amerikanos, but if you're out of options, you might as well see what's inside.' I turned back to the drawing. The mouth, I now realised, was Teterev's way of drawing the cave entrance.

But it still looked like the beak of an octopus.

'One thing's for certain,' Lenka said. 'If Teterev went into that hill, she didn't come back.'

'I didn't notice any footprints,' I said.

'They wouldn't last, not with all the geothermal activity around here. The top of the ice must be melting and refreezing all the time.'

'We should look into the cave, anyway,' Rasht said.

I shook my head, struck by an intense conviction that this was exactly the wrong thing to.

'It's not our job to find Teterev's corpse.'

'Someone should find it,' Lenka said sharply. 'Give her some dignity in death. At least record what happened to her. She was one of us, Nidra – an Ultra. She deserves better than to be forgotten. Can I look at her journal?'

'Be my guest,' I said, passing it over to her.

'Nidra is right – her body isn't our concern,' Rasht said, while

Lenka paged through the sheets. 'She took a risk, and it didn't work out for her. But the Amerikanos are of interest to us.'

'Records say they weren't here,' I said.

'And that's what I've always believed. But records can be wrong. What if Teterev was right with her theory? Amerikano relics are worth quite a bit these days, especially on Yellowstone.'

'Then we return to orbit, send down a drone,' I said.

'We're here already,' Rasht answered. 'There are three of us – four if you include Kanto. Did you see how old Teterev's helmet was? We have better equipment, and we're not down to our last hope of survival. We can turn back whenever we like. Nothing ventured, nothing gained.'

It took something to make our ramshackle equipment look better than someone else's, I thought to myself. Besides, we were inferring a great deal from just one helmet. Perhaps it had been an old keepsake, a memento of earlier spacefaring adventures.

Still, Rasht was settled in his decision. The orbiting ship had been picked clean; the shuttle held nothing of obvious value; that left only the cave. If we were to salvage anything from this expedition, that was the last option open to us.

Even I could see the sense in that, whether I liked it or not.

Don't mind me, for the moment. Got work to be getting on with. Busy, busy, busy.

What am I doing with these things?

Well, that's obvious, isn't it? I'm arranging them around you. Jamming them into the ice, like mirrored sculptures. I know you can't move your head very easily. There's no need, though. There's not much to see, other than the cave mouth behind you and the wreck ahead of you.

What are you saying?

No, it's not for your benefit! Silly Captain. But you are very much the focus of attention. You've always liked being at the centre of things, haven't you?

What?

You're having difficulty breathing?

Just a moment, then. I don't want you to die before we've even begun! It was lucky, what happened with the winch. I mean, I'd have found one eventually, and the line. Of course it didn't seem lucky at the time. I thought I was going to die in there. Did you think of abandoning me?

I think you did.

Here. I'm making a micro adjustment to the tension. Is that better? Can you breathe a little more easily?

Wonderful.

We went outside again. The monkey was having some difficulty with its paw, as if the contamination had worked its way into the servo-workings. It kept knocking the paw against the ground, trying to loosen it up.

'There aren't any footprints,' Lenka said, tugging binoculars down from the crown of her helmet. She was speaking in general terms, addressing Rasht and I without favour. 'But I can see the cave mouth. It's just where Teterev said it was. Must be about five, six kilometres from here.'

'Can you plot us a path between these obstacles?' Rasht asked.

'Easily.'

It was still day, not even local noon. The sky was a pale blue, criss-crossed by high-altitude clouds. Beyond the blue, the face of the gas giant backdropped our view of the hill – one swollen, ugly thing rising above another. We set off in single file, Lenka leading, Rasht next, then the monkey, then I. We were all still on suit air, even though our helmet read-outs were patiently informing us that the outside atmosphere was fully breathable, and (at the limit of our sensors) absent of any significant toxins. I watched the monkey's tail pendulum out from side to side as it walked. Bubbling pools pressed in from either side, our path narrowing down. Every now and then a geyser went off or a pool burped a huge bubble of gas into the air. Toxins or otherwise, it probably smelled quite badly out there. But then again, we were from the *Lachrimosa*, which was hardly a perfumed garden.

I had no warning when the ice gave way under me. It must have been just firm enough to take the others, but their passage – the weight of their heavy, power-assisted suits – had weakened it to the point where it could no longer support the last of us.

I plunged down to my neck in bubbling hot water, instinctively flinging out my arms as if swimming were a possibility. Then my feet touched bottom. Instantly my suit detected the transition to a new environment and began informing me of this sudden change of affairs – indices of temperature, acidity, alkalinity and salinity scrolling down my faceplate, along with mass spectrograms and molecular diagrams of chemical products. A tide of rust-coloured water lapped against the lower part of my visor.

I was startled, but not frightened. I was not totally under water, and the suit could cope with a lot worse than immersion in liquid.

But getting out was another thing.

'Don't try and pull me,' I said, as Lenka made to lean in. 'The shelf'll just give way under you, and then we'll both be in the water.'

'Nidra's right,' Rasht agreed, while the monkey looked on with a sort of agitated delight.

It was all very well warning Lenka away, but it only took a few minutes of frustration to establish that I could not get myself out unassisted. It was not a question of strength, but of having no firm point of leverage. The fringe of the pool was a crust of ice which gave away as soon as I tried to put any weight on it. All I was doing was expanding the margin of the pool.

Finally I stopped trying. 'This won't work,' I said. By then I was conscious that my arms were picking up the same sort of furry red contamination that had affected the monkey's paw.

'We'll need to haul her out,' Rasht said. 'It's the only way. With us on firm ground, it shouldn't be a problem. Lenka: you'll need to go back to the lander, get the power winch.'

'There's a quicker way,' Lenka said. 'I saw a winch in the stores locker, on the wreck. It looked serviceable. If it's no good, it'll only cost me a little longer to fetch ours.'

So Lenka went back to the crash site, detouring around the pool in which I was still trapped, then rejoining our original path. From my low vantage point, she was soon out of my line of sight. Rasht and the monkey kept an eye on me, the Captain silent for long minutes.

'You think this is a mistake,' he said eventually.

'I don't like that hill, and I like the fact that Teterev didn't come out of it even less.'

'We really don't know what happened to Teterev. For all we know she came back to the wreck and was eventually rescued.'

'Then why didn't she say so, or take her journal with her?'

'We're going into the cave to find answers, Nidra. This is what we do – adapt and explore. Mazamel's intelligence proved faulty, so we make the best of what we find.'

'You get the intelligence you pay for,' I said. 'There's a reason other ships never dealt with Mazamel.'

'A little late for recrimination, don't you think? Of course, if you're unhappy with your choice of employment, you can always find another crew.' I thought he might leave it at that, but Rasht added: 'I know how you feel about *Lachrimosa*, Nidra. Contempt for me, contempt for Lenka, contempt for your ship. It's different now though, isn't it? Without that winch, you'll be going nowhere.'

'And without a navigator, you won't be going much further.'

'You're wrong about that, though. I can use a navigator, just as I can use a sensor specialist like Lenka. But that doesn't mean I couldn't operate *Lachrimosa* on my own, if it came to that. You're useful, but you're not indispensable. Neither of you.'

'Be sure to tell Lenka that, when she returns.'

'No need. I've never had the slightest doubt about Lenka's loyalty. She's emotionally weak – all this stupid concern over Teterev. But she'll never turn on me.'

The monkey gibbered. Lenka was coming back.

The power winch was a tool about the size of a heavy vacuum rifle. Lenka carried it in two hands. We had similar equipment, so there was no question of working out how to use it.

The winch had a grapple attachment which could be fired with compressed gas. Lenka detached the grapple from the end of the line, and then looped the line back on itself to form a kind of handle or noose. The line was thin and flexible. Lenka spooled out a length from the power winch and then cast the the noose in my direction. I waded over to the noose and took hold of it. Lenka made sure she was standing on firm ground, turned up her suit amplification, and began to drag me out with the winch. The line tightened, then began to take my weight. It was still an awkward business, but at last I was able to beach myself on the surrounding ice without floundering through. I crawled from the edge, belly down, until I felt confident enough to risk standing.

'Your suit's a mess,' Rasht observed.

'I'll live. At least I didn't dip myself in it deliberately.'

But my suit had indeed suffered some ill effects, as became apparent while we resumed our trek to the cave mouth. The life support core was intact – I was in no danger of dying – but my locomotive augmentation was not working as well as it was meant to. As had happened with the monkey's paw, the organisms in the pond seemed to have infiltrated the suit's servo-assist systems. I could still walk, but the suit's responses were sluggish, meaning that it was resisting me more than aiding me.

I began to sweat with the effort. It was hard to keep up with the others. Even the monkey had no problem with the rest of its suit.

'Thank you for getting the winch,' I told Lenka, between breaths. 'It was good that you remembered the one in the wreck. Any longer in that pond, and I might have had real problems.'

'I'm glad we got you out.'

Perhaps it was just the flush of gratitude at being rescued, but I vowed to think better of Lenka. She was senior to me on the crew, and yet Rasht seemed to value her capabilities no more than he did mine. Whatever I thought of her lack of ambition, her willing acceptance of her place on the ship, it struck me that she deserved better than that. Perhaps, when this was over, I could break it to her that she was considered no more than useful, like a component that would serve its purpose for the time being. That might change her view of things. I even imagined the two of us jumping ship at the next port, leaving Rasht with his monkey. Perhaps we could pass as sisters or twins, if we wanted new employment.

The terrain became firmer as we neared the hill, and we did not need to pick our course so carefully. The ground rose up slowly. There was still ice under our feet, and we were flanked on either side by the steadily widening lava tubes, which were already ten or fifteen times taller than any of us.

Ahead lay the cave mouth. Its profile was a semicircle, with the apex perhaps ten metres above the surface of the ice which extended into the darkness of the mouth. The hill rose up and up from the mouth, almost sheer in places, but there was an overhang above the entrance, covered in a sheath of smooth clean ice – the 'beak' of Teterev's drawing.

The tongue of ice continued inside, curving down into what we could see of the cave's throat.

'Still no footsteps,' Lenka said, as we neared the entrance.

That the ice occasionally melted and refroze was clear from the fringe of icicles daggering down from the overhang, some of them nearly long enough to reach the floor. Rasht shouldered through them, shattering the icicles against the armour of his suit. As their shards broke off, they made a tinkling, atonal sort of music.

Now Lenka said: 'There are steps! This is the way she went!'

It was true. They did not begin until a few metres into the cave, where sunlight must have only reached occasionally, or not at all. There was only a single pair of footprints, and they only went one way.

'That's encouraging,' I said.

'If you want to remain here,' Rasht said, 'we can exclude you from your cut of the profits.'

So he had gone from denial of the Amerikano settlement, to a skeptical allowance of the possibility, to imagining how the dividend might be shared.

We turned on our helmet lights again – Rasht leaning down to activate the light on the monkey, which was too stupid to do it on its own. The monkey seemed more agitated than before, though. It was dragging its heels, coiling its tail, lingering after Rasht.

'It doesn't like it,' Lenka said.

'Maybe it's smarter than it looks,' I put in under my breath, which was about as much as I could manage with the effort of my ailing suit.

But I shared the monkey's dwindling enthusiasm. Who would really want to trudge into a cave, on an alien planet, if they had a choice in the matter? Teterev had gambled her salvation on finding relic technology, something that could buy her extra time in the wreck. We had no such compulsion, other than an indignant sense that we were owed our due after our earlier disappointment.

The angle of the slope pitched down steeply. The ice covered the floor, but the surrounding walls were exposed rock. We moved to the left side and used the grooved wall for support as we descended, placing our feet sideways. The monkey, still leashed to Rasht, had no choice but to continue. But its unwillingness was becoming steadily more apparent. Its gibbering turned shriller, more anxious.

'Now now, my dear,' Rasht said.

The tunnel narrowed as it deepened. All traces of daylight were soon behind us. We maintained our faltering progress, following the trail that Teterev had left for us. Once or twice, the prints became confused, as if there were suddenly three sets, rather than one. This puzzled me to begin with, until I realised that they marked instances of indecision, where Teterev had halted, reversed her progress, only to summon the courage to continue on her original heading.

I felt for Teterev.

'Something ahead,' Rasht announced. 'A glow, I think. Turn off your lights.'

'The monkey first,' I said.

'Naturally, Nidra.'

When Rasht had quenched Kanto's light, the rest of us followed suit. Our Captain had been correct. Far from darkness ahead, there was a silvery emanation. It did not seem to come from a single point source, but rather from veins of some mineral running through the rock. If they had been present nearer the surface, we would probably not have seen them against the brighter illumination of daylight. But I did not think they had been present until now.

'I'm not a geologist,' Lenka said, voicing the same thought that must have occurred to the rest of us. We had no idea what to make of the glowing veins, whether they were natural or suspicious.

Soon we did not need our helmet lights at all. Even with our eyes ramped down to normal sensitivity, there was more than enough brightness to be had from the veins. They shone out of the walls in bands and deltas and tributaries, a flowing form frozen in an instant of maximum hydrodynamic complexity. It did not look natural to me, but what did I know of such matters? I had seen the insides of more ships than worlds. Planets were full of odd, boring physics.

Eventually the slope became shallower, and then levelled out until our progress was horizontal. We were hundreds of metres from the entrance by now, and perhaps beneath the level of the surrounding terrain. It would have been wiser to send a drone, I thought. But patience had never been the Captain's strong point. Still, Teterev would not have had the luxury of a drone either. Thinking back to her journal, with its increasingly desperate, fragmentary entries, I could not shake the irrational sense that we would be letting her down if we did not follow her traces all the way in. I wondered if she had felt brave as she came down here, or instead afraid of the worse fate of dying alone in the wreck. I did not feel brave at all.

But we continued.

In time the tunnel widened out into a larger space. We paused in this rock-walled chamber, leaning back to study the patterning of the veins as they flowed and crawled and wiggled their way to the curving dome of the ceiling.

And saw things we should not have seen.

We should have turned back there and then, shouldn't we? If those figures weren't an invitation to leave, to never come back, I don't know what could have been clearer.

What do you mean, Teterev went on?

Of course she went on. She was out of options. No way off this planet unless she found something deeper in the cave, something she could use to wake up the orbiting ship. To go back to the wreck was to die, and so she knew she might as well continue.

I doubt she wanted to go on, no. If she had a sane bone in her body by that point, she'd have felt the way the rest of us did. Terrified. Scared out of her fucking skull. Every nerve screaming turn around, go back, this is wrong.

Wrong, wrong, wrong.

But she carried on. Brave Teterev, thinking of her son. Wanting to get back to him. Thinking of him more than her own survival, I think.

You say we were just the same? Just as brave?

Don't piss on her memory, Captain. The only thing driving us on was greed.

Fucking greed. The only thing in the universe stronger than fear.

But even greed wasn't strong enough in the end.

The silver veins looped and crossed each other, defining the outlines of looming forms. The forms were humanoid, with arms and legs and heads and bodies. They were skeletally thin and their torsos and limbs were twisted, almost as if the very substrate of the rock had shifted and oozed since these silvery impressions were made. Their heads were faceless, save for a kind of hemispheric delineation, a bilateral cleft suggesting a skull housing nothing but two huge eyes.

The strangeness of the figures – the combination of basic human form and alien particularity – disturbed me more than I could easily articulate. Monsters would have been unsettling, but they would not have plumbed the deep well of dread that these figures seemed to reach. The silver patterns appeared to shimmer and fluctuate in brightness, conveying an impression of subliminal movement. The figures, bent and faceless as they were, seemed to writhe in torment.

None of us could speak for long minutes. Even the monkey had fallen into dim simian reverence. I was just grateful for the opportunity to regather my strength, after the recent exertions.

'If that's not a warning to go,' Lenka said. 'I don't know what is.'

'I want to know what happened to her,' I said. 'But not at any cost. We don't have to go on.'

'Of course we go on!' Rasht said. 'These are just markings.'

But there was an edge in his voice, a kind of questioning rise, as if he sought reassurance and confirmation.

'They could almost be pre-human,' I said, wondering how we might go about dating the age of these impressions, if such a thing were even possible.

'Pre-Shrouder, maybe,' Lenka said. 'Pre-Juggler. Who knows? What we really need is measuring equipment, sampling gear. Get a reading off these rocks, find out what that silver stuff really is.'

By which she meant, return to the ship in the meantime. It was a sentiment I shared.

'Teterev went on,' Rasht said.

Her prints were a muddle, as if she had dwelled here for quite some time, pacing back and forth and debating her choices. But after that process of consideration she had carried on deeper into the tunnel, where it continued beyond the chamber.

By now the monkey almost needed to be dragged or carried. It really did not want to go on.

Even my own dread was becoming harder to push aside. There was a component to it beyond the instinctive dislike of confined spaces and the understandable reaction to the figures. A kind of unarguable, primal urge to leave – as if some deep part of my brain had already made its mind up.

'Do you feel it?' I risked asking.

'Feel what?' Rasht asked.

'The dread.'

The Captain did not answer immediately, and I feared that I had done my standing even more harm than when I questioned his judgement. But Lenka swallowed hard and said: 'Yes. I didn't want to say anything, but . . . yes. I've been wondering about that. It's beyond any rational fear we ought to be experiencing.' She paused and added: 'I think something is *making* us feel that dread.'

'Making?' Rasht echoed.

'The magnetic fields, perhaps. It's strong here – much stronger than outside. What we saw before was just leakage. Our suits aren't perfect Faraday cages, not with all the damage and repair they've had over the years. They can't exclude a sufficiently strong field, not completely. And if the field acts on the right part of our brains, we might feel it. Fear, dread. A sense of the unnatural.'

'Then it's a defence mechanism,' Rasht said. 'A deterrent device, to keep out intruders.'

'Then we might think of heeding it,' I said.

'It could also mean there is something worth guarding.'

'The Amerikanos never had psychological technology like this,' Lenka said.

'But others did. Do I need to spell it out? What did we come to this system for? It wasn't because we thought we'd find Amerikano relics. We were after a bigger reward than that.'

My dread sharpened. I could see where this was going. 'We have no evidence that Conjoiners were here either.'

'They say the spiders liked to place their toys in caches,' Rasht went on, as if my words counted for nothing. 'C-drives. Hell-class weapons.'

Despite myself I laughed. 'I thought we based our activities on intelligence, not fairy tales.'

'I heard someone already found those weapons,' Lenka said, as if that was all the convincing Rasht would need.

But his voice turned low, conspiratorial – as if there was a chance of the walls listening in. 'I heard fear was one of their counter-intrusion measures. The weapons get into your skull, turn you insane, if you're not already spidered.'

I knew then that nothing, not even dread, would deter Rasht from his quest for profit. He would replace one phantom prize with another, over and over, until reality finally trumped him.

'We have come this far,' Rasht said. 'We may as well go a little deeper.'

'A little,' I said, against every rational instinct. 'No further than we've already come.'

We pushed out of the chamber, Lenka setting the pace, following Teterev's course down another rock-walled tunnel. To begin with, the going was no harder than before. But as the tunnel progressed, so the walls began to pinch together. Now we had to move in single file, whether we liked it or not. Then Lenka announced that the walls squeezed together even more sharply just ahead, as if there had been a rockfall or a major shift in the hill's interior structure.

'That's a shame,' I said.

'We could blast it,' Lenka said. 'Set a couple of hot-dust charges at maximum delay, get back to the ship.' She was already preparing to unclip one of the demolition charges from her belt.

'And bring down half the mountain in the process,' I said. 'Lose the tunnel, the chamber, Teterev's prints, probably blast to atoms whatever we're hoping to find.'

'Her prints don't double back,' Rasht said. 'That means there must be a way through.'

'Or this obstruction wasn't here,' I answered.

But there was a way through. It was difficult to see at first, efficiently camouflaged by the play of light and shadow on the rock, almost as if it meant to hide itself. 'It's tight,' Lenka said. 'But one at a time, we should manage. With luck, it'll open up again on the other side.'

'And luck's been so kind to us until now,' I said.

Lenka was the first through. It was tight for her, and would be even tighter for Rasht, whose suit was bulkier. She grunted with effort and concentration. Her suit scraped rock.

'Careful!' Rasht called.

Now most of Lenka was out of our sight, swallowed into the cleft. 'It's easier,' she said. 'Widens out again. Just a bottleneck. I can see Teterev's footprints.'

Rasht and the monkey next. I could see that the monkey was going to take some persuasion. To begin with it would not go first, ahead of its master. Rasht swore at Kanto and went on himself, his suit grinding and clanging against the pincering rock. I wondered if it was even possible for Rasht to make it through. He could have discarded the suit, of course – put up with the cold, for the sake of his treasure. I had known the Captain endure worse, when there was a sniff of payoff.

Yet he called: 'I'm through.'

Kanto was still on the leash, which was now tight against the edge of the rock. The monkey really did not want to rejoin the Captain. I felt a glimmer of cross-species empathy. Perhaps the magnetic emanations were affecting it more strongly than the rest of us, reaching deeper into the poor animal's fear centre.

Still, the monkey did not have much say in its fate. Rasht pulled on the leash, and I pushed it through from the other side. I needed the maximum amplification of my struggling suit. The monkey would have bitten my face off given half the chance, but its teeth were on the wrong side of its visor.

Reunited, our little party continued into the tunnel system.

But we had only gone a hundred metres or more when the path branched. There were three possible directions ahead of us, and a mess of footprints at the junction.

'Looks as if she went down all three shafts,' Lenka said.

Only one set of prints had led to this point, so Teterev must not have returned from one of those tunnels. But it was hard to say which. The prints were confused now. She must have gone up and down the shafts several times, changing her mind, returning. Given the state of the prints, there was no way of saying which had been her ultimate choice.

We selected the leftmost shaft and carried on down it. It sloped a little more, and eventually the ice under our feet gave way to solid rock, meaning that we no longer had Teterev's prints as a guide. All around us the silver patterning continued, streaks and fissures of it, jetstreams and knotted synaptic tangles. It was hard not to think of a living silver nervous system, threading its way through the stone matrix of this ancient mountain.

'Your suit, Lenka,' Rasht said.

She slowed. 'What about it?'

'You've picked up some of that patterning. The silver. It must have rubbed off when you squeezed through the narrowing.'

'It's also on you,' I told the Captain.

It only took a glance to confirm that it was on me and the monkey as well. A smear of silver had attached itself to my right elbow, where I must have brushed against the wall. Doubtless there was more, out of sight.

I moved to touch the silver, to dust it from myself. But when my fingers touched it, its contamination seemed to jerk onto them. The movement was startling and quick, like the strike of an ambush predator. I stared at my hand, cross-webbed by streaks of gently pulsing silver. I clenched and opened my fist. My suit was as stiff as it had been since my accident outside, but for the moment it did not seem to be affected by the silver.

'It's nanotech,' I said. 'Nothing the suit recognises. But I don't like it.'

'If it was hostile, you'd know it by now,' Rasht said. 'We push on. Just a little further.'

But turning around there and then is exactly what we should have done. It might have made all the difference.

The next chamber was a palace of horrors.

It was as large as the earlier place, the shape similar, and a tunnel led out from it as well. But there all similarities ended. Here the tormented human forms were not confined to figures marked on the walls. These were solid shapes, three-dimensional evocations of distorted and contorted human anatomies, thrusting out of the wall like the broken and bent figureheads of shipwrecks. They seemed to be formed not of rock, or the silver contamination, but some amalgam of the two, a kind of shimmering, glinting substrate. There were ribcages and torsos, grasping hands, heads snapped back in agonies of perfect torment. They were not quite faceless, but by the same token none of the faces were right. They were all eyes, or all mouths, hinged open to obscene angles, or they were anvil-shaped nightmares that seemed to have cleaved their way through the rock itself. I was struck by a dreadful conviction that these were souls that had been entirely in the rock, imprisoned or contained, until an instant when they had nearly broken through. And I did not know whether to be glad that these souls were not quite free, or sick with terror that the rock might yet contain multitudes, still seeking escape.

'I hate this place,' Lenka said quietly.

I nodded my agreement. 'So do I.'

And all of a sudden, Lenka's earlier idea of setting a demolition charge did not seem so bad to me at all. The mere existence of this chamber struck me as profoundly, upsettingly wrong, as if it were my moral duty to remove it from the universe.

The charges at maximum delay. Time to get back to the ship, if we rushed, and none of us got stuck in the squeeze point.

Maybe. Maybe not.

That was when the monkey broke free.

So, anyway. About what we've done to your suit.

Its basic motor systems were already compromised when I found you near the cave mouth. You'd got that far, which can't have been easy.

Yes, well done you.

Brave Captain.

The nanotech contamination, the traces you picked up from

the cave wall, was clearly the main cause of the systemic failure. Obviously, if you'd stayed any longer, your suit would have begun to turn against you, the way it happened with Teterev. Allowing itself to be controlled, absorbed. But you still had some control over it, and enough strength to overcome the resistance of the jammed locomotive systems.

It was never as bad for me. I think when I fell in that pool, some of the native organisms must have formed a barrier layer, a kind of insulation against the nanotech. Perhaps they've had time to begin to evolve their own defence measures, to contain the spread of it. Who knows? My good fortune, in any case.

It didn't feel like good fortune at the time, but that's the universe for you.

Anyway, back to your suit.

You're already paralysed, effectively, but just to make sure that the systems don't begin to recover, I've opened your main control box and disabled all locomotive power. Locked it tight, in fact. You might as well be standing in a welded suit of armour, for all the success you'll have in moving.

Why are your arms the way they are?

We'll come to that.

You are standing, yes. Your feet are on the ground. Obviously, with the noose around your neck, the one thing you don't want to do now is topple over. I won't be there to catch you. But your suit is heavy and provided you don't wriggle around inside it too much, you should stay upright.

Of course, if you don't want to stay upright, that's one way out of this for you.

You're cold?

I'm not surprised! It's a cold planet, and you're not wearing a space helmet. Be a bit difficult, slipping a noose around your neck, if you were still wearing your helmet!

Fine, you want some more heat? That's easy. Your life-support systems are still good, and you can adjust the suit temperature. The reason your arms are positioned in front of you the way they are is that I want you to be able to operate your cuff control. That's right. You can do that. You can move your fingers, tap those buttons.

Here's the thing, though. There's only one thing you can do with those buttons. Only one system you can control.

You can turn up your suit temperature, or you can turn it down. That's all.

Why?

The why is easy. You remember those pieces of the wreck I went to so much trouble to position around you?

There was a point to all that.

There's a point to you.

I suppose the terror was too much for Kanto, and that the passage through the narrowing had weakened its leash. Whatever the case, the monkey was out of the chamber, gibbering and shrieking, as it headed back the way we had come.

None of us had spoken until that moment. The chamber had struck us into a thunderous, paralysing silence. Even when Kanto left, we said nothing. Any utterance would have felt like an invitation, permission for something worse than these stone ghouls to emerge from the walls.

Lenka and I looked at each other through our visors. Our eyes met, and we nodded. Then we looked at Rasht, both of us in turn, and Rasht looked as frightened as we felt.

Lenka went first, then Rasht, then I. We moved as quickly as our suits allowed. But even though none of us felt like lingering, I was no longer having to work as hard to keep up with the other two. My suit still felt sluggish, but it had not worsened since I came into contact with the silver contamination. Lenka and Rasht, though, were not moving as efficiently as before.

I still could not bring myself to speak, not until we were well away from that place. If the monkey had any sense, it was already through the narrowing, on its way back to daylight.

But when we reached the junction, the intersection of four tunnels, Rasht made us halt.

'Kanto's taken the wrong one,' he said.

In the chaos of footprints, there was no chance at all of picking out the individual trace of the monkey. I was about to say as much when Rasht spoke again.

'I have a trace on his suit. In case he . . . escaped.' The word seemed distasteful to him, as if it clarified an aspect of their relationship best kept hidden. 'He should be ahead of us now, but he isn't. He's behind again. Down this shaft, I think.' Rasht was indicating the rightmost entrance of the three we had faced on our way in. 'It's hard to know.'

Lenka said in a low voice: 'Then we have to leave. Kanto will find his own way out, once he knows he's gone the wrong way.'

'She's right,' I said.

'We can't leave him,' Rasht said. 'We won't. I won't allow it.'

'If the monkey doesn't want to be found,' I said, 'nothing we do is going to make any difference.'

'The fix isn't moving. I have a distance estimate. It isn't more than twenty or thirty metres down that tunnel.'

'Or that one,' I said, nodding to the middle shaft. 'Or your fix is wrong, and he's ahead of us anyway. For all we know, the magnetic field is screwing up your tracker.'

'He isn't behind us,' Rasht said, doggedly ignoring me. 'There are really only two possibilities. We can check them quickly, three of us. Eliminate the wrong shaft.'

Lenka's own breathing was now as heavy as my own. I caught another glimpse of her face, eyes wide with apprehension. 'I know he means a lot to you, Captain . . .'

'Is there something wrong with your suits?' I asked.

'Yes,' Lenka said. 'Mine, anyway. Losing locomotive assist. Same as happened to you.'

'I'm not sure it's the same thing. I fell in the pool, you didn't. Can you still move?'

Lenka lifted up an arm, clenched and unclenched her hand. 'For the time being. If it gets too bad, I can always go full manual.' Then she closed her eyes, took a deep breath, and reopened them. 'All right, *Captain*.' This with a particular sarcastic emphasis. 'I'll check out the middle tunnel, if it'll help. I'll go thirty metres, no more, and turn around. You can check out the one on your right, if you think Kanto's gone that way. Nidra can wait here, just in case Kanto's gone ahead of us and turns back.'

I did not like the idea of spending ten more seconds in this place, let alone the time it would take to inspect the tunnels. But Lenka's suggestion made the best of a bad situation. It would appease the Captain and not delay us more than a few minutes.

'All right,' I agreed. 'I'll wait here. But don't count on me catching Kanto if he comes back.'

'Stay where you are, my dear,' Rasht said, addressing the monkey wherever it might be. 'We are coming.'

Lenka and Rasht disappeared into their respective tunnels, their suits moving with visible sluggishness. Lenka, whose suit was more lightly armoured, would find it easier to cope than Rasht. I speculated to myself that the silver contamination was indeed having some effect, but that my exposure to the pond's microorganisms had provided a barriering layer, a kind of inocculation. It was not much of a theory, but I had nothing better to offer.

I counted a minute, then two.

Then heard: 'Nidra.'

'Yes,' I said. 'I hear you, Lenka. Have you found the monkey?'

There was a silence that ate centuries. My own fear was now as sharp and clean and precise as a surgical instrument. I could feel every cruel edge of it, cutting me open from inside.

'Help me.'

You came back then. You'd found your stupid fucking monkey. You were cradling it, holding it to you like it was the most precious thing in your universe.

Actually I do the monkey a disservice.

As stupid as he was, Kanto was innocent in all this. I thought he was dead to begin with, but then I realised that it was trembling, caught in a state of infant terror, clinging to the fixed certainty of you while he shivered in his armour.

I made out his close-set yellow eyes, wide and uncomprehending.

I loathed your fucking monkey. But there was nothing that deserved that sort of terror.

Do you remember how our conversation played out? I told you that Lenka was in trouble. Your loyal crewmember, good, dependable Lenka. Always there for you. Always there for the Lachrimosa. *No matter what had happened until that point, there was now only one imperative. We had to save her. This is what Ultras do. When one of us falls, we reach. We're better than people think.*

But not you.

The fear had finally worked its way into you. I was wrong about greed being stronger. Or rather, there are degrees. Greed trumps fear, but then a deeper fear trumps greed all over again.

I pleaded with you.

But you would not answer her call. You left with Kanto, hobbling your way back to safety.

You left me to find Lenka.

*

I did not have to go much further down the tunnel and reached the thing blocking further progress. It had trapped Lenka, but she was not yet fully part of it. Teterev had come earlier – many years ago – so her degree of intregration was much more pronounced. I could judge this in a glance, even before I had any deeper understanding of what I had found. I knew that Lenka would succumb to Teterev's fate, and that if I remained in this place I would eventually join them.

'Come closer, Nidra,' a voice said.

I stepped nearer, hardly daring to bring the full blaze of my helmet light to bear on the half-sensed obstruction ahead of me.

'I've come for Lenka. Whatever you are, whatever's happened to you, let her go.'

'We'll speak of Lenka.' The voice was loud, booming across the air between us. 'But do come closer.'

'I don't think so.'

'Because you are frightened?'

'Yes.'

'Then I am very glad to hear it. Fear is the point of this place. Fear is the last and best thing that we have.'

'We?'

'My predecessors and I. Those who came before me, the wayfarers and the lost. We've been coming for a very long time. Century after century, across hundreds of thousands of years. Unthinkable ages of galactic time. Drawn to this one place, and repelled by it – as you nearly were.'

'I wish we had been.'

'And usually the fear is sufficient. They turn back before they get this deep, as you nearly did. As you *should* have done. But you were braver than most. I'm sorry that your courage carried you as far as it did.'

'It wasn't courage.' But then I added: 'How do you know my name?'

'I listened to your language, from the moment you entered me. You are very noisy! You gibber and shriek and make no sense whatsoever.'

'Are you Teterev?'

'That is not easily answered. I remember Teterev, and I feel her distinctiveness quite strongly. Sometimes I speak through her, sometimes she speaks through us. We have all enjoyed what Teterev has brought to us.'

I had never met Teterev, never seen an image of her, but there were only two human figures before me and one of them was Lenka, jammed into immobility, strands of silver beginning to wrap and bind her suit as if in the early stages of mummification. The strands extended back to the larger form of which Teterev was only an embellishment.

She must still have been wearing her suit when she was trapped and bound. Traces of the suit remained, but much of it had been picked off her, detached or dissolved or remade into the larger mass. Her helmet, similar in design to the one we had seen in the wreck, had fissured in two, with its halves framing her head.

I thought of flytrap mouthparts, Teterev's head an insect. Her face was stony and unmoving, her eyes blank surfaces, but there was no hint of ageing or decay. Her skin had the pearly shimmer of the figures we had seen in the second chamber. She had become – or was becoming – something other than flesh.

But apart from Teterev – and Lenka, if you included her – none of the other forms were human. The blockage was an assemblage of fused shapes, creature after creature absorbed into a sort of interlocking stone puzzle, a jigsaw of jumbled anatomies and half-implied life-support technologies. Two or three of the creatures were loosely humanoid, in so far as their forms could be discerned. But it was hard to gauge where their suits and life-support mechanisms ended and their alien anatomies commenced. Vines and tendrils of silver smothered them from head to foot, binding them into the older layers of the mass. Beyond these recognisable forms lay the evidence of many stranger anatomies and technologies.

'I've heard of a plague,' I said, making my way to Lenka. 'They say it's all just rumour, but I don't know. Is this what happened to you?'

'There are a million plagues, some worse than others. Some *much* worse.' There was an edge of playfulness in the voice, taking droll amusement in my ignorance. 'No: what you see here is deliberate, done for our mutual benefit. Haphazard, yes, but organised for a purpose. Think of it as a form of defence.'

'Against the outside world?' I had my hands on her suit now, and I tried to rip the silver strands away from it, while at the same time applying as much force as I could to drag Lenka back to safety.

The voice said: 'Nothing like that. I am a barrier against the thing that would damage the outside world, were it to be released.'

'Then I don't understand.' I caught my breath, already drained by the effort of trying to free her. 'Is Lenka going to become part of you? Is that the idea?'

'Would you sooner offer yourself? Is that what you would like?'

'I'd like you to let Lenka go.' Realising I was getting nowhere – the strands reattached themselves as quickly I peeled them away – I could only step back and take stock. 'She came back here to find the monkey, not to hurt you. None of us came to harm you. We just wanted to know what had happened to Teterev.'

'So Teterev was the beginning and end of your concerns? You had no other interest in this place?'

'We wondered what was in the cave,' I answered, seeing no value in lying, even if I thought I might have got away with it. 'We thought there might be Amerikano relics, maybe a Conjoiner cache. We picked up the geomagnetic anomaly. Are you making that happen? If so, you can't blame us for noticing it. If you don't want visitors, try making yourself less visible!'

'I would, if it were within my means. Shall I tell you something of me, Nidra? Then we will speak of Lenka.'

Shall I tell you what I learned from her, Captain? Will that take your mind off the cold, for a little while?

You may as well hear it. It will put things into perspective. Make you understand your place in things – the value in your being here. The good and selfless service you are about to commence.

She was a traveller, too.

Not Teterev, but the original one – the first being, the first entity, to find this planet. A spacefarer. Admittedly this was all quite a long time ago. She tried to get me to understand, but I'm not sure I have the imagination. Whole galactic turns ago, she said. When some of the stars we see now were not even born, and the old ones were younger. When the universe itself was smaller than it is now. Young galaxies crowding each other's heavens.

I don't know if it was her, an effect of the magnetic field, or just my fears affecting my sense of self. But as she spoke of abyssal time, I felt a lurch of cosmic vertigo, a sense that I stood on the crumbling brink of time's plungeing depths.

I didn't want to fall, didn't want to topple.

Sensible advice for both of us, wouldn't you say?

The universe always feels old, though. That's a universal truth, a universal fact of life. It felt old for her, already cobwebbed by history. Hard for us to grasp, I know. Human civilisation, it's just the last scratch on the last scratch on the last scratch, on the last layer of everything. We're noise. Dirt. We haven't begun to leave a trace.

But for her, so much had already happened! There had still been time enough for the rise and fall of numberless species and civilisations, time for great deeds and greater atrocities. Time for monsters and the rumours of worse.

She had been journeying for lifetimes, by the long measure of her species. Travelling close to light, visiting world after world.

If we had a name for what she was, we'd call her an archaeologist, a scholar drawn to relics and scraps.

Still following me?

One day – one unrecorded century – she stumbles upon something. It was a thing she'd half hoped to find, half hoped to avoid. Glory and annihilation, balanced on a knife edge.

We know all about that, don't we?

Your finger is moving. Are you trying to adjust that temperature setting? Go ahead. Turn up your suit. I won't stop you.

There. Better already. Can you feel the warmth flowing up from your neck ring, taking the sting out of the cold? It feels better, doesn't it? There's plenty of power in the suit. You needn't worry about draining it. Make yourself as warm as you wish.

Look, I didn't say there wasn't a catch.

Turn it down, then. Let the cold return. Can you feel those skin cells dying, the frostbite eating its way into your face? Can you feel your eyeballs starting to freeze?

Back to our traveller.

We have rumours of plague. She had rumours of something far worse. A presence, an entity, waiting between the stars. Older than the history of any culture known to her kind. A kind of mechanism, waiting to detect the emergence of bright and busy civilisations such as hers. Or ours, for that matter.

Something with a mind and a purpose.

And she found it.

'I've no reason to think you haven't already killed Lenka,' I said, a kind of desperate calm overcoming me, when I realised how narrow my options really were.

'Oh, she is perfectly well,' the voice answered. 'Her suit is frozen, and I have pushed channels of myself into her head, to better learn her usefulness. But she is otherwise intact. She has travelled well, this Lenka. I can learn a great deal from her.'

I waited a beat.

'Are you strong?'

'That is an odd question.'

'Not really.' I reached beneath my chest pack, fumbling with my equipment belt until I found the hard casing of a demolition charge. I unclipped the grenade-sized device, presenting it before me like an offering. 'Hot-dust. Have you dug deep enough into Lenka to know what that means?'

'No, but Teterev knew.'

'That's good. And what did Teterev know?'

'That you have a matter-antimatter device.'

'That's right.'

'And the yield would be . . .?'

'A couple of kilotonnes. Very small, really. Barely enough to chip an asteroid in two. Of course, I have no idea of the damage it would do to you.'

I used two hands to twist the charge open along its midline, exposing its triggering system. The trigger was a gleaming red disk. I settled my thumb over the disk, thinking of the tiny, pollen-sized speck of antimatter held in a flawless vacuum at the heart of the demolition charge.

'Suicide, Nidra? Surely there's a time-delay option.'

'There is, but I'm not sure I'd be able to get to my ship in time. Besides, I don't know what you'd do with me gone. If you can paralyse Lenka's suit, you can probably work your way into the charge and disarm it.'

'You would kill Lenka at the same time.'

'Not if you let her go. And if you don't let her go, this has to be a kinder way out than being sucked into you.' I allowed my thumb to rub back and forth over the trigger, only a twitch away from activating it. There was an unsettling temptation to *just do it*. The light would be quick and painless, negating the past and future in a single cleansing flash.

In that moment I wanted it.

What would you have done, Captain?

Her mistake?

That's easy. The thing she found, in the wreck of another ship, seemed dead to her. Dead and exhausted. Just a cluster of black cubes, lodged in the ship's structure like the remnant of an infection. But it had not spread; it had not destroyed the wreck or achieved total transformation into a larger mass. She thought it was dead. She had no reason to think otherwise.

Can we blame her for that?

Not me.

Not you.

But the machinery was only dormant. When her ship was underway, while she slept, the black cubes began to show signs of life. They swelled, testing the limits of her containment measures. Her ship woke her up, asking what it should do. Her ship was almost a living thing in its own right. It was worried for her, worried for itself.

She had no answer.

She tried to strengthen the fields and layer the alien machinery in more armour. None of that worked. The forms broke through, began to eat her ship – making more cubes. She put more energy into her containment. What else could she do?'

Throw them overboard, you wonder?

Well, yes. She considered something like that. But that would only be passing the problem on to some other traveller. The responsibility was hers alone. She felt quite strongly about that.

Still, the machinery was definitely damaged. She was sure of that. Otherwise the transformation would have been fast and unstoppable. Instead, she had achieved a sort of stalemate.

What next?

Suicide, perhaps – dive into a star. But the data offered no guarantees that this would be enough to destroy the machinery. It might make it stronger!

Not a chance she could take.

So instead she found this world. A ship in space is an easy thing to see, even across light years. A world offers better camouflage – it has mass and heat. She thought she could screen herself – drawing no attention from passers-by.

She was wrong.

The cubes were resilient, resourceful. Constantly testing her capabilities. They demanded more power, more mass. She converted more and more of her ship into the architecture of their prison. She died! But by then her living ship had grown to know her so well that her personality lived on inside it, haunting it as a kind of ghost.

Centuries blasted by.

Her ship protected and enlarged itself. It ate into the surrounding geology, bolstering the containment and consolidating its defences. For the most part it had no need of her, this residue of what she had been. Once in a while it raised her from the shadows, when her judgement was required. She was never lonely. She'd burned through her capacity for loneliness, discarding it like an outmoded evolutionary stage.

But she had visitors, all the same.

Like us?

No, not quite. Not to begin with. To begin with they were just like her.

'They came,' the voice said. 'My sensors tracked them with great vigilance and stealth. I watched them, wary of their intentions. I risked collapsing my containment fields, until they were out of range. I did not want to be found. I did not want my mistake to become theirs. It was always a bad time.' It paused. 'But I did not miss their company. They were not like me. Their languages and customs had turned unfamiliar. I was never sorry when they turned for space and left me undisturbed.'

'I don't believe you.'

'Believe what you like. It hardly matters, anyway. They stopped coming. A silence fell, and endured. It was broken only by the tick of pulsars and the crack and whistle of quasars half way to the universe's edge. There were no more of my kind. I had no knowledge of what had become of them.'

'But you could guess.'

'It did not mean that I could give up, and allow what I had found to escape. So I slept – or ceased to be, until my ship had need of me again – and the stars lurched to new and nameless constellations. Twenty million orbits of my old world, two hundred thousand lifetimes. And then a new visitor – a new species.'

I guessed that we were still in the distant past.

'Did you know this culture?'

'I had no data on anything like them, dead or alive. Frankly, it disturbed me. It had too many limbs, a strange way of moving, and I wondered what it looked like outside of its armour. I wanted it to go away. I quietened myself, damped my energies. But still it came. It dug into me, seeking an explanation for whatever its sensors had picked up. I thought of simply killing it – it had come alone, after all. But there was another possibility open to me. I could take it, open its mind, learn from it. Fold its memories and personality into my own. Use its knowledge to better protect myself the next time.' A kind of shame or regretfulness entered the voice. 'So that is what I did. I caught the alien, made sure it was incapable of escape, and pushed feelers through the integument of its suit and into its nervous system. Its anatomy was profoundly unfamiliar to me. But at one end of its segmented, exoskeletal body was a thing like a head and inside the brittle cage of that head was a dense mass of connected cells that had something of the topological complexity of what had once been my own brain. It was hierarchically layered, with clear modular specialisation for sensory processing, motor control, abstract reasoning and memory management. It was also trying very hard to communicate with its fellows – wherever *they* were – and that made it easy for me to trace the circuits and pathways of expression. Before long, I was able to address the alien through the direct manipulation of internal mental states. And I explained what was to become of it. Together we would be stronger, better equipped both to deal with the thing at the heart of me, and also to make my concealment more effective. I was sorry about what had needed to be done, but I made it understand that I had no choice at all.'

'How did it take it?'

'How do you *think*, Nidra? But very soon the question concerned neither of us. It had become me, I had become it. Our memories were a knot of entanglements. It understood my concerns. It grasped that there had only ever been one path. It knew that we had no choice about what we had become.'

'Forgiveness?'

'Acceptance.'

'But it didn't end, did it? There were more. Always more. Other species . . . dozens, hundreds of them. Until we came!'

'You are no different.'

'Perhaps we aren't. But this alters things, doesn't it?' I still had my thumb on the trigger, ready to unleash a matter-antimatter conflagration. 'You think I won't do this? You've told me what you are. I understand that you acted . . . that you've *been* acting . . . for what you think is the common good. Maybe you're right, too. But enough is enough. You have Teterev. It's too late for her . . . too late for you, if I'm still reaching a part of her. But it stops with Lenka. She's mine. She's coming back with me.'

'I need her. I need to add her library of fears to my own. I need to make myself stronger.'

'It won't work. It hasn't *been* working. You're stuck in a spiral . . . a destructive feedback loop. The more you try to make yourself impregnable, the more *evident* you become to the outside world. So you have to make yourself yet more impregnable . . . add to your library of fears. But it can't continue.'

'It must. I tried to stop myself. But always they came. New travellers, new species. Nothing I did made myself invisible to them. I could not *negotiate*, I could not *persuade*, because that would have been tantamount to confessing the hard fact of my existence. So I did what I had always done. I hid. I made myself as quiet and silent as physics allowed, and willed them to leave. I dug into our mutual psychologies, trawled the ocean of our terrors, and from that sea of fears I shaped the phantasms that I hoped would serve as deterrence, encouraging newcomers to come no nearer. But it was never totally sufficient. Some were always too brave, or curious, and by force of will they reached the heart of me. And always I had no choice but to *take*, to *incorporate*, to turn them to my cause. To feed me their fears, so that I might better my defences. Why do you think I had to take Teterev? She was the first of your kind – a new jewel, to place in my collection. She has been very useful, has Teterev. We are all very glad of her. Her fears are like a new colour, a new smell. We never imagined such things!'

'Good. I'm truly sorry for Teterev. But you don't need Lenka. Give her back control of her suit, and we'll leave you alone.'

'You could make that promise to me. But you did not come here alone.'

'The Captain . . . we'll take care of him.'

See? Thinking of you even then.

Always in our hearts and minds.

'I listened to your babble. The theories of your Captain. He craves his fortune. He will think he can turn the *fact* of me to profit. He will try to sell the knowledge of my location.'

'He doesn't even know what you are!'

'But he will find out. He will ask what became of you, what became of Lenka. Your silence will count for nothing. He *will* return. He will send machines into me. And soon more will come, in other ships, and I am bound to fail. When the machines touch your civilisation, they will scorch you into history. They have done it a thousand times, with a thousand cultures. They will leave dust and ruins and silence, and you will *not* be the last.'

'Lev,' I said quietly.

There was a silence. I wondered if the thing before me would speak again. Perhaps I had shut the door of communication between us with that one invocation.

But the voice asked: 'What do you know of Lev?'

'Your son,' I answered. 'The son of part of you, the son of Teterev. You had to leave him on the orbiting ship. You didn't mean to, but it must have been the only way. You loved him. You wanted very badly to get a message to him, to have him help you. That's why you came as far as you did. But you failed.'

'And Lev is gone.'

I nodded. 'But not in the way you think. Someone got to that ship before us – cleaned it out. Stripped it of engines, weps, crew. The frozen. But they'd have been valuable to someone. If Lev was on that ship, he'd have made it back to one of the settled worlds by now. And we can find him. The Mendicants trade in the frozen, and we have traded with the Mendicants, in many systems. There are channels, lines of enquiry. The name of your ship . . .'

'What would it be to you?

'Give us that name. Let us find Lev. I'll return. I promise you that much.'

'No one ever promises to *return*, Nidra. They promise to stay away.'

'The name of the ship,' I said again.

She told me.

So many names, so many ships. Numberless. Names too strange to put into language, at least no language that would fit into our heads. Names like clouds. Names like forests. Names like ever-unfolding mathematical structures – names that begat themselves, in dreams of recursion. Names that split the world in two. Names that would drive a nail through your sanity.

But she told me some of them, as best as she could.

Lovely names. Names of such beauty and terror they made me weep. The hopes and fears of the brave and the lost. The best and the worst of all of us. All wayfarers, all travellers.

I asked her to try and remember the last of them.

She did.

Tell you?

Not a chance, Captain. You don't get to know everything.

I stepped back from his suited-but-immobile form, admiring my handiwork. He really did look sculptural, frozen into that oddly dignified posture, with his arms coming together across his chest, one hand touching the cuff of the other.

'I suppose you could say that we came to an understanding, Teterev and I,' I said. 'Or what Teterev had become. Partly it was fear, I think, that I'd use the hot-dust. Did I come close? Yes, definitely. Not much to lose at that point. I might have been able to work the ship without you, but certainly not without Lenka. If she didn't survive, there wasn't much point in me surviving either. But Lenka was allowed to leave, and so was I. It was hard work, getting Lenka back here. But she's begun to regain some suit function now, and I don't think either of us will have any trouble returning to the lander.'

The Captain tried to speak. It was hard, with the noose tight around his throat. He could breathe, but anything more was an effort.

He rasped out three words that might have been 'fuck you, Nidra'. But I could not be sure.

'I made a commitment to Teterev,' I carried on. 'Firstly, that we'd make sure you were not a problem. Secondly, that I'd do what I could to find Lev. If that's decades, longer, so be it. It's something to live for, anyway. A purpose. We all need a purpose, don't we?'

He attempted another set of syllables.

'Here's yours,' I said. 'Your purpose is to die here. It will happen. How fast it happens, is in your hands. Quite literally. Those pieces of debris I set around you are curved mirrors. Now, it's not an exact science. But when the sun climbs, some of them will concentrate the sun's light on the snow and ice on which you are standing. It will begin to melt. The tension on your noose will increase.' I paused, allowing that part to sink in, if he had not already deduced matters for himself. 'In any case, the ice will melt eventually, with the change of seasons. It's only permafrost deeper in the cave mouth. But you'll be dead by then. It'll be a nasty, slow death, though. Hypothermia, frostbite, slow choking – take your pick. But you can speed it up, if you like. Turn up your suit's heat, and you can stay as warm as you like. The downside is that the heat will spill away from your suit and melt the ice even quicker. You'll be hanging by your neck within hours, with the entire weight of your suit trying to rip your skull from your spine. At that point, overwhelmed by terror and pain, you might try and turn down the thermal regulation again. But by then you might not be able to move your fingers. Ultimately, it doesn't matter. There are many paths to the one goal. All the scenarios end with your corpse hanging from the mouth of the cave. Swinging there until the ice returns. You'll make an effective deterrent, wouldn't you say? A tolerable invitation to keep away?'

Rasht tried to say something. But Lenka, who had hobbled closer, placed a finger on his lips.

'Enough,' she whispered. 'Save your breath.'

'Where is the monkey?' I asked.

'Tethered where we left it, over by the wreck. Shall we leave it here?'

'No. We'll bring it with us, and we'll take good care of it. I promised him that much. I try not to break my promises. Any of them.'

'Then we're done here,' Lenka said.

'I think we are.'

We turned our backs on our former Captain and commenced the slow walk back to the lander. We would stop at the wreck on our way, collect the monkey, and what we could of Teterev's belongings. Then we would be off Holda, out of this system, and that was a good thought.

Even if I knew I had to return.

'When we we get back to the ship, I want to give it a new name.'

I thought about that for a moment. 'That's a good idea. A clean break. I have some suggestions.'

'I'd be glad to hear them,' Lenka said.

NIGHT PASSAGE

If you were really born on Fand then you will know the old saying we had on that world.

Shame is a mask that becomes the face.

The implication being that if you wear the mask long enough, it grafts itself to your skin, becomes an indelible part of you – even a kind of comfort.

Shall I tell you what I was doing before you called? Standing at my window, looking out across Chasm City as it slid into dusk. My reflection loomed against the distant buildings beyond my own, my face chiselled out of cruel highlights and pitiless, light-sucking shadows. When my father held me under the night sky above Burnheim Bay, pointing out the named colonies, the worlds and systems bound by ships, he told me that I was a very beautiful girl, and that he could see a million stars reflected in the dark pools of my eyes. I told him that I didn't care about any of that, but that I did want to be a starship captain.

Father laughed. He held me tighter. I do not know if he believed me or not, but I think it scared him, that I might mean exactly what I said.

*

And now you come.

You recognise me, as he would not have done, but only because you knew me as an adult. You and I never spoke, and our sole meeting consisted of a single smile, a single friendly glance as I welcomed the passengers onto my ship, all nineteen thousand of them streaming through the embarkation lock – twenty if you include the Conjoiners.

Try as I might, I can't picture you.

But you say you were one of them, and for a moment at least I'm inclined to give you the time of day. You say that you were one of the few thousand who came back on the ship, and that's possible – I could check your name against the *Equinoctial*'s passenger manifest, eventually – and that you were one of the still fewer who did not suffer irreversible damage due to the prolonged nature of our crossing. But you say that even then it was difficult. When they brought you out of reefersleep, you barely had a personality, let alone a functioning set of memories.

How did I do so well, when the others did not? Luck was part of it. But when it was decreed that I should survive, every measure was taken to protect me against the side effects of such a long exposure to sleep. The servitors intervened many times, to correct malfunctions and give me the best chance of coming through. More than once I was warmed to partial life, then submitted to the auto-surgeon, just to correct incipient frost damage. I remember none of that, but obviously it succeeded. That effort could never have been spread across the entire manifest, though. The rest of you had to take your chances – in more ways than one.

Come with me to the window for a moment. I like this time of day. This is my home now, Chasm City. I'll never see Fand again, and it's rare for me to leave these rooms. But it's not such a bad place, Yellowstone, once you get used to the poison skies, the starless nights.

Do you see the lights coming on? A million windows, a million other lives. The lights remain, most of the time, but still they remind me of the glints against the Shroud, the way they sparked, one after the other. I remember standing there with Magadis and Doctor Grellet, finally understanding what it was they were showing me – and what it meant. Beautiful little synaptic flashes, like thoughts sparking across the galactic darkness of the mind.

But you saw none of that.

Let me tell you how it started. You'll hear other accounts, other theories, but this is how it was for me.

To begin with no one needed to tell me that something was wrong. All the indications were there as soon as I opened my eyes, groping my way to alertness. Red walls, red lights, a soft pulsing alarm tone, the air too cold for comfort. The *Equinoctial* was supposed to warm itself prior to the mass revival sequence, when we reached Yellowstone. It would only be this chilly if I had been brought out of hibernation at emergency speed.

'Rauma,' a voice said. 'Captain Bernsdottir. Can you understand me?'

It was my second-in-command, leaning in over my half-open reefersleep casket. He was blurred out, looming swollen and pale.

'Struma.' My mouth was dry, my tongue and lips uncooperative. 'What's happened? Where are we?'

'Mid-crossing, and in a bad way.'

'Give me the worst.'

'We've stopped. Engines damaged, no control. We've got a slow drift, a few kilometres per second against the local rest frame.'

'No,' I said flatly, as if I was having to explain something to a child. 'That doesn't happen. Ships don't just stop.'

'They do if it's deliberate action.' Struma bent down and helped me struggle out of the casket, every articulation of bone and muscle sending a fresh spike of pain to my brain. Reefersleep revival was never pleasant, but rapid revival came with its own litany of discomforts. 'It's sabotage, Captain.'

'What?'

'The Spiders . . .' He corrected himself. 'The Conjoiners woke up mid-flight and took control of the ship. Broke out of their area, commandeered the controls. Flipped us around, slowed us down to just a crawl.'

He helped me hobble to a chair and a table. He had prepared a bowl of pink gelatinous pap, designed to restore my metabolic balance.

'How . . .' I had too many questions and they were tripping over themselves trying to get out of my head. But a good captain jumped to the immediate priorities, then backtracked. 'Status of the ship. Tell me.'

'Damaged. No main drive or thruster authority. Comms lost.' He swallowed, like he had more to say.

I spooned the bad-tasting pink pap into myself. 'Tell me we can repair this damage, and get going again.'

'It can all be fixed – given time. We're looking at the repair schedules now.'

'We?'

'Six of your executive officers, including me. The ship brought us out first. That's standard procedure: only wake the captain under dire circumstances. There are six more passengers coming out of freeze, under the same emergency protocol.'

Struma was slowly swimming into focus. My second-in-command had been with me on two crossings, but he still looked far too young and eager to my eyes. Strong, boyish features, an easy smile, arched eyebrows, short dark curls neatly combed even in a crisis.

'And the . . .' I frowned, trying to wish away the unwelcome news he had already told me. 'The Conjoiners. What about them. If you're speaking to me, the takeover can't have been successful.'

'No, it wasn't. They knew the ship pretty well, but not all of the security procedures. We woke up in time to contain and isolate the takeover.' He set his jaw. 'It was brutal, though. They're fast and sly, and of course they outnumbered us a hundred to one. But we had weapons, and most of the security systems were dumb enough to keep on our side, not theirs.'

'Where are they now?'

'Contained, what's left of them. Maybe eight hundred still frozen. Two hundred or so in the breakout party – we don't have exact numbers. But we ate into them. By my estimate there can't be more than about sixty still warm, and we've got them isolated behind heavy bulkheads and electrostatic shields.'

'How did the ship get so torn up?'

'It was desperate. They were prepared to go down fighting. That's when most of the damage was done. Normal pacification measures were never going to hold them. We had to break out the heavy excimers, and they'll put a hole right through the hull, out to space and anything that gets in the way – including drive and navigation systems.'

'We were carrying excimers?'

'Standard procedure, Captain. We've just never needed them before.'

'I can't believe this. A century of peaceful co-operation. Mutual advancement through shared science and technology. Why would they throw it all away now, and on my watch?'

'I'll show you why,' Struma said.

Supporting my unsteady frame he walked me to an observation port and opened the radiation shutters. Then he turned off the red emergency lighting so that my eyes had a better chance of adjusting to the outside view.

I saw stars. They were moving slowly from left to right, not because the ship was moving as a whole but because we were now on centrifugal gravity and our part of the *Equinoctial* was rotating. The stars were scattered into loose associations and constellations, some of them changed almost beyond recognition, but others – made up of more distant stars – not too different than those I remembered from my childhood.

'They're just stars,' I told Struma, unsurprised by the view. 'I don't . . .'

'Wait.'

A black wall slid into view. Its boundary was a definite edge, beyond which there were no stars at all. The more we rotated, the more blackness came into our line of sight. It wasn't just an absence of nearby stars. The Milky Way, that hobbled spine of galactic light, made up of tens of millions of stars, many thousand of light years away, came arcing across the normal part of the sky then reached an abrupt termination, just as if I were looking out at the horizon above a sunless black sea.

For a few seconds all I could do was stare, unable to process what I was seeing, or what it meant. My training had prepared me for many operational contingencies – almost everything that could ever go wrong on an interstellar crossing. But not this.

Half the sky was gone.

'What the hell is it?'

Struma looked at me. There was a long silence. 'Good question.'

*

You were not one of the six passenger-delegates. That would be too neat, too unlikely, given the odds. And I would have remembered your face as soon as you came to my door.

I met them in one of the mass revival areas. It was similar to the crew facilities, but much larger and more luxurious in its furnishings. Here, at the end of our voyage, passengers would have been thawed out in groups of a few hundred at a time, expecting to find themselves in a new solar system, at the start of a new phase in their lives.

The six were going through the same process of adjustment I had experienced only a few hours earlier. Discomfort, confusion – and a generous helping of resentment, that the crossing had not gone as smoothly as the brochures had promised.

'Here's what I know,' I said, addressing the gathering as they sat around a hexagonal table, eating and drinking restoratives. 'At some point after we left Fand there was an attempted takeover by the Conjoiners. From what we can gather one or two hundred of them broke out of reefersleep while the rest of us were frozen. They commandeered the drive systems and brought the ship to a standstill. We're near an object or phenomenon of unknown origin. It's a black sphere about the same size as a star, and we're only fifty thousand kilometres from its surface.' I raised a hand before the obvious questions started raining in. 'It's not a black hole. A black hole this large would be of galactic mass, and there's no way we'd have missed something like that in our immediate neighbourhood. Besides, it's not pulling at us. It's just sitting there, with no gravitational attraction that our instruments can register. Right up to its edge we can see that the stars aren't suffering any aberration or redshift . . . yes?'

One of the passengers had also raised a hand. The gesture was so polite, so civil, that it stopped me in my tracks.

'This can't have been an accident, can it?'

'Might I know your name, sir?'

He was a small man, mostly bald, with a high voice and perceptive, piercing eyes.

'Grellet. Doctor Grellet. I'm a physician.'

'That's lucky,' I said. 'We might well end up needing a doctor.'

'Luck's got nothing to do with it, Captain Bernsdottir. The protocol always ensures that there's a physician among the emergency revival cohort.'

I had no doubt that he was right, but it was a minor point of procedure and I felt I could be forgiven for forgetting it.

'I'll still be glad of your expertise, if we have difficulties.'

He looked back at me, something in his mild, undemonstrative manner beginning to grate on me. 'Are we expecting difficulties?'

'That'll depend. But to go back to your question, it doesn't seem likely that the Conjoiners just stumbled on this object, artefact, whatever we want to call it. They must have known of its location, then put a plan in place to gain control of the ship.'

'To what end?' Doctor Grellet asked.

I decided truthfulness was the best policy. 'I don't know. Some form of intelligence gathering, I suppose. Maybe a unilateral first contact attempt, against the terms of the Europa Accords. Whatever the plan was, it's been thwarted. But that's not been without a cost. The ship is damaged. The *Equinoctial*'s own repair systems will put things right, but they'll need time for that.'

'Then we sit and wait,' said another passenger, a woman this time. 'That's all we have to do, isn't it? Then we can be on our way again.'

'There's a bit more to it than that,' I answered, looking at them all in turn. 'We have a residual drift towards the object.

Ordinarily it wouldn't be a problem – we'd just use the main engines or steering thrusters to neutralise the motion. But we have no means of controlling the engines, and we won't get it until the repair schedule is well advanced.'

'How long?' Doctor Grellet asked.

'To regain the use of the engines? My executive officers say four weeks at the bare minimum. Even if we shaved a week off that, though, it wouldn't help us. At our present rate of drift we'll reach the surface of the object in twelve days.'

There was a silence. It echoed my own, when Struma had first informed me of our predicament.

'What will happen?' another passenger asked.

'We don't know. We don't even know what that surface is made of, whether it's a solid wall or some kind of screen or discontinuity. All we do know is that it blocks all radiation at an immeasurably high efficiency, and that its temperature is exactly the same as the cosmic microwave background. If it's a Dyson sphere . . . or something similar . . . we'd expect to see it pumping out in the infrared. But it doesn't. It just sits there being almost invisible. If you wanted to hide something, to conceal yourself in interstellar space . . . impossibly hard to detect, until you're almost on top of it . . . this would be the thing. It's like camouflage, a cloak, or . . .'

'A shroud,' Doctor Grellet said.

'Someone else will get the pleasure of naming it,' I said. 'Our concern is what it will do. I've ordered the launch of a small instrument package, aimed straight at the object. It's nothing too scientific – we're not equipped for that. Just a redundant spacesuit with some sensors. But it will give us an idea what to expect.'

'When will it arrive?'

'In a little under twenty six hours.'

'You should have consulted with the revival party before taking this action, captain,' Doctor Grellet said.

'Why?'

'You've fired a missile at an object of unknown origin. You know it isn't a missile, and so do we. But the object?'

'We don't know that it has a mind,' I responded.

'Yet,' Doctor Grellet said.

I spent the next six hours with Struma, reviewing the condition of the ship at first hand. We travelled up and down the length of the hull, inside and out, cataloguing the damage and making sure there were no additional surprises. Inside was bearable. But while we were outside, travelling in single-person inspection pods, I had that black wall at my back the whole time.

'Are you sure there weren't easier ways of containing them, other than peppering the ship with blast holes?'

'Have you had a lot of experience with Conjoiner uprisings, Captain?'

'Not especially.'

'I studied the tactics they used on Mars, back at the start of the last century. They're ruthless, unafraid of death, and totally uninterested in surrender.'

'Mars was ancient history, Struma.'

'Lessons can still be drawn. You can't treat them as a rational adversary, willing to accept a negotiated settlement. They're more like a nerve gas, trying to reach you by any means. Our objective was to push them back into an area of the ship that we could seal and vent if needed. We succeeded – but at a cost to the ship.' From the other inspection pod, cruising parallel to mine, his face regarded me with a stern and stoic resolve. 'It had to be done. I didn't like any part of it. But I also knew the ship was fully capable of repairing itself.'

'It's just a shame you didn't allow for that,' I said, cocking my own head at the black surface. At our present rate of drift it was three kilometres nearer for every minute that passed.

'What would you have had me do?' Struma asked. 'Allow them to complete their takeover, and butcher the rest of us?'

'You don't know that that was their intention.'

'I do,' Struma said. 'Because Magadis told me.'

I let him enjoy his moment before replying.

'Who is Magadis?'

'The one we captured. I wouldn't call her a leader. They don't have leaders, as such. But they do have command echelons, figures trusted with a higher level of intelligence processing and decision-making. She's one of them.'

'You didn't mention this until now?'

'You asked for priorities, Captain. I gave you priorities. Anyway, Magadis got knocked around when she was captured. She's been in and out of consciousness ever since, not always lucid. She has no value as a hostage, so her ultimate usefulness to us isn't clear. Perhaps we should just kill her now and be done with it.'

'I want to see her.'

'I thought you might,' Struma said.

Our pods steered for the open aperture of a docking bay.

By the time I got to Magadis she was awake and responsive. Struma and the other officers had secured her in a room at the far end of the ship from the other Conjoiners, and then arranged an improvised cage of electrostatic baffles around the room's walls, to screen out any possible neural traffic between Magadis and the other Conjoiners.

They had her strapped into a couch, taking no chances with that. She was shackled at the waist, the upper torso, the wrists, ankles and neck. Stepping into that room, I still felt unnerved by her close proximity. I had never distrusted Conjoiners before, but Struma's mention of Mars had unlocked a head's worth of rumour and memory. Bad things had been done to them, but they had not been shy in returning the favour. They were human, too, but only at the extreme edge of the definition. Human physiology, but boosted for a high tolerance of adverse environments. Human brain structure, but infiltrated with a cobweb of neural enhancements, far beyond anything carried by Demarchists. Their minds were cross-linked, their sense of identity blurred across the glassy boundaries of skulls and bodies.

That was why Magadis was useless as a hostage. Only part of her was present to begin with, and that part – the body, the portion of her mind within it – would be deemed expendable. Some other part of Magadis was still back with the other Conjoiners.

I approached her. She was thin, all angles and edges. Her limbs, what I could see of them beyond the shackles, were like folded blades, ready to flick out and wound. Her head was hairless, with a distinct cranial ridge. She was bruised and cut, one eye so badly swollen and slitted that I could not tell if it had been gouged out or still remained.

But the other eye fixed me well enough.

'Captain.' She formed the word carefully, but there was blood on her lips and when she opened them I saw she had lost several teeth and her tongue was badly swollen.

'Magadis. I'm told that's your name. My officers tell me you attempted to take over my ship. Is that true?'

My question seemed to amuse and disappoint her in equal measure.

'Why ask?'

'I'd like to know before we all die.'

Behind me, one of the officers had an excimer rifle pointed straight at Magadis's head.

'We distrusted your ability to conduct an efficient examination of the artefact,' she said.

'Then you knew of it in advance.'

'Of course.' She nodded demurely, despite the shackle around her throat. 'But only the barest details. A stellar-size object, clearly artificial, clearly of alien origin. It demanded our interest. But the present arrangements limited our ability to conduct intelligence gathering under our preferred terms.'

'We have an arrangement. Had, I should say. More than a century of peaceful co-operation. Why have you endangered everything?'

'Because this changes everything.'

'You don't even know what it is.'

'We have gathered and transmitted information back to our mother nests. They will analyse the findings accordingly, when the signals reach them. But let us not delude ourselves, Captain. This is an alien technology – a demonstration of physics beyond either of our present conceptual horizons. Whichever human faction understands even a fraction of this new science will leave the others in the dust of history. Our alliance with the Demarchists has served us well, as it has been of benefit to you. But all things must end.'

'You'd risk war, just for a strategic advantage?'

She squinted from her one good eye, looking puzzled. 'What other sort of advantage is there?'

'I could – should – kill you now, Magadis. And the rest of your Conjoiners. You've done enough to give me the right.'

She lifted her head. 'Then do so.'

'No. Not until I'm certain you've exhausted your usefulness to me. In five and half days we hit the object. If you want my clemency, start thinking of ways we might stop that happening.'

'I've considered the situation,' Magadis said. 'There are no grounds for hope, Captain. You may as well execute me. But save a shot for yourself, won't you? You may come to appreciate it.'

We spent the remainder of that first day confirming what we already knew. The ship was crippled, committed to its slow but deadly drift in the direction of the object.

Being a passenger-carrying vessel, supposed to fly between two settled, civilised solar systems, the *Equinoctial* carried no shuttles or large extravehicular craft. There were no lifeboats or tugs, nothing that could nudge us onto a different course or reverse our drift. Even our freight inventory was low for this crossing. I know, because I studied the cargo manifest, looking for some magic solution to our problem: a crate full of rocket motors, or something similar.

But the momentum of a million-tonne starship, even drifting at a mere fifty metres a second, is still immense. It would take more than a spare limpet motor or steering jet to make a difference to our fate.

Exactly what our fate was, of course, remained something of an open question.

Soon we would know.

An hour before the suit's arrival at the surface I gathered Struma, Doctor Grellet, the other officers and passenger delegates in the bridge. Our improvised probe had continued transmitting information back to us for the entire duration of its day-long crossing. Throughout that time there had been little significant variation in the parametres, and no hint of a response from the object.

It remained black, cold and resolutely starless. Even as it fell within the last ten thousand kilometres, the suit was detecting no trace radiation beyond that faint microwave sizzle. It was pinging sensor pulses into the surface and picking up no hint of echo or backscatter. The gravitational field remained as flat as any other part of interstellar space, with no suggestion that the black sphere exerted any pull on its surroundings. It had to be made of something, but even if there had been only a moon's mass distributed throughout that volume, let alone a planet or a star, the suit would have picked up the gradient.

So it was a non-physical surface – an energy barrier or discontinuity. But even an energy field ought to have produced a measurable curvature, a measurable alteration in the suit's motion.

Something else, then. Something – as Magadis had implied – that lay entirely outside the framework of our physics. A kink or fracture in spacetime, artfully engineered. There might be little point in attempting to build a conceptual bridge between what we knew and what the object represented. Little point for baseline humans, at least. But I thought of what a loom of cross-linked, genius-level intelligences might make of it. The Conjoiners had already developed weapons and drive systems that were beyond our narrow models, even as they occasionally drip-fed us hints and glimpses of their 'adjunct physics', as if to reassure their allies that they were only a step or two behind.

The suit was within eight thousand kilometres of the surface when its readings began to turn odd. It was small things to start with, almost possible to put down to individual sensor malfunctions. But as the readings turned stranger, and more numerous, the unlikelihood of these breakdowns happening all at once became too great to dismiss.

Dry-mouthed, I stared at the numbers and graphs.

'What?' asked Chajari, one of the female passengers.

'We'll need to look at these readings in more detail . . .' Struma began.

'No,' I said, cutting him off. 'What they're telling us is clear enough as it is. The suit's accelerometres are going haywire. It feels as if it's being pulled in a hundred directions at once. Pulled and pushed, like a piece of putty being squashed and stretched in someone's hand. And it's getting worse . . .'

I had been blunt, but there was no sense in sugaring things for the sake of the passengers. They had been woken to share in our decision-making processes, and for that reason alone they needed to know exactly how bad our predicament was.

The suit was still transmitting information when it hit the seven thousand kilometre mark, as near as we could judge. It only lasted a few minutes after that, though. The accelerational stresses built and built, until whole blocks of sensors began to black out. Soon after that the suit reported a major loss of its own integrity, as if its extremities had been ripped or crushed by the rising forces. By then it was tumbling, sending back only intermittent chirps of scrambled data.

Then it was gone.

I allowed myself a moment of calm before proceeding.

'Even when the suit was still sending to us,' I said, 'it was being buffeted by forces far beyond the structural limits of the ship. We'd have broken up not long after the eight thousand mark – and it would have been unpleasant quite a bit sooner than that.' I paused and swallowed. 'It's not a black hole. We know that. But there's something very odd about the spacetime near the surface. And if we drift too close we'll be shredded, just as the suit was.'

It reached us then. The ship groaned, and we all felt a stomach-heaving twist pass through our bodies. The emergency tone sounded, and the red warning lights began to flash.

Had we been a ship at sea, it was as if we had been afloat on calm waters, until a single great wave rolled under us, followed by a series of diminishing after-ripples.

The disturbance, whatever it had been, gradually abated.

Doctor Grellet was the first to speak. 'We still don't know if the thing has a mind or not,' he said, in the high, piping voice that I was starting to hate. 'But I think we can be reasonably sure of one thing, Captain Bernsdottir.'

'Which would be?' I asked.

'You've discovered how to provoke it.'

Just when I needed some good news, Struma brought it to me.

'It's marginal,' he said, apologising before he had even started. 'But given our present circumstances . . .'

'Go on.'

He showed me a flowchart of various repair schedules, a complex knotted thing like a many-armed octopus, and next to it a graph of our location, compared to the sphere.

'Here's our present position, thirty five thousand kilometres from the surface.'

'The surface may not even be our worst problem now,' I pointed out.

'Then we'll assume we only have twenty five thousand kilometres before things get difficult – a bit less than six days. But it may be enough. I've been running through the priority assignments in the repair schedule, and I think we can squeeze a solution out of this.'

I tried not to cling to false hope. 'You can?'

'As I said, it's marginal, but . . .'

'Spare me the qualifications, Struma. Just tell me what we have or haven't got.'

'Normally the ship prioritises primary drive repairs over anything else. It makes sense. If you're trying to slow down from lightspeed, and something goes wrong with the main engines at a high level of time-compression . . . well, you want that fixed above all else, unless you plan on over-shooting your target system by several light years, or worse.' He drew a significant pause. 'But we're not in that situation. We need auxiliary control now, enough to correct the drift. If takes a year or ten to regain relativistic capability, we'll still be alive. We can wait it out in reefersleep.'

'Good . . .' I allowed.

'If we override all default schedules, and force the repair processes to ignore the main engines – and anything we don't need to stay alive for the next six days – then the simulations say we may have a chance of recovering auxiliary steering and attitude control before we hit the ten thousand kilometre mark. Neutralise the drift, and reverse it enough to get away from this monster. *Then* worry about getting back home. And even if we can't get the main engines running again, we can eventually transmit a request for assistance, then just sit here.'

'They'd have to answer us,' I said.

'Of course.'

'Have you . . . initiated this change in the schedule?'

He nodded earnestly. 'Yes. Given how slim the margins are, I felt it best to make the change immediately.'

'It was the right thing to do, Struma. You've given us a chance. We'll take it to the passenger-representatives. Maybe they'll forgive me for what happened with the suit.'

'You couldn't have guessed, Captain. But this lifeline . . . it's just a chance, that's all. The repair schedules are estimates, not hard guarantees.'

'I know,' I said, patting him on the shoulder. 'And I'll take them for what they are.'

I went to interview Magadis again, deciding for the moment to withhold the news Struma had given me. The Conjoiner woman was still under armed guard, still bound to the chair. I took my seat in the electrostatic cage, facing her.

'We're going to die,' I said.

'This is not news,' Magadis answered.

'I mean, not in the way we expected. A clean collision with the surface – fast and painless. I'm not happy about that, but I'll gladly take it over the alternative.'

'Which is?'

'Slow torture. I fired an instrument probe at the object – a suit stuffed full of sensors.'

'Was that wise?'

'Perhaps not. But it's told me what we can expect. Spacetime around the sphere is . . . curdled, fractal, I don't know what. Restructured. Responsive. It didn't like the suit. Pulled it apart like a rag doll. It'll do the same to the ship, and us inside it. Only we're made of skin and bone, not hardware. It'll be worse for us, and slower, because the suit was travelling quickly when it hit the altered spacetime. We'll take our time, and it'll build and build over hours.'

'I could teach you a few things about pain management,' Magadis said. 'You might find them useful.'

I slapped her across the face, drawing blood from her already swollen lip.

'You were prepared to meet this object. You knew of its prior existence. That means you must have had a strategy, a plan.'

'I did, until our plan met your resistance.' She made a mangled smile, a wicked, teasing gleam in her one good eye.

I made to slap her again, but some cooler part of me stilled my hand, knowing how pointless it was to inflict pain on a Conjoiner. Or to imagine that the prospect of pain, even drawn out over hours, would have any impact on her thinking.

'Give me something, Magadis. You're smart, even disconnected from the others. You tried to commandeer the ship. Your people designed and manufactured some of its key systems. You must be able to suggest something that can help our chances.'

'We have gathered our intelligence,' she told me. 'Nothing else matters now. I was always going to die. The means don't concern me.'

I nodded at that, letting her believe it was no more or less than I had expected.

But I had more to say.

'You put us here, Magadis – you and your people. Maybe the others will see things the same way you do – ready and willing to accept death. Do you think they will change their view if I start killing them now?'

I waited for her answer, but Magadis just looked at me, nothing in her expression changing.

Someone spoke my title and name. I turned from the prisoner to find Struma, waiting beyond the electrostatic cage.

'I was in the middle of something.'

'Before it failed, the suit picked up an echo. We've only just teased it out of the garbage it was sending back in the last few moments.'

'An echo of what?' I asked.

Struma drew breath. He started to answer, then looked at Magadis and changed his mind.

It was another ship. Shaped like our own – a tapering, conic hull, a sharp end and a blunter end, two engines on outriggers jutting from the widest point – but smaller, sleeker, darker. We could see that it was damaged to some degree, but it occurred to me that it could still be of use to us.

The ship floated eight thousand kilometres from the surface of the object. Not orbiting, since there was nothing to hold it on a circular course, but just stopped, becalmed.

Struma and I exchanged thoughts as we waited for the others to reconvene.

'That's a Conjoiner drive layout,' he said, sketching a finger across one of the blurred enhancements. 'It means they made it, they sent it here – all without anyone's knowledge, in flagrant violation of the Europe Accords. And it's no coincidence that we just found it. The object's the size of a star, and we're only able to scan a tiny area of it from our present position. Unless there are floating wrecks dotted all around this thing, we must have been brought close to it deliberately.'

'It explains how they knew of the object,' I mused. 'An earlier expedition. Obviously it failed, but they must have managed to transmit some data back to one of their nests – enough to make them determined to get a closer look. I suppose the idea was to rendezvous and recover any survivors, or additional knowledge captured by that wreck.' My fingers tensed, ready to form a fist. 'I should ask Magadis.'

'I'd give up, if I were you. She's not going to give us anything useful.'

'That's because she's resigned to death. I didn't tell her about the revised repair schedule.'

'That's still our best hope of survival.'

'Perhaps. But I'd be remiss if I didn't explore all other possibilities, just in case the repair schedule doesn't work. That ship's too useful a prize for me to ignore. It's an exploratory craft, obviously. Unlike us, it may have a shuttle, something we can use as a tug. Or we can use the ship itself to nudge the *Equinoctial*.'

Struma scratched at his chin. 'Nice in theory, but it's floating well inside the point where the suit started picking up strange readings. And even if we considered it wise to go there, we don't have a shuttle of our own to make the crossing.'

'It's not wise,' I admitted. 'Not even sane. But we have the inspection pods, and one of them ought to be able to make the crossing. I'm ready to try, Struma. It's better than sitting here thinking of ways to hurt Magadis, just to take my mind off the worse pain ahead for the rest of us.'

He considered this, then gave a grave, dutiful nod. 'Under the circumstances, I think you're right. But I wouldn't allow you to go out there on your own.'

'A Captain's prerogative . . .' I started.

'Is to accept the assistance of her second-in-command.'

Although I was set on my plan, I still had to present it to the other officers and passenger-representatives. They sat and listened without question, as I explained the discovery of the other ship and my intention of scavenging it for our own ends.

'You already know that we may be able to reverse the drift. I'm still optimistic about that, but at the same time I was always told to have a back-up plan. Even if that other ship doesn't have anything aboard it than we can use, they may have gathered some data or analysis that can be of benefit to us.'

Doctor Grellet let out a dry, hopeless laugh. 'Whatever it was, it was certainly of benefit to them.'

'A slender hope's better than none at all,' I said, biting back on my irritation. 'Besides, it won't make your chances any worse. Even if Struma and I don't make it back from the Conjoiner ship, my other officers are fully capable of navigating the ship, once we regain auxiliary control.'

'The suit drew a response from the object,' Grellet said. 'How can you know what will happen if you approach it in the pods?'

'I can't,' I said. 'But we'll stop before we get as deep as the suit did. It's the best we can do, Doctor.' I turned my face to the other passenger-representatives, seeking their tacit approval. 'Nothing's without risk. You accepted risk when you consigned yourselves into the care of your reefersleep caskets. As it stands, we have a reasonable chance of repairing the ship before we get too close to the object. That's not good enough for me. I swore an oath of duty when I took on this role. You are all precious to me. But also I have twenty thousand other passengers to consider.'

'You mean nineteen thousand,' corrected Chajari diplomatically. 'The Conjoiners don't count any more – sleeping or otherwise.'

'They're still my passengers,' I told her.

No plan was ever as simple as it seemed in the first light of conception. The inspection pods had the range and fuel to reach the drifter, but under normal operation it would take much too long to get there. If there were something useful on the Conjoiner wreck I wanted time to examine it, time to bring it back, time to make use of it. I also did not want to have to depend on some hypothetical shuttle or tractor to get us back. That meant retaining some reserve fuel in the pods for a return trip to the *Equinoctial*. Privately, if my ship was going down then I wanted to be aboard when it happened.

There was a solution, but it was hardly a comfortable one.

Running the length of the *Equinoctial* was a magnetic freight launcher, designed for ship-to-ship cargo transfer. We had rarely used it on previous voyages and since we were travelling with only a low cargo manifest I had nearly forgotten it was there at all. Fortunately, the inspection pods were easily small enough to be attached to the launcher. By being boosted out of the ship on magnetic power, they could complete the crossing in a shorter time and save some fuel for the round-trip.

There were two downsides. The first was that it would take time to prepare the pods for an extended mission. The second was that the launcher demanded a punishing initial acceleration. That was fine for bulk cargo, less good for people. Eventually we agreed on a risky compromise: fifty gees, sustained for four seconds, would give us a final boost of zero point two kilometres per second. Hardly any speed at all, but it was all we could safely endure if we were going to be any use at the other end of the crossing. We would be unconscious during the launch phase and much of the subsequent crossing, both to conserve resources and spare us the discomfort of the boost.

Slowly the *Equinoctial* was rotated and stabilised, aiming itself like a gun at the Conjoiner wreck. Lacking engine power, we did this with gyroscopes and controlled pressure venting. Even this took a day. Thankfully the aim didn't need to be perfect, since we could correct for any small errors during the crossing itself.

Six days had now passed since my revival, halving our distance to the surface. It would take another three days to reach the Conjoiner ship, by which time we would have rather less than three days to make any use of its contents. Everything was now coming down to critical margins of hours, rather than days.

I went to see Magadis before preparing myself for the departure.

'I'm telling you my plans just in case you have something useful to contribute. We've found the drifter you were obviously so keen on locating. You've been going behind our backs all this time, despite all the assurances, all the wise platitudes. I hope you've learned a thing or two from the object, because you're going to need all the help you can find.'

'War was only ever a question of time, Captain Bernsdottir.'

'You think you'll win?'

'I think we'll prevail. But the outcome won't be my concern.'

'This is your last chance to make a difference. I'd take you with me if I thought I could trust you, if I thought you wouldn't turn the systems of that wreck against me just for the spite. But if there's something you can tell me, something that will help all our chances . . .'

'Yes,' she answered, drawing in me a little glimmer of hope, instantly crushed. 'There's something. Kill yourselves now, while you have the means to do it painlessly. You'll thank me for it later.'

I stepped out of the cage, realising that Doctor Grellet had been observing this brief exchange from a safe distance, his hands folded before him, his expression one of lingering disapproval.

'It was fruitless, I suppose?'

'Were you expecting something more?'

'I am not the moral compass of this ship, Captain Bernsdottir. If you think hurting this prisoner will serve your ends, that is your decision.'

'I didn't do that to her. She was bruised and bloodied when she got here.'

He studied me carefully. 'Then you never laid a hand on her, not even once?'

I made to answer, intending to deny his accusation, then stopped before I disgraced myself with an obvious lie. Instead I met his eyes, demanding understanding rather than forgiveness. 'It was a violent, organised insurrection, Doctor. They were trying to kill us all. They'd have succeeded, as well, if my officers and I hadn't used extreme measures.'

'In which case it was a good job you were equipped with the tools needed to suppress that insurrection.'

'I don't understand.'

He nodded at the officer still aiming the excimer rifle at Magadis. It was a heavy, dual-gripped laser weapon – more suited to field combat than shipboard pacification. 'I am not much of a historian, Captain. But I took the time to study a little of what happened on Mars. Nevil Clavain, Sandra Voi, Galiana, the Great Wall and the orbital blockade of the first nest . . .'

I cut him off. 'Is this relevant, Doctor Grellet?'

'That would depend. My recollection from those history lessons is that the Coalition for Neural Purity discovered that it was very difficult to take Conjoiners prisoner. They could turn almost any weapon against its user. Keeping them alive long enough to be interrogated was even harder. They could kill themselves quite easily. And the one thing you learned never to do was point a sophisticated weapon at a Conjoiner prisoner.'

For the second time in nine days I surfaced to brutal, bruising consciousness through layers of confusion and discomfort. It was not the emergence from reefersleep this time, but a much shallower state of sedation. I was alone, pressed into acceleration padding, a harness webbed across my chest. I moved aching arms and released the catch. The cushioning against my spine eased. I was weightless, but still barely able to move. The inspection pod was only just large enough for a suited human form.

I was alive, and that was something. It meant that I had survived the boost from the *Equinoctial.* I eyed the chronometre, confirming that I had been asleep for sixty six hours, and then I checked the short-range tracker, gratified to find that Struma's pod was flying close to mine. Although we had been launched in separate boosts, there had been time for the pods to zero-in on each other without eating into our fuel budgets too badly.

'Struma?' I asked across the link.

'I'm here, Captain. How do you feel?'

'About as bad as you, I'm guessing. But we're intact, and right now I'll take all the good news I can get. I'm a realist, Struma: I don't expect much to come of this. But I couldn't sit back and do nothing, just hoping for the best.'

'I understood the risks,' he replied. 'And I agree with you. We had to take this chance.'

Our pods had maintained a signals lock with the *Equinoctial*. They were pleased to hear from us. We spent a few minutes transmitting back and forth, confirming that we were healthy and that our pods had a homing fix on the drifter. The Conjoiner ship was extremely dark, extremely well camouflaged, but it stood no chance of hiding itself against the perfect blackness of the surface.

I hardly dared ask how the repair schedule had been progressing. But the news was favourable. Struma's plan to divert the resources had worked well, and all indications were that the ship would regain some control within thirteen hours. That was cutting it exceedingly fine: *Equinoctial* was now only three days' drift from the surface, and only a day from the point where the suit's readings had begun to deviate from normal spacetime. We had done what we could, though – given ourselves a couple of slim hopes where previously there had been none.

Struma and I reviewed our pod systems one more time, then began to burn fuel, slowing down for our rendezvous with the drifter. We could see each other by then, spaced by a couple of kilometres but still easily distinguished from the background stars, pushing glowing tails of plasma thrust ahead of us.

We passed the ten thousand kilometre mark without incident. I felt sore, groggy and dry-mouthed, but that was to be expected after the acceleration boost and the forced sleep of the cruise phase. In all other respects I felt normal, save for the perfectly sensible apprehension anyone would have felt in our position. The pod's instruments were working properly, the sensors and read-outs making sense.

At nine thousand kilometres I started feeling the change.

To begin with it was small things. I had to squint to make sense of the displays, as if I was seeing them underwater. I put it down to fatigue, initially. Then the comms link with the *Equinoctial* began to turn thready, broken up with static and drop outs.

'Struma . . .' I asked. 'Are you getting this?'

When his answer came back, he sounded as if he was just as far away as the ship. Yet I could see his pod with my own eyes, twinkling to port.

'Whatever the suit picked up, it's starting sooner.'

'The surface hasn't changed diametre.'

'No, but whatever it's doing to the space around it may have stepped up a notch.' There was no recrimination in his statement, but I understood the implicit connection. The suit had provoked a definite change, that ripple that passed through the *Equinoctial*. Perhaps it had signified a permanent alteration to the environment around the surface, like a fortification strengthening its defences after the first strike.

'We go on, Struma. We knew things might get sticky – it's just a bit earlier than we were counting on.'

'I agree,' he answered, his voice coming through as if thinned-out and Doppler-stretched, as if we were signalling each other from half way across the universe.

At least the pods kept operating. We passed the eight-thousand-five-hundred mark, still slowing, still homing in on the Conjoiner ship. Although it was only a quarter of the size of the *Equinoctial*, it was also the only physical object between us and the surface, and our exhaust light washed over it enough to make it shimmer into visibility, a little flake of starship suspended over a sea of black.

There would be war, I thought, when the news of this treachery reached our governments. Our peace with the Conjoiners had never been less than tense, but such infringements that had happened to date had been minor diplomatic scuffles compared to this. Not just the construction and operation of a secret expedition, in violation of the terms of mutual co-operation, but the subsequent treachery of Magadis's attempted takeover, with such a cold disregard for the lives of the other nineteen thousand passengers. They had always thought themselves better than the rest of us, Conjoiners, and by certain measures they were probably correct in that assessment. Cleverer, faster, and certainly more willing to be ruthless. We had gained from our partnership, and perhaps they had found some narrow benefits in their association with us. But I saw now that it had never been more than a front, a cynical expediency. Behind our backs they had been plotting, trying to leverage an advantage from first contact with this alien presence.

But the first war had pushed them nearly to extinction, I thought. And in the century since they had shared many of their technologies with us – allowing for a risky normalisation in our capabilities. Given that the partnership had worked for so long, why would they risk everything now, for such uncertain stakes?

My thoughts flashed back to Doctor Grellet's parting words about our prisoner. My knowledge of history was nowhere near as comprehensive as his own, but I had no reason to doubt his recollection of those events. It was surely true, what he said about Conjoiner prisoners. So why had Magadis tolerated that weapon being pointed at her, when she could have reached into its systems and made it blow her head off?

Unless she wanted to stay alive?

'Struma . . .' I began to say.

But whatever words I had meant to say died unvoiced. I felt wrong. I had experienced weightlessness and gee-loads, but this was something completely new to me. Invisible claws were reaching through my skin, tugging at my insides – but in all directions.

'It's starting,' I said, tightening my harness again, for all the good it would do.

The pod felt the alteration as well. The read-outs began to indicate anomalous stresses, outside the framework of the pod's extremely limited grasp of normal conditions. I could still see the Conjoiner ship, and the beyond the surface's black horizon the stars remained at a fixed orientation. But the pod thought it was starting to tumble. Thrusters began to pop, and that only made things worse.

'Go to manual,' Struma said, his voice garbled one instant, inside my skull the next. 'We're close enough now.'

Two hundred kilometres to the ship, then one hundred and fifty, then one hundred, slowing to only a couple of hundred metres per second now. The pod was still functioning, still maintaining life-support, but I'd had to disengage all of its high-level navigation and steering systems, trusting to my own ragged instincts. The signal lock from the *Equinoctial* was completely gone, and when I twisted round to peer through the rear dome, the stars seemed to swim behind thick, mottled glass. My guts churned, my bones ached as if they had been shot through with a million tiny fractures. A slow growing pressure sat behind my eyes. The only thing that kept me pushing on was knowing that the rest of the ship would be enduring worse than this, if we did not reverse the drift.

Finally the Conjoiner ship seemed to float out of some distorting medium, becoming clearer, its lines sharper. Fifty kilometres, then ten. Our pods slowed to a crawl for the final approach.

And we saw what we had not seen before.

Distance, the altered space, and the limitations of our own sensors and eyes had played a terrible trick on us. The state of decay was far worse than we had thought from those long-range scans. The ship was a frail wreck, only its bare outline surviving. The hull, engines, connecting spars were present . . . but they had turned fibrous, gutted open, ripped or peeled apart in some places, reduced to lacy insubstantiality in others. The ship looked ready to break apart, ready to become dust, like some fragile fossil removed from its preserving matrix.

For long minutes Struma and I could only stare, our pods hovering a few hundred metres beyond the carcass. All the earlier discomforts were still present, including the nausea. My thoughts were turning sluggish, like a hardening tar. But as I stared at the Conjoiner wreck, nothing of that mattered.

'It's been here too long,' I said.

'We don't know.'

'Decades . . . longer, even. Look at it, Struma. That's an old, old ship. Maybe it's even older than the Europa Accords.'

'Meaning what, Captain?'

'If it was sent here before the agreement, no treaty violation ever happened.'

'But Magadis . . .'

'We don't know what orders Magadis was obeying. If any.' I swallowed hard, forcing myself to state the bleak and obvious truth. 'It's useless to us, anyway. Too far gone for there to be anything we could use, even if I trusted myself to go inside. We've come all this way for nothing.'

'There could still be technical data inside that ship. Readings, measurements of the object. We have to see.'

'No,' I said. 'Nothing would have survived. You can see that, can't you? It's a husk. Even Magadis wouldn't be able to get anything out of that now.' My heart was starting to race. Besides the nausea, and the discomfort, there was now a quiet, rising terror. I knew I was in a place where simple, thinking organisms such as myself did not belong. 'We failed, Struma. It was the right thing to attempt, but there's no sense deluding ourselves. Now we have to pray that the ship can slow itself down without any outside help.'

'Let's not give up without taking a closer look, Captain. You said it yourself – we've come this far.'

Without waiting for my assent he powered his pod for the wreck. The Conjoiner ship was much smaller than the *Equinoctial*, but still his pod diminished to a tiny bright point against its size. I cursed, knowing that he was right, and applied manual thrust control to steer after him. He was heading for a wide void in the side of the hull, the skin peeled back around it like a flower's petals. He slowed with a pulse of thrust, then drifted inside.

I made one last attempt to get a signal lock from the main ship, then followed Struma.

Maybe he was right, I thought – thinking as hard and furiously as I could, so as to squeeze the fear out of my head. There might still be something inside, however unlikely it looked. A shuttle, protected from the worst of the damage. A spare engine, with its control interface miraculously intact.

Once I was inside, though, I knew that such hopes were forlorn. The interior decay was just as bad, if not worse. The ship had rotted from within, held together by only the flimsiest traces of connective tissue. With my pod's worklights beaming out at full power, I drifted through a dark, enchanted forest made of broken and buckled struts, severed floors and walls, shattered and mangled machinery.

I was just starting to accept the absolute futility of our expedition when something else occurred to me. There was no sign of Struma's pod. He had only been a few hundred metres ahead of me when he passed out of sight, and if nothing else I should have picked up the reflections from his worklights and thrusters, even if I had no direct view of his pod.

But when I dimmed my own lights, and eased off on the thruster pod, I fell into total darkness.

'Struma,' I said. 'I've lost you. Please respond.'

Silence.

'Struma. This is Rauma. Where are you? Flash your lights or thrusters if you can read me.'

Silence and darkness.

I stopped my drift. I must have been half way into the innards of the Conjoiner ship, and that was far enough. I turned around, rationalising his silence. He must have gone all the way through, come out the other side, and the physical remains of the ship must be blocking our communications.

I fired a thruster pulse, heading out the way I had come in. The ruined forms threw back milky light. Ahead was a flower-shaped patch of stars, swelling larger. Not home, not sanctuary, but still something to aim for, something better than remaining inside the wreck.

I saw him coming just before he hit. He must have used a thruster pulse, just enough to move out of whatever concealment he had found. When he rammed my pod the closing speed could not have been more than five or six metres per second, but it was still enough to jolt the breath from me and send my own pod tumbling. I gasped for air, fighting against the thickening heaviness of my thoughts to retain some clarity of mind. I crashed into something, collision alarms sounding. A pod was sturdy enough to survive the launch boost, but it was not built to withstand an intentional, sustained attack.

I jabbed at the thruster controls, loosened myself. Struma's pod was coming back around, lit in the strobe-flashes of our thrusters. Each flash lit up a static tableau, pods frozen in mid-space, but from one flash to the next our positions shifted.

I wondered if there was any point reasoning with him.

'Struma. You don't have to do this. Whatever you think you're going to achieve . . .' But then a vast and calm understanding settled over me. It was almost a blessing, to see things so clearly. 'This was staged, somehow. This whole takeover attempt. Magadis . . . the others . . . it wasn't them breaking the terms of the Accord, was it?'

His voice took on a pleading, reasoning tone.

'We needed this intelligence, Rauma. More than we needed them, and certainly more than we needed peace.'

Our pods clanged together. We had no weapons beyond mass and speed, no defences beyond thin armour and glass.

'Who, Struma? Who do you speak for?'

'Those who have our better interests in mind, Rauma. That's all you need to know. All you *will* know, shortly. I'm sorry you've got to die. Sorry about the others, too. It wasn't meant to be this bad.'

'No government would consent to this, Struma. You've been misled. Lied to.'

He came in again, harder than before, keeping thruster control going until the moment of impact. I blacked out for a second or ten, then came around as I drifted to a halt against a thicket of internal spars. Brittle as glass, they snapped into drifting, tumbling whiskers, making a dull music as they clanged and tinkled against my hull.

A fissure showed in my forward dome, pushing out little micro-fractures.

'They'd have found out about the wreck sooner or later, Rauma – just as we did. And they'd have found a way to get here, no matter the costs.'

'No,' I said. 'They wouldn't. Maybe once, they'd have been that ruthless – as would we. But we've learned to work together, learned to build a better world.'

'Console yourself. When I make my report, I'll ensure you get all the credit for the discovery. They'll name the object after you. Bernsdottir's Object. Bernsdottir's Shroud. Which would you prefer?'

'I'd prefer to be alive.' I had to raise my voice over the damage alarm. 'By the way, how do you expect to make a report, if we never get home?'

'It's been taken care of,' Struma said. 'They'll accept my version of events, when I return to the *Equinoctial*. I'll say you were trapped in here, and I couldn't help you. I'll make it sound suitably heroic.'

'Don't go to any trouble on my account.'

'Oh, I wouldn't. But the more they focus on you, the less they'll focus on me.'

He rammed me one more time, and I was about to try and dive around him when I let my hands drift from the thruster controls. My pod sailed on, careening into deepening thickets of ruined ship. I bounced against something solid, then tumbled on.

'You'd better hope that they manage to stop the drift.'

'Perhaps they will, perhaps they won't. I don't need the ship, though. There's a plan – a contingency – if all else were to fail. I abandon the ship. Catapult myself out of harm's way in a reefersleep casket. I'll put a long-range homing trace on it. Out between the stars, the casket will have no trouble keeping me cold. Eventually they'll send another ship to find me.'

More thruster flashes, but not from me. For an instant the sharp, jagged architecture of this place was laid stark. Perhaps I saw a body somewhere in that chaos, stirred from rest by our rude intrusion, tumbling like a doll, a fleshless, sharp-crested skull turning its blank eyes to mine.

'I'm glad you trust your masters that well.'

'Oh, I do.'

'Who are they, Struma? A faction within the Demarchists? One of the non-aligned powers?'

'Just people, Rauma. Just good, wise people with our long-term interests in mind.'

Struma came in again, lining up for a final ram. He must have heard that damage alarm, I thought, and took my helpless tumble as evidence that I had suffered some final loss of thruster control.

I let him fall closer. He picked up speed, his face seeming to swell until it filled his dome. His expression was one of stony resolve, filled more with regret than anger. Our eyes must have met in those last strobe-lit instants, and perhaps he saw something in my own face, some betrayal of my intentions.

By then, though, it would have been much too late.

I jammed my hands back onto the controls, thrusting sideways, giving him no time to change his course. His pod slid into the space where mine had been only an instant earlier, and then onward, onto the impaling spike of a severed spar. It drove through armour, into Struma's chest, and in the flicker of my own thrusters I watched his body undergo a single violent convulsion, even as the air and life raced from his lungs.

Under better circumstances, I would have found a way to remove his body from that wreck. Whatever he had done, whatever his sins, no one deserved to be left in that place.

But these were not better circumstances, and I left him there.

Of the rest, there isn't much more I need to tell you. Few things in life are entirely black and white, and so it was with the repair schedule. It completed on time, and *Equinoctial* regained control. I was on my way back, using what remained of my fuel, when they began to test the auxiliary engines. Since they were shining in my direction, I had no difficulty making out the brightening star that was my ship. Not much was being asked of it, I told myself. Surely now it would be possible to undo the drift, even reverse it, and begin putting some comfortable distance between the *Equinoctial* and the object.

As my pod cleared the immediate influence of the surface, I regained a stable signal and ranging fix on the main ship. Hardly daring to breathe, I watched as her drift was reduced by a factor of five. At ten metres per second a human could have outpaced her. It was nearly enough – tantalisingly close to zero.

Then something went wrong. I watched the motors flicker and fade. I waited for them to restart, but the moment never came. Through the link I learned that some fragile power coupling had overloaded, strained beyond its limits. Like everything else, it could be repaired – but only given time that we did not have. The *Equinoctial*'s rate of drift had been reduced, but not neutralised. Our pods had detected changes at nine thousand kilometres from the surface. At its present speed, the ship would pass that point in four days.

We did not have time.

I had burned almost all my fuel on the way back from the wreck, leaving only the barest margin to rendezvous with the ship.

Unfortunately that margin proved insufficient. My course was off, and by the time I corrected it, I did not have quite enough fuel to complete my rendezvous. I was due to sail past the ship, carrying on into interstellar space. The pod's resources would keep me alive for a few more days, but not enough for anyone to come to my rescue, and eventually I would freeze or suffocate, depending on which got me first. Neither option struck me as very appealing. But at least I would be spared the rending forces of the surface.

That was not how it happened, of course.

My remaining crew, and the passenger-representatives, had decreed that I should return to the ship. And so the *Equinoctial*'s alignment was trimmed very carefully, using such steering control as the ship now retained, and I slid back into the maw of the cargo launcher. It was a bumpy procedure, reversing the process that had boosted me out of the ship in the first place, and I suffered concussion as the pod was recaptured by the launch cradle and brought to a punishing halt.

But I was alive.

Doctor Grellet was the first face I saw when I returned to awareness, lying on a revival couch, sore around the temples, but fully cognizant of what had happened.

My first question was a natural one.

'Where are we?'

'Two days from the point where your pods began to pick up the altered spacetime.' He spoke softly, in the best bedside manner. 'Our instruments haven't picked up anything odd just yet, but I'm sure that will change as we near the boundary.'

I absorbed his news, oddly resentful that I had not been allowed to die. But I forced a captainlike composure upon myself. 'It took until now to revive me?'

'There were complications. We had to put you into the auto-surgeon, to remove a bleed on the brain. There were difficulties getting the surgeon to function properly. I had to perform a manual override of some of its tasks.'

No one else was in the room with me. I wondered where the rest of my executive staff were. Perhaps they were busy preparing the ship for its last few days, closing logs and committing messages and farewells to the void, for all the hope they had of reaching anyone.

'It's going to be bad, Doctor Grellet. Struma and I got a taste of it, and we were still a long way from the surface. If there's nothing we can do, then no one need be conscious for it.'

'They won't be,' Doctor Grellet said. 'Only a few of us are awake now. The rest have gone back into reefersleep. They understand that it's a death sentence, but at least it's painless, and some sedatives can ease the transition into sleep.'

'You should join them.'

'I shall. But I wanted to tell you about Magadis first. I think you will find it interesting.'

When I was ready to move, Doctor Grellet and I made our way to the interrogation cell. Magadis was sitting in her chair, still bound. Her head swivelled to track me as I entered the electrostatic cage. In the time since I had last seen her the swelling around her bad eye had begun to reduce, and she could look at me with both eyes.

'I told the guard to stand down,' Doctor Grellet said. 'He was achieving nothing, anyway.'

'You told me about the prisoners on Mars.'

He gave a thin smile. 'I'm glad some of that sunk in. I didn't really know what to make of it at the time. Why hadn't Magadis turned that weapon on herself, or simply reached inside her own skull to commit suicide? It ought to have been well within her means.'

'Why didn't you?' I asked her.

Magadis levelled her gaze at Doctor Grellet. Although she was still my prisoner, her poise was one of serene control and dominance. 'Tell her what you found, Doctor.'

'It was the auto-surgeon,' Grellet said. 'I mentioned that there were problems getting it to work properly. No one had expected that it would need to be used again, I think, and so they had taken no great pains to clear its executive memory of the earlier workflow.'

'I don't understand,' I said.

'The auto-surgeon had been programmed to perform an unusual surgical task, something far outside its normal repertoire. Magadis was brought out of reefersleep, but held beneath consciousness. She was put into the auto-surgeon. A coercive device was installed inside her.'

'It was a military device,' Magadis said, as detached as if she were recounting something that had happened to someone else entirely, long ago and far away. 'An illegal relic of the first war. A Tharsis Lash, they called it. Designed to override our voluntary functions, and permit us to be interrogated and serve as counter-propaganda mouthpieces. While the device was installed in me, I had no volition. I could only do and say what was required of me.'

'By Struma,' I said, deciding that was the only answer that made any sense.

'He was obliged to act alone,' Magadis answered, still with that same icy calm. 'It was made to look like an attempted takeover of your ship, but no such thing was ever attempted. But we had to die, all of us. No knowledge of the object could be allowed to reach our mother nests.'

'I removed the coercive device,' Doctor Grellet said. 'Of course, there was resistance from your loyal officers. But they were made to understand what had happened. Struma must have woken up first, then completed the work on Magadis. Struma then laid the evidence for an attempted takeover of the ship. More Conjoiners were brought out of reefersleep, and either killed on the spot or implanted with cruder versions of the coercive devices, so that they were seen to put up a convincing fight. The other officers were revived, and perceived that the ship was under imminent threat. In the heat of the emergency they had no reason to doubt Struma.'

'Nor did I,' I whispered.

'It was vital that the Conjoiners be eliminated. Their co-operation was required for the existence and operation of this ship, but they could not be party to the discovery and exploration of the object.'

'What about the rest of us?' I asked. 'We were all part of it. We'd have spoken, when we got back home.'

'You would have accepted Struma's account of the Conjoiner takeover, as you very nearly did. As I did. But it was a mistake to put her under armed guard, and another mistake to allow me a close look at that auto-surgeon. I suppose we can't blame Struma for a few slips. He had enough to be concentrating on.'

'You were worried about war,' Magadis said evenly. 'Now it may still happen. But the terms of provocation will be different. A faction inside one of your own planetary governments engineered this takeover bid.' She held her silence for a few moments. 'But I do not want war. Do you believe in clemency, Rauma Bernsdottir?'

'I hope so.'

'Good.' And Magadis stood from her chair, her bindings falling away where they had clearly never been properly fastened. She took a step nearer to me, and in a single whiplash motion brought her arm up to my chin. Her hand closed around my jaw. She held me with a vicelike force, squeezing so hard that I felt my bones would shatter. 'I believe in clemency as well. But it takes two to make it work. You struck me, when you thought I was your prisoner.'

I stumbled back, crashing against the useless grid of the electrostatic cage. 'I'm sorry.'

'Are you, Captain?'

'Yes.' It was hard to speak, hard to think, with the pain she was inflicting. 'I'm sorry. I shouldn't have hit you.'

'In your defence,' Magadis said, 'you only did it the once. And although I was under the control of the device, I saw something in your eyes. Doubt. Shame.' She relinquished her hold on me. I drew quick breaths, fully aware of how easily she could still break me. 'I'm minded to think you regretted your impulse.'

'I did.'

'Good. Because someone has to live, and it may as well be you.'

I reached up and nursed the skin around my jaw. 'No. We're finished – all of us. All that's left is reefersleep. We'll die, but at least we'll be under when it happens.'

'The ship can be saved,' Magadis answered. 'And a small number of its passengers. This will happen. Now that knowledge of the object has been gathered, it must reach civilisation. You will be the vector of that knowledge.'

'The ship can't be saved. There just isn't time.'

Magadis turned to Doctor Grellet. 'Perhaps we should show her, Doctor. Then she would understand.'

They took me to one of the forward viewports. Since the ship was still aimed at the object, all that was presently visible was a wall of darkness, stretching to the limit of vision in all directions. I stared into that nothingness, wondering if I might catch a glimpse of the Conjoiner wreck, now that we were so much closer. They had asked me very little of what happened to Struma, as if my safe return was answer enough.

Then something flashed. It was a brief, bright scintillation, there and gone almost before it had time to register on my retinae. Wondering if it might have been a trick of the imagination, I stayed at the port until I saw another of the flashes. A little later came a third. They were not happening in the same spot, but clustered near enough to each other not to be accidental.

'You saved us,' Doctor Grellet said, speaking quietly, as if he might break some sacred spell. 'Or at least, showed us the way. When you and Struma used the cargo launcher to accelerate your pods, there was an effect on the rest of the ship. A tiny but measurable recoil, reducing some of her speed.'

'It's no help to us,' I said, taking a certain bleak pleasure in pointing out the error in his thinking. 'If we had a full cargo manifest, tens of thousands of tonnes, then maybe we could shoot enough of it ahead of the ship to reverse the drift. But we haven't. We're barely carrying any cargo at all.'

Another flash twinkled against the surface.

'It's not cargo,' Magadis said.

I suppose I understood even then. Some part of me, at least. But not the part that was willing to face the truth.

'What, then?'

'Caskets,' Doctor Grellet said. 'Reefersleep caskets. Each about as large and heavy as your inspection pod, each still containing a sleeping passenger.'

'No.' My answer was one of flat denial, even as I knew there was no reason for either of them to lie.

'There are uncertainties,' Magadis said. 'The launcher is under strain, and its efficiency may not remain optimal. But it seems likely that the ship can be saved with the loss of only half the passenger manifest.' Some distant, alien sympathy glimmered in her eyes. 'I understand that this is difficult for you, Rauma. But there is no other way to save the ship. Some must die, so that some must live. And you in particular must be one of the living.'

The flashes continued. Now that I was attuned to their rhythm, I picked up an almost subliminal nudge in the fabric of the ship, happening at about the same frequency as the impacts. Each nudge was the cargo launcher firing another casket away, the ship's motion reducing by a tiny value. It produced a negligibly small effect. But put several thousand negligibly small things together and they can add up to something useful.

'I won't sanction this,' I said. 'Not for the sake of the ship. Not murder, not suicide, not self-sacrifice. Nothing's worth this.'

'Everything is worth it,' Magadis said. 'Firstly, knowledge of the artefact – the object – must reach civilisation, and it must then be disseminated. It cannot remain the secretive preserve of one faction or arm of government. It must be universal knowledge. Perhaps there are more of these objects. If there are, they must be mapped and investigated, their natures probed. Secondly, you must speak of peace. If this ship were lost, if no trace of it were ever to return home, there would always be speculation. You must guard against that.'

'But you . . .'

She carried on speaking. 'They would accept your testimony more readily than mine. But do not think this is suicide, for any of us. It has been agreed, Rauma – by a quorum of the living, both baseline and Conjoiner. A larger subset of the sleeping passengers was brought to the edge of consciousness, so that they could be polled, their opinions weighed. I will not say that the verdict was unanimous . . . but it carried, and with a healthy majority. We each take our chances. The automated systems of the ship will continue ejecting caskets until the drift has been safely reversed, with a comfortable margin of error. Perhaps it will take ten thousand sleepers, or fifteen thousand. Until that point has been reached, the selection is entirely random. We return to reefersleep knowing only that we have a better than zero chance of surviving.'

'It's enough,' Doctor Grellet said. 'As Magadis says, better that one of us survives than none of us.'

'It would have suited Struma if you butchered us all,' Magadis said. 'But you didn't. And even when there was a hope that the repairs could be completed, you risked your life to investigate the wreck. The crew and passengers evaluated this action. They found it meritorious.'

'Struma just wanted a good way to kill me.'

'The decision was yours, not Struma's. And our decision is final.' Magadis's tone was stern, but not without some bleak edge of compassion. 'Doctor Grellet and I will return to reefer-sleep now. Our staying awake was only ever temporary, and we must also submit our lives to chance.'

'No,' I said again. 'Stay with me. Not everyone has to die – you said it yourselves.'

'We accepted our fate,' Doctor Grellet said. 'Now, Captain Bernsdottir you must accept yours.'

And I did.

I believed that we had a better than even chance. I thought that if one of us survived, thousands more would also make it back. And that among those sleepers, once they were woken, would be witnesses willing to corroborate my version of events.

I was wrong.

The ship did repair itself, and I did make it back to Yellowstone. As I have mentioned, great pains were taken to protect me from the long exposure to reefersleep. When they brought me back to life, my complications were minimal. I remembered almost all of it from the first day.

But the others – the few thousand who were spared – they were not so fortunate. One by one they were brought out of hibernation, and one by one they were found to have suffered various deficits of memory and personality. The most lucid among them, those who had come through with the least damage, could not verify my account with the reliability demanded by public opinion. Some recalled being raised to minimal consciousness, polled as to the decision to sacrifice some of the passengers – a majority, as it turned out – but their recollections were vague and sometimes contradictory. Under other circumstances such things would have been put down to revival amnesia, and there would have been no blemish on my name. But this was different. How could I have survived, out of all of them?

You think I didn't argue my case? I tried. For years, I recounted exactly what had happened, sparing nothing. I turned to the ship's own records, defending their veracity. It was difficult, for Struma's family back on Fand. Word reached them eventually. I wept for what they had to bear, with the knowledge of his betrayal. The irony is that they never doubted my account, even as it burned them.

But that saying we had on Fand – the one I spoke of earlier. *Shame is a mask that becomes the face.* I mentioned its corollary, too – of how that mask can become so well adapted to its wearer that it no longer feels ill-fitting or alien. Becomes, in fact, something to hide behind – a shield and a comfort.

I have come to be very comfortable with my shame.

True, it chafed against me, in the early days. I resisted it, resented the new and contorting shape it forced upon my life.

But with time the mask became something I could endure. By turns I became less and less aware of its presence, and then one day I stopped noticing it was there at all. Either it had changed, or I had. Or perhaps we had both moved towards some odd accommodation, each accepting the other.

Whatever the case, to discard it now would feel like ripping away my own living flesh.

I know this surprises you – shocks you, even. That even with your clarity of mind, even with your clear recollection of being polled, even with your watertight corroboration, I would not jump at the chance for forgiveness. But you misjudge me if you think otherwise.

Look out at the city now.

Tower after tower, like the dust columns of stellar nurseries, receding into the haze of night, twinkling with a billion lights, a billion implicated lives.

The truth is, they don't deserve it. They put this on me. I spoke truthfully all those years ago, and my words steered us from the brink of a second war with the Conjoiners. A few who mattered – those who had influence – they took my words at face value. But many more did not. I ask you this now: why should I offer them the solace of seeing me vindicated?

They can sleep with their guilt when I'm dead.

I hear your disbelief. Understand it, even. You've gone to this trouble, come to me with this generous, selfless intention – hoping to ease these final years with some shift in the public view of me. It's a kindness, and I thank you for it.

But there's another saying we used to have on Fand. You'll know it well, I think.

A late gift is worse than no gift at all.

Would you mind leaving me now?

OPEN AND SHUT

Not many months after the Aurora crisis, Dreyfus was summoned by Jane Aumonier. She was in a room of her own in the medical section, lying on a sloping platform with her head and upper body fixed into an alloy framework. Around her the walls churned with images and status summaries, display facets swelling and shrinking in restless succession.

Dreyfus walked to her side.

'You asked for me, Supreme Prefect.'

A quilt of mirrors floated above Aumonier's face, forming an adaptive network trained to respond to intentional cues. With a smooth flutter of co-ordinated motion the mirrors angled themselves so that her eyes were brought into line with his own.

'I read your report on the Chertoff case,' Aumonier said, her lips moving while the rest of her remained still. 'Terse and to the point, Tom, as I expect from you.'

'I filed that report weeks ago,' Dreyfus said, biting into the apple he had collected on his way to the medical section. 'Was there a problem with it?'

'Do you think there might have been?'

Dreyfus had returned to Panoply after a routine polling core inspection in one of the habitats orbiting near the edge of the Glitter Band. Tired, he loosened his belt and removed his whiphound and holster. He set them down on a nearby medical cabinet, glad to be rid of the dragging weight around his paunch.

He took another bite.

'I thought it was a simple open-and-shut. That's how I treated it in my report. If you want waffle and obfuscation, other prefects are available.'

'You've been active since Chertoff. Twenty three days of uninterrupted duty, with no more than thirteen hours between any two assignments, and several taken consecutively.' The mirrors fluttered again, redirecting Aumonier's gaze to an area of a breakdown of schedules and rosters scrolling down a wall. 'You've failed to take your normal rest intervals, and you've rushed to fill in for other prefects whenever there was a risk that you might have time on your hands.'

'I enjoy my work.'

'Sparver says you've been showing signs of stress and irritability since Chertoff. Thalia said the same thing, although it was harder to get it out of her.'

'Anything else you'd like to ask my team while I'm not around?'

'I asked them both direct questions, and gave them no choice but to answer me. Is that understood?'

He bit into the apple again.

'Perfectly.'

'Then we'll get to the crux of the matter. Something rattled you during the Chertoff case. I don't doubt that your report is entirely factual. But my unavoidable conclusion is that you've been burying yourself in your duties ever since, because something broke through that usually implacable facade.' The mirrors fluttered again, bringing their eyes back into alignment. 'I reviewed your service history. Not because I have the slightest doubt about your competence, but because I wondered if this was your first open-and-shut.'

'I've served my share of lockdowns.'

'But, until now, never had to deal with the direct consequences of that action.'

'I fail to see the significance.'

'Then it's fortunate that one of us is able to. Would you please stop eating that apple? It's bad enough lying here listening to myself breathe, without your crunching.'

Dreyfus dropped the half-eaten apple to the floor, where it was quickly absorbed into the quickmatter substrate under his feet.

'You spent eleven years locked in a room with no possibility of human contact. I would have thought a few months here was a breeze.'

'Are you telling me to stop complaining?'

'Put bluntly.'

A faint smile played across her lips. 'And I thought Demikhov's bedside manner needed work.'

'He's an excellent physician. But he isn't one of your oldest colleagues and friends.'

'Fetch me a glass of water, will you? Demikhov says it's safe for me to swallow.'

Dreyfus went to the wall, conjured a glass of water and brought it back to the bedside as Aumonier mouthed a command and the platform beneath her increased its tilt, until she rested at about thirty degrees to the horizontal. Dreyfus brought the glass to her lips, letting her sip a small amount at a time.

'Demikhov must be pleased with your progress.'

'He puts on a brave face, but he thinks I should be regaining peripheral motor control by now – able to move my hands and fingers at least.'

Dreyfus's gaze slipped to the pale line around her neck, the barely visible trace of the surgery that had reattached Jane

Aumonier's head to her own body. The operation and the circumstances surrounding it had been entirely unprecedented. No one, least of all Demikhov, had been willing to make specific predictions about the course of her recovery. Yet there was now an unavoidable sense that only the more pessimistic range of outcomes remained, though Dreyfus still hoped for the best.

'There's no rush,' he said.

'That's what I try to tell myself.' She licked the last drop of water from her lips. 'Thank you – that's enough. You're not off the hook, though. Remind me of the circumstances of the original lockdown order.'

Dreyfus sighed. He had no desire to rake over this old ground. Equally, she was correct that the Chertoff case had been playing on his mind, driving him into a familiar pattern of overwork, as if he sought to revalidate his own professional credentials. Not just those, he reflected, but the entire ethical basis of Panoply and its methods. Overwork, fatigue, shortness with his colleagues and peers, then a gradual loss of effectiveness in his own decision-making. It was a self-reinforcing spiral that he recognised all too well, yet seemed unable to avoid.

'It was a forty-year lockdown,' he said, speaking slowly and carefully. 'I was only a few months into Field Two when Albert Dusollier sent me to investigate a polling anomaly in House Chertoff. Looking back, I was as green as they come. But I felt confident – ready for anything.'

'Dusollier wouldn't have sent you in if he had anything less than total faith in your abilities. He'd also have had a shrewd idea that the polling glitch might be grounds for lockdown, and that you were fully competent to make that call on the spot. What were the essentials?'

Dreyfus's eyes wandered to the wall, to the constant shuffling play of summaries. The majority of the locales were unfamiliar to him. There were ten thousand orbiting habitats under Panoply's care, and Dreyfus doubted he could name more than one in ten of them, even after thirty years of service. But that was only because most habitats never came to Panoply's direct notice.

That did not mean that the citizens in them were all saints, or that serious crimes went uncommitted. But Panoply's remit was highly specific. The organisation – with its tiny cadre of prefects – was dedicated to ensuring that the machinery of democratic participation ran flawlessly throughout the habitats. The hundred million citizens of the Glitter Band lived with embedded neural connections, implants that enabled mass participation in a real-time voting process, as well as theoretical access to many layers of abstraction. Whether they lived in an abundant utopia, a rustic pre-industrial throwback or a Voluntary Tyranny, each citizen was guaranteed their right to vote.

Panoply protected that right with surgical force, and punished infringements with a merciless impartiality. Sometimes those punishments were directed at individuals, but very occasionally an entire habitat was implicated in some aspect of vote rigging.

In such instances the consequences were particularly severe.

'Chertoff is – was – a small habitat, with less than five thousand permanent residents at the time I visited. I didn't have to dig very deeply to find evidence of high-level collusion in a vote-tampering.'

'What was the loophole?'

'Pietr Chertoff had identified a tiny flaw in our error-handling routines. Once in a while a legitimate vote would suffer packet corruption and be discarded. The system would prompt a vote resend. Chertoff had found a way to fool the apparatus into accepting both the corrupted and the duplicate packet, effectively amplifying his voting influence.'

'Grounds for action against Chertoff, certainly, but there'd be a limit to the damage he could have done, or the personal benefits he could have accrued.'

'Chertoff had allies. He stuffed the habitat with friends, and they shared the vote-spoofing scheme. There were at least two hundred of them in on it, and when they voted in a co-ordinated fashion, in marginal polls, they had enough cumulative influence to shift results. They needed to be very careful about it, to avoid garnering suspicion, and for several years they were. But our pattern filters eventually picked up the anomaly, and Dusollier instigated a full traceback which identified Chertoff and his associates.'

'What was in it for them?'

'Cash for votes, as banal as it sounds. Chertoff feathered his nest with wealthy clients who needed those marginals to swing one way or another. We got them all eventually – lone fish for the most part. But Chertoff and his friends constituted an organised syndicate operating at the highest levels of House Chertoff's local administration. It was grounds for immediate lockdown.'

'How did they take it?'

'As well as they ever do. Outrage, indignation, fear and panic.' Dreyfus laced his fingers, conscious that his palms were damp with sweat, feeling as if he had been asked to account for himself. 'They had the usual six hundred second margin before the lockdown became binding. Time to send messages to loved ones, before we imposed the total communications blackout. Time for a very lucky few to make it to docked spacecraft and get away from the habitat, before we sealed the locks and enforced an exclusion volume. I think about a hundred got out – maybe fewer. There was some rioting near the shuttle docks, as they tried to squeeze aboard.'

'Did it cross your mind that some of those citizens about to be locked inside House Chertoff for forty years were innocent of any wrongdoing?'

He shrugged.

'Of course.'

'And you still instigated the lockdown, even with that knowledge?'

'There is a thing called due diligence,' Dreyfus said, after a moment's consideration. 'Many of those citizens had no direct complicity in Pietr Chertoff's crime. But they should have been suspicious of him. I saw what the place was like. The whole habitat was a palace, with Chertoff on the throne, his friends in high office and everyone else living the life of pampered courtiers. Gold everywhere. Molten rivers of it flowing in channels through the palace grounds. They even had fountains spraying liquid gold into the air. Anything that wasn't gold was jewelled. There wasn't a square centimetre of the place that didn't scream of obscene concentrations of money and power. All real, as well. Nothing holographic or virtual. No plumage or abstraction layers, because Chertoff wanted you to know that this was the real thing, wealth you could reach out and touch. No one who lived there could have failed to wonder where all this wealth came from. Yet they silenced their qualms, turned a blind eye, and enjoyed the fruits of Chertoff's vote rigging. They took a gamble, and they lost.'

'Some of them,' Aumonier said. 'Those who at least had the foresight to consider that there might be something rotten at the core of House Chertoff. But what of those citizens who were simply naive, or excessively trusting?'

'I regret that they were caught by the lockdown. But there can't be any half-measures. Besides, forty years is not the longest such sentence we've ever imposed.'

'Were you confident that House Chertoff had the internal resources to keep its citizens alive for that span of time, with no outside assistance?'

'No,' Dreyfus said. 'But again, the citizens knew the risk and had ample time to satisfy themselves that the arrangements were sufficient. If they doubted House Chertoff's capability to sustain itself through a lockdown, they should have relocated.'

'You take a very unforgiving line.'

'I'm employed to.' Dreyfus unlaced his hands, drying his palms against his trousers, which immediately absorbed and reprocessed the sweat. 'We aren't without a conscience. That's why we have the open-and-shuts. Dusollier ordered a mid-term inspection, twenty years into the lockdown. If I'd found anything untoward . . . anything that warranted a suspension of the punishment . . .'

'And did you?'

'You read the report.'

'As I said, terse. Just the dry facts, and a recommendation that the lockdown continue until its scheduled expiration. No colour, no emotional context. Despite the fact that it's playing on your mind three weeks later. What did you see in there, Tom?'

Dreyfus settled his hands behind his back, breathed in deeply through his nose. Through the play of mirrors her eyes met his own, a little too intently this time. He glanced away, then despised himself for that moment of weakness.

'It's not meant to be an easy ticket.'

'Were you seen?'

'Not to begin with. I went in covertly, as we always aim to do. Dock silently, and open a lock without detection. Send in a whiphound or two as an advance scout, then conduct a field survey. It doesn't have to be exhaustive – just enough to satisfy the basic criteria. If we'd found that these had degenerated beyond some threshold . . . if things had got too bad . . .'

'Had they?'

'Not quite.' Dreyfus swallowed, clearing a tightness in his throat. 'Not quite enough. Chertoff and most of his circle were dead, probably at the hands of aggrieved citizens who had no one else to blame when the lockdown took hold. The palace's inner sanctum had been stormed and taken over. The ornaments and prizes looted and smashed. Clearly there'd been a period of violent anarchy, then a gradual stabilisation to a new social order. The habitat's life-support infrastructure was still just about operable. It maintained breathable air and recycled the waste products efficiently enough to provide food and water, albeit at a much reduced level. The citizens had to make do with daily rations, just enough to sustain them, and some very low-level medical provision. Most of them needed to work, just to keep the life-support system from breaking down. It was very cold, and the power budget only allowed for twilight illumination.' He studied Aumonier's face, wondering how well his own words were painting a picture. 'Imagine a permanent, shivering gloom, and never a moment without hunger, thirst and exhaustion. Imagine the constant fear of suffering illness or injury.'

'You've just described nine tenths of human history.'

'Perhaps. I've seen worse, too, in the VTs. But this was enforced on those citizens, not adopted by them as a conscious lifestyle. Even so, it didn't meet our thresholds for lockdown suspension.'

'If we intervened to revoke lockdown as soon as conditions turned a little trying,' Aumonier replied, 'we might as well not have lockdown at all.'

Dreyfus thought on her reply for a few moments before continuing.

'I met a man, hobbling over a garbage mound of broken gold. He had lost a leg below the knee. His clothes were rags. He had a stick, and there was a crude bandage over his stump. He smelled very badly. I think he may have been looking for food scraps, or something to barter with.'

'What did he make of you?'

'Surprised to see me, of course, and suspicious and hopeful at the same time. If he recognised me, he showed no sign of it. I explained that I was there to review the situation, that I would appreciate his co-operation, and that it would be much better for both of us if I avoided drawing further attention.'

'And was he willing?'

'Yes. He took me further into the habitat, choosing a route that would keep us away from too many prying eyes. He began to ask questions, and slowly it dawned on me that he had no idea how long he had been inside the habitat. He thought I was here to end the lockdown.'

'He thought forty years had passed, not twenty?'

'It seems incredible, but once I'd seen the state of the place I found it much easier to accept. No clear distinction between one day and the next, in that endless twilight, and no means of checking. The days and months must have slipped into one endless drudge of misery and squalor. But in me he saw hope. He thought that the time of punishment was nearly over, and the more assistance he gave me, the quicker that end would come.'

'Did you . . . correct him?'

'I never lied,' Dreyfus answered. 'At the same time, I thought he would be more useful to me if I had his co-operation, so I sidestepped his questions. When I was ready to leave, he still had a flicker of hope in his eyes. I thought at the time that telling the truth would have been far crueller than allowing him that hope, if only for the few hours it took to realise we weren't coming back. But I was wrong.'

'I understand why you might have felt that way,' Aumonier said. 'And why it might have gnawed at you since. But you needn't be too harsh in reviewing what you did or didn't say to him. For all you know, he could have been one of Chertoff's closest allies.'

'Perhaps. I'm fairly sure he wasn't Chertoff himself.'

'Your whiphound ran an ident?'

'It didn't need to,' Dreyfus answered. 'He took me to see Chertoff.'

'You said he was murdered.'

'I'm sure he was, and that it happened in the immediate aftermath of the lockdown. It was in one of the formal gardens of the palace, just about recognisable after twenty years. The place would have been busier, but that was about the time when the habitat was releasing the latest allocation of food and water rations, and most of the survivors were gathering in the dispensary area. The man led me to Chertoff's corpse.'

'They hadn't disposed of him?'

'There was no need. He wasn't a disease risk. They had thrown him into one of his rivers of gold. Judging by the posture in which I saw him, and the expression on his face, he was still alive when they did it. The gold was in the process of cooling, becoming solid metal – whatever machine kept the gold molten and flowing must have been broken – and had encased him like a molten cast. He was caught in that hardening river like a drowning man, thrashing with his last breath. They'd left him like that. I don't imagine he'd have lasted long if any of the survivors had any use for gold.'

'No, I doubt that they would have. And in twenty years we'll have the great pleasure of deciding what to do with that corpse.' Aumonier's expression turned rueful. 'Although I rather suspect that will be my successor's problem, not mine.'

'I hope we can count on your leadership for just a little longer.'

'That will depend on . . . many factors.' The quilt of mirrors fluttered, as if Aumonier were trying to stare down the length of her own body. 'We'll see. Perhaps it will be your little headache in twenty years, who knows. I take it you're ready to put this behind you now?' She did not wait for his answer. 'You won't stop remembering that ragged man, nor the hope in his eyes. And you being you, you won't stop questioning your own judgement in that regard. I'd expect nothing less. But you'll draw a line under it now, take at least two days immediate rest, and consider your conduct to have been judged fully satisfactory.'

Dreyfus sighed, some portion of the recent days' tension leaving him at last. He still carried his share of it, and that would leave him slowly if at all, but he realised it had been an error not to share this experience sooner. He had been impaired, his work had been impaired, and by extension so had the work of his immediate colleagues Thalia and Sparver. Panoply was a small but very tightly-knit mechanism, and it only functioned properly when all its components were operating smoothly.

He ought to have seen that sooner, instead of waiting for this pep-talk . . .

'Thank you,' he said, beginning to reach for his whiphound.

'Two more things. The first is that you're not the only one to have served a lockdown and then followed through with the open-and-shut. I have, too, and I had just as much trouble dealing with the consequences.'

Dreyfus cocked his head, surprised that his old friend still had the capacity to surprise him. 'You've never mentioned this, and I thought I had a reasonably good idea of your service history.'

'Back in the day, my reports were as terse and to the point as your own. If not more so. It was a similar set-up. I was green when I served the lockdown, and about twenty years *less* green when I revisited. What I found was . . . similarly challenging.' A tightness crept into her face. 'It was the Carter-Suff Spindle habitat. Three thousand citizens at the time of lockdown, and every expectation that most of them would still be alive when I went back in again.'

'And?' Dreyfus asked.

'They took a grave exception to my decision. Things had turned a little harder than anticipated, as well. It got very bad, very quickly. Famine had set in, then cannibalism, and they ate themselves into oblivion – first the newly dead, then the old and the weak, then the less old, the less weak. By the time I got there, all that remained were a few gangs of feral children.'

Dreyfus shook his head in wonder and horror. 'It must have crossed our thresholds.'

'Of course. Immediate revocation of the lockdown, followed by rapid humanitarian intervention. But by then it was much too late. The few living children were beyond conventional rehabilitation. We sent the best of them to the Mendicants. There was very little we could do for the others, except keep them from sharp objects and other human beings. Can I tell you the worst of it, though?'

'You may as well.'

'They made a bone pile for me. A sort of statue, in my honour. A figure of me, made from corpses, or what was left of them. It must have been one of their last acts before the final generation, before they forgot language, writing, or any sense of why they were there. And I still remember it. There isn't a day when it doesn't push itself into my thoughts. Even those eleven years when I couldn't sleep . . . it was always *there*. And it was a blessing, in a way, because it was a part of me that the Clockmaker couldn't touch. Something worse.'

After a silence Dreyfus said: 'If there's one thing I've learned, it's that there's always something worse.'

'Yes. Odd that *that* should be what keeps us going, but there it is. We take our comforts where we may.'

'We do.'

'There were two things. Demikhov will be back shortly, but I'd rather you were the first to know.'

Dreyfus smiled through his misgivings. 'What is it?'

'Touch my fingers.'

He reached down and placed his hand in contact with her own. 'Can you feel anything?'

'Yes – it's faint, but not so faint as it was a week ago. A little better all the time, I think. This harness is starting to bother me below the neck, too, and that must be a good thing, because at least I can feel it. There's something else, though. I did it for the first time this morning, but I want to be sure it isn't my mind playing tricks. The mirrors can't give me a good enough view to be certain.'

'Certain of what?'

'This, Tom.' She drew a breath, relaxed her fingers, then closed them slowly around his own. 'Open and shut.'

PLAGUE MUSIC

A volantor descended through the air of Chasm City.

The flying machine navigated a tricky, winding path through the thickening tangle of diseased buildings. Searchlights stabbed out from its belly, scissoring through rain, fog and smoke, glancing off the nearing obstructions. There seemed no end to the city's descending levels; no end to the profusion of entanglements and mutated architecture.

A sudden vertigo gripped the nervous young man who had his face pressed to the volantor's side-window. Merignac had never been good with heights. It was why he had chosen this line of work, above the other possibilities offered him. He had been assured that the sterilisation crews mostly worked the lowest levels.

Had they lied to him?

At last something like a floor appeared in the down-pointing searchlights. It was a ledge, buttressed off from one of the buildings, rather than the true base of the city. Ramps and bridges fed away to other ledges and plazas, suspended at about the same height. There were still levels beneath this one, dark and mist-wreathed. Not many blocks away was the nearest edge of the swallowing emptiness of the Chasm itself, the natural abyss around which the city had accreted. Merignac's stomach churned at the idea of the depths still under him. But if they kept to the plazas, away from the edges of things, he imagined it would not be too hard to forget about the empty spaces underneath.

'Shit,' Molloy said, clicking her fingers impatiently. 'Your papers. Nearly forgot.'

Greer looked up from the breather mask he was adjusting. 'You left it until now to check his papers?'

'My neck on the line, not yours,' Molloy muttered.

Merignac fished out his documents, the ones he had brought down from orbit after his arrival. Molloy uncreased them. Her fingers were bare, her heavy fireproof gloves still in her lap. She was team leader, Greer the next most experienced.

They had not told him what had happened to the one he replaced.

'In from Sky's Edge,' Molloy said.

'Yes,' he answered guardedly.

Her nails were chewed to the quick. She tapped one against the paper. 'Says here you were a soldier.'

He shrugged easily. 'Not too many other lines of work.'

'Why'd you leave?'

He studied Molloy's head, her close-shaven, scarless scalp. 'The opportunity arose, so I took it.'

'You swapped a warzone for a plague-ridden shithole. Good move?'

'At least the plague isn't trying to kill anyone because they were born at the wrong end of a peninsula.'

Molloy nodded slowly, seemingly accepting the logic of his answer. Anything, indeed, had to be better than a soldier's life. 'Well, he's clean. Welcome to the squad, Skyboy. Don't fuck up, and you might just fit in.' She began to slip on the gloves. 'Greer, you got the schedule?'

'Mm-hmm. Pretty light, all told. Three to sweep, all in the same sector.'

On her with breather mask, crunching it down onto her scalp. Her voice came through muffled, and she said a word that was unfamiliar to Merignac.

'Sprokers?'

'Maybe one or two. Actually almost certainly two.'

'Thought you said it was pretty light.'

'Neither should be a problem.' Greer tapped a fireproofed pouch on his overalls. 'I have the association test for the first, the one we'll find in the second location. That'll ease in Skyboy nicely.'

'And the one after?'

'Building three. Inactive, according to the last squad through. Should be an easy burn.'

'I still hate sprokers. Shit, they give us two on the same shift, *and* a newbie? My day just gets better.' She gestured at her shoulder. 'Check my supply valves, will you? Right one feels slack.'

Greer began to fiddle with the armoured oxygen hoses feeding around from Molloy's backpack to her breather mask.

Merignac asked: 'What's a sproker?'

The other two laughed: Greer with an easy-going sympathy, Molloy with contempt.

They helped him with his protective gear, then the three of them trudged down the volantor's belly ramp. Each had a sled's worth of equipment to drag behind them. When they were down on the ground Molloy signalled the volantor to pull back into the air. Quickly it lost itself in the higher levels.

They fussed around the sleds for a minute or two, making sure the gear was tied down and properly balanced. They had explained none of it to Merignac. Not that it mattered: a child could have figured out most of it. There was cutting and demolition equipment, ranging from mallets and axes to high-powered drills and plastic explosives. There were propellant tanks for the incinerators, and the incinerators themselves – long, rugged, riflelike implements that could be carried slung over a shoulder but which were now racked onto the sleds, until they were needed. They looked easy to use: just a simple trigger and regulator. Merignac's sled had the tools, tanks and incinerators, but also a top-heavy stack of electrical instruments and cables, protected from the rain under a makeshift awning.

Merignac realised that he had not yet breathed the open air of Chasm City. While Greer and Molloy were examining a rain-proof map, plotting the route to the first building, he shrugged back his hood and lifted off his breather mask.

He took a cautious breath, but as soon as it was in his lungs he wanted to cough it out. The city was diseased, its atmosphere foul. The rain was no improvement. It stung his eyes and left an abrasive, rust-coloured residue on his gloves.

He spat into the goggles, settled the breather mask back over his face, taking care with the skin-tight seals.

'Follow,' Molloy said, already leaning into her sled.

The first stop on their schedule was almost routine.

They got to it after about forty minutes of hard hauling, up and down ramps and bridges, veering close to the crumbling edges of things but never to the point where Merignac felt real vertigo. Sweat pooled around his goggles, and his muscles and bones already felt strained to their limits. The awkwardly-laden sled was hard work on the rough, sodden ground. His protective garments, stiffened with heavy fireproofing, seemed to wilfully resist his efforts.

At the base of the building Molloy and Greer halted their sleds and looked back to him as he caught up. Molloy's eyes swam behind her goggles. They were the only part of her face Merignac could see.

'You struggling already, Skyboy?'

He raised a glove. 'I'm fine. Just finding my feet.'

'I thought a soldier would be fitter.'

'I'm only a few days out of reefersleep.' He forced grit into his voice. 'I'll manage.'

'You'd better. No room for slip-ups here. Be throwing fire around soon enough.'

He looked back at the distance they had come.

'Why didn't they set us down nearer?'

'Only stable ground was that ledge,' Greer answered. 'Things get a little sketchy this close to the Chasm. When we've cleaned this zone, the surveyors'll move in and see what can be reinforced, what needs to be knocked down and remade. Only sure thing is that someone will make money off of it, whatever happens.'

He looked up at the flank of the building, as much as he could see of it before its higher levels were lost in mist. It was treelike, with swelling, rootlike footings. There were lightless windows in the bark, scattered along queasy alignments. Merignac guessed that they had been neatly ranked once, but distorted by the building's mutation, the way the symmetry of a human face could be pulled apart by disease.

Greer swept a torch into the cleft between two of the major roots. A wide, glass-paned door nestled in the darkness, battened over. Next to the door was a scrawl of reflective colour, sprayed directly onto the building's surface.

'See that?' Molloy asked.

'I do.'

'Gang tag, Skyboy. You'll be needing to read these, to be any use to us.'

Merignac's eyes made no sense of the swooping, tangled scrawl. It almost looked like writing, but in some alphabet not quite known to him.

'What does it say?'

'The idiot's version?'

'Please.'

Molloy sighed, as if to answer his question required herculean reserves of strength and fortitude.

'The building's been swept by Bizley's squad. They've certified it for sterilisation. It also says that the only reason they didn't finish the job was that they ran low on incinerant. So we – the next team along – get to have the pleasure of burning.'

Merignac raised his eyes to the edifice. 'We're meant to burn this whole thing to the ground?'

Molloy turned her mask to Greer and sniggered. 'He really did come to us green.'

Greer chuckled quietly, but with some glimmer of tolerance for the newcomer. 'We don't burn down the whole building, no. That'd need a lot more than these incinerators and burner tanks. What we do is make it safe for the surveyors and heavy demolition crews, just by burning away any last traces of plague. Bizley's tag says they finished the interior cleansing, and the higher levels need specialist access. All we're required to do is sterilise the lowest part, on the outside.'

'Then it's . . . helpful, to be told that,' Merignac ventured.

'When you've learned to read the tags,' Molloy said, before correcting herself. '*If* you learn . . . you'll understand that there's a fuck of a lot more to it. It's not just what's written, it's how it's written. The way Bizley's left it . . . there's a tone to it. A cockiness. Doesn't just say "this is what you need to do". It says "look what we've left for you to finish off, pussies. Hope it's not too much for you." Fuckers.'

'There's a healthy rivalry between gangs,' Greer said. 'Helps productivity. And it has to be said that we give as good as we get. Don't we, Moll?'

'We've earned it,' Molloy said gruffly. 'Earned it several times over. Bizley's gang hasn't.'

She strode to her sled and unhitched her incinerator, Greer following suit. Merignac watched and copied their actions with a fierce attentiveness. Checking the armoured fuel lines, opening safety valves, working the spring-loaded trigger and fuel-mixture regulators to make sure nothing was going to jam on them, especially when the incinerant was in full flow and ignited. Something in Molloy and Greer's methodical deliberations suggested to him that there had recently been some slip or omission that had cost them badly.

'Light your pilot like this,' Greer said, showing Merignac how to turn on the permanent little flame at the tip of the incinerator. 'Then open her up slowly, and watch for wind deflection. Don't want that fire curling round back at you.'

They pointed the incinerators to the sky. The main flame was blue, a very particular blue, shading to a dark purple near the core, which in turn cusped a curious dancing black. Greer showed the optimum regulator setting, then how to open the trigger to increase the flow. The flame licked out metre by metre, until it was a searing blue banner ten or twelve metres in extent.

The rain sparked through it, and the breeze made the flame's furthest extent buckle and quiver unpredictably, as if it was a snake that he held by the tail alone.

The flames cleared some of the mist around and above them, revealing more of the building's flanks.

'See those silver filaments?' Molloy said, dabbing her flame in the direction of the building's wall. 'Veins of plague matter, risen to the surface. Concentrate your burn around those nodes where it's thickest. Once the flame takes hold, it'll burn along those filaments by itself. Don't go dousing it around where it won't help. I don't want us running dry like Bizley.'

They let Merignac take the first stab at it, a test of sorts. He lowered the burner until the flame was nearly horizontal, and then eased back the trigger to reduce the flame to a controllable eight or nine metres. He advanced pace by pace, and brought the blue fire into contact with the one of the nervelike nodes where the silver filaments tangled together. He held his position, waiting until the flame brought the plague matter up to combustion temperature. It took suddenly, the silver flashing to a river of blue, and the blue began to thread out along the filaments, advancing slowly but steadily.

Merignac stepped back, selected another tangle and continued the burn. Molloy and Greer watched him without comment. After a minute, they lowered their own burners and began to join in the work, striking at the nodes scattered some way from those he had already torched.

He supposed by their wordlessness that he had passed the test, or at least not failed it.

With the burning complete, Molloy unclipped a selection of coloured aerosols and daubed her own message across the tag left by the previous gang. The tag she left was distinct from the first, but recognisably formed from the same elements of coded grammar. Not much was left visible of the tag beneath it.

'Fuck you, Bizley,' he heard her say. 'Piss on our patch again, and . . .'

Greer checked the map, turning it this way and that until he had the right orientation. They leaned into their sleds and set out for the next building.

'So,' Greer said, as if they were all old friends by now. 'What did you do during the war, Merignac?'

'Tell me a little about sprokers,' he answered. 'And I'll tell you a little about Sky's Edge.'

The story he told them was sparse in its details, but sufficient. He was glad when they kept their questions (most of which came from Greer) to generalities.

He had been a soldier in the Northern Coalition, he said. The last surviving son of a family decimated by incursions from the forces of the Southland Militia.

'I was in Kessler's brigade, for a while. But I soon got out of it. I'm proud to have been a patriot, but even I knew that Kessler's methods were too extreme.'

'I guess you were conscripted,' Molloy said, making it sound like a character judgement.

'No, I volunteered. The Southers killed my brothers, and then took my father. I was too young to join up when my mother became a widow, but from that point on I was counting the days until they'd have me.'

'Did your mother agree with that?' Greer asked.

'No, as you can imagine.' Merignac grunted his sled on, catching his breath between exertions. 'But she respected my decision to honour the family. It was even more significant because by the time my father died, I was given automatic exemption from conscription. I didn't have to do what I did.' He grunted again, countering a tendency of the sled to begin toppling over as its rails scraped over buckled ground. 'I went to see his body. They'd tried to fix him up in one of the private hospital compounds, but his injuries were too severe. They were keeping him alive, in the medical sense, so that some of his organs could be harvested and sent back out the field clinics. You had to be pretty badly injured on Sky's Edge before you got a ticket home, or even away from the front line.'

'I can see why coming to Chasm City might not be such a jolt after all,' Greer said.

'As I said, I was lucky to get a chance to leave. There was a lottery for conscripted and voluntary soldiers, something to pin our hopes onto. Once in a while one of us got offered a slot on an outbound ship, to some better world.'

'Guess you'd rather be back home now,' Molloy said.

'No,' he said. 'Not in the slightest. Nothing for me there, by the end. Mother had died, and the graves marking my brothers turned to rubble. I'd done my part for the North. When I saw my name on that reefersleep slot, I took it.'

'Sorry about your mother,' Greer offered.

Molloy scoffed but said nothing.

'It wasn't the war that got her in the end,' Merignac said. 'Just disease. But I suppose disease was a side effect of the war, too. She'd have been happy that I made it out, I think. Even if it meant coming here.'

Greer asked: 'You think about her much?'

'Not so much about the times after father died. But when I was smaller, and she had to break the news to me that I'd lost a brother . . . she used to sing me to sleep, and tell me that everything would be all right in the end.' Merignac laboured his sled over a black fissure wide enough to fall into. 'She sang very beautifully, and I won't forget that.' Then, consciously breaking the spell of his own words: 'That's my part. Tell me about sprokers.'

*

Blue torches aloft, they emerged into what had once been a high-ceilinged lobby, but which now had something of the oppressive damp gloom of a hothouse. It was a dense, tangled volume, criss-crossed at all levels by branchlike projections that had grown out of the main walls. They went up and up, growing ever more interconnected and impenetrable. There was no power or light left in the building, but some grey radiance filtered down from far above. Rain penetrated the interior, too. The branches were dripping, and a glossy mosslike growth had taken hold on many of them.

'We have to go up there?' he asked, trying to make the question sound matter-of-fact.

'You volunteering?' Molloy asked.

'Actually I think I'd rather stay down here.'

They dragged their sleds further into the lobby, stooping under the lowest of the branches. The lobby's floor had collapsed into a shallow bowl, taking them ankle-deep into grey water. Merignac kept an eye on the instruments on the sled, making sure they stayed out of the water. His goggles were starting to fog over again, but he thought better of taking off his mask. He wanted to look as if he was keeping up, fitting in.

He jumped as something moved in the grey water, a sinuous swimming shape just beneath the surface. Merignac dipped his burner, ready to incinerate. For a second all he could think of were the lethal serpentine creatures of Sky's Edge.

'Easy,' Molloy said, with a mocking undertone. 'Just a rat. They've grown bigger lately. But they aren't our problem.'

They ducked beneath a thick, low-hanging spar, wading deeper into the water. Then up a gradually rising slope, until the water was again only ankle-deep, surely too shallow for swimming horrors.

Something snagged his foot. He staggered into the fall, letting out a sharp surprised gasp. His boot had caught on some cabling that must have been left by one of the earlier teams. He extricated himself, found his balance, continued forward without a further word.

It was almost a relief to come to the objective. Molloy had brought them through the chaos and water to the back wall of the building, roughly opposite their point of entry. Here the light was even more attenuated than before. The rain worked its way down not in drips but in continuous forceful rivulets, more than seemed reasonable to Merignac. The rain splashed off every surface, airborne drops transfigured to blue glories in the radiance of their pilot flames.

'Wakey-wakey,' Molloy called out.

The sproker was a man, half buried in the wall. He seemed to have been trying to claw his way out of it, as if the wall were a perpendicular sea, the man a drowning swimmer. Only the upper part of his body was visible at all: his chest, his flailing arms, his head caught in a neck-straining fight for one last breath, before the building consumed him. It had not succeeded, not entirely, but the process had been sufficient to leave the man embedded, petrified, incapable of gesture or reaction, turned into this half-formed sculptural tableau.

He seemed to be cast from some pewterlike metal. His face was an alloy mask; his eyes blank surfaces, his mouth a shallow concavity. Where the edges of his flesh and clothes met the wall, silvery curlicues suggested an extension of the man into the architecture, a diffusion of his nervous system into the building's own network of sense and reaction.

They came nearer, blue flames aloft, so that all the highlights and shadows of the sproker appeared to move, evoking a sense that the man was flinching away, trying to flatten himself or perhaps sink entirely into the wall.

'He wasn't going down without a struggle,' Greer said.

'Don't they all struggle?' Merignac asked.

'You'd think. With some there's a look of resignation or surrender. They know what's coming and they don't resist. Others . . . seems they went willingly. Eagerly, even, as if it's a kind of bliss. Mostly, we'll never know what was going on in their heads.'

'Mostly we don't want to,' Molloy said, curtailing this line of discussion. 'Stow your burner, Merignac. You can help me with the test lines. Clean out the inputs, where they've begun to close up.'

He fixed the burner back onto the sled, but with the blue pilot still licking from its end. Molloy did the same, then began to spool out lengths of coiled electrical cable. Merignac unloaded his drill. It was a heavy, rugged item worked by a manually-operated handle on a gear wheel.

An earlier team had already drilled input points into the sproker. Five whitish craters showed where they had gone in: one in the cranium, two in the chest, another two in the forearms. The active Melding Plague still present in the sproker had begun to heal up those drill points. Now they needed to be rebored so that Molloy could drop in the test probes.

Merignac presented the drill, braced himself and began to turn the handle. Coils of silver spun out of the slow-turning bit. Rather than anything that resembled human tissue, the sproker seemed to be made up of soft glistening clay. The plague had infiltrated his anatomy to an extreme level, so that what remained was more like a fossil than a corpse. Merignac found it almost easy to forget that he was drilling into a human body.

He completed his work and stepped back.

Molloy made a sniffing examination of the input holes, but seemed unable to find obvious fault. One by one she plugged each hole with a tight-fitting probe, with five cables running back to the equipment on the sled Merignac had been dragging. She began to work switches and knobs, watching as dark-coloured screens lit up with fuzzy, wavering traces. Despite the awning the rain had still found its way onto the equipment. Sparks flickered across poor connections; hums and crackles came out of grilles. Some of the plugs and cables had been crudely repaired after damage, bandaged in insulating tape. Molloy cuffed the side of a screen when it kept blanking out, as if reprimanding a child.

Molloy tipped back her hood and settled on a pair of battered-looking headphones. She had very short hair, cropped tight against a scarless skull.

Merignac felt his own scalp prickle.

'Mother,' Molloy said, raising her voice. 'Father. Child. Home. School.'

Greer was observing the glowing traces. 'Nothing.'

Molloy continued. 'Work. Society. Capital. Prestige.'

'Still just noise.'

'Admiration. Esteem. The City. The Glitter Band.'

'No change.'

Molloy tried the same test phrases in a few different languages besides Canasian. Greer reported no alteration in the potentials. Molloy switched to specific association phrases.

'Victorine, Gladius, Nerval-Lermontov, Overwatch Heights, the Third District Bastion and the Outer Peripherique. Summer Falls and the White Regard. The Impartial Knife. The Quicksilver Delegation and a meeting with the Tropic Sisters.'

'Nothing,' Greer said, but with the tiniest trace of doubt. 'All right. Maybe a flicker on Nerval-Lermontov. Run it again.'

'Sybil, Victorine, Gladius, Nerval-Lermontov, Overwatch . . .'

Greer shook his head.

'Nothing that time.'

Molloy tapped her headphones. 'Just getting wind and static here. Think we're ready to unplug.'

She took off the phones, slipped her hood back over her head, disconnected the test lines and reeled them back onto the sled. She powered down the humming equipment, then unhooked her burner, with its pilot still wavering. She raised the incinerator, seemed on the point of dousing its fire over the sproker, then turned to Merignac. 'Go ahead: treat yourself.'

He retrieved his incinerator.

'We're sure?'

'We're sure.'

Molloy and Greer stepped back, their incinerators held aloft like the torches of some arcane initiation ceremony. Merignac moved nearer, tightening his grip, opening the valve, extending the flame, dousing the sproker. The fire took an immediate, consuming hold, much faster than with the filaments. Tongues of it wreathed the sproker and began to lick away from the margins, where the human form emerged from the wall.

Merignac made sure that the job was well done. Fire warmed his mask and goggles, prickling through to his skin. The raindrops became beautiful in the flames' light, a dance of cobalt gems. The sproker was melting away, parts of it breaking free, no longer a human form but an indistinct, flame-wreathed nub, losing definition by the second.

Eventually a heavily-gloved hand touched his shoulder.

'Good enough,' Molloy said. 'Plenty more to come.'

'Have you ever made a mistake?' Merignac asked, while they were on their way to the third building.

Molloy's tone was one of immediate suspicion. 'Such as?'

'I don't know. Those tests you did with the sproker: the word associations. Are they always reliable?'

'In what sense?' Greer probed.

'You were testing for sentience, for some trace of the sproker's past consciousness. Suppose there was sentience going on, but you just didn't hit on the right trigger words, or the instruments weren't sensitive enough to pick up the response.'

'If the instruments don't pick it up, it's not there,' Greer said.

Merignac thought about the way the equipment had sparked and shorted in the rain; how badly maintained it had looked, how no part of it looked as if it belonged to any other part.

'Then no one's ever missed a trace of sentience?' he asked, trying to generalise his question so that it sounded as if he was referring to the gangs as a whole, rather than add offence to Molloy and Greer. Then, answering himself: 'Although I suppose it would be difficult to tell, if the building's been burned.'

'Look at it a different way,' Molloy said. 'If you were one of those poor souls trapped in a building, and part of you was still living . . . but you couldn't say or do anything, couldn't communicate in any way with the outside world? What the fuck kind of life is that? Wouldn't you rather be burned?'

'I think I would want it to be my choice,' Merignac replied thoughtfully.

'Choice was a luxury,' Greer said. 'We're past all that.'

They went inside the third building, through a short, low-ceilinged passage and into the main atrium. They halted their sleds and played their torches around.

It was dry inside this time, with no rain dripping down from the high, vaulted ceiling, and no build-up of water on the floor. Merignac heard the rain's patter somewhere above, but it was distant and muted. In place of the rain's usual sound, in fact, was a low, shifting moan, coming not just from above and below but all around. Merignac did not remember there being much of a breeze when they had been outside, but clearly whatever movement of air existed was in some way channelled and amplified by the ducts and passages still threading the building, producing an almost musical ululation.

The open space of the atrium made the sproker easier to find than the first, almost as if she were a work of art given an uncluttered setting of her own: a whole room for a single masterpiece. Like the first, she was located at the entrance level, and was also in a state of partial fusion with the wall behind her.

There the similarities ended.

Merignac was the first to reach her, the first to illuminate her form with his torch and the blue flicker of his pilot. He stopped, halted in his tracks.

He was transfixed, locked in a perfect rapture of paralysis.

It was not merely that she was beautiful, even in death. It was that he did not think he had ever seen someone more beautiful, nor ever imagined that such beauty were possible.

Simply to blink, simply to think of averting his eyes – even for one instant – was beyond all consideration, a crime against nature.

If the first sproker had been caught in an instant of desperate struggle, thrashing to escape the consuming surface of the wall, the repose of this woman suggested something entirely different. She had not resisted any part of it. More than mere acceptance, in her expression and posture Merignac detected a languorous, ecstatic submission, a willingness that shaded beyond enthusiasm into something nearer to lust.

She had not just come to terms with the transformation, she had been embracing it with all the fervour and avidity of a drowsy lover. There was, Merignac supposed, no reason why the last signals reaching this woman's dying mind should not have been messengers of pleasure and delight, rather than torment and fear.

About two thirds of her form was visible, caught not so much in the act of escaping the wall, as backing into it, as if the wall were some fragrant waterfall and she wished to prolong the delicious coolness of its first tingling contact upon her flesh, savouring to the fullest degree each nuance of its balming touch. The plague had turned her to an iridescent green (or perhaps she had always been green) and about her form, cloaking nearly all of it but her head and neck, lay an abundance foliage and fruit: shimmering green leaves, vines and bunches of grapes, all of it gleaming with the same metallic lustre as the rest of her. Her face was serene, her smile patient, the direction of her gaze not quite his to fathom, but seemingly averted from him no matter how he varied the angle of his scrutiny.

He stared and kept staring. The initial shock of her beauty was abating, but it still left him reeling, wondering what strange alchemy of light and form could do this to him, and so easily. He had never been as moved by a living form so thoroughly as he was by this corpse.

If she were indeed a corpse.

'Skyboy's in love,' Molloy said.

Something in him snapped. He spun around, raising his fist as if to strike Molloy's mask from her face. But at the last instant he recovered himself, opening his hand in a feeble attempt to disguise his intentions. 'The drill,' he said, flustered. 'Give me the drill, damn it. You're the one saying we haven't got all day.'

Molloy regarded him, and perhaps in her eyes there was some recognition of what he had been about to do, or at least about to attempt. Not some new-found respect, but a grudging understanding that she might have overstepped some mark, and would need to be more careful around him in future.

'Sure,' she said, speaking slowly and deliberately. 'The drill. All yours.'

She passed it to him, and he closed his fingers around it and twisted it out of her grip.

If the sproker had been drilled before, the bores had healed up invisibly. He did not want to be the one who now violated that perfect form. Equally, he could not stand by and let either Molloy or Greer do it instead, which was exactly what would happen if he refused. So like a surgeon forced to perform some agonising procedure on the person he was most desirous of not harming, Merignac commenced his work. He selected his drill sites, none of them close to the flawless, alluring mask of her face, boring a pair through the shroud of leaves and grapes beneath her neck and another pair above her forehead, where the metallic foliage formed a towering wimpled crown. He put another bore into her wrist, where her arm emerged from the foliage in a gesture of beckoning enchantment, as if it were her will that he followed her back into the wall. Five drilling sites in all, just as with the first sproker: if it had been sufficient then, he reasoned, it ought to be sufficient now.

'Over to you,' he said to Molloy, lowering the drill.

She gave his handiwork a doubtful glance before turning her attention to the equipment on the sled. She reeled out five listening probes and sunk one each into the holes Merignac had bored, tapping them down gently until they reached their limits. She flicked power switches, screens and dials lighting up as before. When one flickered, she wiggled a connection in and out until the instrument stopped crackling and the dial gave off a steady illumination.

Molloy put on her headphones again, and stood close to the sproker.

'Mother. Father. Child. Home. School.'

Next to the sled, Greer squinted at the read-outs. 'Nothing.'

'Work. Society. Capital. Prestige.'

'Nothing.'

'Admiration. Esteem. The City. The Glitter Band.'

'Still nothing.'

Molloy wrenched off the headphones. 'Nothing also. All right, let's burn.'

'Wait,' Merignac said, surprised by the speed of the diagnosis. 'The first one, you ran a lot more tests. There were keywords, much more specific than those general associations you just tried.'

'We don't have those for every sproker,' Greer said. 'Mostly we don't know who these people were, what they did or who they knew. The plague took out ninety-nine percent of all civic records for this sector. That last sproker was one of the rare cases we had some biographical leads.'

'But you've got to try something,' Merignac pleaded. 'We can't just condemn her because there wasn't a reaction to that first set of keywords.'

'There's no "her" to condemn,' Molloy said, already stepping past him to drag the listening probes out of their bores. But as her fingers reached out she hesitated. 'Although if you really want to go the extra mile, Skyboy, no one's stopping you. Drop a bore straight into her cortex, right between the eyes.'

He glanced back at her. 'I don't want to.'

'Yeah, we noticed. But you're the one saying you want this done properly.' She made to reach for his drill. 'Happy to do it for you, if you don't think you've got the nerve.'

Merignac jabbed the drill at the ceiling, holding it high and upright like a duellist's pistol. 'No. I'll do it. Not you.'

Molloy stepped back, offering her palms in surrender. 'Be my guest. Make it good and deep, though, if you want this to be definitive. Make sure you reach whatever's left rotting in there.'

While Greer looked on, seemingly content to let Molloy and Merignac settle this one between themselves, Merignac steeled himself for the sacrilegious act he must now perform. He presented himself before the face, kneeling slightly because of its averted gaze, and for the first time looked at it square-on. Her beauty stalled his breath: if anything it assailed him harder than before, as if to make the next deed even more difficult than he had imagined. And yet, even with the face aligned with his, her sightless green gaze seemed to slip past him, as if she dared not meet his eyes.

Fighting a tremble in his hands, he elevated the drill until its cutting tip was poised just above her nose. He squeezed the trigger and made the drill whirr. He advanced it into contact, telling himself that the damage he was about to do to the face was localised, symmetric and need be no more disfiguring than an ash-mark.

The drill skidded, gouging a glittering cleft across the woman's brow. Startled and horrified, Merignac pulled it away.

Molloy made a snickering sound behind her mask.

Greer coughed and said: 'Start again, slower this time. Keep the pressure on, but not too much. Let the drill do the work.'

He had damaged her, but not ruined her beauty. Did the glittering wound in some way throw the rest of her into even more perfect contrast, adding the necessary imperfection she had been lacking until this moment?

'In your own time, Skyboy.'

He steadied his hand, heeded Molloy's advice, and recommenced. This time there was no error, and after a few moments he felt the drill beginning to bite, gaining traction. Flakes and coils of shimmering green wisped away from the drill, and the cutting tip advanced further into her brow. He kept it slow and steady, and did not make the mistake of backing out before he was deep enough to reach critical brain structures, if any trace of them now remained.

He stopped the drill, withdrew it, and snapped his hand at Molloy.

'Probe.'

'Yes, sir.'

Molloy unreeled a sixth line from her equipment and jammed the end of it into Merignac's palm. Merignac took the listening probe and tapped it into position. He glanced back at the equipment on the sled, at the dials and traces.

'Try again.'

Molloy put on her headphones and mumbled her way through the test words, almost slurring them into each other.

'Mother, father, child, home, school . . . Still nothing. Greer? I got nothing.' She barely paused. 'Good, then we're done.'

'There was a flicker on "father",' Greer said doubtfully. 'Try again, from the beginning.'

'Seriously?'

'We're just being thorough. Good for the kid to see we don't take this lightly.'

'Do it,' Merignac insisted.

'All right, just this once. Mother. Father. Child. Home. School. And again. Mother. Father. Child. Home. School. Work. Society. Capital. Prestige. You getting anything, Greer? Just noise through these phones.'

Greer sighed. 'No, there's nothing. Must've been a glitch, first time around. We can go again, you want to be doubly sure . . .'

Molloy began to extract the listening probes. 'No, we've gone the extra mile here, for Skyboy's sake. She's a pretty one, to be sure. But pretty doesn't get this city back up and running.'

'I can hear her,' Merignac said.

*

I can hear her.

The others froze, regarding him silently. The moment stretched: Molloy with one hand on her headphones, Greer monitoring the glowing traces, all of which were steady and flat. The tableau remained like that for several seconds, Merignac feeling as if he had violated some grave dictum of professional etiquette, a boundary that until then he had had no idea even existed.

'I said I can hear her,' he repeated. 'It started when you said the words the second time.'

Molloy had the listening probes bunched in her hand. She spooled them back into the equipment. Greer flicked power switches, turning off the humming modules until the sled was dark.

'Neither of us heard anything,' Greer said quietly.

'You're not listening. It's not coming through Molloy's phones, or the equipment on the sled. It's all around. The building's singing.' Merignac frowned behind his mask. 'You can hear it. It's not loud, but it's there. It's there and it's growing. It's singing. A woman's voice, coming through. There aren't any words, just the sounds she's making . . . you hear it now, don't you?'

Greer said softly. 'There's nothing, kid. Just some rain in the high levels, some wind whistling through ducts . . . it's only the same sounds that were here when we arrived.'

'It's singing.' He nodded to the green woman. 'She's singing. It's coming from her, out of her and into the fabric of the building.' His tone turned fiercer. 'She's singing! You can't tell me you don't hear it. It's just as beautiful as she is. More beautiful. She reminds me of . . .'

'Greer, check his pressure lines, see he hasn't mixed them up. Thinking Skyboy might be breathing fumes.'

'There's nothing wrong with my lines, or my head. I feel fine, and I know what I'm hearing. You can stop pretending you don't hear it now. She's communicating to us, the only way she can.'

Merignac did not need to lie about the music. If he had doubted his senses at the very onset of it, when it first began to rise above the sounds of rain and wind, now it filled his soul. The woman's voice sang a long, closely recurring phrase that climbed with each iteration, spiralling like a staircase into ever more vertiginous heights of outward expression. It was heartache and ecstasy, desperation and fulfilment, hope and hope's annihilation, each extreme of emotion buttressing the other, and just when Merignac swore that the progression must have reached its soaring limit, that his sanity could take no more, so it kept going. It was a kind of torment, but one he would have gladly endured for the rest of eternity.

In its purest distillation beauty had always been merciless.

'There's no music,' Molloy said, and for once it was concern, rather than mockery, that he heard in her voice. 'Nothing's coming through, Merignac. Whatever you think you're hearing . . .'

He had to force himself to speak, for fear of shattering the spell. 'I know what I'm hearing.'

In a low voice Greer said: 'Maybe he is hearing something, in his own head. Revival psychosis. Could be that they thawed him out too fast. I hear things were getting backed up there in orbit when the last few ships came in, too many to process, corners being cut.'

Molloy unhitched one of the incinerators. 'It's possible. It's also possible that corners got cut in another way.' She thrust the tip of the incinerator in his direction, its flame not yet lit. 'That what happened, Skyboy? Those papers that said you were clean?'

'What're you saying?' Greer asked solicitously.

'That maybe he came to us with something still inside his skull. Some tricky little implant that should've been scooped out before he came down from orbit.'

Greer sounded appalled. 'Oh, Merignac. Not that. Tell me that's not how it happened. Tell me you're not still walking around with that stuff in your skull, in a plague zone!'

Merignac did not care to see Molloy with the incinerator, when he was unarmed. Before she or Greer could stop him, he ducked to the side of the sled and unhitched his own unit.

'I'd only be a danger to myself, so what would it matter?'

'Little shit's admitting it!' Molloy declared excitedly.

'I'm not admitting anything. It isn't true, anyway. I'm as clean as I say I am. You can't *bribe* those people up in orbit . . .' Merignac activated his pilot flame, the dancing blue imp at the end of the incinerator. Then, on a falling note. 'They can't be bribed.'

'Which I guess you'd only know if you'd tried,' Molloy said.

'I didn't.' He jabbed the incinerator. 'Now get back. You too, Greer. We're done here. She doesn't burn. We go outside and you spray one of those signs on the outside, a message that says this building has to stay the way it is, now and forever.'

'There's no such instruction,' Greer said deliberately, reaching to unclip his own incinerator.

'Then you'll make something up.'

'It's over, Merignac. Put down the incinerator.' Greer was speaking very slowly, holding his own incinerator by one hand while he gestured with the other, palm lowering. 'What happened here, that can stay between us. Molloy and me, we can get you fixed up with one of the other teams.'

Merignac nearly laughed. 'One of your rivals, you mean?'

'Whatever it takes. Our paths don't have to cross again. No hard feelings. There are teams all over the city . . . you'd never have to come near this sector again.'

'That's all very good, Greer. But what if I never wanted to leave this sector? The music reaches me now. But I've no guarantee that I'll hear it when I'm half way across Chasm City.'

Merignac stopped himself, his focus drawn back to the green woman. Her ghost was leaving her body. At least, that was how it looked to him. A green phantom detached itself from her form, rising into the air until she hovered above Merignac, looking down on him with the same face, the same radiant loveliness as her mortal remains, except undamaged by the work of the drill. The leaves and grapes clad her, but diaphanously, veils of green that parted and sheared in teasing glimpses.

She spread her arms and paddled herself higher, regarding him with a serene but distant fondness. The structure of the ceiling loomed through her translucence.

Another phantom slipped out of the body, then a third. They were equally lovely, equally bewitching as they rose into the air and began to swoop and circle above him. Greer and Molloy must have noticed the tracking of his gaze, but that did not concern him. Now the music seemed to emanate from the moving forms rather than the sproker, and if anything it tightened its clutch on him, becoming even more wondrous.

'Kid's gone,' he heard Greer say to Molloy.

'Merignac,' Molloy snapped with a sudden finality. 'Get clear of the sproker. We've work to do here.' Molloy elongated her incinerator's flame, reaching half way to Merignac: her last warning.

Merignac opened his incinerator as far as it would go and swung the flame into Molloy. The blue fire curdled around her for an instant, gloving her from head to foot. For a moment, it was if Molloy and the flame were to be symbiotic partners, neither encroaching on the other. But the flame's greed was not to be sated. It found its way into her incinerator, touching the unlit fuel, and Molloy became a thrashing horror, screaming, flailing out, stumbling to her knees. All that in a few moments, during which time Merignac also torched Greer. Greer had not been as bad to him as Molloy, but once he struck out against his principle tormenter, it would only have been a matter of time before Greer responded. Greer therefore had to burn as well.

Merignac shut down his own incinerator as soon as Molloy and Greer were ablaze. No sense in wasting fuel. Molloy was on the floor: a blue-wreathed, hummocklike form no longer easily recognisable as a person. She had stopped making sounds.

Greer was on his way to the same fate, but lagging by a few seconds.

Merignac watched with diminishing concern, quickly satisfied that there was no immediate risk of either localised conflagration spreading to the sproker. The floor under them, and any part of the building's nearby fabric, did not seem to be taking to the flame. But to be sure, Merignac walked around the burning pyres to the sleds, and uncoupled the remaining lines and cables linking them to Molloy and Greer. Then he dragged the sleds one at a time back to the entrance, so that there was no chance of a stray spark catching the remaining incinerant tanks.

He went back to the theatre of his work.

Molloy and Greer were two slumped beacons of spectral blue, Greer now as still and silent as his partner. He wondered if they gave off a smell, burning like that. Perhaps it was for the best that he kept his mask and goggles on.

There would be repercussions of this deed, Merignac knew. Difficult repercussions, which would need all his wits to negotiate. He would come up with a story, some plausible account of an accident, a terrible thing, Molloy and Greer so kind to him, new on the job. Had they been cutting corners, horsing around? Well, how was he to say? He was new to burning.

For now, such concerns could be set aside. The main thing was that the music had not been silenced. It was still as beautiful as when it had first touched him: all the more so, now that he was its sole audience. The green phantoms were above, still circling, the ceiling above them, gently reradiating the blue glow of the fires beneath.

'I'll do whatever it takes,' he said, raising his voice with confidence. 'You have my word. You can sing and dance like this forever, and I'll make sure no one ever stops you.'

A change happened to the music. The ever-soaring motif, the uplifting swell that had borne his soul with it, ceased its ascent. It was only the tiniest shift in register, but now there was something pensive about the singing, a crack of doubt where before there had been glorious self-assurance. The circling phantoms slowed their orbiting, and began to spiral inward and downward, slowly converging over the two sets of human remains. The incinerant had nearly exhausted itself, with only a few smouldering wisps of blue flame still clinging to the combusted forms. The phantoms seemed drawn to the burned bodies, but as they stretched out their arms to skim the ashen mounds, their curiosity switched to something else. They flinched back, surprised or repulsed, and their circling became flighty and agitated. The music, meanwhile, moved from diffidence to slumping collapse. The singing faltered and faded, and as its last notes played across him, they were strident rather than harmonious: the wail of banshees rather than the chorusing of angels.

The phantoms accelerated into a circle of green, and then the circle snapped itself back into the sproker, and Merignac was quite alone, in silence and stillness.

He walked back to the sproker. He bent down, as he had done before, to present his face to hers. Still her gaze seemed to slip past him, as if constrained by entirely different geometries than those that held firm in reality. He saw that her brow was now unmarred, with no trace of the drill site or the mark he had gouged on his first attempt. Nor was there any trace of the other places where she had been drilled.

Something in her countenance had shifted, he judged. Where before there had been a coquettish aversion of her gaze, now her expression was troubled. The change was subtle, like that first shift in the music's register, but it was equally impossible to ignore.

There was judgement in that expression: disappointment; condemnation; perhaps even revulsion.

'No,' Merignac said, holding the face two-handed, trying to force it to look at him, trying to bend its features into the form he preferred. 'No – you can't make the music stop. Not after what I did for you.' It was unnecessary to nod to the handiwork still smouldering behind him. 'Not after this.' Then his discontent became pleading. 'Sing again. Make them come out of you. I want to hear the singing, and see their faces. Once wasn't enough!'

Nothing happened. For all that fires had lately burned in this space, the sproker was as cold and immutable as iron. He felt as if was begging forgiveness from a boulder.

His pleading became rage. He began to pound his fists at the green woman, breaking away brittle shards and bunches of the grapes and foliage which encased her. The more he damaged her, the more her expression seemed to harden.

'You tricked me,' he cried, voice breaking on his anguish. 'You tricked me! They burned for you!'

When there came a point where his rage had subsided to a slow-burning despair, and his fists could take no more of the revenge he wished to bestow on her, Merignac stumbled past the corpses of Molloy and Greer and out beyond the sleds, to the entrance, and out into the eternal night of Chasm City.

He wrenched his mask and goggles off and lifted his face to the night and the rain. The higher fog had broken apart. The rising murk of twisted and disfigured buildings dragged his focus all the way to the uppermost heights of the inhabited city. Lights still glimmered up there: a lacy, spitlike suspension of civilisation strung beneath the canopy's ceiling. He thought of the clean-up gangs that must still be up there, toiling day and night to scrub the panels clean, or merely cleaner.

Perhaps that might have been the better vocation for him.

Voices sounded out of the night. He turned his gaze from the canopy, back to the level where he stood. About a hundred metres away, moving between shadow and half-light, was a small party of hooded and goggled figures, picking their way across the jumbled and deceptive ground. He counted five of them. They had torches, beams scissoring out into the rain. They were dressed just like a burner squad, but they moved without sleds or heavy equipment.

One of the torch beams glanced across him. He ducked, trying not to be seen as the beam returned.

'Molloy, is that you?'

'It's Greer,' he called back, realising he had no chance of not being seen. 'Greer,' he emphasised.

'Everything all right, Greer?'

'Who is it?'

'Farkas. We got word that . . .' Farkas broke off as a piece of masonry crumbled beneath the party, forcing them to scramble for firm ground before the city swallowed them whole. Farkas caught his breath, wheezing audibly. 'We got word . . . is Merignac still in there, Greer?'

'Yes, Merignac's still in there, with Molloy. They're just . . . finishing up. We're good here.'

Farkas and his party only had about thirty metres to cover before they were at the entrance. Merignac was considering his options, surveying the possible escape routes and trying to decide which if any of them were the least treacherous.

'Greer,' said one of two people at the rear of the squad. 'There's a problem with your recruit.'

'What sort of problem?' he asked innocently, squinting against the torch glare.

A woman's voice said: 'My name's Kolax. I'm a constable, just down from orbit. I'm here with . . . another sleeper, another incomer thawed off the same ship your recruit came in on. Came here as fast as I could, then got Farkas and his team to lead me down to you.'

'Why?'

'Your man Merignac . . . he's not who he claims. He's here on falsified papers. All of it, his whole identity. A colleague of mine nearly died because of him.'

'I don't understand.'

'He's not clean,' Kolax went on. 'Residual structures in his head. Plague susceptible. My colleague was the one who should have scanned him and stopped him getting anywhere near Chasm City, at least until he had those implants scooped out. But your recruit obviously didn't like the idea of that. He attacked my colleague, left him for dead and forged his own clearance documents.'

'We checked his papers,' he said.

'Not well enough, it seems.'

'Well, you can't blame him for not wanting the kind of back-room surgery they'd have offered him in orbit, fresh off the ship. Never mind the cost that would have been his to bear, when he was already fresh out of reefersleep without a single credit to his name.'

'Greer . . .' Farkas said doubtfully. 'You *sure* everything's all right with your squad?'

'Yes, everything's absolutely fine. We're done with this building.' He twisted around to look back it, as if with fondness. 'It was . . . a good burn.'

He heard Kolax utter: 'It's him.'

Whether she knew it, or was guessing, no longer mattered.

He had to leave.

He darted without warning, selecting the least problematic of his possible directions of escape. The ground was still laden with hazards, but without a sled behind him he moved more easily than before, and with a sort of desperate, fear-driven confidence, leaping between areas of level ground, stumbling on loose scree then recovering his gait. The others were trying to follow – he could hear their excited cries, the crunch of rubble under their feet – but he had the element of surprise and quickly turned a corner of the building, blocking him from their sight. By the time they rounded the same corner, he would be lost down any number of possible routes.

If he had the remnant of a plan, after murdering the others, now his only thought was to buy time and distance. There would be no explaining away what had happened in the building, not now that Kolax had exposed his earlier crime. But that did not mean he was done. The city was huge and dark and mostly lawless, and if he kept going he could soon lose himself in it.

Granted, he would need to adapt very quickly to the life of the fugitive. But as he had already demonstrated to himself, a lack of adaptability was not one of his shortcomings. If the ferals could live in the city's underbelly, so could he. But unlike them, he would not settle for that existence.

He rounded another corner, ducked under an overpass, and caught himself just before he planted his foot onto an impaling spike, ramming up out of the ground. His breathed hard. The rain was the dominant sound, sluicing down in continuous greasy veils from a higher overhang of the building. He strained for indications of pursuit: their cries and footfalls. Perhaps there was something, just at the limit of his hearing, but the more he concentrated on it the more it seemed to be receding, as if they had indeed misjudged his direction of flight.

He calmed himself.

He could afford to be more cautious now. All he needed to do was make methodical progress, putting a sector or two behind him. If he moved slowly and quietly, there was no need to give himself away. If they were really serious about catching him, they would have sent more than just this one hapless constable. He supposed that the death of a minor functionary – the unhelpful official he had murdered – was not really worth the trouble of an organised manhunt. What was the point of putting right one crime, when there was a whole city gone to chaos and madness?

He slipped through dark alleys between buildings, unchallenged. Now and then he spotted the sprayed tags of burner teams, the prideful boasts glowing faintly against shadow and grime, and he wondered at the work that had been done in them, the dreaming sprokers that had been roused to a parody of consciousness. If the dials twitched, they might live. If not, quick blue fire was their exorcism.

His shadow leapt ahead of him. All around was light. Merignac froze, pinned into a circle of brilliance. He looked up, into the howling downdraught of a volantor, lowering out of the rain.

They had found him after all.

An amplified voice said: 'Stop, Merignac – if that's what you're calling yourself. There's nowhere for you to go.'

He looked around. Where there had been darkness – sanctuary – there was now only a blinding confusion of light and shadow, moving and squirming as if to trick his perceptions. Spectral figures emerged from the glare. For an instant his eyes made green angels out of them, until the forms coalesced into Farkas, Kolax and the three other two pursuers.

Kolax shouted over the volantor's roar: 'Give up now, Merignac. This is the best chance you get.'

He laughed. 'The best chance for what?'

'To avoid the worst. My prosecutors will look at mitigating circumstances. You weren't long out of reefersleep. That'll count in your favour. This man here . . . he's a soldier, another incomer from Sky's Edge.'

'I'm Merignac,' said the fifth one, in an accent that immediately identified him as a citizen of the Northern Coalition. 'You took my identity, took my memories. You were never a soldier. Your family ran a private hospital, making money out of the war. When I was in there, badly injured, you ran an illegal memory trawl. Took what you needed from me, including my own past. Just enough to pass yourself off as me and take a slot on that ship. You thought I'd die, and no one would be any the wiser. But I survived. I made it out. And when we learned what you'd done, another soldier volunteered his slot on the ship, just so that I could follow you.' He paused, breathing heavily. 'But not to punish you. Just to . . . have back, what you took. My name. My past.'

'It's a lie,' he called back.

But Kolax answered calmly: 'No, it's not. He's really Merignac. But you left his memories shredded. Done too quickly, no safeguards. But what you know, you can give back to him.'

'Trawl me, you mean?'

'No – we can't do that very easily now. But Merignac just wants the pieces filled in. You can talk to him. Tell him what you remember, and that'll help him with the missing parts, the holes you left him in with. Just talk.'

'Why would he not want to punish me?'

The real Merignac called back: 'Because I've seen too much of that. I just want to remember her again. That's all I ask.'

'Her?'

'My mother, and how she sang to me.'

Kolax spoke up: 'It's not too late. There's nothing that can't be forgiven here. You made errors, but they're understandable. The traumas of war . . . you didn't need to be on the front line to be touched by them. And my colleague's hurt, but he'll be all right. So will Merignac, if you help him. Nobody's died here. We'll look at therapeutic rehabilitation. Believe it or not, we need people alive more than we need them dead. This city's broken. It's going to take a lot of hands to put it right.'

He took off his mask and goggles so that he could address her properly. They were not far apart now.

'You said nobody's died.'

Kolax cocked her head.

'What's so funny?'

'It's just that you wouldn't have said that if you already knew about Molloy and Greer.' He stared at her wonderingly. 'But you don't, do you? You haven't had time to go back into that building. You don't know what I did to them.'

'Did what?' Farkas asked.

'They wanted to stop the music,' he explained. 'I couldn't allow that. So I burned them both.'

'Don't run!' Merignac called. 'I need you! I need *her*!'

So he ran.

It was impossible, and he knew it, but he had to run anyway. The volantor followed him with an almost leisurely interest, like the kind of predator that had already injected its venom, needing only to wait for its quarry to succumb. Somewhere behind, he did not doubt that Farkas, Kolax and the real Merignac were following, guided by the light.

He came to the edge of something. Beyond the moving circle of light, the city fell away into void. Buildings teetered on the edge, top-heavy galleons circling a black-bottomed whirlpool. The absence was so wide and vast that he could not see the other side of it, nor gauge any trace of its depth. But he knew full well what he had reached. It was the lip of the Chasm.

He could not go back, and any way to his left and right would soon be blocked. But a thin thread of masonry arced out into the void. It was a bridge, narrow as a footpath, bordered by hip-high railings of buckled metal. The light lingered on the bridge's nearest end, encouraging him to step onto it.

'Don't do it,' Kolax called. 'It's a dead end. The bridge goes nowhere.'

'Listen to her!' Merignac called, with a rising desperation in his voice. 'I was ready to forgive – I'm still ready!'

He stepped onto the structure. Perhaps it went somewhere, perhaps it did not, but there was certainly no future for him at the Chasm's edge. Their noble ideas of rehabilitating him would wither at the first glimpse of those smouldering bone-piles. Then they would want to burn him as well. Better to be running, no matter where running took him.

Under his feet the bridge felt firm, but only to begin with. The further he got from the edge, the more he felt the bridge swaying, with the amplitude of its motion seeming to increase with each thud of his boots. He looked back, expecting to see Kolax and the others – even poor motherless Merignac – beginning to follow him. But they had come no nearer, content to observe him from the relative safety of the Chasm's edge. Even the volantor had given up the pursuit, hovering just above the party.

He ran until the shaking of the bridge made it impossible, and then he slowed into a lope, gripping the buckled rail for support. The bridge quivered violently, sickening him with its undulations. He had no choice but to walk now, spreading his legs for stability. But the railing's support was already betraying him. The metal felt loose, only tenuously connected to the structure it was meant to be protecting. Far from the volantor's illumination, and the torches of the party, he could make out very little of the bridge's extent; how far it extended across the void.

With a shudder the railing flapped away in a continuous arc, leaving him with nothing to hold onto. He gasped and dropped to his knees, gripped by a monstrous dread of falling.

A green angel swooped out of the night. It came very close to him, hovering momentarily so that he was exposed to the full and dreadful spectacle of its beauty. Then it sped off again, circling high above him. A second came, then a third. They dived past him, arcing beneath the bridge and then back up and around. The three fell into their gyring dance, the one he had seen already. Their coiling motion began to converge on him, tightening and lowering.

Their was an aspect to their faces he had not seen before.

They were not happy with him.

He flinched and twisted as they swept ever nearer. He felt the cold turbulence of their passing. Their displeasure was hardening now, becoming a green-eyed rage.

'They wanted to stop the music,' he pleaded again, but this time to a different audience. 'But I needed to hear you sing.'

The green angels became green furies of vengeance and punishment. Their skin was ablating away to bone and sinew. He screamed as he tried to bat them away. He thrashed and moaned and lost his fragile balance on the bridge.

He fell.

He paddled the air, helplessly. He screamed into the uprising mist. The three green furies swooped around him, forming an escort, and at last they began to sing.

It was a different song this time, one that no mother had ever sung to her last living son.